ERIC

In the Company of Snipers

Book 15

Irish Winters

COPYRIGHT

Eric; In the Company of Snipers, 15

Cover design and author photo by Kelli Ann Morgan, Inspire Creative Services

Interior book design by Bob Houston, eBook Formatting

Editor: Linda Clarkson, Black Opal Editing and Proofreading

ISBN Paperback: 978-1-942895-45-9
ISBN eBook: 978-1-942895-46-6
Library of Congress Control Number: 2017945628

Irish Winter's websites: http://www.irishwinters.com
and irishwinters.blogspot.com

In the Company of Snipers

You can find Irish Winters on Facebook:
https://www.facebook.com/author.irishwinters

On Twitter: https://twitter.com/irishwinters1

For news on upcoming releases, sign up for Irish Winters' Newsletter at IrishWinters.com.

For more information about all my books, visit IrishWinters.com.

IN THE COMPANY OF SNIPERS

This series revolves around ex-Marine scout sniper, Alex Stewart, and his covert surveillance company, The TEAM, home-based out of Alexandria, Virginia. An obsessive patriot and workaholic, he created the company to give ex-military snipers like him a chance at returning to civilian life with a decent job.

This is not a serial with each book ending at a cliffhanger. I wouldn't do that to you. *In the Company of Snipers* is a collection of passionate love stories involving women and men who are tough enough to take on the world alone. Each is a stand-alone read, where in the course of an active TEAM operation, one agent comes face to face with his or her demons. The men and women I write about are all patriots and warriors, dealing with what they've lived through or the mistakes they've made

Spoiler alert: Every novel contains adult scenes including sexual situations (some explicit), language, and violence. I don't write sweet romance, so be forewarned.

At the end of each story, it's my hope that you, along with my heroes, will come to realize...

Love changes everything.

"I fled Him, down the nights and down the says;

I fled Him, down the arches of the years;

I fled Him down the labyrinthine ways

Of my own mind; and in the midst of tears

I hid from Him…"

Excerpt from *The Hound of Heaven,* by Francis Thompson

CHAPTER ONE

"Sit room. Now!"

Eric stiffened at the snap-to in Alex Stewart's command. A chill prickled up his spine and his gut clenched like it used to at the call of 'man down' when he'd been active-duty, right before they'd scrambled to the helos to save lives.

Something wicked had come to The TEAM. He felt it as surely as if it had zeroed down on him alone, probably because it had. Most of the other agents were already assigned and out in the field. Zack Lennox was in Cuba. Seth McCray was somewhere in South America. Hunter Christian and Lee Hart were only Alex knew where. Even Senior Agent Harley Mortimer had been out of the country for the last two weeks, no doubt monitoring the spike in opium production in Afghanistan for the UN. *Who didn't see that coming after decades of war and failed promises from the international community?*

Others were assigned to local operations and security details. That left two senior agents, Mark Houston and David Tao, and two junior agents, Eric Reynolds and Jordan Hannigan. Techies Mother and her assistant, Ember Dennison, didn't count. They didn't do field work.

Eric no more than parked his butt in the Sit Room, when the big screen overhead flashed, revealing the bastard running the show. Who didn't recognize Abdul-Mutaal? Dressed in the black robes of the current terrorist plague sweeping the planet, he'd masked the lower half of his face. A scimitar in his right-hand cast blinding laser flashes at the camera lens. He grunted as he gripped his victim's long, bloodied hair into a cruel topknot, twisting the kid's neck, forcing his head back.

Eric tilted forward, scanning every detail. As a prior Navy Corpsman who'd opted to join the Marines he served, he found his keen mind automatically diagnosing. Triaging.

The victim couldn't have been more than twenty-five. Strangled whimpers scraped past his swollen, cut lips. He couldn't seem to catch a decent breath. His nose was broken, several teeth, too. *Torture. Probable punctured lung. Definite dehydration.*

Dark, black lines crisscrossed his bare torso. *Bloody welts, possible burns. Hard to know for sure.*

His hands were bound in front of him, bloody stumps where three fingers had been clipped off. Both index fingers. One pinkie. *Severe extremity trauma. Internal bleeding. God knows what else. Pain control's a given, along with a damned rapid evac.*

Hemorrhaging required sustained massive transfusions and tourniquets. Shock, hypothermia, and the victim's unknown medical history would work against Eric no matter how fast he could get to the kid. This was a race against time. Eric's boots automatically shifted under his chair, needing to be off and away. In transit. Running.

Even as adrenaline triggered his body to act, his brain told him this was a pre-recorded death scene. Somewhere out there, it had happened again. Someone's child had died.

"I am Abdul-Mutaal!" the bastard towering over the victim postured, thumping his chest with the handle of that scimitar like a Neanderthal. "You have forty-eight hours to deliver Finn Powers to me. No more!"

Powers? That got Eric's undivided attention. It was his ex-wife's maiden name. Shea Powers Reynolds. A proud name—until she ran away. Ditched him. Filed for divorce.

"F-Finn," the young man ground out, the shuddering panic in his voice unmistakable, and his teeth chattering. "I'm... I'm sorry." Wide, fear-filled eyes, the whites red with blood, rolled about the room as if looking for something.

Eric latched onto that. Who was he looking for? Someone beyond the camera? If Finn Whoever-He-Was was there in the same room, why hadn't he tried to help his friend?

Then...

Time ran out. With one brutal stroke, the wicked deed was done. The camera caught the blood spray as a young man a world away was murdered in cold blood. Abdul-Mutaal pushed the body aside while he picked up the decapitated head and shook it with a vigorous, "Forty-eight hours!"

The video blacked out. *Thank God.*

Eric dug his fingernails into his palms, willing his soul back to center, and his heart to stop jackhammering out of control. He'd seen crap like this before. What combat medic hadn't? It wasn't the first beheading on live TV, and it wouldn't be the last. Frustration at not being able to do what he did best filled his gut with the need to strike back.

Until that last act of cruelty, he could've saved that young man. If nothing else, he could've simply been there so that kid hadn't died alone.

Working for Alex Stewart, the owner of the elite covert surveillance company of ex-military snipers, The TEAM, often brought the harsh realities of the world into the Situation Room. *But that?* No different than a gruesome slash film.

Whatever contract Alex had just signed, whatever promise he'd made to save the world like the hero he thought he was, Eric wanted in. Abdul-Mutaal needed one of those up-close-and-personal come-to-Jesus meetings the Corps offered free of charge. *With a .338 Lapua Magnum. 16.2 grams ought to do it. Now, damn it.*

"The young man whose death you just witnessed was Phoenix Berglund, a student at the University of Amsterdam and an American citizen. We believe his murderer is Abdul-Mutaal," Alex said, his palms flat on the conference table. "Berglund's body was found in the research lab where he worked, but he was tortured elsewhere."

"Mutaal's damned nervy to carry out a beheading in the middle of a busy university," Jordan muttered, his voice subdued, his complexion a pasty gray.

"He's an asshole is what he is. Who sent the video?" Senior Agent Mark Houston pushed back from the conference room table, his arms across his chest. He was a hard one to rattle, but even he'd turned a whiter shade of pale.

"As far as we know, Mutaal made the video alone, but one of Berglund's friends stole it," Mother answered, her voice tight and edgy. It wasn't often The TEAM's genius techie came unraveled, but she was close, her manicured nails tapping a relentless clatter on the tabletop. "Phoenix and his friends were involved in a research project at the university, something to do with solar energy. They called it dynamic energy displacement."

"Your hacker friend got a name?" Eric asked point blank.

Hackers. The twenty-first century's version of Robin Hood, at least until the the folks at Langley caught up with them and turned them into federal agents or inmates at Leavenworth. Mother worked with gamers and hackers all over the world. No doubt these were friends from her other life. She walked a thin line between providing superior technical support and outright breaking the law to provide that support. That she wasn't behind bars proved her unique expertise at not leaving breadcrumbs in her wake.

Glancing at the agents sitting around the table, she made eye contact with everyone. Him last. Her hands trembled. *Wasn't that interesting?* Eric's sixth sense sprang to life. She didn't want to name her hacker friend. *Why not?*

"Finn Powers," Alex divulged what she couldn't or wouldn't. "He's the one Mutaal wants, and he's also one of three young men Mother works with as a freelance game developer. All are Americans living abroad on a research grant in Amsterdam."

The name alone—Powers—was more than enough to make Eric wonder, like he had every day for the last two years, where on earth Shea had gone. The why no longer mattered. He'd take her back in an instant if she'd let him.

Alex drummed his fingers on the table, pulling Eric's attention back to the Sit Room. "Mother received this video an hour ago. From what we know now, Finn witnessed Berglund's murder and stole the SD card out of Abdul-Mutaal's camera. That one act of courage preempted this bastard's plan to release it to the Al Jazeera news network. Abdul-Mutaal lost the advantage of shock and awe. He's got to be pissed."

"Finn was in that room?" Eric bit out. "Why didn't he help his buddy then?" *The jerk.*

"He... he's not like that," Mother said softly. "He doesn't have a mean bone in his body."

Eric let that slide. Having your buddy's back had nothing to do with being mean, but everything with acting like a man instead of a coward. He changed the subject. "How can we be sure he's lost his advantage?" Terrorists liked nothing more than to bully the civilized world with their acts of bloodlust and perverted cruelty. Beheadings on live television guaranteed a grim kind of respect, notoriety, and an influx of stupid, idealistic recruits.

Alex eyed Eric a full minute before he spoke. "Ember's monitoring all newsfeeds out of the Mideast in case he made a copy, but our source, Finn Powers, was pretty sure he didn't."

A coward would know, wouldn't he? Eric stifled his opinion.

"There hasn't been a word of this on any news network yet," Ember assured everyone. "Our State Department hasn't caught wind of it, either. I called one of my friends over there to be sure."

Not like that meant anything. The State Department didn't often offer up intelligence until they had to. The CIA, either. Both federal agencies might know what had just gone down in Amsterdam, but this poor guy's parents shouldn't have to wait until top-secret records were declassified decades in the future.

Hell, this could be a CIA undercover operation gone horribly wrong for all anyone knew.

Mother expelled a breath slowly in one long sigh through pursed lips.

"What are you not telling us?" Eric asked her directly. "What's going on? Why'd Abdul-Mutaal kill Berglund to get at Finn? What's Finn got that Mutaal wants?"

She rested her chin in her fist, breathing hard before she blurted it out. "Finn told me a couple days ago that he and his friends were onto something big. Maybe illegal."

"What'd they hack into?" Eric growled, hating that someone from The TEAM might have to put his life in danger to save people who took stupid chances.

"Nothing. This isn't about hacking, at least not as far as I know, but Hugh Carlson paid them a visit at the university a couple days ago. He made all three of them impressive job offers if they'd work for him. When they refused, he threatened to steal their invention."

"The narcissist billionaire from France? Why? What's so great about this…?" Eric waved his hand, "…dynamic energy displacement thing?"

Mother should never go into black ops, not the way *LIAR* lit up in her blue eyes like a neon sign.

"For hell's sake, tell him," Alex growled. "If you want Eric to save your boyfriend, then tell him everything he needs to know."

"He's your boyfriend?" Eric asked. Why was that not a shock?

"No, no, it's not like that. It's just that…" With another deep breath, Mother spilled. "You won't believe it, but they've built the perfect force field." She swallowed hard. "I know this is going to sound like science fiction, but it's not. Dynamic energy displacement is a naturally occurring repulsion based on passive energy. You know, the sun. Think of DED like a giant magnet with a north and a south pole. Two magnets attract each other when their opposing poles align. It's basic science."

DED. Wasn't that the perfect acronym?

"And they repulse each other when you force north to north or south to south. Got that. Natural repulsion. I understand all things are energy, but how does any of that equate to a force field?" Eric asked.

"Because these three guys created a unique amplifier that boosts that natural attraction or repulsion. They've found a way to compress solar energy, turning DED into a—"

"Jesus Christ, a weapon," Eric finished for her. *Just what the world needs.* "Carlson wants to weaponize whatever they came up with."

She nodded, her nails clattering on the table top enough to drive a man crazy. "Yes. It could be used as a weapon. In fact—"

"It could effectively be used as a long-range laser, nearly as powerful as a controlled solar flare, if what Finn told Mother can be substantiated," Alex interrupted, two fingertips to his left temple. The man dealt with horrendous migraines, something Eric could help him with if he'd let him.

"Carlson's dangerous. You've all heard his tag line: *One Nation. One Network. One World.* He's bent on the notion that the man-made constraints of nation, country, and state have fallen to the wayside. They're obsolete. Like castles and national borders." Alex paused, his brows furrowed and the cords in his neck rigid. He made marble look relaxed. "He sees cyber-technology as the go-to for world domination of market and resources. *His* world domination. Think about it. If not for his monopoly on the CC, none of us would have cell service today, would we?"

"Right." Eric got that much. The CC, or Carlson's Chip, as Carlson himself named it, had done away with local cell providers in every country nearly overnight in a brilliant coup that took even Wall Street by surprise. Hence the slogan: *One Nation. One Network. One World.*

To say the least, the man was pompous. He held an over-inflated opinion of himself and his abilities, so much that the bastard had outright told the United Nations he intended to take over the world, that his chip was just the beginning. Get out of his way. So far they had, but the chip had only been active six months. As far as Eric was concerned, that wasn't long enough for an honest beta test of a toy gun, much less a reason to roll over and admit defeat to a tyrant with money.

Alex growled, "We won't know the extent of his madness until we get Finn Powers and Gordie Mikkelson out of Amsterdam and into U.S. custody. The Secretary of Defense is willing to send his Seal Team operatives in, but Finn asked for you, Eric. By name. You're lead. Jordan will accompany you. By the way, how the hell do you know this guy?"

Eric shrugged, as baffled as everyone else. The only connection to Finn was that last name. *Powers,* and it wasn't much. "Never met him in my life, Boss. Where is this Finn person now, and how do you know all this?" he asked Mother.

She glanced over her shoulder at Ember. "Go on. Show him."

Ember tapped her keyboard, bringing a final video to screen. It had to have been taken via Finn's cellphone, and a cheap one at best. At least the bumbling oaf knew enough to set it down to take a steady video clip. An obese young man with Coke-bottle glasses peered into the screen. Unibrow. Crooked teeth. Big, wide nose. The guy was no looker. Typical geek type. Squinty-eyed. Unkempt. Probably used techno-speak like Mother and Ember. Too bad he didn't look as good as they did.

Eric cringed when Finn stuck his face too close to the screen, magnifying a horrific boil on his chin that needed to be lanced. No way in hell was this guy related to Shea. *She was perfect in every way. Flawless. A gorgeous brunette with starlight in her eyes*—until the day she left.

Eric's attention blinked back to the case at hand. Finn's voice didn't improve Eric's first impression. He had a quavering, effeminate voice that pitched across the Sit Room, grating on Eric's nerves. "Sasha. You know that boss of yours? The one you're always talking about? I need him, like uber fast. Time's scary short." He looked over his shoulder as if checking to see if he'd been followed. "Tell him to check his dedicated savings account, the one he pays his personal taxes from. I transferred enough to get the job done. If that isn't enough to get me out of the country, I can get more. Help me, Sasha. They're coming. Tell your boss to send his best. Send Eric!"

Your best? Me? How the hell do you know me, 'cause I sure don't know you. Eric's throat couldn't have gone any drier at that odd request.

"Three-million dollars was deposited in my bank account at midnight," Alex said, those slender fingers of his, playing at his temple like drumsticks. "Ember tracked the transaction through a dozen Internet cafes and IP addresses across the globe. Finn or Mikkelson or whoever sent this video is a damned good hacker. Ember lost him somewhere in…" He glanced at her.

Ember scrunched her shoulders like a little girl. "Sorry, Alex. Dhaka, Bangladesh. That was where I lost the trail, and you're right. He's good."

Alex blew out a long-suffering sigh. "S' okay. The real question is where'd the money come from to begin with. Those three guys were on grants. They had to be living together to make it in Amsterdam."

Eric lifted a palm to slow the information download. "Correct me if I'm wrong, but we've got two things going on here. Carlson wants the force field and Abdul-Mutaal wants Finn. I get Carlson. He's a rich bastard who wants to rule the world, but what's Abdul-Mutaal's stake? How are the two connected?"

"At this point, I'm not sure they are." Alex lowered his voice. "All we know now is that Finn needs our help, and we're going to give it to him. According to the time stamp on the video, Berglund was murdered at sixteen hundred hours yesterday. That puts us inside a very tight forty-eight-hour window. An international flight will eat up most of what's left. Eric. Jordan. Gear up. You're going to Amsterdam."

CHAPTER TWO

Shea fingered the dirty linen curtain aside to view the rainy street. Everything looked so normal. Mundane. All except for the man in the black tweed hat on the corner. He might be watching the internet cafe, the way his eyes kept shifting in her direction. He might have seen her dash inside the front door.

The gray-haired guy in the ratty gray sweater looked suspicious, too. Even the young couple with their hands all over each other on the park bench across the street looked like they were putting on a show.

Who are they trying to kid? They're all after me.

She bit the inside of her cheek and closed the curtain. She'd told Gordie to meet her here, that she'd bring Phoenix's laptop, but now she wasn't so sure it was a safe place. She was scared out of her mind, no longer able to distinguish good people from the evil ones, not after witnessing the barbaric death of Phoenix. That awful man in the black robe. He'd killed Phoenix right under her nose. She could still see the despair in Phoenix's blue eyes.

Taking two full steps back from the curtain, she clutched his laptop to her chest, her stomach ready to heave. This murder had to be about the research he'd stored on this computer, the invention they'd all sworn to protect from prying eyes, and now a killer.

The café was quiet for a change, but the smell of espresso and lattes spiked her nausea. She'd never forget the despair in her friend's eyes as long as she lived. Poor Phoenix. Why would anyone want to hurt him, a harmless, cute guy with shaggy blond hair that hung into his eyes? The kind of guy most girls wanted to take home and play house with.

Only he didn't care for girls.

Phoenix had come to Amsterdam from Buffalo, New York, the same as Gordie Mikkelson, another wannabe scientist. Gordie was the athlete, the primper, and the weightlifter. He shaved from head to foot every single morning, said it made his body sleeker. The coconut scented oil he slicked himself down with every day didn't hurt. It had surely made Phoenix take notice.

Lust hit them hard. Then destiny.

While uncomfortable at times, their openly gay relationship had allowed Shea to maintain her anonymity. Her friends were too caught up in each other and their energy displacement project to look beyond her dumpy clothes long enough to realize she wasn't just another geeky man. She wasn't a guy at all.

Finn, the fat suit she wore every day, was the person they thought they'd asked to room with them. She went along with it, content to be the third wheel to two fun loving geniuses who needed someone to cook for them. Better yet, a friend who knew how to midnight requisition a few extra dollars now and then. Never from honest, hardworking people though. That wouldn't be right. She was very selective whose bank account she pilfered.

Living with Gordie and Phoenix had taught her a few lessons about life. Respect for personal borders. One hundred percent honesty. Compromise. Always compromise. Most importantly: Money could buy most things. Friends. Influence. Access to more money.

That was the reason Gordie and Phoenix were selected to participate in the solar energy project. Because of Finn's *dabbling*, they were able to bring a certain level of capital with them. The cost to the university went down. They got the equipment and the lab they needed to continue their work.

All three of them had spent long hours at the university, not because they had to, but because they were onto something. Call it serendipity. Phoenix called it a gift from the universe. Even Professor Grover, their research mentor, named them his lucky stars the day Phoenix inadvertently stumbled on a way to bounce back expended energy, a paradox of sly Mother Nature.

At least that was what Phoenix said. He hadn't been exactly forthcoming with how his force field worked, not that Shea would've understood it if he had. Dabbling she could do. Not science.

Professor Grover's bright gray eyes had all but glowed with pride, but holy crap, did that discovery open up a new field of science no one saw coming. Einstein's theory came to life in a big new way. Everyone already knew that matter consisted of energy, but mankind's problem was always how to harness that energy without unleashing the power of the atom.

At least that was what Phoenix had said. He might not have discovered affordable solar energy, but he'd done the impossible. He'd discovered dynamic energy displacement, a natural bounce back effect that focused and reflected dissipated energy back onto the force expending it, neutralizing the point of origin in the process. By any other name a natural force field. One anyone could manipulate if they possessed the means to focus and amplify the initial source of energy.

At least that was what Phoenix said.

Shea wondered now. She'd always detected an undercurrent of something she couldn't pin down to his claims. Doubt niggled at the back of her mind. Was this discovery all he'd claimed or had he gotten himself killed for something else?

Gordie never appeared to notice, and that always quelled Shea's touch of anxiety. He was the practical side to Phoenix's hyper. She dabbled in hacking and came up with more funds. Phoenix and Gordie dabbled in science. It was the same thing. Kind of.

But why did that monster demand that Finn be turned over within forty-eight hours? *For what? Another execution? Why me? I know nothing.*

The only thing that came to mind was the *dabbling* she'd committed against one particular Mideasterner, Basheer Bagani. Shea shivered at the rash of goose flesh rippling over her shoulders, just thinking of waking up on his satin sheets. It still gave her a morgue-like chill. The man was a predator—for flesh. The female kind.

True, it was her fault for being in a drunken stupor when he'd found her, but it was his fault for tying her spread-eagled to his four-poster. Finn thanked *God* for whoever had interrupted Bagani's evil plans that night.

Later, after she'd pulled herself out of her inebriated state, she'd Googled him. *What do you know?* Bagani was none other than a Saudi prince, one of many sons of a powerful wealthy sheik. The only difference between father and son? The father was decadently rich. Basheer was just decadent.

He'd been investigated in the whereabouts of two missing starlets. Shea had her suspicions where those two women were, especially if the lines of white powder on his coffee table were what she thought they were.

At first, she'd taken just enough out of his bank account to maintain get back on her feet and to maintain a decent lifestyle. Then, like a modern-day Robin Hood, she'd given some to Phoenix and Gordie to keep their research afloat and to get them to Amsterdam.

When confronted with the spectacle of cold-blooded murder, she'd infused a large amount into the bank account of one honorable Alex Stewart, the one he used to pay his taxes, judging by the quarterly allotments going to the State of Virginia and the Internal Revenue Service. He might not qualify as a charity or a research grant, but she needed his kind of assistance.

She knew if Mr. Stewart wanted to find someone, he could and would do it. He had a hard reputation in the covert ops world, but was known to work miracles when others could not. The man had phenomenal resources. He leased satellite time. He also employed her ex-husband.

Eric.

Shea's heart fluttered with palpitations at the name that always stole her breath. Just thinking about the man she'd left behind reduced her to befuddled and—chilled. Never to be warm again. She'd hurt him in the cruelest way possible. She'd lost hope and faith in the darkest of times, when she should've been holding on tight to him. Trusting him. Instead, she'd deserted him without warning or an honest reason, like a captain deserting her sinking vessel without regard to her sole shipmate.

The day after Phoenix discovered dynamic energy displacement, their professor, Morell Grover, went missing. That was when their world had changed forever. They'd no more than heard that disconcerting news, when Gordie called her at the university's research lab and told her some bad-assed dude was after her. She needed to run for her life. *Hurry! No time to explain. Just run! Hide!*

How he knew, he'd never said, but by then, that bad-assed dude was already in the hall. With nowhere to run, she'd forced her bulky fake body into the cabinet under the lab sink. Poor Phoenix had been cruelly tortured. He was barely able to walk. The black-robed assassin kept asking one question, "Where's Finn?"

Phoenix kept crying, "I don't know. I thought he was here. You've got to believe me."

The killer's question never changed. Neither did the answer. Only the level of terror in Phoenix's sad voice.

Shea couldn't close her eyes any more. She couldn't sleep. Every time she tried, the sounds and smells and sights came back to her. Every detail of his brutal death had been carved into her mind. After his head had been severed from his body, his eyes had kept blinking while a pool of red poured from his neck. It spread under his cheek. His lips kept moving, but there were no words. Only gurgles. When he'd needed her most, she had cowered like a—coward. Shaking like a little girl. Like she was now...

Paralyzed with fear, her thoughts had flown across the Atlantic to that one man in a million who would've fought to rescue Phoenix if he had been there.

Eric.

That was the way he was made, to stand up to bullies. To take down despots and despicable men. To fight the world if need be.

The murderer had made one mistake. After he had killed Phoenix, he'd placed his head in a plastic gym bag, then walked across the expansive lab to wash his hands at the sink. In those precious few seconds of heart-pounding terror, Shea had summoned every last ounce of her courage and light-fingered the SD card from the assassin's camera while he wasn't looking.

While Phoenix's body twitched, and although her fingers shook so much that she'd almost dropped the card, she'd still done it. Then she'd hid under the sink again, her trembling arms wrapped around her padded legs, praying she hadn't been seen. That the murderer wouldn't check his camera before he'd left.

Whoever he was, he had a good reason to want her dead now, but that was the mystery.

Unless he works for Bagani...

Even that didn't make sense. Bagani couldn't possibly know she'd transformed herself into an over-weight, bumbling man with bad hygiene. *Could he?*

Unless he followed you...

She eased the curtain aside and peered down at the street. Maybe it did make sense. Bagani had the resources. He could've had her followed.

Gordie had better hurry it up. They needed to talk and they needed to plan a quick getaway. Maybe it was time she came clean and admitted to him that she was nothing more than an American housewife on the run. A fool running from the man who loved her, maybe running from the only one who could save their lives.

Oh, hurry Gordie!

She almost sighed in relief, until those fake lovers on the park bench glanced directly at her draped window. A guy in a black turban had just crossed the street, coming her way. His gaze rolled to where she stood as if he too knew exactly which window to look at.

He's found me.

CHAPTER THREE

"Ladies and gentlemen, this is your captain speaking. Please return to your seats and fasten your seatbelts. We're in for a bumpy ride."

Again?

There was no need to return. Eric Reynolds never unbuckled once he'd lowered his butt to first-class seating and strapped in. Didn't matter the airline. Didn't matter the destination. Only when all wheels touched planet Earth would he consider unfastening that buckle, even to use the restroom. Screw physics. The science behind jet propulsion couldn't compete with the cataclysmic force of attraction behind Newton's law of gravity.

Look around. There were no service stations in the clouds, no place to land or park. A rock was still a rock, even if it flew thirty-five thousand feet above the planet. Didn't matter what colorful eye-catching logo was splashed across the tail or under the belly of this jumbo bird, jets fell out of the sky more often than they should.

Could be acrophobia, the anxiety of great heights. Could be claustrophobia, that inexplicable sense of suffocating in restricted, tight places. Could even be plain old anxiety. *Whatever!*

Facts didn't mean squat when a guy could, at any moment, drop twenty thousand feet—a minute, mind you—out of a clear blue sky with nothing to say about it but hold onto your ass. Splat and goodbye. Add pelting rain, thunder, and lightning to the mix, and Eric was as wired as he'd ever been.

Despite having flown in an odd assortment of military aircraft during his military career, Eric's blood pressure spiked the moment he set foot in the terminal. Any terminal. Didn't matter how many times he'd already done this. He hated every minute of it.

Screw physics and bring on the Dramamine. *Or a Jack and Coke.*

To make what was a godawful morning worse, this flight to Amsterdam from JFK had been one jolting bump after another. Up and down. Side to side, and every so often, he swore the jet shifted in all four directions at the same time until his stomach screamed to stop.

He steeled what was left of his ragged nerves and dug his fingers into the armrests just in time. The aerodynamically designed aircraft bucked like a wild mustang, and anyone not strapped in, hit the ceiling, and they deserved it, too. What were they thinking walking around like this was safe?

Black clouds taunted at every window. Lightning flashed, too close and personal. The atmosphere sounded like a warzone.

Regularly scheduled, my ass. Flying fifteen hours straight wasn't part of his regular schedule, not by a long shot. He clenched his jaw and gritted his teeth, bound for glory because, once more, his compassion got the best of him.

The jumbo jet liner dipped, jolting Eric. He glanced at his companion agent, Jordan Hannigan, Army Ranger in his past life, directly across the aisle. He'd stretched his long legs under the seat ahead of him and was sound asleep. Had been since the flight left D.C. Snoring. Damn him.

Eric tightened his seat belt. He had just three more hours to the land of windmills and Hell.

Finally. Oomph. The jetliner touched down on one wheel before the others engaged the runway. *Didn't it figure?* Bumpy flight. Rough landing.

Before it rolled to the gate, Eric jumped to his feet, ready to get both boots on the ground, and be out of that flying death trap called modern air transportation. He thumped his buddy Jordan's shoulder. "Wake up. Time to move."

Stretching with one bleary eye half-open, Jordan groaned. "We there yet?"

Not funny, wise guy.

An athletic ex-Army Ranger, Jordan handled life as it came and rarely got rattled. From the frozen tundra of wild Alaska, he stood a strapping six-feet five in his stocking feet. He'd graduated from the University of Alaska after he'd graduated from enough deployments to last a lifetime. The happy-go-lucky man gave up all that fancy education to serve his country a couple more years with The TEAM. Yeah, Jordan was crazy like that. But then, so was Eric.

All the economy class passengers had already jumped to their feet, anxious to disembark the minute the exit doors opened. Eric snagged his sole carry-on, a battered and well-used backpack, out of the overhead compartment while he tapped his cell off airplane mode. The thing chirped and vibrated in his hand the second he did. *Alex. Damn. Already? What now?*

Eric stifled his irritation with his OCD employer and answered politely, "Hey, Boss."

"You guys find anything yet?"

"Not yet. We only just landed. We're still on the plane."

"I need a Sit Rep, damn it. The State Department wants answers. The sooner the better."

"Understood. We all want answers. Give us a minute. I'll—"

Alex hung up in his usual curt manner. No big surprise there. He tended to charge full throttle into battle, and when he charged, all hands had better be ready to charge with him, or they'd get left in the dust.

Eric stowed his phone and rolled the cramp out of his neck. Talk about a migraine. Alex never knew when to back off. Men with demons tended to act like that. Obsessed. A tad maniacal. Impatient as hell. In other words, Alex Stewart to a T.

"He have more news on these guys we're supposed to hook up with?" Jordan asked.

"No. He's just antsy. Alex wants Powers and Mikkelson back in the States in record time. You know how he is. He wants everything done yesterday. Let's move."

They shouldered their backpacks and beat feet down to the airport entrance, hailed a cab and headed to the University of

Amsterdam. They were no sooner on their way, when the weather cleared. The rain stopped. The sun came out. *Didn't it figure?*

According to Mother's instructions, they were to rendezvous with Powers and Mikkelson at a private flat, off campus. She'd given fairly accurate descriptions. Mikkelson, weightlifter. Powers, overweight. The original odd couple. Yeah, there ought to be no problem spotting them in a line up. Eric pulled up the image of Powers from the selfie Finn had sent Mother. Anyone that *interesting* would be hard to miss.

The *Universiteit van Amsterdam* boasted one of the most forward-thinking research departments in the world, something Eric appreciated no end. There was a day not too long past when he'd come to the Netherlands on a different mission, a quest for the cure to one of the rarest cancers known to afflict mankind. No matter how old or young they were…

The child of his heart, Cheyenne Rose, a tender angel of seven, seized one sunny afternoon while playing *Chopsticks* on the piano with Shea. Her fingers failed. The rest of her poor little body swiftly followed suit.

She fell writhing to the floor, and despite all Eric had seen and lived through during his many overseas deployments with the Corps, that day he knew real fear for the first time in his life. Fortunately, he'd been home when everything fell apart, undecided whether he'd stay with the Corps or opt out for Shea and Cheyenne's sake.

The seizures made the decision for him. He opted out. Never looked back. Never had a chance to. *Meningioma.* God, the name still struck terror in his soul, but that was what it was called. A brain tumor had developed in the soft tissue surrounding Cheyenne's brain and spinal column. Her prognosis went from bad to worse quickly, leaving Eric and Shea to watch their only child's sweet personality change with that first discordant chord at her fingertips.

Nothing but finding the best care and the quickest cure mattered after that. The illness reduced their only child to steady migraines and nausea, neither controllable. Medicine didn't help. Local options failed. National options, too.

When all seemed lost, an experimental drug in a far-off country declared itself the only light at the end of a very bleak tunnel. Dr. Hendrikx, the Danish researcher who'd developed the miracle drug, offered the slimmest chance. Eric grabbed hold and took the gamble, along with his wife and child, to Amsterdam.

He never saw it coming. Never thought the day would come he couldn't fix a person or a problem if he gave it his all and worked fast enough and hard enough and long enough. Especially if that person was his only child. Guess he'd been lucky up to that point. No more. Lady Luck failed him in his hour of greatest need.

Cheyenne never met Dr. Hendrikx. Never even made it to his high-tech research lab. Never got the first injection. No radiotherapy. No steroids or surgery, either. After coming so far and sinking everything he owned in a one-in-a-million chance, Eric lost the battle. Hell, he lost the war. His sweet baby girl died in her sleep the first morning in the Netherlands.

A dedicated full-time mother, Shea couldn't cope with the loss. Shortly after the funeral, she ran off on a singles cruise by herself, thinking to put distance between her and the heartache. She didn't return. Sent a lawyer instead with divorce papers and a declaration of the bitterest regret for having married for love.

Eric fingered the rolled edge of his gear bag. Shea was right. She should've chosen wiser and none of this would've happened to her. She should've married better. Should've never gotten pregnant. *Should've. Would've. Could've. Poor Shea.*

His heart still ached for her. His body and soul ached, too, if a guy could call the hole at the center of his being an actual physical ache. Felt more like Fate had injected a shot of living-Hell-on-earth straight into the heart of him, and he was meant to carry it until the day he died. So he did. Like a rucksack full of junk that he might figure out how to handle some day. Like that as yet unsigned divorce decree in his in-basket at home, a daily reminder of the greatest unfinished business of his life. His wife.

But that was a different time and a different heartache. A different person named Powers. Slapping the door shut on his pain, Eric chose to see the colorful sights of Amsterdam's upbeat urban culture passing by the cab's windows. Canals. Gabled row houses. Museums. The city reverberated with the busyness of *Amsterdamers* on bicycles, and history at every glance.

They all flew by in a blur. One charming city looked the same as another without someone special to share it with. Jordan didn't count.

Eric couldn't seem to move on, and that near fatal stabbing in South America last year had reduced him to light-duty for months. Yes, he'd survived, but he wasn't living. Not like when he'd been part of a family. *My family.*

It never stopped hurting, the missing them. But there was no going back. Only forward. Into one relentless day after another.

He slipped his fingers into a pair of black latex gloves as the cabbie drew near the University. Jordan did the same. Leaving trace evidence behind wasn't allowed.

The cabbie dropped them at the front of an ornate brick building with bars on the basement windows. Several grandiose, carved stone porticos opened onto the street. If all went well, this ugly operation would end soon, and Eric would be back on that jumbo jet and bound for home. Gordie and Finn would be safe. Better yet, he'd finally meet the odd duck who claimed he knew him. It could happen. The only problem with that thought process was that once a guy expected an op to go down smoothly—it didn't.

Jordan led the way, taking the second-floor staircase two steps at a time. With enthusiasm. *The showoff.* All that reckless abandon came to a screeching halt at the fourth door along the left hall, when blood on the hardwood floor declared their usual meet-and-greet wasn't happening.

The weapons they'd concealed beneath their heavy TEAM jackets jumped automatically to their hands. Eric maneuvered to one side of the already jimmied door. Jordan took the other.

With pistols cocked and ready, they assumed defensive positions: one man on point, the other close behind. Eric signaled his intent to enter with a quick nod, his eyes forward. Jordan tapped his shoulder once to acknowledge a go, what to them was SOP.

As one, they rushed inside, Eric first, weapon straight ahead, Jordan on his six. Blood was everywhere. The cloying scent of it hung heavy in the enclosed space. Seconds mattered.

Jordan went left while Eric advanced swiftly to the hall straight ahead. Cautiously, he entered an equally trashed bedroom. Coffee-brown walls. White ceiling. Picture frames shattered. Dresser drawers dumped and the dresser overturned. Duffel bags sliced and their contents scattered.

He proceeded carefully, looking for the source of the smell. Two full-sized beds, both upended. Mattresses sliced as well. Chrome dumbbells gleamed from beneath the mess. A weight bench lay on its side. The busted photo on the floor of Berglund and Mikkelson chest-to-chest smiling at the camera, declared whose room this was as it outed them as a couple.

But no sign of Powers or Mikkelson. Still wary about what might be lurking around the next corner, he advised Jordan with a hushed but firm, "Clear."

A firm "Clear here" came swiftly back to him.

Stepping over the destroyed personal belongings, Eric proceeded out the way he'd entered, still amped for trouble. Only one more door at his right. Turning the crystal knob, he entered a second bedroom in similar ruin. Same paint scheme. Single bed. Still ransacked. The mattress had been gutted and a dark brown ceramic lamp was crushed. Had to be Powers' room. Want to bet the guy bailed on Mikkelson like he had Berglund back at the lab.

The closet validated Eric's suspicion. No suitcase. No duffle bag. Just a mound of extra-large button-up shirts on the floor. Socks. The yellow silk nightgown hanging on a hook inside the closet was interesting. He filed that detail to share during his Sit Rep with Alex.

"You need to see the kitchen," Jordan reported. "The icebox is on its side, and the stove's pulled away. Someone sliced the wallboard behind them down to the studs. Big, square hole back there. Nothing in it."

But something had been in it. Something one of these three men didn't want the others to know about? Or were they all into some illicit activity together?

Eric's cellphone vibrated on his hip, instantly tweaking the pain in his butt, Alex by any other name. "Reynolds," he barked. Yes, barked. Alex could take it. He certainly dished it out.

"So?"

"So we've arrived on scene." Eric strove for patience. "Looks like a B&E with intent within the last half hour or so. The place is torn to hell. It stinks. Still searching for the—"

"Eric!" Jordon's voice boomed. "Found the b-b-body. Damn it to hell."

Eric ran to join his buddy at the kitchen sink. Puking his guts up, Jordan pointed behind him. "He's… it's… in there."

The head. Aptly named.

Eric's cellphone vibrated in his hand at the same time. *Give it a rest, Boss.*

Without preamble, Alex bit out, "Al-Jazeera aired a video three minutes ago. Gordie Mikkelson is dead."

"Decapitated," Eric said quietly, his stomach roiling at the gore in the tub and the odor of blood, excrement, and all those nasty things that crime movies on television failed to pass along to their avid viewers. "Yeah. Found him." In the—*head*. "What's left of him."

"Three A.M. your time." Alex's voice softened. "You okay?"

Dumbest question ever asked, but Eric understood where it came from, and why most people asked it. No person in their right mind would be okay at the sight of something like this, but he answered with "Yeah, I'm good," nonetheless. Alex needed to know if he could handle this op or not. He could. In a minute or two.

"I'm…" Jordan again. "I'll be out in the hall."

"Shut the door on your way out," Eric advised.

Striving for balance and the courage to finish his job, he breathed through his open mouth. He stepped closer to the scene, carefully avoiding the evidence pooled beside the tub or the boot print in the middle of the puddled blood beside the commode.

Definite arterial spray. Shit. Arterial spray up the walls and off the ceiling. Not dripping though. Tacky, by the looks of it. The boot print's solid evidence. The local constable needs be contacted, but first...

Eric hung up on his boss. He pushed his humanity and his natural aversion to tortured bodies aside to focus on the clinical perspective of the victim, and the stumps where both index fingers and one pinkie finger had been clipped off.

Now Eric knew what had caused those black lines on poor Phoenix Berglund. Bloodied welts left by a whip crisscrossed the headless body. Even its neck. The back of its shaved head. *Jesus Christ, what kind of animal does this?*

Abdul-Mutaal.

Eric crouched at the tub and strove to see the gore from a purely forensic view. Everything matched the Berglund murder scene, except the location. Abdul-Mutaal must have tortured his victims elsewhere, then forced Mikkelson back to the apartment to locate whatever that elusive *something* was that he'd killed for.

It didn't make sense. Abdul-Mutaal clearly wanted more than just Finn, or he wouldn't have destroyed the place. What was Mutaal looking for and why kill Finn's friends to get it? That alone seemed counter-productive.

All questions. No answers.

Eric lifted the commode lid with the barrel of his pistol. Mikkelson's head wasn't in there, but someone had hurled and forgot to flush.

More questions. Like Berglund, Abdul-Mutaal took Mikkelson's head with him. Why? And who the hell else was in here? And when? Was it Powers or someone helping Mutaal? *Disturbing. Damned disturbing.*

Pushing to his feet, Eric needed more room and a helluva lot more air than the already occupied head afforded. He snapped several shots of the scene with his cellphone camera and called his work done. Duty demanded he be thorough, so he made a final sweep through the pillaged apartment, swallowing down the bile creeping up his throat.

His head buzzed with revulsion. The sympathetic taste of copper clung to the back of his tongue. He needed to spit, but got another shock instead. There, at the juncture of the hallway and kitchen, a familiar face smiled up at him. *His.*

Holy shit. How'd that get here? In Amsterdam of all places. He dropped one knee to the floor, surprised to see his USMC picture staring back at him. Needing to be sure it was his dumb face in the middle of a gruesome murder scene, he picked it up and turned it over. That was his signature on the back of it all right. *Definitely me. What the hell? Why here?*

There was no way he'd leave that behind, so Eric tucked the photo into his jeans pocket and vacated the premises. He shouldered both of their packs since Jordan stood pale and breathless beside the apartment entry, his back and palms flat to the wall behind him. "You good?"

"Yeah. I guess." Jordan was nowhere near good, not blowing through his open mouth like he was, and not with his butt still pressed against the wall for support. The guy was downright gray. Sweaty.

Retrieving a small plastic pill jar from his bag, Eric rolled two tablets to his palm and offered them to Jordan before the guy upchucked and made everything worse. "Here. Swallow. These will settle your gut so you can move."

Jordan tossed his head back, gulped the anti-nausea meds dry, still panting hard. "You finished in there?"

"There's nothing more we can do. Let's move. Let the local authorities deal with it."

Jordan blew out a big breath through pursed lips, jerking his head at the mess beyond the apartment door. "I don't know how you do it. One look at shit like that and I turn into the vomit comet."

Eric stuck a firm palm to his buddy's shoulder. "It all depends on what you see. You saw the horror. Once I settled down, I saw the man. Breathe in. Breathe out. Think of something else. Let it go."

Jordan wilted to his knees, his head between both palms. "That's no *man* in there. That was nothing but a meat sack in a slaughterhouse. I don't ever want to see anything like that again."

"Come on. We've got to get moving. Someone has to have called this in." Eric tugged him back on his feet. Only fresh air and distance cured this kind of shock.

It could've been worse. They could've found two bodies.

CHAPTER FOUR

Please pick up. Pick up!

Still in her fat suit, Shea pressed her knuckles to her teeth as the phone rang. Five pm at the Amsterdam airport meant eleven pm on the East Coast of the United States. All she owned now rested in a carry-on at her feet.

When Gordie hadn't shown at the Internet cafe, she'd gone back to their flat looking for him. The second she'd pushed her broken door open, she'd smelled it, but in she went, hoping she could save her last, and maybe her only, friend.

It didn't work out that way.

She'd found what was left of Gordie in the bathtub, and panic set in. She threw up, barely able to get to the commode in time. With fear ratcheting up her spine like a devil with spurs, she'd stuffed a few necessities into her carry-on along with the laptop, and she'd run for her life. The only smart thing she'd done was to wipe her bloody boots before she left tracks.

Come on! Sasha has to be home!

Nearly a full year ago, Shea had linked up with Sasha Kennedy. It happened after her encounter with Bagani. Afraid for her life and hiding out in a cheap hotel room, she and Sasha had played the latest, greatest computer game, *Vengeance and Hell, version 2.0,* for months before they'd hooked up in an online chat room about the flaws in the game. They'd collaborated on a better version of *V&H* to link gamers all over the world while enhancing action and rewards.

But talk about it being a small world. Shea knew instantly whom she'd accidentally bumped into: *Mother,* the genius who worked for Alex Stewart. Possibly the only man in the world who could locate a missing ex-wife.

Goose bumps lifted over her body the moment she'd realized who she was chatting with, but Sasha had never let on. Still, Shea kept a watchful ear. If Sasha had ever suspected, she was good at hiding it.

On the fifth ring, Shea gave up and dialed her friend's work number.

Please, please be there!

"The TEAM, Sasha Kennedy speaking. Finn? Is this you?"

"Yes!" Relief leapt off Shea's tongue. "Gordie's dead!"

"I know. It's on all the news channels. Where are you?"

"I'm at the airport in Amsterdam. Is Eric coming? I can't stay here any longer!" She wiped her sweaty palms on the baggy pants of her fake persona. Right then and there, she resembled a three-hundred-pound guy with red hair and an eating compulsion. Her fake buckteeth were in her sloppy coat pocket along with more spirit gum if any facial appliances decided to move. Like her over-sized nose. Her furry eyebrows. The wart on her chin.

"Yes, he's on his way to you right now. Where are you travelling to?"

"England. Flight number sixteen twenty—" A bump from behind interrupted her, pushing Shea's angst into overdrive.

She whirled on her attacker, but the elderly man in wire-rimmed glasses who'd stuck the pointed end of his umbrella in her left butt cheek didn't look so dangerous. His nose crinkled under craggy, white brows. A cute smile lit up his wrinkled face. "Sorry, young man," he said with a perfect British clip. "I'm afraid my bumbershoot got away from me. I didn't hurt you, did I?"

Her gut clenched. This sweet gentleman might not have a mean bone in his body, but that other guy, the man in the black robe, couldn't be far behind. She couldn't help the creepy sensation that he lurked in every shadow, watching and waiting. That he could get to her whenever he wanted.

Stifling her terror, she muttered in her deepest Finn-voice, "No problem."

Her cellphone screamed, "Finn! Speak to me, damn it!"

Shea turned her back on the gentleman, every last speck of saliva gone from her tongue and throat. "Sorry. I thought... I mean, I thought I saw... Never mind. W-what did you want?"

"I asked where you're going?"

"England. I'm, ahh..."

Oh, hell on earth. A tall swarthy man in a long flowing robe strode toward her in the crowd of passengers disembarking a just arrived flight into Amsterdam. *It's him.*

Three women in veils followed him, and the robe was cream-colored, not black, but there was no mistaking the grim fire in his eye.

Her phone clattered to the floor.

Eric called Mother the minute he hit the sidewalk outside Powers' flat. "Where the hell is he?"

Sirens approached from the south, so he and Jordan headed north away from the murder scene, their weapons concealed, their gloves off, and no idea where their remaining quarry was.

"I'm not sure. He was at the Amsterdam airport and he mentioned flight number sixteen twenty-seven. England. If he actually made the connection. He hung up on me before he said."

Eric tipped his cellphone from his ear to check the local time, a chilly inkling of premonition tiptoeing up his spine. A successful op didn't run on *maybes*. The precious forty-eight hours of this wild goose chase were slipping away, and he hated being one lousy step behind the man he was supposed to be saving. "When?"

"It departs in thirty minutes." Mother sounded edgy. *She should.*

"Call him back. Tell him to stay at the airport." *So we can catch up with his dumb ass.* "We're on our way now, but there's no way we'll make it in thirty minutes." Eric pocketed his cell, that annoying premonition poking him to move faster or risk losing another client to the bloodthirsty killer on the loose. Fifty percent was one helluva loss rate for any op. Alex had to be as pissed as Eric.

Jordan had recovered his professional demeanor if not his stomach. The poor guy's eyes still resembled two pieces of coal on a stark white face, but he was operational. He flagged a cab, but busy rush hour traffic reduced their fifteen-minute ride back to the airport to a slow crawl. People were everywhere. On foot. In taxis and boats. Bicycles and putt-putt scooters flooded the streets and alleyways.

Eric stared at the mad dash home, one he could relate to. He used to be that way, ready to run to Shea at the first opportunity, and… *Don't go there.* He bowed his forehead to his clenched fist and forced his mind from the ghosts of his past. Thinking about *them* took too much out of his soul, and now wasn't the time for past regrets. He needed to be on his A-game. For *Finn* Powers, not—Shea.

Truth be known, he didn't relish another flight so soon after the first. There'd been no sleeping on the flight over. Forty winks might see him through the rest of this op—if he ever got the chance. Finding Powers alive wouldn't hurt either.

He and Jordan arrived back at the Amsterdam airport fifty-five minutes later, and one more time, they hit the ground running. If Powers was semi-smart, and if he exercised a half-ounce of common sense, he'd be hiding inside the terminal, waiting for them to show. He'd contact Mother and let her know where he was. The airport was big enough. There ought to be a dozen or more places to hide.

But if he were really smart, he'd come looking for them. Eric doubted a civilian on the run had that much sense though. Once fear and adrenaline kicked in, anything could happen. This op was like herding cats.

After a quick talk with airport security and showing their U.S. federal credentials, Eric and Jordan were allowed access to the departure gates for outgoing flights to London. No luck. Flight number sixteen twenty-seven had already taxied away from the gate. First in line for takeoff might as well be on the moon.

They scanned the other departure gates for every dumpy, ill-dressed man in sight. Plenty fit the bill, but none were the man they were looking for.

Eric rang Mother, that eerie sense of foreboding ramping into a full-blown migraine. "Where is he? Do you know? Have you heard from him?"

"He's not there?"

"I wouldn't be calling if he was, would I?"

"I'll bet he's already left then."

No shit! "Didn't you tell him to stay put like I asked?"

"I couldn't get in touch with him. He's running for his life. He must've gone onto England."

Eric rolled the cramp out of his neck. This disastrous op hadn't let up since Alex's staff meeting. The long flight, the missed contacts, and Mother weren't helping. "Call him back. We need to know where he'll be when we hit Heathrow. I'm not chasing his dumb ass around London just because he's scared, damn it."

"I will. I promise. I'll monitor the flight, and the minute I know anything, I'll send you a text. Umm, Eric?"

"Yes?" he asked with extreme patience. Mother always meant well, but chasing a chicken with its head cut off didn't bode well for Mr. Powers.

"He asked for you by name again. He wanted to know if you were coming. I told him yes."

Great. Just damned great. High expectations for a stranger he didn't know from Adam.

"Can you at least try to be nice to him?"

That sparked Eric's temper. "When haven't I been? I haven't even met the guy yet."

"It's just that he might be gay. I know Phoenix and Gordie were, and, umm, I don't know how you feel about the whole issue."

He could hear her cringe all the way across the Atlantic. The whole gay issue was such a non-player in his opinion. People were people, damn it, and this one was scared witless. Gay or straight didn't mean squat. "Listen up, Mother. I don't give a shit if he's transsexual, bisexual, or if he sports a third eye in the middle of his forehead. Tell him to keep his ass out of sight until we get to Heathrow. I can't save him if I can't find him!"

Eric hung up before she threw another problem his way. Scowling at Jordan, he wondered why Mother had thought he'd treat Powers any different than everyone else. *I'm a nice guy, damn it. Most of the time. Aren't I?*

"Get in line," he barked at Jordan. "We're going to London."

Shea all but ran out of the main terminal once she arrived at Heathrow, sure she'd stumble on her big Finn-feet if she peered over her shoulder one more time. She needed to catch a cab without being seen. She needed a safe place to hide until Eric showed, but even then, she didn't know what she'd do when he did.

Run to him?

Run from him?

Either scenario had its merits.

Would he recognize her? Not in this get up. Fingering the unibrow that until now, had kept her safely hidden from her past, she waited patiently in the queue to catch a cab. She couldn't stay inside the terminal. Eric would have to understand that eyes were everywhere. She could feel them on the back of her neck just as surely as if a bulls-eye was painted there.

At last it was her turn, but as she took a step to the cab, a hand clamped onto her sleeve, paralyzing her heart. It had finally happened. Her whole body cringed. She stumbled, scared to turn around for fear Phoenix and Gordie's killer had followed her to London. He'd caught her, and now she'd be killed, just like—

"Excuse me, sir, but you dropped this." Standing there with her airline ticket stub was a businessman dressed in a three-piece suit. A Caucasian businessman. In a red tie.

How un-Mideastern of him.

Relief shivered up her spine. She snatched the stub from his fingertips with a hurried, "Th-thank you."

He lifted a perturbed brow and continued on his way.

Professor Grover's brow used to lift like that, often at the speed with which the Lucky Stars problem solved. Her heart ached for him. For Phoenix and Gordie. She could barely catch a full breath. Karma seemed determined she pay for past mistakes. She'd lost everyone. *Again...*

The need to see Professor Grover filled her with an inexplicable longing. He'd often spoken of Dungarvin Bay in Ireland, his home away from home. And Ireland was just a hop, skip, and a jump across the water. Maybe that was where he'd gone. Maybe he'd know who killed Phoenix and Gordie. At least, he'd give her safe refuge until they reasoned it out together. *If he's there.*

It was worth a try. Shea waved the cabbie off, determined to unravel the mess she'd created. Stiffening her resolve and her spine, she left the cab behind and marched back into Heathrow. She was going to Ireland.

CHAPTER FIVE

Eric knew the moment the jet touched down at Heathrow. *Finn isn't in jolly Olde England, either.* Before the *Jetway* engaged with the *British Airways* Airbus, he had Mother on his phone.

"Oh, I'm so glad you called. Guess what?"

God, he hated that question.

"Finn isn't in England anymore."

"Where is he then?" Whatever else this Powers creep might be, he'd been nothing but a royal pain in the ass since this operation started. A genius maybe, but he was obviously one of those quirky guys without a lick of sense to back up their brilliance. The kind who never showered and didn't know how to tie their own shoelaces. *That* kind.

Jordan hunched over the back of Eric's airline seat. They'd travelled in typical military-style this flight, dead last in the rear of the aircraft with their seats against the galley wall, no option to recline or stretch their long legs. "You're kidding me, right? He's not here?"

Eric stilled so he could hear Mother over Jordan's question. "He's gone to Ireland to find his professor, Morell Grover, but I've got an address. Finn won't run this time. He promised."

Eric simmered. *And I'm supposed to believe that why?*

This continual game of cat and mouse had grown thin. He'd been awake for over thirty-five hours straight. No sleep. No decent food. And no Finn.

The forty-eight-hour window was blown. One more round of hide-and-go-seek, and *Operation Find Finn* could go to hell. He and Jordan would head back to Virginia where they belonged, and Finn could cover his own sorry ass.

"Where in Ireland?" he bit out more sharply than he intended.

Mother provided the address in southern Ireland, but before she could get another word in, he ended the call. He'd run out of patience for the idiot on the run. Her, too.

"Where next, Bro?" Jordan asked, his easy-going demeanor intact once more. Why not? He'd slept those fifteen hours over the Atlantic to Amsterdam, on this puddle-jumper flight, too.

Eric pushed back in his chair, bone-tired with nothing to show for the day but another flight he didn't want to take. "Dungarvin, Ireland."

Jordan took the seat across the aisle while the flight attendants assisted the last passengers. "Powers is in Ireland? Why the hell?"

"Mother thinks he's hooking up with his professor, Morell Grover. Don't ask why because I don't know much more than you do."

"Doesn't sound very Irish to me. Morell Grover. Does it to you?"

Eric couldn't answer. He stared, his brain starved for sleep he couldn't allow. Not yet. Once he gave in to the overwhelming urge it'd be *all she wrote*. He drew in a deep breath, needing to move before he lost the battle. Summoning the image of those two dead young men did the trick. Berglund and Mikkelson deserved justice.

Mentally kicking his own butt, Eric heaved up and out of his seat. *Operation Find Finn* was back on. Fortunately, they had their pick of flights into Cork. They ended up in the back of the bus again. The Airbus. Touchdown went as smooth as silk, probably because Eric couldn't have cared less by then. It was an interesting way to cure one's fear of air travel: fly until jetlag numbed your brain.

While the other passengers disembarked, he dragged his backpack out of the overhead compartment one last time, prepared for another search, and hopefully a quick in-and-out extraction.

Jordan clapped his back, urging him on. They opted for a rental with GPS instead of a cab. Jordan drove. Might have been a mistake. A nap during the drive would've been nice, but Jordan needed a navigator to get them out of all those blasted Irish roundabouts and onto the correct exits. *And* to keep him on the left side of the road. For some reason, the guy from Alaska thought driving in Ireland would be a breeze. It wasn't. Besides acclimating himself to the controls being on the wrong side of the car, he kept hanging a right when he should've been turning left.

After a circuitous ride through winding roads that resembled one-lane sheep trails and more roundabouts than Eric realized existed in the world, they arrived at the address Mother had relayed. Eric stepped out of the car, his jacket once again concealing two loaded firearms and one beat-to-hell body. The destination Powers gave Mother ended at a well-kept, white clapboard home with a green-shingled roof that lapped the drip line, creating a homey cottage effect. The matching green shutters, white picket fence instead of stone, with bushes and trees in bloom added to the courtyard. Roses. The flowery scent of roses—lots of roses—mingled with the fresh salt air lifting off the Irish Sea to the south.

The hour was late, well after twenty hundred, eight pm Ireland time. He'd already made reservations at a local hotel chain, in the event they actually caught up with Powers this time.

Eric forged ahead, his senses on high alert. Despite its genteel appearance, evil could still be afoot even at this quaint Irish cottage. His covert training came back to him as easy as turning a corner. Hyper-vigilance had its place in the world.

Knocking on the front door rewarded him with a prompt response by a plump, dark-haired, middle-aged woman, her tresses streaked with gray and twisted into a bun at the top of her head.

"May I help you?" she asked with a definite Irish lilt and an unabashedly cheery smile. The white apron covering her blue dress and the fuzzy strands dangling down her neck declared she'd been busy in her kitchen, and *what did he want at this late hour?*

"Excuse us, ma'am, but we were told to meet Finn Powers at this location. Is he here?"

She cast an appraising glance up and down Jordan. Then did the same with Eric. Her smile widened. "He did say visitors would be along the bye, but he didn't say they'd be as charming as the likes of you two young men. Please come in." She stood aside and beckoned them to enter.

A delightful sensory overload hit Eric's nose and stomach the second he set foot inside. Fresh baked bread. Soup or stew, definitely beef stock. Onions for sure. The blend of aromas elicited a rumble from his empty stomach.

"Are you hungry?" she asked as if she already knew the answer.

"Yes," Jordan answered with emphasis. *When wasn't he hungry?*

"No," Eric corrected instantly, intent on maintaining a professional distance from this kindly woman. "Thank you for your offer, ma'am, but we're not here to bother you. We came for Powers, and we need to leave as soon as possible."

Jordan's grumble at his six didn't go unnoticed by their pleasant hostess. She interlocked her fingers over her rounded stomach, a definite twinkle in her eye. "I'll have you know I'm Rosie O'Banner, and this is the 'Edge of O'Banner', the finest bed and breakfast on the far side of the Isle. Your friend left the minute he arrived. He said you're not to leave 'til he returns. And for your information, it's no inconvenience to care for the weary and tired, nor the hungry, young man. You're welcome to wait, and if you need a place to stay while you're here, I have two empty rooms waiting for you. Meals are included, and there's no charge for the hospitality nor the welcome."

Damn. She'd pegged him dead on. Weary. Tired as hell. Hungry enough to eat airport fast food and tempted to accept her offer of a room with a bed. And dinner. How was a guy supposed to refuse all of that? He tried. "That's very kind, but no thank you, ma'am. We've already made arrangements in Dungarvin. We'll be leaving as soon as Powers gets back."

"But you'll eat while you wait, will you not?" Rosie O'Banner had a delicious openness about her. When she cocked her head, her blue eyes twinkled with a dash of mischief, as if she dared him to turn her down one more time.

It didn't help that Jordan elbowed him and said, "I can always cancel the hotel."

"And I'll just bet my last lamb in the meadow that you poor boys haven't eaten all day now, have you, eh?" Mrs. O'Banner reinforced her argument.

Eric's stomach growled at the temptation within reach. Perhaps this out-of-the-way B&B would suffice for dinner and the night, but no more. In the morning, he was out of there. With Finn. For sure. "Thank you. We have travelled far today. A meal would hit the spot."

Oh, the smiling eyes this woman had been blessed with all but beamed at the chance to feed them. Like that was anything but more work for her. She reminded Eric of his mother out in Washington State and her willingness to serve others. There never was a crotchety child or a grumpy man she couldn't get around with her endearing ways and lighthearted banter. Rosie had to be related, if not by blood, then by spirit.

"Well, good. That's settled." She nodded to the staircase at her left. "First room at the top is open. You take that one," she said to Eric then turned to Jordan. "The one across the hall from it is available as well. 'Tis yours. Now call that stuffy hotel with its scratchy bedding and boxed meals, and cancel those reservations. You're to be my guests for the night, and I challenge either of you to argue."

Eric relented. His charming host had quite a way about her. "One night will suffice. Thank you, ma'am."

"Off with you and wash your hands then. I've just finished tomorrow's stew and another batch of bread. I'll have a table set with a hot meal and a hearty mug of Guinness for you before you're back. Hurry along. Don't dilly dally."

He had to smile. She'd won him over with food and a cheerful welcome. Him. A stranger with a gun. All the more reason he and Jordan couldn't stay more than one night.

They obeyed their charming hostess like two sons might have obeyed their mother. Eric took the door to the right of the staircase. He set his backpack on the floor next to the bed, and his stomach growled in anticipation of its first meal in nearly two days. He'd gone without food or sleep longer on black ops, but it always ended the same. He'd be comatose for a day or two, then hungry enough to eat anything not tacked down.

The room was larger than he'd expected. Clean in a fresh breeze kind of way, the window was open and a gentle evening wind tossed the sheer white curtain panels. A patchwork quilt of all shades of blues and creamy whites covered the queen-sized bed. Braided rugs littered the polished wooden floor.

Eric closed the window and deliberated doffing his shoulder holster as well, but didn't. Instead, he covered the weapon with a light jacket to keep it out of sight. What Rosie didn't know wouldn't hurt her.

Setting his backpack beside the bed, he opened the side pocket and tugged out a flat metal case. Opening the tablet-sized item, he pushed his thumb to the one sided-hinge to lock it in place before he set it on his nightstand. And there she was, a dark-haired little girl with adoration for him in her brown eyes. *Cheyenne.*

Eric pressed the pad of his thumb to his lips, then to hers. "I love you, Angel," he whispered like he'd done every night since his world fell apart, "and I still remember."

Along with his daughter, his parents, Lara and Rex Reynolds smiled back from their own photo. And like it or not, so did Shea on her wedding day. God, she'd been a radiant bride. So full of hope. Love. All good things.

The only other item in his portable shrine was the key to a Cape Cod style home on Vashon Island in the middle of Puget Sound, Washington. His and Shea's first real home and their refuge until things got too tough. He hadn't had the heart to sell it, so it waited—like him—for the day she came back. For now, a couple with seven kids rented it, which was good. It deserved to live.

Tugging the photo he'd found in Mikkelson's flat out of his pocket, Eric slid it between Cheyenne and Shea's photos. "Keep her safe for me," he told his daughter. "If she's already up in heaven with you, please tell her I miss her. Tell her I never stopped loving her. Give her a kiss for me." His prayer. Every night.

Brushing a quick hand under his eye, Eric let the silence between heaven and earth stretch. It had been so long since he'd seen or talked with Shea, maybe it was time to face the truth. She could very well be dead. He just wished he knew how and where or—if. A husband deserved to know something like that.

Ending his one-sided conversation the way he had for two years now, Eric whispered what he'd once said to his sleepy child, "Goodnight, Angel. Sweet dreams."

Off he went to use the en-suite head. One glance in the mirror over the washbasin explained how his hostess had read him like a book. The man in the mirror stared back with definite black circles around his glassy eyes. The tired ass had hunger and exhaustion down to a fine art.

He turned the faucet on and lowered his head under the cold stream long enough to revive him. Eric towel dried his face and spruced his short black hair into a few spikes until he looked halfway decent. The grumpy man in the mirror didn't appear to be quite so dead by the time he hit the top of the stairs.

Jordan's cheerful voice could be heard below, bantering from one room to another with Rosie about the weather in Amsterdam. All conversation ceased when she hurried from her kitchen with a basket of steamy rolls in her hand.

Eric crossed the cozy dining area with its tablecloth covered tables and wooden captain's chairs, to where Jordan sat in the corner with his face in a steaming bowl of beef stew. Rolls dripping with melted butter lined his plate. He had a half-finished pint of what looked like ale in one hand and a spoon in the other. "Come on," he said with a mouthful. "This stuff's good. Dig in."

"You'd better hurry," Rosie tossed over her shoulder on her way back to her kitchen. "There may not be anything left but crumbs and dirty dishes in another minute."

Eric took a seat with his hungry buddy, but faced the doorway, an old habit from active duty days. Rose might know how to cook, but he doubted he'd relish the fare as much as his buddy did. He'd lost the zest for life over two years ago. Mostly, he ate take-out or order-in. Cheap food. Fast food. He never sat in the kitchen or at the dining room table when he ate. Wouldn't think of it.

Oddly, one spoon full of the meaty broth encouraged another. His stomach calmed. He dipped his chin toward the aromatic aroma lifting from the bowl, and he settled down to all but inhale the tastiest and simplest fare he'd consumed in a long time. Chunks of tender, seasoned beef swam with carrots and baby red potatoes in a richly flavored broth. Yeast rolls, tender and warm. Creamy butter. A pint of Guinness that went down smooth and rich.

By the time he finished, he'd polished off three bowls of stew and hadn't spoken a word. There wasn't time. As long as he'd kept eating, Rosie kept serving.

At last, sated and comfortably full, he tipped back in his chair to watch Jordan sop a bread roll to the last speck of stew in the bottom of what had to be his third bowl, not that Eric counted.

Dessert appeared in the form of a hearty spoonful of apple cobbler topped off with thick vanilla custard and a drizzle of cream. Eric eyed the tantalizing dish, not certain he had room for more, but that aroma...

Maybe just one bite.

Jordan made swift work of his, moaning and groaning that the dessert was too good to pass up. The guy had to have been born with a hollow leg. After smacking his lips, he stuck his elbows to the table and eyed Eric's plate. "You gonna eat that?"

Eric lifted his fork, daring his buddy to make another move. "What do you think?"

Decision made. Just like the stew and biscuits, after the first savory bite, Eric polished off the dessert. The apples retained a bit of crispness, and the custard added a hint of cinnamon mingled with another flavor he couldn't identify. Rum? Irish whiskey? It was good, whatever it was. For a change, he'd enjoyed eating. His stomach didn't complain, either.

Rosie spied him licking his bottom lip after the last delicious morsel. "I have more if you're still hungry."

He chuckled. "No, thank you, ma'am. I haven't eaten this much home-cooked food in years." *Two years, one month and seventeen days to be precise. Shake-n-Bake chicken. Wild rice and buttered asparagus. Razzleberry pie with a dollop of vanilla bean ice cream. The night before we flew to Amsterdam. The last day of my life. And then they both left me...*

"You're a mighty fine cook, Mrs. O'Banner," Jordan declared, his chair tilted back and one hand on his full stomach, the other on the edge of the table. "Mr. O'Banner must be one happy man. Where's he off to?"

She blushed to the roots of her pleasantly graying hair. "I'm afraid he's singing with the angels. I planted him over at Saint Peter's twelve years back."

"I'm sorry." Now it was Jordan's turn to blush. "I didn't mean to—"

"Never you mind." She brushed his apology off. "'Twas the day before Easter he got it in his head to row out for a bucket of oysters all the way at Galway. Should've gone to Holy Saturday Mass like I told him to, but no. Tsk, tsk. He liked his chowder, and me? Well, I liked to make it for him, so off he went. When he didn't come back, I took me car and went to find him. Poor Paddy. He'd had a heart attack. Hadn't shucked a single oyster. Hadn't even gotten into his dinghy. Just dropped dead on the shore under a clear, blue sky."

Eric took over for Jordan who'd gone redder than Rosie and looked to be ten times more uncomfortable. "That had to have been hard for you."

She dabbed at her eyes with a corner of her apron. "Yes and no. Life is made up of a long line of comings and goings, like people in a queue at the church buffet. 'Tis the way of things, is all 'tis. Paddy went a tad earlier than I expected, but one day 'twill be my turn at the table. How about you? You've had your share of bad times. It was difficult, but you survived, didn't you?"

Her piercing question shot a spear straight to Eric's heart. This woman seemed able to see inside him. He chose not to engage in her charming, but probing way. Some things were better left unshared. "When did Finn say he'd be back?"

Rosie offered a sly wink as if she knew he'd dodged her inquiry, when she knew absolutely nothing at all and never would. "Whenever you're ready, I'm here to listen. Just remember. We can nah share a sorrow we have nah finished grieving. Nor can we share joy 'til we've learned the real cost of a smile. Life is hard, but 'tis the hardness of it that makes the goodness of it shine like a glimmer of sun breaking through a cloudy day. As for Finn, he didn't give me a definite time. 'Tis dark now and another storm cloud has rolled in, so maybe soon."

Eric averted his gaze. Rosie had an uncanny insight and a glib tongue. He needed to avoid her.

"What do you think?" Jordan asked. "Go looking for him?"

"Stay." Eric glanced at the rain hitting the window, typical for southern Ireland in spring. "Let him come to us for a change."

CHAPTER SIX

Shea had left Rosie's cottage within seconds of her arrival. She'd no more than stashed her suitcase next to the dresser in her room before she'd advised Rosie that she was going for a walk, but to expect visitors. Mother had said another agent was with Eric, but Shea had forgotten the name.

Professor Grover's eyes widened to see her on the doorstep of his cottage. "What are you doing here?" he asked, his wire-rimmed glasses perched on the end of his nose. He'd fussed, sputtered a moment, then waved her inside. "Come in, child, it's raining. Are you alone?"

"I am, but I can't stay long." She entered quickly with one last measured glance to make sure she hadn't been followed. Only when she was safely behind his heavy wooden door did she allow a deep breath of relief.

His home was none the worse for wear considering his long absences to Amsterdam. Embers glowed at the hearth where a black cat lay curled on a golden velvet pillow. Yet the professor seemed caught off guard. Edgy. He reopened his door to peer outside.

"Did I catch you at a bad time?"

One bushy brow lifted. "No, I don't get many visitors, that's all. Let me look at you. What's going on? You're thinner. Have you lost weight?"

This wasn't the time to look thinner. Shea used her deepest Finn voice as she adjusted her very large paunch. "You tell me what's going on. You're the one who left without saying a word. Did you know Phoenix was killed right after you left? Gordie's dead, too. They were beheaded. With a sword!" The words rushed out of her.

He blinked in surprise. "Murdered? A sword? Oh, dear me, no. I hadn't heard that, not that anyone knew where I'd gone. You see, my sister took ill. I rushed home, but she passed before I could get here. I'm... I don't know what to say. I'm sorry."

Shuffling to the rocking chair by the fireplace, he shook his head and slipped out of his penny loafers. "To tell you the truth, I was so frazzled when I got the news about Eloise that I honestly didn't think to tell anyone I was leaving. Once I got here..." He gestured at the room in general as he sank into the chair. "I'm sorry. I simply forgot about everything, but her."

Of all people, Shea understood how dazed a person could become after the death of a loved one. She crouched at his knee. "No, I'm sorry. I didn't realize you were dealing with a sick sister, nor her death. I wouldn't have come, but now..." Her gaze shifted to the closed door behind her. "Do you know anyone who would want to murder Phoenix and Gordie?"

"Murdered?" he asked again, squinting at her through the smudged lenses of his glasses. "What happened to you? You're different tonight. Come, let me make you a cup of tea." He seemed confused instead of upset at the deaths of his favorite students.

Shea lifted to the chair beside his, confident that her padding was still in place. A knitted cream-colored afghan hung off the back of his chair, no doubt his sister's. Maybe that was why this home seemed well taken care of. His sister must have lived here with him. She'd been keeping house for him while he commuted back and forth between Ireland and Amsterdam. How weird.

"Professor. Didn't you hear what I just said?"

"Umm, what?" Stretching forward, he asked yet again, "What's wrong with you?"

Me? What's wrong with you? Oh, hell on earth, Shea should've guessed. Her unibrow, the only item that had failed in the past, must be coming undone. Tentatively, her fingers ran over the perfect line of a long, furry caterpillar spirit-gummed over her own delicate brows. *Nothing wrong there.* She fingered the wart on her chin. *Still in place.* Her shaggy red wig was next, but it was as good as ever, hopefully as ugly.

What was he seeing that she wasn't? "Why do you think I'm different?"

He squinted through his spectacles, his entire face wrinkling. "I don't think I've ever noticed the color of your eyes before. They're quite lovely for a young man. What color are they? Green or turquoise?"

Crap! My glasses. She patted her pockets, not sure where that part of her ensemble had gone. Talk about scatterbrained. "I must've lost my glasses. My eyes are greenish blue. Sometimes," she admitted. *And I'll get another pair the first chance I get. Extra thick. Twice as geeky. So no one can see them. Especially not Eric.*

"Don't worry about it. Come in and sit awhile, child. Tell me what you've been up to." He leaned back in his rocker with his hands folded on his stomach. "It's been a long time since we've talked, hasn't it?"

She leaned in closer, frustrated that he couldn't seem to absorb the awful news she'd just shared, and *oh, by the way. I'm already in and sitting.* "Professor. Are you okay?"

He rocked forward and backward. "I'm fine. Why do you ask?"

Because you're freaking me out. "Phoenix and Gordie are dead, but you act as if you haven't heard me."

"They are? What happened?" His rocking chair squeaked on the forward thrust as he came to a stop. His lips curved with an oddly disjointed, lopsided smile that didn't reflect any concern. He might as well have asked about the weather.

She caught herself. There was no sense in repeating what he didn't seem capable of understanding. Her professor's appearance was different, too. His left eyelid sagged. His smile drooped on the left side of his face, too. Had he suffered a stroke? "Professor, you don't look well. Is there someone I can call?"

A crease narrowed between his brows. "Heavens no. Just sit with me. Sometimes grief is too much to take in all at once. It takes time to process it."

As she well knew. "Are you hungry?"

He nodded in time to the sway of his rocking chair. "Yes. I believe I could eat."

Shea bit her lip, the hope of any explanation into the murders of her friends lost in the blink of an aged man's eye. "I'll fix something before I leave."

"But Finn. You must stay. You only just got here."

"I'll be back another day when you're feeling better." She lifted from her seat, disappointed, but determined to do what she could.

Considering his state of mind, his kitchen was quite orderly. She couldn't locate the cat's food dishes, but fed it anyway since the friendly beggar kept rubbing its long svelte body against and between her pant legs. Once the cat had its face in its bowl, she fixed toast and opened a can of noodle soup from the professor's well-filled pantry.

Someone must have helped him with the housework or there would've been more mess. While he ate, she contented herself with petting his cat. It all but scrubbed its furry face on her chin, seemingly starved for attention.

The banked embers in the hearth glowed, while she stroked the purring feline on her lap. A wisp of smoke curled into the chimney, and her mind drifted with it, back in time

Two years of running and pretending to be someone she wasn't, had taught her well. All the disguises in the world couldn't hide her stretch marks, nor Eric's pride when she'd gained weight while she was pregnant. He'd patted her backside right up to the day Cheyenne was born.

"I put that baby inside of you," he'd breathed between kisses to her sweaty forehead in the delivery room. "Just bring her to home base, and it'll all be worth it. You'll lose every last, pinchable ounce, and you'll be in love with yourself again. Like I am. You'll see."

She'd made him happy that day. The grin on that handsome face when the nurse placed his newborn daughter in his arms haunted her.

Delivery wasn't the problem. The funeral was.

After a particularly heartbreaking visit from her neighbor, she'd run from all that reminded her of that perfect smiling angel she'd never hold again. *Never read another bedtime story to. Never smell her minty toothpaste breath at goodnight's kiss. Never another giggle. Another Christmas morning. Another tooth fairy. All those nevers!*

The day she lost Cheyenne, she lost her way. Something inside of her broke, and for once in their perfect married life, she and Eric weren't in sync. There was no comfort to be found in his arms, and some days, she couldn't stand to look at him. Like a vinyl record set too long in the sun, the diamond needle of his love couldn't reach the scream buried in the tracks of her warped and desolate heart.

Yet not a day passed that she hadn't thought of Eric. Didn't need him. Didn't wish he'd look for her and find her.

Professor Grover's spoon clattered to the floor, drawing her out of her depressing past. He'd fallen asleep with the empty soup bowl on his lap.

Shea rubbed her chilled biceps. Carefully, she extracted it from his grasp and took it to the kitchen. She washed the few dirty dishes in the sink, straightened the counters, and filled a bowl with water for his cat. It seemed a lonely but friendly animal. She lifted it into her arms. "I'm going to call you mittens until I know your real name. My little girl would've loved a sweet kitty like you." *And I'd give the world to have her back. Just to see her play with you. Just once...*

The feline rubbed its nose against Shea's chin. Its body arched into the curve of her palm, seeming to crave her touch. *So much like another tiny little body...*

Time shifted in the quaint little cottage. For a split second, comfort invaded that barren hole in her heart. Holding the cat felt a lot like holding Cheyenne. Mittens was warm and soft. Alive.

A smattering of rain kicked up outside the cottage windows. The professor snored lightly, his head bowed, while the chunks of peat in the fireplace barely glowed anymore, but Shea made a decision. She'd go her way when the rain stopped.

Eric stood at the open door to Rosie's B&B, mad as hell, with his arms crossed. Sleepy from what had to be a carb overload, Jordan had already gone upstairs to his bedroom while Eric took first watch. Rosie had retired earlier. She'd kindly left a full pot of coffee on the stove. There were no other guests in the home, and no damned Finn Powers.

For hours Eric watched and waited. Midnight came and went. By zero two hundred hours, the rain stopped. Eric doubted Abdul-Mutaal's ability to track Powers to the 'Edge of O'Banner', as far off the beaten path as it was. Unless the genius still carried a GPS enabled cellphone and made it easy. Anything was possible.

When the coffee was gone, Eric called it a night. He climbed the stairs to wake Jordan for his turn at watch. Naturally, Jordan was sound asleep, but he'd left his door unlocked. That saved Eric having to knock and risk waking Rosie.

Jordan roused easily and snapped to like a good troop.

Finally flat on his back in bed, with his pistol on the nightstand beside him, Eric let his mind relax. Jordan would wake him at the first sign of trouble.

Eric stretched, his legs too long for the mattress. Angling his body corner-to-corner, he adjusted the pillow at his neck and strove for sleep. Though short, the bed in Rosie's B&B was a godsend after a tremendously wasted day.

He tossed. He turned. Eric punched his pillow, cussing at those last two cups of coffee. As every night before, the moment he closed his eyes, his mind drifted back in time. It had only taken once to get Shea pregnant, he was sure of it, not that they'd made love just once in Rio. More like every morning, noon, and night. She couldn't keep her hands off him, and he'd felt the same about her. Smitten. Totally smitten. *Downright intoxicated.*

Yes, sex with her was out of this world, but that wasn't the only way they were good together. Loving Shea was as easy as opening his eyelids in the morning and looking at the sunrise. As easy as breathing in and breathing out. He'd always believed it was at the peak of their first mind-blowing orgasm together that his perfect child came to be. Life only needed one spark.

Despite the caffeine in his blood, Eric fell asleep.

Shea came to him in a dream. His nose filled with the light fragrance of her vanilla musk as she climbed up his body the way she had on their honeymoon. Delightfully bare-naked and tantalizingly horny. Luscious and dripping wet. For him.

She held him down with her anxious lovemaking, not like she'd weighed anything. But being at the mercy of this woman was, at best, Eric's favorite wet dream. He cupped her hips as he filled her to the hilt, her soft moans and grunts and groans his favorite erotic playlist. "You're back," he whispered.

"I never left," she whispered back.

Even in his dream, he knew better, but she rode him hard, as if she couldn't get enough, and he let her. Not until she collapsed on his chest with her nails dug into his shoulders, did she kiss his neck and moan, "Eric. Eric. Eric! Ahh…"

His palms found the back of her head, the tangles of her dark brown swirls. Some women screamed in the throes of passion, but Shea always ended with a sexy, throaty moan that climbed up her body from her toes and clenched every muscle along its way, him along with it.

In return, he thrust into her warmth over and over. The dream was good, just not good enough. *I love you, Shea. Why can't I find my rhythm? My release?*

She slipped out of his hands and lifted into nothingness. Only the anguish in his heart remained, that bottomless hole he risked falling into. There was no way out. Only—

Shea! Come back! Eric woke covered in sweat and the taste of her in his mouth. Her scent in his nose. The moisture from her hot, silky skin still on his fingertips. *It can't be!*

But it was just a dream. He squeezed his eyes shut, sick at heart, his tongue certain he'd just tasted the honey of her lips and the cream of her body. It was enough to make him doubt his sanity. Enough to make him cry. *She'd felt so real!*

Cheyenne's pretty face, so much like her mother's, added to the heartache. Eric bowed his head at the daily struggle he lived with, scrubbing the back of his hand over his eyes.

Goddammit, he'd lost everything that made inhaling another breath—any breath!—worth taking. No one had a clue how tough just the simple act of getting out of bed at the start of every day was. Hell, how impossible pasting a smile on his face was. Yet he'd done it, hoping someday he might actually mean it. For now, all it did was keep people from asking.

The black hole at the core of his soul reached out with long tentacles of despair and melancholy. There was a time he'd fallen. Been sucked into it was more like it. But booze only added more depression to an already bleak time in his life, so he'd worked harder at his job, and he volunteered for longer hours until he was fit for human company. After all, a man had to look himself in the mirror every day. He had to see something looking back at him to *keep on keeping on.*

Eric pushed out of bed and strode to the window overlooking Rosie's front yard. The rain had ceased, but left a shimmering blanket of misty fog.

And there she stood...

Just beyond the picket fence in a swirling shadow of mist. Waiting. Beckoning him to come hither. Needing him. Calling for him. *E-r-r-ric...* Her voice drifted along with the clinging fog. One word. The right word. She'd come back to him. *E-r-r-ric...*

His heart jump started to an impossible beat. It couldn't be real. Not here. Not her. He blinked, and when he did, the fog swirled. The dark mists claimed her, and Shea dissolved into nothingness. Like before.

He swallowed the ache in his heart before it climbed up his throat and screamed for all the world to hear. Crying didn't help. This bottomless hurt never healed. Couldn't begin to. Might never. Not with this kind of crap digging at him!

Why should it? He was a fool to still want the woman who'd cruelly deserted him, but God, what he wouldn't give to have Shea back. Let her tell her lies. Living without her was a thousand times worse. He'd take anything at her hand if she'd only come back. Just one more day. One more hour. *Just call me and talk to me for a minute or two. I'll understand. I promise I will. I'll listen.*

Eric leaned his forehead to the glass, his knees weak and his heart broken. He was a fool for still loving Shea. He always would be, but he honest to God didn't know any other way.

The grief groaned out of him. Why now? Why after all this time had he dreamt of her, then seen such an enticing apparition? A nightmare of Berglund or Mikkelson made better sense, but Shea? So full of life? So incredibly beautiful? *Why the hell now?*

It had to be this 'Edge of O'Banner' place. *Edge of insanity* seemed a better name. Something in its precocious owner had stirred the deepest currents of his soul and brought these wickedly sad memories to the surface. It was as if she knew what he'd suffered and why. As if she'd recognized a kindred spirit.

He huffed out the excess adrenaline mucking up his mind. That had to be it. Rosie had lost her husband. She'd simply recognized another's grief. That made better sense.

He padded to the door and down the steps, sleep robbed and gone for another night. It made better sense to offer up what little was left of a good night's rest to Jordan. No demons bothered him. Hell. He could sleep anywhere. He might as well do it now.

"I'm going for a walk," Eric announced at the front door of the best B&B in all of Ireland. "Go to bed. I won't be gone long."

Jordan lifted his cup of coffee in a silent toast. "Later, bro."

Eric stepped into the mist. He closed the door behind him and took a deep breath of the cool air. Shea wasn't out there, but peace of mind might be.

CHAPTER SEVEN

Shea woke with a start, the warm spot on her lap cold. Barren. Mittens had deserted her, and her professor wasn't in his chair. The fire had gone out and the darkened room closed oppressively around her. Eerily silent. Chilling.

I need to get back to Rosie's. Eric will be there by now.

She pushed to her feet, cocking her head to hear any indication where her mentor might have gone. The afghan she'd covered him with now lay folded over the back of his chair, and his shoes were missing. He'd probably gone to bed.

"Professor?" she asked the darkened hallway opposite the kitchen, and, just in case the feline remembered, she called out quietly, "Mittens?"

Nothing. Not even a purr answered.

The floor creaked under her feet as she pressed forward. A man in her professor's dazed condition might have fallen on his way to bed. She needed to be sure he was tucked in safe and sound before she left.

"Are you in here?" she whispered at the first doorknob. When it wouldn't budge, she tried the last, but it wouldn't open either. Locked doors inside? Wasn't that odd? Could he have gone out? On a drizzly night like this?

Retracing her footsteps to the large window between his chair and the fireplace, she peered through the drawn curtains. A dense fog cloaked the ground. Everything was dark, adding to the eerie ambience of the place. Even the gas lamp at the corner of his well-kept yard, bright and cheery when she'd arrived, was off.

The place felt deserted. Hollow. Shea swallowed hard, her senses now on high alert. *He wouldn't have run off and left me, w-w-would he?*

"Professor?" she asked, her tone thin and needy as she stepped away from the window to the front door. *Please answer me.*

Her fingers had barely touched the knob, when the kitchen doorway behind her filled with a hulking black shadow, punctuated at waist level by the silvery glint of a shining scimitar.

Run!

Like a thief caught red-handed, Shea burst through the professor's front door, her boots pulverizing the soggy moss beneath them, and her heart jackhammering. Every muscle blazed with sheer adrenaline as she sprinted toward Rosie's.

Run faster!

Heavy footsteps pounded behind her. The over-sized boots of her bumbling disguise hampered her speedy getaway when she needed it most. She stumbled to one knee, but quickly righted herself before she touched ground. A quick glance over her shoulder revealed more than one monster behind her. Another loomed out of the mist behind them. *Who are these people?*

Run! Run! Run!

With her lungs on fire, she put her all into escaping. The three men on her heels must have already killed the professor. Beheaded him. Maybe Mittens, too.

I'm next. God, why did I let myself fall asleep! Faster!

The path glistened ahead, wet with rain. Tendrils of inky fog swirled close to the ground, but there was nowhere to hide and nothing to hide behind. She had to keep going and hope a late-night driver or walker intruded upon this desperate scene. Her side cramped, and the coppery taste of blood climbed up her throat, but still she willed her clumsy feet to fly.

Deep male grunts followed. So did the steady slap, slap of heavy boots behind her. They'd gotten closer. A whimper climbed up her throat. Nobody knew her in this country. Poor Professor Grover, if he were still alive, might not even remember her. What an awful way to die, unloved and alone and…

Why is this happening to me!

With one last frantic look over her shoulder, she could see that her pursuers were very nearly on her. In minutes, they'd have her. Maybe seconds! Shea dug for her last ounce of energy and—

Oomph!

She'd hit a wall. A very solid, warm wall that grunted upon impact. A man. Steel bands clenched her biceps as he pulled her behind him, and ordered her to, "Stay here."

Her heart leapt to her throat. *That voice. It couldn't be. Eric?*

"You guys looking for someone?" he barked, his voice hard and a pistol suddenly in his hand, the business end pointed at her pursuers.

Three lethal looking men skidded to a stop, maybe twenty feet away. All of them were hulking brutes, larger and heavier than Eric. One stepped forward, jerking his chin at her. "Walk away, Yank, and mind your business," a definite French accent answered. "He's our problem. Not yours."

Who in France who wants me dead? She raked her brain for anybody she knew from that country. None came to mind. *Oh, wait. Hugh Carlson. Do these guys work for him?*

Didn't that notion just make her stomach jump up her throat.

Her rattled brain connected what dots she thought she knew. Phoenix and Gordie were killed after Carlson's visit. Could he be behind this? But that black-robed monster hadn't once mentioned the DED. All he'd wanted was—*me.*

Could these French guys work for Bagani? That made no sense, either. She'd taken on her Finn disguise after she'd eluded Bagani. How could he know where she'd gone when she'd dressed as an overweight man the past year?

Eric leveled his pistol at the man who'd spoken. "Make me, wise guy." He widened his stance, his shoulders squared, and his chin stuck out. Releasing her wrist, he kept his arm across her body as if drawing a line where his territory began and the French guys ended.

Eric never had a problem facing down a bully, but three against one? She clenched her fist into a tight hard knot, prepared to help as much as she could.

Her three assailants approached, but the robes she thought she'd seen had transformed into military-style uniforms. Berets on their heads. Night sticks in their hands, not shiny and certainly not scimitars. She gulped. *Okay, so maybe I was scared, and I saw things that weren't real.*

The guy who'd spoken took a step forward then stopped, smacking his open palm with the stick. "How about you and me settle this like gentlemen, *monsieur*?" Sarcasm laced his tone. "You walk away, and I won't beat your rich American ass to a wretched, bloody pulp."

"How about you die trying?" Eric shot back, his weapon pointed at the man's upper body. The guy outweighed him, but what Eric lacked in size, he made up for in sheer willpower and guts. "You're mighty brave for a guy with a little stick."

"And you're dreaming if you think you can take on the three of us and live through it."

"He's got help."

Shea jumped as another man walked out of the mist, a gun in his hand that was also aimed at the Frenchman. She pressed closer to Eric, panic choking the life out of her. The thought of a gunfight was more than she could stand, but two guns against three bully sticks seemed immensely better odds.

The Frenchman dropped back with his two buddies, all hulks now that she had a chance to look at them. They didn't resemble the demon from Hell at all. Square heads. Buzz cuts. The worst type of ex-military—mercenaries.

She pressed a hand to Eric's back just beneath his left shoulder blade, needing some of his strength. The instant her palm felt the warmth of his rock-solid muscles, her heart remembered, and tears threatened. Whether he knew it or not, he'd finally come for her.

The leader of the thugs pointed his stick at Eric. "I'll remember you. Don't think I won't."

"Count on it," Eric snarled back.

"And you'd better bring more than sticks next time," his buddy declared.

The three attackers backed away until the mist swallowed them.

"Assholes," Eric muttered, his weapon still drawn and ready. "Sure glad you showed up."

The other man holstered his pistol. "Can't explain it. I had a crazy feeling I needed to follow you. What'd you do? Start a war all by yourself?"

Eric blew out a long deliberate breath. "It's been that kind of a day." He finally turned on her as he tucked his pistol under his left arm. A two-pistol holster if she remembered correctly. His weapons were always loaded, always prepared to stand up to evil. Like him.

"You wouldn't happen to be Finn Powers, would you?" he asked, his brows narrowed to an angry V. "I sure hope so because I've been up all night waiting for you."

She dropped her head and pulled her jacket collar up to hide her neck and face, sure he'd recognize her the minute he looked into her eyes. Those facial appliances had better stand the crucial test of his scrutiny. She coughed, the lump in her throat making it difficult to speak. Brushing the back of her right hand across both eyes to dispel her tears, she froze. *Oh, crap. My glasses.*

Muttering in as deep a voice as she could muster, she offered him nothing but the top of her head. "Yeah," she muttered. "I'm Finn."

Gah! No gruff voice came out of her mouth. She'd squeaked like a frightened woman. He'd never believe she was a bumbling male at this rate. Wiping her tear-dampened hand on her baggy pants, she stuck it out for a handshake. "Glad you got my message," she mumbled, striving for baritone. At least alto.

She'd never had a problem deceiving Phoenix and Gordie. Why was it so hard fooling Eric? "Been a…" She cuffed a fist to her mouth and coughed. "…a helluva long day."

He gave her hand a quick shake, his focus on the direction her would-be assailants had gone. "Who were those guys? Do you know them?"

"Sure don't," she admitted hoarsely, stealing a quick glance in his direction. Short black hair. Soft. Sexy. The kind of hair women liked to run their fingers through. Her nostrils flared, drinking in the scent of his shaving lotion.

Standing close to him worked magic on her body. Heat pooled between her legs. Her stomach churned along with everything else inside of her trembling body. Even her fake jowls quivered against her neck. Frazzled, she took a step back and tripped on her over-sized feet.

He caught her elbow and pulled her upright. "Don't go falling—"

Whatever else he meant to say got caught in his throat. The man had the kindest, darkest brown eyes in the world. Bedroom eyes that could melt a woman's panties as quickly as they'd light up her world.

He licked his lips, soft lips she remembered nipping and tasting. Kissing like there was no tomorrow. She'd never needed alcohol with him. She could get drunk on Eric for days.

A distinct shadow graced the hard angle of his jaw, giving him a definite bad boy look. That was so unlike him. Whether in the Navy or the Corp, he'd always strived for the clean-shaven look.

His chest expanded, drawing her gaze to his open collar. His neck. The hollow under his chin where she used to snuggle in peace and love.

He blinked then, staring down at their joined hands, her small fingers caught in his much larger grip. She knew well the comfort of that hand, but he'd also just latched onto Finn's greatest weakness. A face was simple to disguise with make-up and appliances, but hands and fingers were a sure giveaway.

Pulling back, she stuffed her fingers inside her long shirtsleeves. "I gotta go."

Eric's brows furrowed and that was the last straw. She headed back to Rosie's before he had time to recognize her. She'd be safe there in her private room. Maybe in the morning, she'd come up with a way to tell him who she was.

Even Sasha didn't know she was Eric's ex-wife, the crazy woman who'd left him at the worst moment in his life.

Shea stepped up her pace only to find Eric at her right, her other savior at her left. She focused on him, the guy she didn't know. "W-who are you?"

"Junior Agent Jordan Hannigan. Why didn't you wait for us in England, Finn? I've got to tell you, we've been running after you all day. You're a royal pain in the ass."

She lifted her sleeved arm to her mouth and faked a cough. "Had to leave. No choice."

"Come on. We need a better answer than that," Eric said. "You're on the run. Why come here?"

"Had to get to Professor Grover," she offered hoarsely, still not meeting his eyes. "Might be too late."

"What are you saying?" he asked. "Is he dead, too?"

Damn. I hope not. Shea stopped and glanced over her shoulder at Grover's cottage. A frisson of fear lanced her foolish attempt at confidence. "Not sure. I, umm, I saw those guys inside his place, and I just... ran." *Like I always do.*

Both men stopped with her. "Take Powers back to Rosie's. Make sure *he's* safe," Eric ordered, a hint of sarcasm lacing his words. "I'll be along shortly."

"No," flew out of her mouth before she had time to think. "God, no. I mean..." She strove for baritone. "...they'll kill you."

Eric peered at her in that inquisitive way he had, his head cocked, his gaze incredibly sharp. As a scalpel. "Why would you care?" He stabbed his finger eastward. "You had no problem watching your buddy die in that lab."

He couldn't have hurt her worse if he'd struck her face with his fist. "I—"

"And what about Mikkelson?" An angry gaze fell to her boots. "You were there too, weren't you? What'd you do, step in his blood on your way out the door?"

She shook her head even as her heart screamed. *It's me, Eric. It's finally me!* "N-n-no! I hid in the lab because—"

"You know what?" Eric bit out, his hand raking over his scalp, tossing his hair. "I don't care. Jesus Christ, this has been a godawful day and..." He huffed, his signal that he'd reached the end of his patience. "We're going back to the States first thing in the morning."

Shea couldn't leave well enough alone. "I don't want anyone else hurt because of me. Call the police. Let them take care of it."

"Yeah, that's why I freakin' traveled all the way to Ireland, to call the police to do *my* job." Eric shifted a cynical gaze over her head to his friend. "Like I said, I'll be back. Don't let anyone get close to our friend here. Not even Rosie. And you…" He stabbed his index finger in Shea's face. "Stay put. I have no problem leaving your sorry ass behind if you take off on me again."

All she could do was nod at that scathing order.

"Hurry back," Jordan answered.

"But you shouldn't go by yourself," Shea shot at the back of Eric's stubborn head as he walked away. This was so like him to take matters into his own hands, to go hunting for trouble. Those three guys had to be waiting for him. He could be walking into an ambush. *Because of me.*

Eric didn't respond or look back, just kept walking until the fog swallowed him up, too.

Jordan cupped her elbow, tugging her to walk with him toward Rosie's. "You picked a good one."

I know…

"The 'Edge of O'Banner' serves some fine food. Let's go see if there's any of that apple dessert left."

Oh. Rosie's place. "Yes, ah, O'Banner's is the best." *Or so, Professor Grover had said.*

He made more small talk, but her heart was on the moor behind her and the man who always thought he was tough enough to take on the world by himself. She cast a glance over her shoulder just as an orange glow pierced the mist. The professor's lovely cottage was burning.

"Fire! We have to go back! He'll be killed!" She would have run, but Jordan intercepted her.

He spun her back around, his grip tight on her elbow. "Enough! Who the hell are you?"

She pointed at the glowing sky behind her, knowing full well she'd spoken out of panic, and that she'd used Shea's voice instead of Finn's. She used it again. Now wasn't the time for deceit. Not with two lives in danger. "Don't just stand there. We have to save him!"

Jordan yanked the wig off her head and tossed it to the ground. "You're no guy. Answer me. Who are you?"

She grabbed the front of his shirt and shook him as real fear poured out. "Why don't you listen to me? Eric needs your help. Go to him! Help him!"

Jordan glanced over her shoulder, his dark eyes shining with reflected orange glow. "You care more about Eric Reynolds than your professor? You want to explain that?"

"No, I... Yes, but..." She gulped her subterfuge away. He'd caught her, and she didn't care. "It doesn't matter. They both need our help. Please! We need to go."

Jordan snagged both of her wrists and pulled her into his face, his sharp gaze raking over her features. He took in everything, from her gummed-on eyebrows to her high cheekbone appliances to her flabby double chin. "I'm not worried about that man, ma'am, and you shouldn't be either. Eric's a straight operator, and he's good as hell. He'll get your professor out of that fire if he can. That's why you're scared, isn't it? You already know him. You mind telling me how?"

She faced the glow, her heart in her throat for what Eric might be walking into. The entire western sky had turned so orange and bright that the blaze could've passed for the morning sunrise. All out panic climbed up her throat. "I can't just stay here and wait. Please. He's my... my ex-husband," she admitted, a catch in her throat. *And God help me, I still love him.*

"Holy shit," Jordan hissed. "You're Shea? Then I'm getting you back to Rosie's before anything else happens. Come on. Stop looking over your shoulder. I know Eric and so do you. He'll be okay."

It felt good to finally tell someone who she was. Shea swallowed. The charade was over and Jordan was right. One Eric was worth a hundred other men. A siren sprang through the distance. Still... she couldn't tear her eyes away from the yellow-orange smoke filling the western sky.

"Trust him, Shea," Jordan urged. "He knows how to take care of himself."

"I know but..." She knew too well the cost of running away.

Jordan tugged her to go with him, and reluctantly, Shea retrieved her wig and allowed him to steer her eastward. Eric didn't take unnecessary risks and chances. Always methodical and focused, he'd never come home wounded from any deployment. He was the lifesaver. The one everyone else relied on to rescue them, and if possible, he'd rescue the professor tonight. Maybe Mittens, too.

"I can't believe this. You're the guy we've been looking for. You're Finn, only you're not. Shea, you've got to tell him who you are," Jordan stated the obvious.

Her words stuck in her throat. "I... can't."

"Bet me. He's no dummy. Once he sees you in the light of day, he'll see right through that clown suit. Tell him. Go on. Rip the scab off and get it over with."

She shook her head as the hollow life she'd lived caught up with her. "You don't understand." *It's not that easy.*

"Then make me. I've got time."

Time wasn't the problem. Forgiveness was.

"Let me tell him in my own time," she said with a conviction she didn't feel. *And when I do, he'll never want to see me again.*

"Make it quick. That man's no dummy."

I know. And therein lay the real problem. Eric was the kind of man who ran into burning houses while others ran out. Only the burning 'House of Finn' had the potential to destroy him.

Sir Walter Scott's words whispered through the foggy mist: *Oh, what a tangled web we weave when first we practice to deceive...*

CHAPTER EIGHT

What the hell's going on?

Eric hopped the stone fence to his right, intent on saving the professor if at all possible. The three guys who'd run him down were definitely not Abdul-Mutaal's men. Not with that French accent, but what the hell had they done? Set fire to the place as a parting gesture?

Eric crouched behind the low hedge surrounding what he guessed was Grover's property. The sky ahead glowed with all the colors of fire, an eerie sight in the thickening fog. *Damn. I'm too late.*

He dropped one knee to the soggy moss and watched, needing to be sure. The front door stood wide open. White smoke billowed upward from the door and the thatched roof. Out every window. There was no one around except for a black cat skulking in his direction. When the roof caved with a hissing groan, the cat jumped high in panic and landed sideways, it's back arched, and its tail twitching like a whip. It hissed at the scene on its heels, then walked straight up to Eric.

He stroked its silky fur from its skull to the tip of its question mark tail. "Is that your home going up like a torch?"

It rubbed against his fingers, purring as it marked him with its whiskers.

He scratched behind its ears, sick at heart that he'd arrived too late to help. If Finn's professor was in that conflagration, there was no getting to him. The place was unapproachable. Any evidence of his murder, if that was what had taken place tonight, was already lost.

"This just isn't our day," he told the cat, his gaze on the fire. Burning to death was a damned hard way to die.

A siren sounded in the distance. Emergency response vehicles were en-route, and before long, the crime scene would be overrun with firemen and the local *Garda*. It was time to go.

The only thing he'd saved was this black cat, the ultimate sign of bad luck. Scooping the friendly feline up, he tucked it inside his jacket. Maybe Rosie would keep it.

"Where is he?" Eric whispered as he entered Rosie's and dropped the cat to the floor. If she was still asleep after all the comings and goings of the night, more power to her.

Seated at the wooden bench just inside the entry, Jordan pointed upstairs. "Taking a shower. Who's your friend?"

The crazy cat wound itself through Eric's boots like a long-lost friend. "Found him at the professor's place, what's left of it. Couldn't leave it. Hope Rosie won't mind that I brought home a pet."

"Was that his place that burned? Grover's?"

Eric nodded. "Thatched roofs burn fast. The whole place was fully engulfed by the time I got there. No sign of anyone but this cat."

"I thought we were going after Abdul-Mutaal. Those French jokers weren't Mideastern."

"Could've been *ex-Berets Verts*, you know, France's version of our Green Berets. I've worked with them before overseas. They're bad-ass operators."

"But why were they after Finn?"

Eric shrugged. "Damned if I know. They might be contractors like us, working for someone without Alex's ethics. He talk much on the way back?"

Jordan pursed his lips. "No, but he's an odd duck. Kept looking over his shoulder like he was worried for you. Did you notice his hands?"

There was no way Eric could've missed Finn's little hands. Delicate was what they were. Dainty. Weirder still, along with that limp handshake, came a sizzling jolt of energy that raised the hair up the back of his neck. Felt like an electric shot of déjà vu. Things got weird then. He'd nearly thrown that little hand back at Finn.

"What time is it?" he asked.

"Do you mean Virginia time or Greenwich mean?"

"I don't care, smart ass. Local time, I guess." Eric ran a quick hand through his hair, his temper rising, another odd response for the man he knew he was. Ever since '*Operation Find Finn*' had commenced, he'd been antsy and out of sorts, not himself at all. Downright edgy. What was up with that?

"Zero three hundred. Hit the sack. I'll take the rest of the watch tonight."

"Good enough. I'll spell you in two." Eric shot a quick glance up the stairs. "Which room is he in?"

"The one next to yours."

Finn was on the other side of Eric's bedroom wall, which for some peculiar reason felt a little too close for comfort, but Eric was damned if he knew why. A yawn overtook his answer. He scrubbed a hand over his face, waved Jordan off, and headed upstairs.

"He's not a bad guy. You oughta try talking to him, you know, be nicer."

Eric paused halfway up the staircase at that out of the blue comment. "When haven't I been?"

Jordan lifted one shoulder. "Just saying. You were pretty rough on him tonight, but you'll catch more flies with honey than vinegar."

Whatever the hell that meant. Eric turned his back on his suddenly verbose buddy and aimed for his room. Sleep was calling, and for once, it wasn't asking for Jordan.

Back in her room with the door locked, Shea couldn't settle down. She'd wanted Eric to save her because he was the only one who could, but now that he'd arrived and done just that, she didn't want to deal with her deceit. Her failures. The truth. They'd all caught up with her.

With all of her heart, she wanted nothing more than to run downstairs and ask after Professor Grover. Did Eric get to him in time? Was he hurt? Burned? Heaven forbid, was he even alive? But she couldn't. Eric would see through her. He'd detect the Shea in Finn's voice and he'd know. She stalled the inevitable.

After two days of running, the padded suit of Finn smelled of sweat, and, well, it just plain stunk. If she could detect the body odor emanating off the layers of foam and cloth, Eric and Jordan surely could. She and Finn needed a bath.

Easing out of her extra-large clothing, she commenced the arduous process of reverting to Shea. Constructed of lightweight foam sewn inside a flesh-colored adult-sized suit, her Finn disguise was similar to a baby's onesie. It snapped at the crotch, and vented mesh panels down the sides allowed ventilation. Plain and simple, her alter ego was a fat suit. Finn zipped up the back and he was easy to care for, but he was still mostly stuffing. Heavy. Sweaty. Stuffing.

By the time she'd laid Finn on the bed, she was down to bra and panties, and shivering. After she finished with her bath, he'd get his, then she'd hang him on a hanger over the tub to drip dry until morning. Shea shivered at the loss of all those layers. She'd been Finn too long this time. The inside of her legs were chafed. Her armpits, too.

Turning the faucet to warm, she removed her facial disguise while the tub filled. Carefully, she wiped each appliance with the bottle of astringent she'd kept in her bag. Once Finn's nose, cheeks, brows, and wart were cleaned, she set them on the counter to wait until the process began anew in the morning. She cleaned her extra pair of thick glasses and attached an elastic to the stems so they wouldn't get lost again. What Eric couldn't see, wouldn't hurt him.

Once she'd unveiled her face, the gaunt woman she'd become stared back at her. Short dark chopped brown hair. A beautician she was not, but the close cut simplified getting in and out of Finn. Long hair would've been too much work.

Shadows curved under her eyes. She'd lost the pretty naiveté of her youth. Loneliness stared back at her with its hollowed cheeks and expressionless eyes. Her brows never lifted in surprise anymore. She'd forgotten how to smile.

The cost of my betrayal...

At the edge of the tub, Shea knew with all of her heart that Jordan was right. Eric had the right to know everything. In her hurried escape from her flat in Amsterdam, she'd actually thought to bring a light cotton dress along for the day of reckoning that was sure to come. The best way might be to waltz down the stairs in that dress tomorrow morning and simply declare, "I'm back, Eric. We need to talk." The truth would shock Eric, but it'd be out. Either he'd forgive her or not.

A hard knot filled her chest at the prospect of hurting him once more. *There has to be a better way.*

Testing the temperature, Shea dragged one fingertip under the running tap, watching her nail slice through the ribbon of water, dividing it into two silvery streams. She was that water, divided. There had to be a way to bring those two streams back together before both Finn and Shea went down the drain.

CHAPTER NINE

Eric laid his pistol on the nightstand. Undressing down to his boxers and climbing into bed, he was glad to be off his feet. The cool sheets soothed as he listened to Finn moving around in the next room. He expected cloddish thumping across the floor, but the fellow was actually light-footed and quiet. Considerate. Therein lay the disconnect. Finn didn't act like a man.

The man hadn't seen Eric until he'd plowed into him and nearly knocked him down. Eric had only meant to steady the guy, but in the process, he'd inadvertently grabbed a handful of something that didn't feel like human muscle or fat.

He replayed the moment while he stared at the dark ceiling. Not cellulite, either. Eric knew his way around guys' and gals' bodies. He'd treated enough of them on the battlefronts in Afghanistan. This texture was something softer, but firm at the same time, more like—foam.

And the glimmer in that guy's shocked eyes? *Damned familiar.*

The faucet turned off in the next room. Water splashed. Finn must've gotten into the tub, and now the guy was humming? Eric lifted to one elbow to listen to the gentleness in that very un-masculine voice.

He'd always been a sucker for the underdog. His mother called it empathy, but sometimes it got him into trouble. Like on his eighth birthday party when he got his first toy doctor's kit. That was the day he found out the hard way other kids' parents didn't appreciate his need to help, especially not their little girls.

But come on, what was a serious minded little guy supposed to do? Little Ginny Weaver had an itch. He'd seen his mother apply ointment to his baby brother's *itch*, but applying it on Ginny opened a whole new world of wonder for Eric. The poor girl was missing one very important piece of her anatomy, which required further investigation. Purely medical, mind you. He'd applied more ointment, hoping she hadn't scratched her peeper off, because the little guy was surely missing.

Funny thing about young, inquisitive doctors. They got their butts whipped for practicing ANY medicine on little girls without peepers.

Eric blew out a deep breath, releasing the worries of the day. It was no wonder that Finn ran from the lab and then from his flat instead of offering any kind of an assist to his friends. He was like most civilians when confronted with pure evil. Untrained. Unarmed. Helpless. That explained a lot.

Setting his alarm clock, Eric punched his pillow one last time, and rolled to his side, part of the puzzle solved. The underdog in his portly client had triggered that streak of empathy, that was all.

Eric's shoulders relaxed. His eyes grew heavy. With Jordan standing guard, a couple hours of shuteye were all but guaranteed. If only Eric knew why Finn had asked for him in the first place.

Rumbling purring woke him, though how that black cat he'd found had gotten inside his room, Eric didn't know. It stretched until its front paws settled against his chin, its warm belly to his chest. Crystal blue eyes peered into his. "I came for you," it said in the softest whisper of a dream.

Why he answered made no sense, but he did. "It doesn't matter. You'll stay here when I go."

It curled one paw to its furry lips and licked its toes with a pink tongue. The damned thing winked like a cat could do such a thing. "But it does matter. Where you go, I'll go."

Whatever. He huffed in his sleep and offered the noncommittal answer of all parents with precocious children, "We'll see."

Two seconds later…

Eric jolted straight out of bed and jumped to his feet. Two hours had somehow morphed into—ten? *What the hell?* He blinked at the alarm clock on the nightstand. *It couldn't be noon. No way!*

Scrambling into his clothes, he ran a quick hand over his bed head, angry he'd let Jordan down. Guys do *not* sleep through their turn at guard duty. It wasn't done.

He secured his holster and pistols, and in two seconds flat, his booted feet dropped like rolling rocks down the staircase at the 'Edge of O'Banner'. Not hearing any voices, he turned to the kitchen, if only because that tended to be the gathering place at his mother's house.

Rosie stood at her stove, stirring something in a big stockpot. His nostrils flared at the delightful cacophony of scents. Onions. Celery. Fresh ground pepper.

"It's about time you woke, sleepy head," she said without turning around. "There's coffee on the warmer behind you. Cream's in the icebox. Lunch is near ready. I've fixed your favorite, clam chowder with toasted ham and cheese sandwiches."

How did she know that? "Where is everyone?"

Rosie turned to him, her lips curved with a smile. "Jordan knew you were exhausted, so he let you sleep. He and Finn are out back chatting. Your friend is one spoiled princess."

"Excuse me?" *Jordan? A princess?*

The light in Rosie's eyes darkened. "I'm glad ye brought Aishling home with you last night instead of leaving her to fend for herself now that Morell's home burned to cinders. Poor wee lass would've turned to begging for scraps and fighting for her life if a kind heart like you hadn't come along."

Oh. The cat. The spoiled princess was busy wrapping her svelte, black body around Eric's ankles and rubbing her chin on his bootlaces. *So it was Grover's house that burned.* "Thanks for understanding. You're right. I couldn't leave her."

The creature tipped her happy face up at him, and he had to look twice. It was too dark last night to notice, but damn. Aishling had blue eyes, just like in his dream. *Interesting.*

"'Tis a good man, ye are, Eric Reynolds. A fine, good man. Now fix a cup and go talk with your friends. I'll call for lunch in a few, and 'twill have to serve as your breakfast, since ye could not be bothered to rise with the sun."

He did as he was told, and the cat followed, purring as if she meant what she'd said in that crazy dream.

Opening Rosie's door revealed lush flowering bushes covered in yellows and pinks, and a fence that ran the length of the property. A white painted arbor stood nearly hidden in the far corner beneath trailing vines with orange trumpet flowers. Jordan and Finn were sitting on the arbor bench. They were so deep in conversation that neither noticed the squeak of the screen door behind Eric.

For some reason, a flash of envy rolled over his shoulders. He felt obliged to announce his arrival, so he coughed. Then he coughed a little louder.

Jordan jerked his head up, startled. That was just plain weird. What were he and Finn discussing that put a definite red glow to his ugly face? To make it worse, Jordan put a clenched fist to his mouth and choked as if he'd swallowed his tongue.

Eric took a long hit off his coffee before he said, "Nice day."

"I. Gotta. Go." Jordan pointed to the back door and made a hasty retreat. *The dog.*

Finn lifted up from the arbor seat. Thick glasses obscured the guy's eyes this morning. He pursed his lips as if he had something to say.

"You leaving too?" Eric teased, just to get a rise out of him.

"Thank you for saving Mittens," Finn squeaked out, his boots shifting as if he was nervous.

"Who?"

Finn's gaze fell to the feline in love with Eric's bootlaces. "The cat."

"Oh, you mean Aishling," Eric nodded. Yes, he'd saved a cat. Not Finn's professor, though. Damn. That was why they were seated together, whispering. Jordan must've been breaking the bad news. "I'm sorry, Finn. The house was in flames when I got there. I couldn't get inside to save Grover."

Finn sniffed, the side of his dainty index finger to his nose like a woman might do if she'd been crying. "S' okay. I understand."

Eric took a step closer, compassion swelling for this gentle giant. "I know you and Grover were close."

The distraught man turned away to face the flowering pink shrub at his left, his jaw clenched.

"Listen, we need to get moving. How long before you'll be ready?" Eric asked.

A soft, gravelly voice came back at him with, "For what?"

Eric dropped his gaze to the ground at that less than intelligent question, remembering this was a civilian. Sometimes they needed more time to get with the program. "To leave for the airport. You brought luggage, didn't you?" Maybe not. Finn was still wearing the clothes he'd been in the night before.

The guy glanced at the cat, still snug between Eric's boots. "I'm ready now," he said, his voice deeper. More baritone. Kind of fake.

The change in tone caught Eric by surprise. Canting his head, he looked closer at his reluctant friend. Maybe there was a way to bridge this uncomfortable gap between them. "Did you catch a cold last night? I've got some decongestant in my gear if you need something."

"Ah, yeah. A cold. Right."

"Hey, Finn. Umm…" Remembering the odd texture he'd grabbed last night, Eric took firm hold of the man's broad shoulder. "Are you feeling okay? I'm a medic. Maybe I can help."

Padded shoulders? On an already overweight man?

Finn shrugged the suggestion—and Eric—off.

What was up with this guy? Not that it mattered. In the end, Finn would go home where he belonged, and the FBI or State Department would assume care for him. They'd stash him in a safe house, maybe bury him in the WPP, the Witness Protection Program, and bottom line, Eric would never see Finn again.

Somehow, that gave him the oddest sense of—disloyalty? What was it about this poor, oafish man that got to Eric? As big a pain in the ass as he'd been to locate, Finn still needed a twenty-four-hour bodyguard, and Eric wanted to be that guy. Yeah. It made no sense.

Shea walked upstairs to her room. If she could hold it together for twenty or so more hours, she'd be back in America and out of Eric's life. Wasn't that what she wanted? She honestly didn't know anymore. All roads pointed to more heartache.

Her head pounded at the predicament she'd gotten herself into. Poor Jordan. He'd all but swallowed his tongue when he'd seen Eric watching them out in the yard. As odd as it seemed, her heart had rallied at the dark shadow that shifted over Eric's face. For a second there, it was almost as if he'd recognized her. Almost as if he'd wanted to knock Jordan's head off, too.

If he'd only known he was the subject of their whispered conversation, not Professor Grover's death.

"He already suspects who I am," she whispered. "I can't let him figure it out by himself. That will be worse. I have to be brave and tell him. At least I'll know where I stand."

To say she was torn was the biggest understatement of her life. Mashed was more like it. God, she loved him so hard her chest ached.

Just standing beside him in the dark had ignited every nerve in her body. She'd wanted him then as much as she'd wanted him their first time together, only—everything had changed. Their 'happily-ever-after' lay in a graveyard in western Maryland.

She'd told Jordan that she couldn't turn back time, a flimsy excuse at best.

To which Jordan had growled like an angry dog. "Bullshit. If my woman loved me enough to bare her soul and admit she'd made mistakes, I'd give her another chance."

"You would?"

"Hell, yeah. You were out of your head with grief two years ago. I don't have any kids. Heck, I don't even have a woman, so I don't rightly know what you were going through, but trust me. Eric's not a hard ass. At least give him the chance. He deserves that much."

Jordan had an easy way about him, and Shea wanted to believe, so she'd decided. As soon as they were safely on United States soil, she'd tell Eric the truth. He might hate her, but at least then he'd know why she'd done what she had.

Drawing a deep breath, she took one last look at her alter ego in the mirror. It was easy to see. Finn had to die so Shea could live. The minute they landed. And then...

I'll get exactly what I deserve...

CHAPTER TEN

Rosie *tsked, tsked.* "I don't know what this world's coming to. Have you heard the news?"

"What's that?" Eric asked, only half paying attention. He'd already vacated his room. Jordan had too. Spec ops guys packed light, so it hadn't taken long. Their backpacks were by the front door.

But then there was Finn. Eric couldn't tear his eyes off the bumbling oaf clomping down the stairs with one hand on the railing, a small carry-on in his other. As if he might fall, Finn placed each boot on each step with deliberate care. When he reached the last two steps where Jordan sat with Aishling on his lap, Finn asked, "Excuse me, umm, sir, but could you move so I can get by?"

What guy does that?

But then things got weirder. Jordan jumped to his feet with a quick, "You bet," and offered a hand to Finn. *Just to climb down the last two steps.*

"The police haven't found the professor's body," Rosie muttered. "'Tis a shame."

That got Eric's undivided attention. "You mean Grover?"

"Aye. 'Tweren't a body in the whole house according to the fire marshal. Not even a single charred bone, for the love of Saint Michael. Can you fathom that?"

Eric shot Jordan a look, his brain pinging over what he thought he knew. "Then why the fire? What'd those three guys do with the professor if they didn't kill him?"

Jordan shrugged. "I'm still trying to figure out why we've got Frenchmen in the middle of what looks like an ISIS terrorist drill in the first place."

"Do you know?" Eric directed his question at Finn. "Do you have any idea why those guys were chasing you?"

Finn lifted both shoulders and grunted. And that was another thing. The guy lacked confidence. Or testosterone. Or something. He pursed his lips. "Well…"

Eric zeroed in on that perfectly peaked Cupid's bow, pinkishly tan and probably moist. Probably tender, too, and—*What the hell's wrong with me?*

He snapped his fingers at Finn, annoyed for… for… *Oh, hell. Just annoyed, okay?* "Well, what?" he barked. "They didn't just drop out of the sky and decide to chase you. They had to have a reason for what they did. What happened last night? Spit it out."

"I, umm…" Finn stuck his dainty fingers into his messy red hair. "I fell asleep 'n then they were there."

"Where?"

"Inside his house."

"Whose house? Grover's?"

"Ah-uh. Only I thought they had, umm, a big knife."

"How many of them were there?"

"One, but then there were three of them and I—"

"What'd the knife look like?"

"Um, a sword?"

"What kind of sword? A rapier? Katana? Broadsword? Long swor—"

"A scimitar, okay?" Finn nearly yelled.

Oooo. Touched a nerve, did I? "How do you know it was a scimitar? It could've been a—"

"Lay off," Jordan barked. "God, Eric. What's wrong with you? He's been through enough already."

Eric clapped his mouth shut, not sure what had just come over him. He didn't badger awkward guys with bad taste. He didn't badger or bully anyone. Ever. He swallowed hard, seriously worried he might be on the verge of a breakdown. Even Rosie's brows had lifted.

"Sorry, I, umm…" What could he say to save face? Nothing but the truth. He fixed his gaze on Finn. "This operation's got everyone rattled. I'm just…" He ran his fingers through his hair, not precisely sure what he was feeling, not with Finn's lower lip quivering like it was. "I'm sorry for being an ass. You didn't deserve that."

Both of the big guy's shoulders lifted. "S' okay," he whispered, which was yet another very un-guy thing to do. Didn't this man have an ounce of fire in his gut? What was he, a walking, talking doormat? Eric shook all the annoying and unsolved puzzles of the day off. He'd worry about them on the other side of the ocean. He had a plane to catch. "You call a cab?"

Jordan set the cat gently to the floor with one more pat between her ears. "He should be here in ten. You ready?"

"Yes." *I'm past ready.*

"You boys be safe," Rosie said. "May your glasses be ever full. May the roofs over your heads be always strong, and may you be in heaven a half hour afore the devil knows you're dead."

Eric had to smile. His Irish hostess had gotten into his heart in the short time he'd known her. She alone made the trip worthwhile. "Goodbye, Ms. O'Banner. It's been a pleasure."

"Ah," she waved his comment off. "'Tis you the pleasure is. You've been a joy, m'boy, and a handsome joy. I pity the girl that let you slip through her silly fingers. What a fool she must've been to let the likes of you get away. I can see it in your eyes. You've got a pure soul in ye, son. A pure and shining soul, as bright as the nuggets of gold in a leprechaun's treasure, and you're as good-looking as my Paddy was the day we wed. Do nah forget the loves of your life, though. They have a way of coming 'round about when you least expect them, do they nah?"

Extending his hand in friendship, he meant to end the delightful nonsense she seemed full of. Rosie pulled him into an embrace instead. "'Tis not goodbye I'll be saying to ye, Eric Reynolds," she whispered in his ear. "'Tis only *'til then*. God bless ye, and may Saint Patrick bless ye, too. May the blessings of the day be the blessings you need most of all."

He eased away from her but still held her forearms, needing to see beyond the whimsy she spouted. Mischief gleamed back at him, but something else he couldn't read. Looked a lot like pride, but why she'd be proud of him—a stranger—he didn't know. "Thank you for everything. You set a fine table, and I slept well last night for the first time in quite a while."

"As well ye should have, what with all the running around in the middle of the night ye were doing." Mischief again. Crimson spilled up from her neck. She gave him a quick peck on his cheek and let him go. "Now be gone, and be good, and if ye think on it, send me a note to tell me when you're finally safe at home."

"I will," he promised, releasing her arms. "Ready?" he asked Jordan who now stood at the door with Finn.

The sight of them together irked Eric for no good reason, but the odd look on Finn's face? He'd gone blotchy pale. The big guy's mouth hung open. He had that *I've-just-seen-a-ghost* pallor.

Eric calmed, needing to set things right with his client. "Hey, are you okay?"

Finn shifted away. "Yeah, I'm... fine." Cough, cough. "Just fine."

No. You're not, Eric thought.

"Cab just pulled up. Let's roll," Jordan announced.

Rosie shook Jordan's hand and stuffed a paper bag in his other. "Just a wee bit to tide you over, lad. Mind the gravy. There's a spoon in there, too. Eat it before you get to the airport with all their blithering security nonsense and such. 'Twill do you good."

The brown paper bag crackled as Jordan peered into it. "Shepherd's pie? For me?" For that she got swept off her feet and pulled into a big Jordan-type, three-hundred-and-sixty-degree, whirling hug. "Thank you, ma'am. I'll never forget you."

Wasn't that the truth? Jordan knew every mom and pop diner from the Florida Keys to Anchorage. Now one in Ireland.

By the time Rosie landed on her feet, her face beamed red as a beet.

Finn stuck out his hand, but got an odd blessing from her instead. "Don't you be a stranger," Rosie said, her index finger waggling under his wide nose. "'Tis a long road ahead of you, darlin', but all is nah lost. Don't be afraid to spread your wings and fly. Now go on. Yer secret's safe with me."

Whatever that meant, it proved the guy's undoing. He wrapped his arms around Rosie and whined like a girl, "I'm sorry."

"There, there," Rosie soothed as she patted his broad back. "'Twill all work out if you let your heart do the talking. I'm sure of it."

Another sad whine and Finn pulled away, wiping a delicate finger under his nose. Adjusting his glasses. Shuffling those two big feet. Eric looked away, feeling like an even bigger ass for badgering an obviously broken man who'd lost three friends in less than forty-eight hours. He vowed to be kinder to poor Finn.

By then, a cab had pulled into Rosie's narrow drive. Gray-haired and whiskered, a little old man exited the right side of what had to be the first Toyota sedan on the island by the scratches and dents on it. The driver's side mirror was missing, something Eric had noticed on quite a few cars.

The pleasant man extended a hand toward Eric's bag. "Might I stow your things in the boot?"

"You mean the trunk?"

"Aye. The trunk. The boot. 'Tis all the same." The cabbie nodded with a smile. "'Tis clean enough for the likes of your fine American bags. I swept it meself this mornin'."

"If you don't mind, we'll keep our gear with us," Eric replied, hoisting his backpack to one shoulder. "Finn?"

"No," Finn said. "It's small. I got it."

"Are you sure?" Eric asked. "It'll get crowded."

Finn tugged his carry-on against his pant leg. "It stays with me."

"Have it your way." The cabbie shrugged his shoulders and grinned at Rosie as he slammed the *boot*. "You wouldn't be needing a ride anywhere this morning would you, Mrs. O'Banner? I'm sure to be goin' your way."

Rosie surprised them all. "I was just about to ask, Gerald. I need to check on old Mrs. Sweeny. She's been down with a titch of the gout in her big toe. Might I go to the corner with you? I can pay."

Eric opened the car door for her and waved her into the front seat. "No problem. Glad to help."

Without locking her B&B behind her, she all but skipped to the cab and climbed inside. Jordan waved Finn into the center of the back seat, then climbed inside. Eric dropped his butt into the other side of Finn and closed the door.

And they were off.

How awkward. Shea could barely catch a breath sandwiched between these two virile males like she was. Shea could feel both men's hipbones, but Jordan's was just a hip.

Eric's was… Warm. Strong. *Heaven.*

His muscular thigh pressed alongside hers up to Finn's baggy knee, flooding her already stretched-to-the-limit nerves with a crazy cocktail of embarrassment, lust, and desire. Her fingers tapped the carry-on she'd tucked into her dumpy men's jacket, in frantic tune with her heart.

It had been so long since she'd sat next to Eric, and being this close to the only man she'd ever loved? Talk about torture. Could he hear the staccato beat of her frantic heart or the way her breath caught with every muscle he flexed? Every twist of his torso when he moved? Could he feel her shivering beneath all her layers of Finn?

Tensing her shoulders, she dared not look at him, not even to see out the windows.

Eyes forward. Senses on neutral. You can do this.

No, I can't. The familiar male scent of him filled her nose and settled in the hungry cellar of her starving soul. Two years she'd been without this man.

He'd shaved and showered. The alcohol in his aftershave drifted like a tantalizing male finger under her nose, spiking her poor libido into overdrive as if she were in control of the brakes. Not now. Not here.

Eric was home and refuge to her. He was sex, love, and manly comfort. Lazy Saturdays in bed until noon. Beer and pizza for Monday night football games. Hot passionate baths and desperate-for-each-other sex after any and all deployments.

But that blessing for Eric from Rosie? God, how had the woman read him like a book? Why did she tell him not to forget the loves of his life? Was she talking about Cheyenne and Shea when she said they have a way of coming around about when you least expect them? How did she know about—*me?*

Finn's thickly padded knee set to twitching, Shea's nerves strung too tightly. Her inner muscles clenched, weeping with frustration for the love she'd lost. Moisture pooled where it had no business pooling. Her head buzzed. More and more, she looked forward to Finn's demise.

He had to die so she could live.

It made for a crowded ride to the corner with Finn's suitcase squarely on his lap and two backpacks taking up all available foot space. No problem. Eric was plenty used to crowded travel. He latched his seat belt, then shifted his hips to make room for three guys' big butts on the narrow bench seat.

The weather had cleared. Rosie and the cabbie made small talk, while Eric sought to make amends with Finn. "It'll be good to get back to America, huh?"

Finn kept his eyes on the road ahead. Typical. Geeky. Reclusive.

Eric tried again. "So where'd you live before Amsterdam? Where are you from?"

Finn coughed into his sleeve. "New York."

"Ah, a New Yorker. The Queens? Manhattan? Buffal—"

"Look out!" Jordan bellowed, lifting his arm to cover his face.

BLAM! A large vehicle had come out of nowhere. Glass flew sideways from Eric's window to Jordan's and everywhere in between. Metal screeched against metal. Someone screamed, and for a split second, Eric thought he heard Shea.

Chaos took over. He caught a glimpse of the vehicle that had crashed grill first into the driver's side of the cab. A Hummer. Heavy duty push bar. Wire enclosed headlights. The damned thing was still powered up, pushing the cab sideways. *What the hell?*

Over they went. In the blink of an eye, everyone and everything shifted to the opposite side of the vehicle. Eric clamped onto Finn, shouldering the brunt of the impact without thinking. Rosie shrieked, and Jordan cursed as the cab rolled. Once. Twice. Three times until, at last, it came to rest on its roof, rocking.

Holy shit. The five of them were now suspended upside down, held in place by their seat belts. Eric shook the roar out of his head, blinking through the dust stirred up from the road, his palms on the roof, which was now where the floor should've been. The cab windshield remained intact, but neither the side nor rear windows had withstood the impact. The acrid creep of petrol fumes filled his nostrils, urging him to do something and do it fast.

"Jordan," he croaked, coughing the dust from his lungs. "You okay, buddy?"

"Here," came a hoarse answer. "Shit. Think my arm's broke. Leg hurts, too."

Eric squinted to see through the mayhem. Finn struggled next to him, moaning. A good sign. But Rosie and the cabbie were quiet. Grabbing for the strap of his backpack, Eric dragged it to the roof above his head and went for his knife.

Of all the days not to have worn it on his ankle holster. Dizziness washed over him like a thick, numbing blanket, and that silver snap on his backpack pocket was tough to undo. He blinked when something warm ran into his eyes, obscuring his vision. *Head wound. Not to worry. They were typical bleeders.*

Finally, he brushed the daze away and worked the snap free. His knife slid out of the pocket into his palm. With slow, deliberate slashes, he freed Finn, then Jordan without cutting either of them. Then himself. Finally, they were on their backs on the ceiling turned floor. It took a couple minutes to get squared away and upright with the backpacks and that roller bag in their way, but at last, they were ready to crawl.

Jordan pushed one backpack out his shattered window, then wormed one shoulder through, but Eric didn't have the option. His side of the vehicle had gotten the worst of the crash. Both windows were crushed to narrow slits. He caught movement to his right. Three pairs of boots. Men's boots. Headed toward the cab.

"We've got to get out of here," he ordered Jordan. "Get Finn out that window and on his feet. Fast." He eased his sore body forward, needing to check Rosie and the cabbie even though he'd told Jordan to run.

"You, too," Jordan urged, on his feet now and dragging Finn out by one arm. For a moment, the big guy's butt blocked the whole window, and Eric thought he'd get stuck. He coughed on the blood thickening in his mouth. "I can't leave. Rosie's out cold. So's the cabbie."

Finn was on his feet. At least he was safe, but Jordan was stressed. "Move it, man!"

Eric shifted forward and felt Rosie's neck for a pulse. Blood dripped from a gash in her cheek. Both she and the cabbie were unconscious. Eric didn't dare cut their seatbelts for fear of what dropping them on their heads might do if either had spinal injuries.

"Damn it, Eric. Get your ass out of there!" Jordan sounded winded and in pain.

Eric tuned him out and unholstered his pistol. "Talk to me, Rosie," he urged, patting her cheek and forehead. At last she mumbled. The cabbie, too. But they were in no condition to be moved.

When a gunshot whistled over the undercarriage of the cab, now exposed to the sun like an upended turtle, Eric ducked. The men who'd killed Grover meant business, but he couldn't leave Rosie and the cabbie. The possibility of the cab catching fire and burning them to death scared the hell out of him.

Jordan fired back, and Eric knew he had no choice. To save Rosie and the cabbie, he'd have to draw the three assassins away from the wreck before one of their rounds set the thing ablaze. It didn't happen as often as Hollywood said it did, but he couldn't take the chance.

Climbing out of the cab, he scrambled to his feet. The earth tilted the moment he was upright. He braced one hand to the wheel to make it stop. *Sprained or broken ankle. Definite head trauma and whiplash.*

He sucked in a deep breath and shook it off. *Work first. Whine later.*

Finn seemed uninjured. He was still wearing those glasses with those geeky straps, another bonus. The poor guy hugged his suitcase to his chest. Eric didn't remember it flying around the inside of the cab. No, just two damned heavy backpacks loaded with weapons and ammo. No wonder his head hurt.

"Move it," he growled. "Let's lead these assholes away from Rosie."

"I can't run." Jordan leaned against the wreck. Blood soaked his left pant leg. "You go. I'll never make it."

"Yes, you can," Eric insisted. "Finn and I will help you."

Jordan turned his head and spat a mouthful of blood into the dirt. "No use arguing. I can't leave Rosie and her friend, and you can't stay. Our primary job was to get Finn back to the States. Looks like it's up to you now."

"I'm not leaving you behind," Eric ground out.

"Give me a break, Superman." Jordan jerked his head toward the quickly approaching Frenchmen. "You've seen what they're packing? One's got a sawed-off shotgun, the other two, ARs. You've got no choice. Save Finn, and let me do my job and cover your sorry ass while I still can."

Another shot zipped overhead, and damn it, Jordan was right. There was no choice. Finn had to get to America and Eric had to make it happen. He gave his buddy one last once over. Jordan had sunk to his butt, both pistols up and ready, his cellphone stuck between his shoulder and his ear. Calling for help in the middle of Hell.

Finn dropped to his haunches beside Jordan. "I can't leave you," he said in a weirdly tragic voice.

"You'd better," Jordan shot back at him. "The only reason I'm hanging back is to cover you. Now go. Do what you're supposed to do. Be quick about it for god's sake. Tell him."

Tell who what?

Finn leaned into Jordan and kissed his whiskered cheek. Damned if Jordan didn't close his eyes at the contact, just for a second.

Eric jerked Finn to his feet. There wasn't time to worry about what was going on between those two. Yanking his backpack out of the cab, he tossed his spare magazines to his buddy and did the unforgiveable. He left his partner behind.

CHAPTER ELEVEN

Eric ran with Finn at his side, downhill, then along a stone fence with one helluva briar patch between it and the road, the briars so tall, they resembled a wall as much as the fence. Finn dragged his suitcase all the way.

Gunshots roared behind them, and Eric's gut clenched tight. He'd committed the worst sin imaginable and could only pray Jordan wouldn't die because of it.

A flat green field lay ahead, surrounded by more stone fences. To the right lay a murky bog lined with reeds and brush, with a flock of sheep to the left. Eric headed for the bog, certain he could keep Finn alive. Maybe return for Jordan, Rosie, and the cabbie when the coast was clear.

Another shot sounded. A man's outraged bellow rent the air. *God! Not Jordan.* Three more shots boomed in quick succession, and Eric's blood froze at what he'd just heard. Three executions. *Civilians, for god's sake! Rosie and the cabbie weren't even armed!*

Grabbing hold of Finn, Eric ran for the bog, shaken at the horror that had just been committed against civilians. Whoever these French guys were, they were twisted sons-of-bitches. No way were they getting Finn.

His frightened partner stopped at the swampy edge of the bog, his suitcase still held to his chest. "I can't go in there," he whined in his odd, girly voice.

"You will," Eric ordered, disgusted this guy dared pitch a fit after what had just happened to everyone else. Without mercy, he shoved Finn into the muddy drink. "Get your ass in. Now!" *And shut the hell up.*

Just in time. Suitcase and all, Finn submerged to his chin as the three men crested the hill. Commandos in green and black cammies. Berets perched on their square heads. Not one of them was less than six feet tall or lighter than two hundred fifty pounds, give or take a few. They stood for a moment scanning the meadow filled with sheep and stone fences, their weapons tight to their chests. Watching. Daring anything to move.

"Very slowly. Go lower," Eric commanded out of the corner of his mouth.

Finn obeyed. As before, his hip and thigh brushing Eric's, up close and personal. God, the guy was clingy.

Carefully, without creating ripples, Eric pushed his prone body backward and away from the bog's edge, into deeper, thicker goo. Predictably, Finn followed suit. Something slimy slithered against the back of Eric's neck. Felt like a snake or lizard. He didn't care, but Finn had better not let out a girly scream because of any damned bugs or reptiles.

Eric sank to his nose and held his breath. This just might work. Blast. The thought was no sooner hoped than jinxed as a gurgle of bubbles erupted to the surface in front of Finn, most likely from his carry-on.

Eric tensed, but thankfully, the thick muck didn't allow much sound. The French Legionnaires, his nickname for the assholes on his six, approached, their heads on swivels. God, they were tense. Twitchy. Ready to fire at anything that moved. One pointed the barrel of his rifle left. That direction would've taken them away from the cab. Another growled, and Eric wished his ears weren't filled with gunk, not that he would've understood French anyway. It'd sure be nice to know if he had time to get back to Jordan and the others, though.

Finn did one better. He sucked in a big breath and submerged entirely without being told to. *Right on.* Must've been scared witless. The big guy couldn't stay under for long, but it gave Eric one less thing to worry about.

Finally, after what seemed like hours, one of the French fellows bellowed. "*Merde! Va te faire foutre, trouduc!*"

Eric only recognized the one word. *Merde. Shit.* These guys were annoyed, just the way he liked them. Good enough. They ran back the way they came.

Unfortunately, Jordan, if he was still alive, was now on his own.

Easing to his feet, Eric cleared the mud out of his nostrils. Keeping an eye on the direction the enemy had gone, he reached under the surface and pulled Finn up by his collar. Leaning into his face, he murmured, "Time to go."

Finn snorted and shook his head. Mud flew from his drenched hair, spattering Eric in the face, not that it mattered. They were both covered. Adrenaline shakes set in. The chilly bog didn't help. They needed to move quickly and without being seen. *How the hell are you going to do that with a guy the size of Finn?* Eric meant to find out.

"We're going back to Rosie's," he told his sputtering companion.

Finn nodded, his lips pressed into thin lines and slime sliding out of his hair. It'd be harder to move as waterlogged as they both were. Boots would squish and might give them away. Running with any speed would be impossible. Eric had to give it to the guy, though. Finn had finally manned up.

Eric took what he thought was the quickest way out of the meadow, along the far stone fence line. His boots squished all the way, and Finn's carry-on streamed a trail of brownish slime. He followed so closely that he kept stepping on Eric's boot heel.

In another hundred yards, they'd reach the trees and shrubbery alongside the wall and they'd be out of sight. Rosie's place wasn't far. She hadn't locked her doors when she'd left. He could stash Finn there and get back to Jordan and Rosie. Eric knew he could do it.

"Stay low, Finn," he cautioned as they rounded the end of the fence and headed into shadow. "How you doing?"

"Good," came back to him on a breathy, lighter than air, voice.

Empathy crept into Eric's mind. Finn was too heavy for all this running. He seemed able enough to keep up, but he was breathing hard and shaking. Yes, the poor guy needed exercise, but in a gym, not running for his life. There it was again, some indefinable need that tugged at Eric's heartstrings to save this guy from himself.

At last, the rear of Rosie's home came into view. Everything appeared quiet and calm. Eric broke cover, waving

Finn to keep up as he closed the distance to the picket fence. *So far, so good.*

Finn crouched alongside Eric like a shadow. Still panting like a fish out of water, but alive. Now the hard part. They were almost home free. Eric needed to get Finn inside that house and locked up tight before he could accurately determine his next strategy, the one he was making up as he went. But almost only counted with horseshoes and hand grenades…

"Stay here," he ordered Finn.

"Nah-ah, you're not leaving me. I'm coming with you."

Eric lost it. "No. Do as you're told and stop arguing!" He ended the discussion by slapping one palm to the top rail and jumping the pickets, a tricky maneuver with boots and pants that weighed a ton. Cautiously, he crept to the back window. A smart man didn't take chances. Those French guys could've set up an ambush here as easily as back on the road.

He sucked in a calming breath, then slowly, Eric lifted his head. *What do you know?* Aishling was sitting smack in the middle of Rosie's kitchen table, licking her paws like a princess. The cat stopped long enough to look right at him, those curious blue eyes unblinking. Her whiskers twitched as if she recognized him. Easing lazily up off her hind end, the feline version of a drama queen strolled to the edge of the table, her long tail twitching over her head like a welcome home flag.

Eric took her feline nonchalance as a good sign and waved Finn to come forward.

Of course, Finn failed to obey. "I... I can't," he said, both shoulders raised and that soggy carry-on still tight against his chest.

Eric waved him forward, emphatically this time. "Now, damn it. Get your ass over that fence before your buddies with ARs show up."

The man just stood there. What'd he want? A boost over? *Oh, for crying out loud.* That was exactly what Finn wanted. He couldn't climb the fence because he was waterlogged and extra heavy now. "Use the gate then. Make it quick."

Finn's head bobbed, but the sight of him when he cleared the gate startled Eric. The guy—shit, he sagged and his double chin drooped to his chest. Had to be all the mud. Couldn't be skin, could it?

What-the-hell-ever! Eric didn't have time to worry about his clumsy client's weight problem. He needed every last pound of this guy inside the house!

At last! Finn clomped into Rosie's, panting as if he'd run a mile. Eric slammed the door and locked it, lowering the shades at the windows, his heart pounding. Of course, Aishling jumped down to greet him with a noisy purr. *What'd she have to worry about?*

With a grunt, he lowered his backpack, surprised he and Finn were still alive. While Finn stood there in a puddle on the polished floor, Eric proceeded to double check that all rooms were clear, upstairs and down. Finally satisfied, he headed back to the kitchen, slapping at his pockets, feeling for more ammo. He'd given Jordan his last loaded magazine, and there were only nine rounds in his pistol. He needed backup, ammo, and a cellphone.

Rounding the corner, he came face to face with—

Holy. Shit.

There stood a half-naked woman in a puddle of muddy ooze, her elegant back turned to him, in Rosie's kitchen.

His heart leapt up his throat. More like burst. Exploded. He couldn't breathe.

Whoever she was, she'd stripped down to a black bra and bikini panties that were plastered nicely to her wet ass. A pile of sodden clothing lay in a muddy heap at her bare feet along with Finn's boots. The bog-filled roller suitcase had been opened, and a laptop sat with its screen up where Aishling had been grooming herself only minutes earlier. The woman appeared to be peeling skin away from her face and neck. Thick, fluffy skin. And flesh.

Prominent vertebrae punctuated her bare back, but what an ass. A guy knew *fine* when he saw it. Her cheeks were a little hollow, but still.

Where had Finn gone? Now wasn't the time for one of his *feminine* moments.

Or maybe it was...

The strange woman glanced over her shoulder. Chopped brown hair. Waifish. Eyes too big for her delicate face. A lot on the scrawny side. The unibrow from hell jutted off her forehead, evidence that a fine ass does not necessarily translate into Miss America. Her knees knocked together. The murky water had left trails of sediment in streaks down her bare body. Tears streamed down her sweet, sad face, but those eyes. Those big, sad turquoise eyes...

Eric couldn't breathe much less swallow. His heart screeched to a hard stop. It couldn't be. And yet...

It is. It's her.

His memory served him still. So did the single, dark black mole at the top of her left butt cheek just above the elastic of her panties. The rosy remnant of a birthmark on the back of her left calf. The gentle shell of her ears. Her neck.

It's her. My God, it's Shea.

She turned to face him then, scrubbing a hand over her short hair as if she didn't know what to say.

Relief flooded his gut. He tucked his pistol into its holster under his left arm and he had her in his arms without a second thought. Lifting her off the floor, he held her tight and prayed to God this wasn't a concussion speaking.

"Shea?" he asked because he needed her to answer in the affirmative that she was real this time. Seeing was believing, but hearing her speak and confirm it wouldn't hurt.

"Yes, Eric, it's me." She held back, her fingers tapping nervously on his chest.

That one word was his undoing. The sorrow of years choked him. His name had never sounded sweeter. Dearer. All he'd missed swelled up inside, flooding him with sad, bitter joy. Eric pulled her under his chin and held on tight to this woman who might have been a dream or his latest nightmare. But she felt real. Cold. Wet. Covered with goose bumps. Shaking like a reed in the wind, but real, damn it.

His heart started beating again. Smoothing one hand over her sodden hair, he was mindful of the lack of curves on what had once been a voluptuous woman. God, she felt like an armful of sticks. So thin. His heart leaked out of his eyes. "You're finally here. You've come back. Are you okay, baby?"

Of all the damned things, his reason for living had returned. Nothing had ever felt better. Her body molded to his and he couldn't let her go. Wouldn't. Never again.

She'd wrapped her arms around his neck, her slight frame shuddering. Her breasts pressed against his chest. Her ribs, too.

For the first time in years, Eric breathed. Truly breathed. Oxygen filled every last starved-for-Shea cell in his body, his soul, and his brain. Miracles did happen. "It's over, baby. I'm here, and I'm never letting you go again."

Gently, he pulled the awful unibrow away from off her own thinned brows. Why that made her tears fall faster was beyond him, but it didn't matter. Together they could figure everything out. He knew it to the roots of his sad, sorry soul.

It all made sense now. Those gentle eyes he thought he'd seen in the dark that first night Finn had all but run over him. The girly fluctuations in the big guy's voice. That odd feeling of a connection with Finn Powers. Shea had always been Eric's magnetic north. Pulling him. Drawing him into her orbit. Of course he'd been drawn to Finn.

God, he wanted to eat her up. "You're back, Shea. You're finally back."

She choked, her face still pressed into his neck. "Not really."

"Yes, you are." He squeezed his eyes shut and chose to believe. She was wrong. She was where she belonged, and whatever the problem was, he could fix it for her. He could! They would be a family once more. They could! All she had to do was believe.

Shea lifted her face, her eyes seeking his. "We need to talk."

"Yes." He agreed wholeheartedly, but he wouldn't let go of her. Not even to talk. Her breasts had shrunk to nothingness. Hell, her entire body had shrunk, and his heart hurt for her. He needed to know what she'd lived through, but he couldn't for the life of him make his fingers release her. Not after missing her for two years.

His mouth rattled off the feelings of his swelling heart. "I love you, Shea. I've never stopped. Not for one single minute. I knew you'd come back to me."

That she didn't answer with a like sentiment proved nothing. He could fix this. That was what he did. He fixed people's bodies and sometimes their attitudes. By the time he handed them off to a surgeon or a chaplain, they lived, or at least they had a fighting chance.

"You need to save Jordan and Rosie first," she whispered.

Eric jolted back to reality. He swallowed hard and set her feet to the floor, his heart banging against his ribs. He placed his index finger under her chin and tipped her pretty face upward. "Wait here."

She nodded, tears still brimming in the prettiest greenish-blue eyes in the world.

"I'm just going to call the police. Get some help. Please be here when I get back."

She nodded, but damn it. With a rush, he pulled her back into his arms and she came willingly, daring his heart to hope. He dipped his head to her lips, needing a kiss to seal her to his heart again. Desperation clawed up from his gut. *Lie to me, damn it. Lead me on. Tell me anything. Just don't leave!*

Sad eyes peered up at him. Instead of offering the kiss he so desperately needed and wanted, she murmured against his mouth, "You have a job to do, Eric. Don't let Jordan down."

A hard light glinted behind the greenish-blue. The woman he'd lost hadn't returned. Not completely. This version of Shea was made of sharper corners and tired lines, something tougher than the woman who'd walked away from him. *My sweet and lovely Shea is gone.*

A scary thought intruded. *Maybe I can't fix this.*

CHAPTER TWELVE

At last, she was herself.

Shea toed the discarded fat suit she'd named Finn aside, thankful that part of her confession was behind her. It took everything not to kiss her ex-husband. To not give in to Eric's thrill at seeing her and ride the crest of the passion they'd once shared. But after all she'd done to him, she couldn't pretend nothing had changed these last two years. She couldn't allow herself to be the welcomed prodigal, not when she was merely the opportunistic sinner who needed Eric's unique brand of salvation.

Yes, her mind and heart had been headed in his direction for the larger part of the past year, but it was the loss of her friends that had pushed her to make the call for help. Once he understood that, he'd forget his excitement at seeing her. He might even push her away and tell her to go sleep in the bed she'd made. Without him.

Eric stood in the hallway at Rosie's wall phone, his gaze still sweeping hungrily up her legs and over her stomach to her breasts, or lack thereof. What she'd lost in weight and curves, she'd gained in cynicism. He'd be glad to leave her once she told him the rest of her story. About Bagani. About that little girl on the shore. Eric might even run from *her* this time.

So many lies.

"The authorities are coming. They'll be here within minutes," he said as he hung the receiver back on its hook, his voice void of all that welcome-home feeling.

"I have no clothes."

A stern gaze dipped over her, feature by feature, from her quivering lips to her neck to her scant cleavage. He'd been hurt in the collision, too. Trickles of blood streamed down the side of his face into his shirt collar. He wiped the back of his hand over the line of blood and glanced at it. His upper lip curled in annoyance at the sight right before he wiped the blood on his sodden pant leg. Of course. He never worried about himself. Only others.

The silence stretched. Shea shivered at the awkwardness of their reunion. There was a time she'd been thrilled to stand naked in front of him. There were times she'd posed in all the erotic, naughty, suggestive ways of Playboy models, just because he enjoyed the show.

Not now. She felt exposed to her soul. Cheap. Incredibly unworthy of this man.

"Find something to wear," he said before he pivoted on his heel and returned to the front window, his pistol once more in hand. "Hurry. We don't have a lot of time."

His change in demeanor took her by surprise. "I have no clothes," she repeated. How did he not understand?

"So? Find some." His gaze didn't stray to hers this time.

This is what rejection feels like.

Shea couldn't blame him. He'd had time to think and to remember.

Scampering into Rosie's bedroom, Shea located a faded-blue henley in the closet, its buttons missing, and a pair of navy-blue twill pants with frayed cuffs. The fit wasn't perfect, but it was close enough. She dressed hurriedly, her pulse pounding in her ears. A heavy vehicle engine had just rumbled into the front yard of the 'Edge of O'Banner' and right up to Rosie's front door.

Eric shoved the bedroom door open as she zipped the pants. "We've got to go."

His gaze faltered at the sight of her trembling fingers on the zipper pull, but only for a fraction of a second. He'd turned from a loving ex-husband to an emotionally detached bodyguard. This was business. Nothing more. She was just the client he'd come to bail out of a tight spot. He waved her forward with the tip of his pistol, his mask in place, and his backpack once again on his shoulder.

She followed him into the kitchen. There lay the soggy remnants of Finn on the floor. No longer needed, but more forensic evidence than Shea expected to leave behind. The fat suit held a wealth of skin cells and DNA in the now sodden folds of cotton and foam. She could be traced, only this time by murderers instead of the man she loved, *but who might not love me.*

Life had an awful sense of humor. *Lose a child; lose your mind. Find your mind; lose everything else.*

Stepping over what was left of her alter ego, Shea shut Phoenix's laptop, and hugged it to her chest. At least, the plastic bag she'd sealed it in had kept it safe and dry in that awful swamp. Everything else she'd traveled with was lost.

Her pursuers could do what they wanted with Finn, but they couldn't have what her friends had died to protect.

"Keep moving," Eric growled, his hand firm on the small of her back, steering her toward a door off the kitchen. "Rosie's garage is out this way."

I didn't know she had a garage.

Always prepared, Eric pulled an LED penlight out of one of his pockets and lifted it to the side of his head, his weapon still in his other hand. Opening the door, he ushered Shea past him and into a dark, musty smell of motor oil and dirt.

The flashlight's bright, narrow beam caught the interior of an orderly, but small garage with a dirt floor. No car. A lump of something beneath a canvas tarp in the corner. A shovel and a rake leaned against the wall. Gas cans. Rags. Burlap sacks full of something or other. The usual clutter of all good garages.

Aishling mewed at his feet. "You're not coming," he growled, easing her off his boot with a gentle nudge. He left Shea standing there while he secured the door with a length of rope he'd found on the floor. Winding two loops around the knob, he tied it off on a nail pounded into the adjoining wall.

Shea headed toward whatever lay beneath the canvas, filled with the need to repent, to at least be helpful. What a surprise. A motorcycle. The orange and black Harley emblem she recognized, clear and crisp on the bike's dusty, black tank. Sturdy leather saddlebags hung at the rear wheel. She secured the laptop in the right pocket, needing it out of sight.

Eric bumped the back of her bicep with his shoulder. "You know how to ride?"

"No." She gulped, the sensation of his breath on her cheek too delicious to ignore. His question sounded as if he meant for her to leave while he stayed behind and defended her. Even if she'd known how, she would've lied and said she didn't. Her leaving-him-behind days were done. She knew who she could live without. He wasn't one of them. "Do you?"

"I will in a minute." He holstered his weapon and crammed his pack into the other saddlebag. Grunting, he nudged one of the gasoline tanks near the bike carefully with his boot. It nearly tipped over, but he caught it before its noisy clatter could give them away. The other can didn't budge. Had to be full. She hoped.

A loud crash at the front of Rosie's B&B urged Shea into action. She unscrewed the bike's gasoline cap while Eric removed the lid from the can and extended the spout. With another grunt, he hefted the heavy can off the floor and filled the tank. Gasoline glugged, but slowly. Eric seemed calm while anxiety ratcheted up her spine. *Hurry.*

Heavy footsteps sounded inside Rosie's home. Men's harsh voices. Professor Grover's murderers were back. Shea swallowed hard. *Hurry. Hurry.*

Eric jerked the tarp away from the rest of the bike, revealing a helmet and two leather jackets setting on a wooden stand beside it. What were the chances that Paddy and Rosie O'Banner were bikers once upon a time?

He handed her the helmet. "Here. Put this on."

"Where's yours?" she asked as she accepted it, needing him protected, too.

"Don't worry about me. Put it on," he growled, a hard light in his eyes as he shrugged into the larger of the two jackets. "The jacket, too. Do it."

She didn't want him at risk, but she had no choice but to obey. After wiping the dust off the helmet, she secured it over her head and adjusted the strap. Her fingers trembled as she hurriedly worked the zipper of the leather jacket. It fit, although a size too large.

Loud banging sounded from inside. She glanced back at the door when someone jerked at the handle. A loud French voice roared on the other side, quickening her pulse.

They're here. Whoever stood on the other side of that door meant business. It shuddered. The rope stretched tight. The man yelled again.

Eric swung one leg over the bike's leather seat and offered her a hand. "Get on."

Shea grabbed onto his wrist and forearm, but climbing up onto a motorcycle presented more obstacles than she'd expected. Once her butt hit the leather seat, she asked, "Where do I put my feet?"

"There." He pointed at the metal bar protruding from the side of the bike near the wheels. "On the pegs. Whatever you do, don't bump the exhaust pipe." He meant the wider tube-like pipe extending from the engine. "Once this baby starts up, it will burn your skin off. Be careful."

She positioned her bare feet as he'd directed.

"Where are your shoes, damn it?" he snapped.

"My boots were full of water. I didn't have time to look for shoes in Rosie's closet before they—"

"You can't ride a bike with no boots. What were you thinking?"

"Of living," she answered honestly, "I guess I didn't know I'd be riding on the back of a motorcycle today or I'd have come prepared."

"Shit," he snarled, but what else could she do? Resting the balls of her feet on the pegs, she wasn't sure how close she should sit to him or what she should hang onto. He radiated nothing but hostility at the moment. How did a woman grab onto *that*?

Instead of him, she grasped the edge of her seat, hoping that would suffice. No way. She teetered the instant he toed the kickstand free. With another growl, he planted his boots on each side of the bike. Reaching both hands behind him, Eric grabbed beneath her knees and jerked her forward. Into him. Intimately into him. Her heaving breasts to his very solid leather covered back. Her twill covered pubic bone to his denim-clad butt.

The male body she'd craved for too many lonely months was now perfectly aligned with hers. Heat flooded her to her core even as she cringed. Tentatively, she circled his waist and placed her palms flat against his stomach, afraid to breathe.

He had come for her. He didn't know it when he did, but here he was. Angry, yes, but saving her just as he'd once saved men on far off battlefields and villages of Afghanistan.

Eric turned his head, his voice deep and gravelly. "Once I start this bike, they'll be all over us. Hang on tight. They'll be shooting. Don't be afraid. We'll be hard to hit while we're moving. You ready?"

"I am," she declared boldly, clutching him.

Aishling chose that moment to jump onto Eric's lap.

He brushed her off. "I said no. You stay here."

The crazy cat jumped back up as quickly as her paws hit the dirt floor.

"Damn it, cat, take off," Eric growled, taking hold of her with both hands this time and settling her back to her feet. "I don't have room. You have to stay."

Aishling lasted a half second at his feet, this time using her claws as she climbed his thigh like a tree truck. Huffing, he glanced over his shoulder. "I guess the cat's coming with us."

Shea relaxed her grip while he unzipped his leather jacket and stuffed Aishling inside. "But if you scratch me one time, kitty, you're outta there," he warned her as if she might understand. "I will leave your fluffy butt behind."

No, you won't, Shea thought. She couldn't help the tiny smile stretching her lips. This was Eric, through and through, thinking he could start up a motorcycle with a cat under his arm. She grabbed hold of him, this time with more confidence as she pressed her cheek between his shoulder blades. When he covered her interlocked fingers with one big hand and squeezed, the warmth of that simple contact took her by storm. She blinked away the glistening moisture clouding her vision. Eric might be angry, but deep down, he was still the only man she loved.

Releasing her, he grabbed hold of the handlebars. Two kicks from his right boot and the engine sputtered to life with a growling roar, alerting the whole world of their whereabouts. Apparently Aishling didn't mind the noise. Eric hadn't sent her flying.

Shea squeezed him tighter, panic skulking up her spine again. Hurry. Hurry. *Hurry!*

He yanked an overhead chain, one she hadn't seen until the muscles rippled across his back and the single, garage door lifted. She closed her eyes and remembered those handsome muscles stretched over her. Every last one of them.

Sunlight poured into their last stronghold. Shea closed her eyes as the powerful man beneath her arms commanded the motorized beast to fly. With another thunderous rumble, the Harley lifted its front wheel from the ground before it dug in to do what it did best.

And they were off.

CHAPTER THIRTEEN

Run like hell. That was all Eric had on his mind. What was it Aishling had said in his dream? *And then you'll need to fly.* He brushed the insane notion that she'd known beforehand he and Shea would need to fly down the back roads of Ireland—on a Harley.

Gunning the motorcycle, he lowered his face, hoping the mud smeared Aviators he'd found in the jacket pocket would keep the wind out of his eyes. There'd only been one helmet in the garage, so of course, it went to Shea. Things might get dicey, but she needed to live. So did the damned cat purring inside what had to be Paddy O'Banner's leather bomber jacket.

The bike was small and had no fairing around the handlebars to protect its rider from bugs and road debris, not like that was Eric's first concern. All he needed was speed.

Swerving around the big, bad Hummer rumbling in Rosie's front yard, he squeezed the handgrip into second gear. A heavy-duty push bar hung off the front of the chassis. No wonder the cab rolled so many times. It never stood a chance.

The Harley rapped into third. Finally, fourth. Eric didn't look back, just hunkered into the wind, held onto Shea's arms with one hand, and let the bike's pistons do their thing. The gentle purr of a contented feline against his ribs soothed one worry away. *Crazy cat.*

Finding Shea in place of Finn in Rosie's kitchen was the surprise of a lifetime, and God, he'd wanted nothing more than to haul her off to the nearest flat surface and claim her once more. But he was pretty sure he'd scared her with that initial, passionate hug. She'd stiffened enough that he'd reevaluated what he thought he'd seen in her eyes. She'd seemed skittish, as if she'd run, and bottom line—he couldn't lose her.

If she even meant to stay. He didn't know, so he'd backed off with the I'm-so-glad-to-see-you, and restrained his runaway heart. He'd closed down, not willing to be hurt like the last time. They needed to talk, but not now.

He raced the motorcycle along the road that ran to Grover's burned out cottage and into the dirt path beyond. For miles the Hummer followed, until Eric took a sharp right into a narrow country driveway and ended up in someone's backyard. The problem with most Irish yards was the country's love of stone fences.

Eric and Shea were quickly boxed in, but no matter. Leaning backward, he urged the front wheel of the Harley onto a carefully stacked pile of peat bricks, and from there, onto the stone fence. The irregular shapes made for a rough ride, but it also ensured the Hummer couldn't follow, not unless the French Legionnaires intended to use that vehicle as a battering ram for all the other fences that would surely stand in their way.

Eric thought himself safely out of their reach until another black motorcycle raced around the Hummer, kicking up grass as it slowed in a wide arc. By then, two of the Frenchmen were boots on the ground, their weapons drawn. They bellowed and waved the intruder off.

The cocky rider didn't comply, but instead dug a rutted circle in the soft turf with his rear wheel, spattering both men. This new intruder was a slender man dressed completely in black leathers. His face was hidden behind the darkened shield of a topnotch helmet. His bike was top of the line, too, complete with protective windshield. Larger gas tank. A scabbard at his right for the automatic rifle strapped in it.

This operation kept going from bad to worse.

"Anyone you know?" Eric asked over his shoulder, keeping his eye on that AR while they made their exit. All he had was a pistol tucked under his left arm and barely enough ammo, a popgun in the face of that bullet-spitting machine.

"I don't know any of them," Shea answered. "Do you?"

"Hell, no." *Time to go.*

Accelerating along the top of the narrow wall, Eric balanced the bike as long as he dared. Out of that yard, into the next. Once out of the Hummer's reach, he dropped both wheels off the edge and gunned the Harley. It responded with a roaring burst of power, but now Eric had more than a weaponized four-wheeler and stationary tough guys to worry about. The intruder to this nightmare had no problem clearing stone fences. His bike soared overhead and landed in front of Eric and Shea.

Shea stiffened, her arms tight around Eric's waist, while he gave the intruder an outright challenge and charged the guy, forcing him to serve to avoid being run over. Twisting the handle grip, Eric commanded the Harley to fly, and—*just like Aishling said they would*—they did. Over stone walls. Through shrubbery and thorny brambles. Under low-lying branches and around nervous sheep that went in ten different directions when spooked.

But Eric couldn't shake the guy. Still in the lead, he raced through the field behind the row of homes, the biker following. More stone fences, all about three feet high and all covered with greenery, created a surreal obstacle course. There were no straight lines to this Irish madness, just meandering piles of stone, some slipshod, some perfectly stacked. Intermittent breaks with a single board for a gate kept the sheep from straying into fields of crops and others of weeds. A taller fence, maybe five feet high, bordered the others as far as Eric could see. There was no way out!

Divots of dirt flew up from the stony ground at his right, and he ducked. Damn it! The intruder had upped the ante. Those were bullets!

"Hang on tight," Eric growled to Shea, the feel of her slender body tucked against him a blessing he was prepared to die for. He gunned the bike and flew, the wind in his hair, but there was nowhere to run. Not unless he could find a break in that outer fence. Still he pressed forward. *Never give up. Must go faster.*

Rounding yet another corner, he banked hard to the right, missing the only trail he'd seen in this maze. The Harley ended up in a field of corn. Tall stalks covered his bike. But the field wasn't American-sized. The end of the line lay straight ahead in the form of what was, no doubt, yet another wall of stone beneath miles of green ivy.

He powered the bike down, hidden from sight for the moment. The intruder had taken the trail, roaring off at Eric's right, while Eric and Shea went nowhere. Patting the warm bulge under his jacket, Eric thought, *what now, Aishling?*

Shea's slender fingers intertwined with his and Eric let them work their magic. For a minute. Too soon, that guy would be back. He'd see the crushed stalks of corn, and he'd know where Eric had gone. With Shea riding in back, she'd take the first bullet. *Not going to happen.*

Eric turned the bike and headed back the way they had come. With their intruder racing in the opposite direction, it'd take him a couple minutes before he caught his mistake. Puttering along in low gear, Eric thought he'd seen metal posts along this stretch of what he hoped was the general boundary fence that bordered the others. Metal posts might mean a gate. He kept his ear tuned for their latest assassin.

Shea's thighs trembled against him, but wasn't she in the perfect womanly position? Her legs spread wide, holding onto him like a lover. He cupped her kneecap, then ran his hand over her sun-warmed thigh, offering what little comfort he could. If only they were facing each other.

Ah, there they are. Two round metal posts. Up ahead.

"I think I know a way out of here," Eric said as he hunkered low, peering beyond the tangled ivy between the posts. At last. Some fine Irishman had added a metal gate, not like it worked as thickly wrapped with green vines as it was.

Eric didn't dare leave the bike behind. No, somehow they had to get through this gate to whatever lay on the other side. Sidling the Harley to the gate, he reached through the ivy until his fingers met rusted horizontal rails. It had been here a long time, but there was give to it. Rusted hinges maybe. Oxidized rails. Good enough. Still on the Harley, Eric leaned his weight into it. He shoved the gate, then shoved harder. At last, it creaked, rustled, and groaned. *If I can just hit it hard enough to...*

"Hold on," he told Shea as he revved the Harley into a wide circle until it faced what he hoped was a weak spot in the wall. Hunkering low, he spurred the bike forward. Lifting the front wheel at the last second, he hit the center of that ivy-covered passage.

Oomph. It was Harley time, along with plenty of dust and moths. But gradually, the gate gave enough that the bike won. Both wheels cleared the fence. The good thing about Irish ivy? It didn't break, and this plant—or plants—had been growing forever. Its many creeping branches and arms, fingers and toes, were dense and woody, downright fibrous, and all had intertwined like a massive net. Once Eric cleared the opening, the pernicious ivy sprang back into place, nearly pulling the gate upright.

He killed the engine, his heart hammering loud enough to wake the dead. "Get off," he ordered Shea. Her bare feet had no sooner hit the dirt than he pulled Aishling out of his jacket and handed her to Shea. She cradled the cat like a baby, and the crazy thing snuggled.

Laying the bike on its side, Eric scrambled back to the wall. He dropped to his knees and hefted the sagging doorway firmly back into place, bracing it with his shoulder so that it appeared solid, at least on his side. *God, this has to work.*

A few minutes later, the intruder approached the wall slowly, still revving his engine as if taunting them. Eric held as still as he could, given the adrenaline pumping through his veins. This madman had to believe they'd gotten away.

Yeah. Not likely. The Harley had left a clear set of tire tracks straight up to the breach in the wall. No guy was dumb enough to believe his adversary could just disappear. The intruder was probably deciding whether or not to search on foot. Eric would have. *Just to be sure.*

With only hope on his side and a helluva lot of nerve, Eric strained to listen. There on his knees. In some farmer's pasture. *If this insane idea works, it'll be the biggest miracle ever.*

The bike rumbled along the fence line and away. Eric lowered his head, thankful for the reprieve, but still tracking yet another man who seemed to be gunning for Shea. How many were after her? Abdul-Mutaal for sure. The Frenchmen. Now some guy with a gun on a motorcycle? The scary thing was they all now knew it wasn't Finn riding with Eric.

Poor Shea crouched beside him, her eyes wide and her teeth clamped over her bottom lip. She'd let Aishling down and where the cat had gone, Eric didn't know. He had Shea on his mind. The poor thing wasn't cut out to be an undercover operative, not shaking like she was. He'd always known she was high-strung, but she seemed close to coming undone.

She'd dropped the helmet to the ground, letting loose her sweaty hair. He couldn't tear his eyes off her. Where had all her chocolate brown tangles gone? He used to love getting lost in the delicious scent of the coconut and vanilla shampoo she'd used. The feel of all that cool silk, like ribbons, spiraling off her head. Reduced to a boyish cut, not even a good handful remained. His heart hurt seeing her like this.

The throbbing pulse at the hollow of her neck revealed her fear, and like it or not, the instinct to protect her spiked Eric's gut with a vengeance.

His gaze strayed to that slender neck and all its ticklish spots. He knew where to breathe hard to make her shiver. Where to nibble to get a moan out of her. *Before.*

Without warning, she ducked into him, trembling like a deer caught in a trap. Her head sank below his chin like it used to do. Her hands slid beneath his open jacket. Over his ribs.

"Shh," he whispered, instead of *'Shit!'* He didn't need the gentle distraction of her fingers smoothing over his pecs and seeking assurance he wasn't so sure she deserved.

She nodded, bumping his chin with the top of her head, or maybe she just shook so hard that it seemed she'd agreed. God, he wanted to hold her, to pull her beneath his arm. To keep her safe, but she'd given up that option when she'd walked away. Was he stupid enough to believe she truly wanted him in all the ways he still wanted her?

Not likely. She needed help. That was all. She might have asked for him by name, but he'd read her body language back at Rosie's. She'd seemed sorrowful, but maybe she just seemed caught. Once again, she'd deceived him, pretending to be Finn to get him to come save her. Why should he forgive and forget?

I haven't.

Yes, you have, his heart declared as quickly as he'd denied it.

No. I haven't. I'm not that stupid.

Even he knew better.

A slow burn commenced in both biceps from the strain of holding the fence, matching the slow burn in his pants. God was real funny, creating men like he had, their bodies ever eager for sex even at the worst of times, springing to attention at the slightest possibility of action, or the slightest scent of their woman. Even now with some killer on the other side of a silly green wall. Even now with the woman who'd destroyed his heart. Hell, his whole life. *Even now…*

Tension tightened his back muscles into planks. Sweat trickled down his forehead. Still, he held his position. Someone had to protect Shea. *I might as well be the dumb jock who…*

Still.

Loves.

Her.

Damn it. I do.

Eric swallowed hard, convinced he had to be the stupidest man on the planet. He tipped his chin to the top of her head and offered what little comfort he could.

The sound of the intruder's motorcycle reduced to a putter and headed back toward their hiding place. No doubt the guy couldn't decide if his prey had truly gotten away or if he'd been duped. Maybe he was still sizing up the wall, intending to jump it. That made more sense. Yeah. He was doing exactly what any predator would be doing. Probing for a weak spot.

Eric held his breath, his mind in a reluctant argument over the woman hugged up against him. *Why should I forgive her? She's the one who left, damn it. Not me. Hell, I searched for her for months after I got served with divorce papers. I never contested it. Never even retained a lawyer. Just left the POS on the kitchen counter and there it stayed. Just sucked up the hurt. Went back to work. Kept hoping she'd get in touch. Prayed. And now she needs me?*

His mind flittered across time and space to Jordan and Rosie, and instantly, blocked the worst-case scenario of what might have happened. The seconds turned into minutes. Eric lifted his head to keep an eye on the edge of ivy above him and his tenuous hiding place. His arms shook in their extended position. His biceps burned. Yet he didn't shrug Shea off. Didn't even ask her to help. Just kept his chin on top of her head and hoped they got out of this alive.

To make matters worse, she'd pressed her nose into his neck, almost as if she'd read his thoughts about protecting her. Her fingers climbed up his back beneath the leather jacket, clinging to his shoulder blades. Her breath came hard and warm against his skin. Her lashes fluttered against his Adam's apple.

He squeezed his eyes shut and fought the overwhelming feelings of his heart, a sucker for all things Shea. *Poor damned thing. God, I prayed for you to come back. I do love you, baby.*

And there in the middle of nowhere, with certain danger and death only feet away, the sweetest memory surfaced. That night in Rio. Their honeymoon. Their first time making love. No clothes. Didn't need them. They had a crazy pagan lust for each other and... love. Hours and hours of passionate, sweaty love.

After an exhaustive exploration of each other's bodies, and possibly one too many orgasms, (if there were such a thing), she'd fallen asleep with her face mashed against his chest. With each flutter of her lashes, she'd tickled the daylights out of his nipple.

Instead of disturbing her, he'd held still for hours, content to watch the tired beauty in his arms. The angel he'd worn out with nothing but love. He pressed a kiss into the crown of her head. *I still love you, Shea. I always have. I always will.*

That night he'd brushed the silken tresses of her fudge-colored hair away from her swollen, well-kissed lips and out of her eyes. That was the most perfect moment of his life. He'd slowed his breathing so he didn't disturb her. He'd wondered how a guy like him had gotten lucky enough to marry a hot babe who'd wanted to spend the rest of her life with him. He wondered still. *Why did you call for me, Shea? What do you want, just a ticket home?*

The sound of the intruder shutting down his bike motor on the other side of the wall sucked Eric out of Rio and back to Ireland. His senses heightened as the meadow calmed.

Insects buzzed. A dog barked off in the distance. But the biker didn't make a sound, not one footfall.

Eric strained to hear any indication the man had gotten off his mount and might be headed their way. He planned for worst-case scenarios and wished for his knife, but it lay sharpened and ready in his gear bag a good five feet away. His pistol was still holstered, his arms and hands raised supporting the gate, not much of a defensive position at all. More like submissive.

Silence stretched while he waited for the scrape of a fresh magazine being slammed into that deadly AR, anything that would tell him the intruder's next course of action. A suspicious killer might spray the bank of ivy with rapid fire just to make sure.

Instead, a black and gray jackdaw fluttered off a branch overhead and flew to the nearby patch of trees lining this side of the wall. Eric accepted what the universe had just provided. The bird's presence might actually convince the intruder there was no one here. He sucked in a steadying breath and hoped.

The sun climbed higher. The leather jacket grew warmer while he breathed into Shea's hair and wished the men hunting her would all go far, far away.

Come on, you bastard. Start your bike up and get the hell out of here. Don't make me have to kill you.

At last, a low grumble from the other side of the fence in— Arabic? Okay, that made sense. This guy had to be in league with Abdul-Mutaal, though how he'd known where Shea was made no sense. But if he was with Mutaal, who were the Frenchmen with? Eric hadn't discounted what Shea said the night she'd run from Grover's cottage. She'd been so sure she'd seen a scimitar. What the hell was going on?

A couple seconds passed, but finally, the Arab restarted his bike. He gunned the engine and rumbled off in the direction he'd come from.

Eric blew out a sigh of relief. They just might live after all. He let the gate sag into its web of ivy and he leaned back enough to peer down into Shea's face. Still nestled under his chin, she looked up, her bluish-green eyes wide with answers to questions he wasn't sure he wanted to ask. Not yet.

Where have you been?

Why did you leave?

Mostly—*do you still love me?*

Ivy dripped from the tallest trees, swarmed the trunks, and blanketed the lowest branches. Green on green. Lovely. Questions could wait. They needed a safe place to lay low until he was absolutely certain the coast was clear. Then they'd start the bike up and venture back onto a paved road. Then they'd find a way to contact Alex. Jordan, too.

Twisting his neck, he looked beyond Shea to the lush, green forest of this fenced communal pasture. His stupid heart was still tender from the deepest hurt a woman could inflict on a man, but it was also hopeful for the first time in years.

Damn it. Love shouldn't hurt so damned hard.

He held an index finger to his lips, needing Shea to maintain a code of silence until they'd gotten farther into the woods. Their adversary might still be nearby. No bounty hunter would've given up so easily. He'd be back. If not him, Abdul Mutaal or the Legionnaires.

CHAPTER FOURTEEN

Shea snagged her helmet and helped Eric lift the heavy motorcycle to its wheel, then followed while he pushed and grunted it over moss-covered rocks and rotted branches. The greenery beneath her bare feet proved sharp and prickly, but none of it prickled as much as her conscience.

She avoided its nagging by watching him work. There was a time she thought he might have been of Hispanic descent, his skin the color of caramel and his hair dark and sexy. Now she knew he was simply one of those guys who tanned easily. At the first hint of summer sun, he'd turn brown. Sweat glistened at the back of his neck. His short black hair curled under his ears, just barely, just enough that she wanted to run her fingertips over his head and mess with it. He must've gotten cut in the accident.

Dried blood still etched the side of his face and jaw, but not once had he complained at the task he'd set himself to. He just kept pushing and grunting. A fallen log covered with moss required more effort. His booted toes dug in. Muscles bunched beneath the back pockets of his denim jeans. His arms stretched forward. He grunted when the leather jacket rode up, lifting his shirt and revealing the tanned muscles of his lower back, his leather belt, and the black band of his underwear advertising *Hanes*.

If this had been another time and if the circumstances were different, she would have snagged that elastic advertisement and snapped it—just for fun. Eric would have been all over her in play. They would have laughed and wrestled and...

But this was not that other time. Shea kept watching and remembering, until at last he cleared the log and leaned the bike against the trunk of a huge, old oak, itself beset with the climbing nemesis of Irish ivy. Shrugging out of his leather jacket, he tossed it aside and brushed the sweat and blood from his forehead with the back of one hand. They both smelled like bog, but poor Eric hadn't had time to change clothes like she had, much less boots. It hadn't slowed him down. Not once.

Shea stalled the inevitable. "You're hurt."

"I'm fine," he growled, his face flushed, but his gaze filled with the sincere need for truth. "Do you want to explain to me why you've got three assholes from France on your ass, and now some jerk from the Mideast? I'm pretty sure he just cursed you out in Arabic. What the hell are you into, Shea? Heroin? Hashish? Meth? God, just tell me. I need to know what I'm fighting."

Judgment day had come. There was nowhere to run and nowhere she'd rather be.

"No drugs," she murmured, hesitant how far back she should go or what to tell him. There was so much. She wished she were invisible.

Eric lowered his butt to the lush green forest floor and sat cross-legged, his wrists on his knees and his holster on the ground beside him. "I've got all day, Shea, and it's quiet at the moment. That guy might return. Might not. Tell me what you do know so I can figure what to do next. Who's chasing you and why? What do you have that they want?"

She swallowed hard, the lump in her throat a bigger hurdle than she expected. Dropping slowly to her knees a few feet opposite him, she slid out of Rosie's leather jacket and tucked her bare feet beneath her. Leaning onto one hand, she met meet his gaze.

"I miss Cheyenne," she said softly, needing Eric to understand the impetus that had propelled her from his life.

He bobbed his head once and gulped. "I miss her, too," he said, his voice husky and tight.

Shea stifled the sob that always choked out of her at the mention of her daughter. She gathered her courage and kept going. "Remember the story you made up about the three, dirty, little pigs? You told it to her that night she decided she wanted to sleep in her sandbox."

His eyes filled with tenderness for the child they'd created and lost. "I do."

She lowered her head and studied the myriad of plant life beneath her hand. Baby ferns curled around her fingers. Soft, green moss cushioned the heel of her palm. A thousand spears of tiny pink flowers shot up through the velvet carpet. Everywhere she looked, she saw Cheyenne. She would've loved picking those flowers and pinching them into a bouquet to give—*me*.

"Remember when the mother pig dropped out of heaven one day and made them wash their hands before they could eat dinner? Remember how surprised they were that they even had a mother? Remember when she fixed them buttered corn and roast beef and mashed potatoes and wouldn't let them eat the Twinkies and cotton candy and all the junk food they'd been eating?" Her heart swelled with the sweet memory of her handsome husband with his tiny daughter on his lap. He'd cocked his head to peer into Cheyenne's face while he told the story, his baby girl nestled inside the circle of his arms. Dressed in his uniform of the day, he'd been the perfect Prince Charming for that little girl. *And I miss him.*

Eric cleared his throat, and Shea didn't have to look to know the cords in his neck were strung tight, or that he'd wiped his face on his sleeve. Eric's heart was as soft as those Twinkies in his make-believe fairytale, but twice as sweet. *Maybe three times.*

Shea struggled to control her ragged emotions, a difficult chore every day of her life. The green tendrils hanging from the tree branches overhead all seemed to have reached a point where they ceased falling and curled upward again, stretching for the sun. She was the same as that ivy. She'd reached the lowest point in her lifetime. To continue, she needed the comfort of the only one in her pitiful life who understood the canyon of her grief.

The laughing jackdaws in the forest broke the stillness. Water dripped somewhere nearby. Suddenly, Cheyenne was there in spirit, if only because she would've loved a picnic in this magical setting. She would've climbed up every low branch and invented her own stories of unicorns and leprechauns, because she was so much like her father. Full of light and life.

Shea opened her mouth, but all that came out was a creaky, "I..." She tried again, positive she deserved nothing this kind man had to offer, but just as sure she needed him to understand why she'd left him.

"I..." was all that lifted from her parched throat. Her paralyzed brain had refused admission to her vocabulary. She'd been struck dumb by her own sin.

Eric seemed not to have noticed her failure. He rolled to his knees and crawled over the weeds and flowers between them. He didn't stop until he cupped one hand to her chin. "Hey. It's me. Remember?"

She blinked the tears off her eyelashes and held her breath. He had every reason to hate her, but there he was, reaching for her. She sucked in a sob and took the chance she'd been given and looked into his eyes. The rest of her life came down to this one defining moment. Either he loved her still and would find a way to forgive her, or she had no reason to live.

"Do you remember the name I chose for that mother pig?" he asked, his thumb tenderly rubbing a circle on her chin.

Of course, she remembered. It was the reason the Reynolds family had giggled together all those years ago. The reason they'd all snorted like those three dirty, little pigs. Not now. She tried to speak it again, but the simple, one word answer caught in her throat.

He edged closer, his lips inches away. "I gave that mama pig a very special name, one that belonged to the smartest, prettiest, most loving mother in the whole world," he whispered. "That's the only mama our little girl loved. I named her after you, Shea. It made Cheyenne laugh. Remember?"

God, how could I ever forget? A tiny cry for rescue crept up from her soul, needing to be heard. "Tell me that story again," Shea cried, her voice tight with the pain of losing her child. "I... I really want to be that mama pig again."

With a groan, Eric bowled her over, his hand behind her head to cushion her fall, and his tears raining down on her face. Strong fingers skimmed over her cheekbones. The length of his body and legs pressed the length of hers. "Talk to me, Shea. Please. Tell me where you've been, and what you've been doing. We could've gone through everything together. Why did you leave?"

"I... I couldn't stay." The pain in her chest twisted upon itself. "You were so sad when we lost her, and I... I let you down."

He leaned his forehead to hers. Nose to nose they faced each other. "No, you didn't. Life let us down, baby. It let us both down. I needed you then, and I need you now." The soft cushion of moss beneath Shea comforted her nearly as much as the weight of the sweaty, sensuous male body crushing her. The pads of his thumbs caressed her temples while his fingers threaded into her hair. "Maybe more."

The pain eked out one word at a time. "I… I couldn't stay. I was afraid."

A shadow shifted over his face. "Of what? Of me?"

She stroked his cheek. "No. Of me. I couldn't think straight. You greeted everyone at the viewing like you were glad to see them, and I wanted to be strong like you, but I… I couldn't. I was so angry. So mad. I hated everyone back then, and every hand you clasped and every other person you comforted pushed me farther away until… I broke."

Shea didn't want to relive the day she'd run, but she needed him to understand "I tried to act strong, Eric. I tried to be brave and I tried to help everyone else when they cried, when they said they didn't know how I could live without her. What a stupid thing to say to me. God, Eric, to me! The mother of that little girl! I still can't live without her."

He pulled her forehead to his lips. "I know, baby. I know." For the first time, he sounded as broken as she felt, only that wasn't right. He'd sounded heartbroken before, only this time, her ears were opened wide. Shea finally heard Eric's pain through the noisy grief in her mind.

There was painful courage in the realization that they shared the same depth of grief; that he understood precisely what she meant. "But one morning, I couldn't pretend I was strong anymore, Eric. I couldn't live without Cheyenne, and I didn't care about anyone else. Cheyenne was my baby, and I... I..." She closed her eyes and wished the unthinking world of people who meant well away. "I just let go. I fell off the tightrope I'd been walking, and I... I..." *Left.*

Rolling to her side, Eric pulled her into the crook of his arm, cradling her as if she'd never deserted him when he'd needed her most. "It's okay. Sh-h-h. Trust me, Shea. Everything's going to be okay."

"But it's not," she insisted, fighting to breathe. Eric needed to see who she'd become, not who she once was. The Shea he'd fallen in love with had died with Cheyenne. She didn't exist anymore and Eric had to love her now for the woman she'd survived into, not who she used to be. He had to open his eyes and see the updated version of Shea Powers Reynolds. The ex-wife. The ex-mother. The ex-everything.

The moment her fingertips touched his scruffy face, he closed his eyes. A shudder raced through him, melting her heart, but Eric had to know everything, and he had to know it now. Before she chickened out. "I kept falling," she whined. "Nothing helped. Not distance. Not booze. I thought I had to go far, far away before I... before I..."

A wicked tsunami of guilt crested high over the top of her endurance, threatening to crush her. But Eric didn't seem repulsed one bit, his fingers gently stoking the back of her neck as if offering a prelude to foreplay. He ran his hand over her dirty, short hair, exhaling a deep breath. "I should've seen it coming. It's my fault. I knew the signs. You had a bad case of baby blues after Cheyenne was born, too. Remember?"

"Yes," she admitted, recalling it well. Those were some other, very dark days. "I had awful mood swings. One minute I was over-the-top-happy to be a mom, and the world was perfect, but the next, I felt as if I wasn't good enough or perfect enough or—"

"Or happy enough or thin enough or *anything* enough," he finished for her. "You cut your hair then, too." He smoothed a hand over her scant locks, the kindest gleam in his eyes. "You had a natural hormonal reaction, and believe me, I understand, Shea, I do. The pressures of being a new mom are enormous. It didn't help that I deployed and left you to deal with a newborn all by yourself. I worried about you the whole time I was overseas. Remember how often I called home?"

"I do." She snuggled against his ribs, relishing how her body awakened to the corners and angles of the only man she'd ever made love with. Twining her bare feet around his ankles, she needed to be as close to him as possible.

"God, what was I thinking," he murmured against her forehead. "I'm sorry. I should've seen it coming. I knew how happy Cheyenne's birth made you, even if it made you a little crazy afterward." He placed a soft, moist kiss in the middle of her grimy forehead. "I saw this type of thing happen enough overseas."

His fingertips carved through her grimy hair. "It's called complex bereavement. Untreated, it turns into severe depression. I should've recognized it and gotten help for you sooner. Faster. Before you ever felt that you needed to leave me in order to protect me. I should've protected you first. You're all I've ever wanted, baby. I hope you still know that."

Gah. Her heart opened wide at the gift he'd just poured into her soul. *Forgiveness.*

She lifted her chin, needing to reclaim the man she'd once run from. "Kiss me."

He dipped his head and pressed his lips to hers, igniting the ember that had lain cold for too long. Shea parted her lips and let the warm coffee-taste of his mouth and the calluses on his palms fill her up and break her open. She'd almost forgotten the pleasant rub of his whiskers on her chin and lips. The way he asked for more without speaking, and the way her body responded with an eager, *Yes.*

His fingers moved lightly over her clothes, peeling the henley and pants away. She shifted her weight to accommodate every last tug until he traced her bare stomach, his fingertips as hot as branding irons, his palms wide and strong.

Shea had no will nor resistance to the only man she'd ever loved. Her body clenched at the contact. Eric had always been her one obsession. The taste of his skin was a heady single-barrel kind of craving.

Easing away from her mouth, he cocked his neck to look down at what he'd bared. She'd left her wet bra back in Rosie's room. Her panties, too. His breath caught as his gaze scrolled over her breasts down to her nakedness below. A glowing smile brightened his handsome face. "You're stunning," he whispered, more gravel to his tone than she'd remembered. There he was once more, the happy, hungry man she'd fallen in love with.

"You came for me," she murmured, her love for him turning into warm anticipation.

He licked his lips again. "And now baby, you're going to come for me," he teased as sweetly as if they'd never parted. He closed the distance and covered her mouth with his. His fingers danced over her stomach on their way to her core, filling her with an aching need to absorb every last bit of him.

Her body remembered his lips and tongue. She tugged his shirt out of his jeans, her tongue making mad passionate love with his. He couldn't kiss her hard enough, deep enough, or long enough.

Easing away from him, she melted. The sight of his sculpted body drew her like a moth to the fire. This man's body was pure porn. The need to feel him deep inside urged her hands up his abdomen and over his chest, shoving his shirt out of her way in record time. His clothes had to go. The snap on his jeans took little time. His zipper. She licked her lips as she pushed his jeans out of her way. He assisted, kicking off his boot and then his pants.

Pushing his back to the moss-covered floor, she couldn't wait. Soft morning light spilled across his handsome face, taking her to another day when she was the anxious virgin.

Make that the anxious *and* rowdy virgin. God, she'd wanted his body so badly that first night on their honeymoon. He'd been too much the gentleman, and all she'd wanted was him stripped bare and inside her. Spreading her legs, Shea straddled him once more, her palms flat to his chest, wanting every bit of exposed flesh until…

What's this? Five vertical lines marred what had once been a glorious six-pack. *Scars.* The last time she'd seen this belly it had been tan and unblemished. Perfect. "What happened? Tell me."

Eric shrugged, his eyes still big and black with lust, his hands on her hips. Tugging her downward, a smile curled his lips when her breasts flattened to his chest. "Brazil happened. An operation went bad. That's all."

"But someone stabbed you. I want to know the whole story."

"And you shall, but not now." He bucked up from the ground just enough to get his *point* across. A salacious grin replaced his gentle smile. "I want inside, Shea. Now. No more talk."

She demurred; ready to give this man whatever he wanted. He was right. Words could wait. Most of them. "I love you, Eric. I never stopped. You need to know that."

A spark flashed down deep in the brown. He clutched the sides of her face and lowered her to his mouth. "And I love you, baby. Only you."

He kissed her hard, tangling his tongue with hers and reclaiming her mouth. Then her chin as he lifted her body over his.

She hugged his head to her while he latched onto her nipple. Energy snapped through her body in a fever pitch. Every last muscle clenched with anticipation. She clamped her knees, not completely claimed, but bursting with an inner explosion of electric fireworks that could. Not. Wait.

Ah! He wasn't inside, yet already he'd lit her body with the delightful detonations of coming. Shea sunk her nose into his hair. How she craved this wonderfully delicious man.

No sooner had her unexpected climax slowed, when he rolled her onto her back. "So soon?" he asked, a dashing glimmer in his eye, and his thumb running laps around her wet nipple. "I thought you'd want more than just nipple kisses after all this time."

"I do." She grabbed the cheeks of his ass, breathless as the storm within her.

He lowered himself with excruciating slowness. Onto her. Into her. Watching as he sank lower and deeper. Filling her. Reminding her of the woman she used to be.

"I've missed you, Shea," he whispered, nuzzling her ear. He remained over her in pushup position and didn't stop watching while he plundered her body, inch by incredible inch. Up and down he flexed. In and out.

"Eric," she moaned, needing all of him. Fast. Hard.

"Tell me what you want," he murmured, his eyes big and dark and taking her all in, his fingers trailing over her ribs and down to clutch her hips. "Tell me what you need, Shea."

"You," she growled, her hands in his hair. "Only. Ever. You."

It happened again. Energy arced. The storm surge built to a thunderous, crashing crescendo. "Now baby?" he asked, his voice tight and needy. "Are you ready for me? You feel like it. Now?"

She couldn't speak. Digging her fingernails into his back, they came together, claiming each other, right down to their souls.

Growling, he sucked a moist trail of fire down her jaw to the crook of her neck. And there he stopped, his breath hot against her skin. The corners of her mouth lifted into the first real smile in months. Aftershocks set off another round of clenching mini-fireworks. She held on tightly, sure that she and Eric had just set a new record for pleasure. This was more than make-up sex. This was *legendary sex.*

Just as her heart filled with love and relief, grief swept in, an undertow she couldn't escape. The memory of Cheyenne's death eclipsed the afterglow. It hurled Shea back to the day she thought she'd lost everything. The vision of her beautiful baby's bright brown eyes full of light and life, so much like her father's eyes, shimmered into view. The same clear color as the man who held Shea in a loving hold—who couldn't seem to face her.

'What have I done?' cried up from her broken heart as she held Eric tight. But then she knew. They'd made their perfect child during another moment of fiery, playful passion. That was why he hadn't yet lifted his head. He was remembering Cheyenne, too. *Tough men don't cry.*

A hiccup wrenched out of her at the knowledge of all he'd suffered. Pressing her lips to the side of his head, she whispered, "I'm so sorry I hurt you, Eric, and I'm sorry Cheyenne died, but please let me be strong for you."

He groaned, and her whole being filled with compassion for the tender warrior wrapped in her arms, the one with the heart of gold. She offered his words of comfort back to him. "I'm here, baby, and I'm never letting go again."

He growled. He grunted. But finally, easing away from her neck, he cupped her face between his hands and blinked away his tears. "I'm supposed to be the strong one."

"No," she corrected gently because now she knew. "We're not strong alone. Only together. Trust me on this."

He blew a deep breath through pursed lips. "God, these last three years have been hell." And then he kissed her. It seemed he couldn't kiss her hard enough or deep enough. He moaned in her mouth, his fingers clamped onto her head in a gentle vice. Their teeth bumped, and she let go of Cheyenne's memory for—just a second. Or two. Because Cheyenne's father needed his wife. And Shea needed her man.

Once more there was nothing in the world but two people who still loved each other. Other tears trickled out of Shea's eyes. Tears of forgiveness for herself. Tears of love for Eric. It was okay to let go of Cheyenne in order to hold onto Eric. It was good.

Drawing in a deep breath, Shea relinquished her mistakes of the past. Absolution swept through her from the passionate kiss Eric seemed intent on branding her with. Every last doubt melted away. He loved her and he didn't blame her.

At last Eric lifted to one elbow beside her. Tears still glistened on his thick lashes, and he didn't wipe them away. "Never again," he ground out, gently cupping her cheek. "From this moment onward, we go forward. Together. We never forget our daughter, but we don't forget us either. We share the good *and* the bad times. All of them. We help each other endure whatever life throws at us. It's you and me against the world. Agreed?"

She sniffed her need to repent away. It might always be there, but with Eric willing to open up and share his grief, her guilt was manageable. "I have no secrets. Never again. Ask me anything."

He pressed his forehead to hers. "And I'll do the same, but know this. I've never been afraid to die, but I am afraid to live—*without you.*"

Ah, he was tearing her heart out. But Shea knew. There in the middle of an Irish glade somewhere between Dungarvin and Kilkenny, she had finally come home.

CHAPTER FIFTEEN

"Come see this," Shea called quietly. She'd barely dressed and stepped out of view.

Already clothed except for his boots, Eric ducked into his shoulder holster and scrambled to join her, his heart pounding at what—or who—she might have encountered. He'd already stashed the Harley beneath a cover of ivy and branches, concealing it from obvious view. He'd made sure the intruder was gone. She didn't sound panicked, but his heart hammered anyway. Call it over-protectiveness. Call it paranoia. He needed her safe.

Eric kept an eye out for Aishling, too. She'd wandered off, but he hoped not too far. The cat had to be deaf the way she'd settled down inside his jacket despite the noisy motorcycle. She'd purred, she'd actually purred. Something wasn't quite right with that nosy feline.

Rounding a line of mighty trees that had to be hundreds of years old, their branches reaching up high and their trunks stretching wide, he paused. There, caught in the golden shafts of sunlight stood what was left of an ancient Irish castle. *Breathtaking.*

Thick green moss coated the one gray wall, now crumbled into ruin. A single stone turret reached above the treetops.

Other branches and vines hid the ornately carved remnant of yesteryear. Despite the trees and ferns surrounding it, a steady stream of water trickled from somewhere above the door.

Brushing a tangled curtain of ivy out of his path, Eric halted in his tracks. There was no enemy nearby. Only a very naked Shea. She stood alone facing the other way, caught in a golden beam of sunlight. *Enchanting as hell.*

She could've passed for an elfin sprite, as thin as she was. As perfect as she was. Her short hair had been mussed good and proper during their lovemaking. Kind of spiky. So damned sexy.

His mouth went dry.

Shea reached upward to catch a narrow stream trickling off an overhead arch in her cupped palm. The golden drops slid down her arm and dripped off her elbow while others slid over her breast and nipples. Better yet, a portion of the water sluiced over the rounded globes of her bare-naked backside.

He stood there entranced while motes of dust filled the beam of sunlight he was caught up in. Could've been fairy dust. Looked like magic. It certainly worked a spell on him.

His body steeled with the need to hold her again, an appetite he didn't want to control. She hadn't explained everything, but what she had offered spoke loud and clear to his father's heart. His husbandly heart. He couldn't have turned aside from this woman if he tried.

Love will do that to a guy.

Slipping the holster off his arm, Eric stretched one hand behind his head as he stripped his shirt up and off. He hopped out of his pants one leg at a time, maybe a little too eager, but hell. This had to be how Adam felt in Paradise when confronted with the temptation of the only woman in the world, and about to fall for her all over again.

"Shea," he whispered, not wanting to disturb the bewitching scene. It was as if he'd never met her before, as if they were starting over at square one.

She turned, her face lit with a gentle smile as her gaze smoothed over him, head to toe. "Join me?"

A man did not have to be asked twice to join a naked woman in a shower. He set his weapon and his clothes on a cushion of moss beside her carefully folded pants and shirt. In two steps, he had her wrapped up tight in his arms. She melted into his chest with a sigh, her deliciously soft breasts crushed against him.

There he stood at the edge of eternity one more time, only wiser, infinitely more in love, and yeah, scared to death. He knew real loss and pain this time around. To walk back into that fire probably made him the dumbest man on earth by some folks' standards, but not his. For Shea and for the sweet memory of Cheyenne, Eric went willingly. He couldn't say it enough. "I love you so damned much that it hurts."

"I know," she murmured, lifting her gaze to his. "I don't understand how you can, but I believe you do. I believe in us."

"I like that word. Us."

He glanced upward to understand where the water came from. It was warmer than he'd expected. There was no hill or plumbing in this wooded glen, but high above the arch, a stone trough had been built into what appeared to be a solid granite walkway to this single wall. Thick with green moss, the underside of it was dripping wet. It had to be an ancient cistern, a water collection system of some sort. Cracked over time, it allowed for this mini-shower in Paradise.

He glanced downward. Those two creamy breasts mashed up against the dark hair on his chest shot a spike of pure lust to his groin. Eric nuzzled her neck, wanting nothing more than to make love to his wife again, but they'd already courted danger. Still…

His pistols were close at hand and the Arab biker hadn't come back. *This could work.*

Shea made the decision for him when she circled her arms around his neck, her fingers light on his shoulder blades. The turquoise in her eyes seemed greener. Her pale skin nearly luminous. Shea glowed. For the first time, no guilt or worry etched her brows, and she was right. They did need a shower. Why not take one together?

He tipped her backward under the trickle, letting it run over her hair and face while he gloried in the sight of the naked body in his arms. Running a hand over her small but firm breasts, he massaged and pinched those tender rosebuds that tasted like wine. Fine wine. Definitely a blush, one that matched the pinkish-hue spreading over the rest of her creamy skin.

She blinked with water in her eyes, trusting him. A profound sense of peace invaded his core even as heat flamed up his legs. Every male muscle sprang to attention. Focusing on bathing her body had created a physical firestorm neither he nor she would be able to ignore. A hard-on wasn't much for subtlety *in* his pants, less so without them.

Stroking her wet cheek, he cupped his hand to let enough water pool to soak her skin, then her hair. Adam never had it so good.

Eric let nature take over. His palms slid down her back until they came to rest on her ass. She closed her eyes, breathing in short, fast bursts, her arms still fastened around his neck. He lifted her body up to mesh with his and impaled her in one smooth, quick thrust. Ah. She was so ready for him to be inside her. So deliciously wet and wanting.

This parallel universe of Paradise felt supernaturally close. Too close. The temptation of this woman's delectable body could lead to certain trouble. An unthinking man might be lulled into a precarious situation under the tender ministrations of a woman, but not Eric. He kept one ear alert for the slightest crackle of a branch or footstep, one eye on the shadows around him, and the other on his reason to live. He knew precisely how many footsteps between him and his pistol even as his senses strayed over and into Shea.

She wiggled, tightening all those wonderful feminine muscles. Pulling him in with every clench, every sigh. He took his time, savoring her mouth, but it happened quicker this time. He honestly hadn't thought he had it in him, but now that he had *it* in her... he went up in flames.

Heat roared up from his thighs and spilled into her. She dug her nails into his shoulders while her butt muscles clenched tight beneath his fingers. Ahh. He stiffened and gave her every last bit of himself again. And again.

Burying her face under his chin, she breathed, "I love you so much."

And Eric honestly believed her because of that one word. Love. *We're going to make it.*

After a gentle scrubbing, he stepped out of the mini-shower a relaxed man. As it was, he couldn't keep his eyes off her, or anything else in the immediate area. The trees beyond her. Every shaft of sunlight and every shadow. Just in case. A former Marine never completely relaxed, not unless he was dead.

They'd moved farther inside the wall of the crumbling castle, hidden from prying eyes for the time being, but moving in sync. She stretched into her dirty clothes. He did the same, the feeling surreal that they'd so easily picked up where they'd left off two years earlier.

The birds quieted in the branches overhead. Sunlight filtered through the greenery, casting just enough shade to shelter them. Better yet, the assassin on the motorcycle hadn't returned. The calm of this hidden glade made it easy to believe their troubles didn't exist, but Eric tuned his inner sniper to stand guard. Like always. A man didn't survive months in war zones and suddenly forget to keep track of his surroundings. Hyper-vigilance never faded away.

Shea caught him looking at her. A rosy hue flushed her neck and cheeks, and he found it incredibly cute after what they'd just done together. "Come sit with me," he offered once he'd tied his bootlaces and secured his pistols where they belonged.

She came easily to his side and the best memories kept popping into his male mind. There was a time when he'd been fully dressed and ready for work when she'd cuddled up with him without a stitch on, tempting him. The tease. He'd gone into work late that day. Smiling, but late.

Eric stifled the heated *'games back on'* signal from his groin. Pulling Shea down with him to a nearby fallen tree, he made himself as comfortable as he could. "So talk. Why is everyone after you?"

Shea shifted on his lap to make better eye contact, like that helped. She had to have noticed his *feelings* for her, but she'd gotten serious.

"Those three French guys might work for Hugh Carlson. He's from France, and he was angry when Gordie and Phoenix didn't accept his job offers. I think he thought he could buy anyone who got in his way."

"How so?" Eric circled his arms around her waist, needing her to feel safe enough to tell him everything.

Shea rubbed her biceps with both hands. "I was in the research lab when it happened. Carlson shoved Gordie. He said he'd have their discovery at all cost. Five million euros, that was what he offered Gordie if he'd come work for him. Can you believe that?"

"I can. He's a megalomaniac, intent on power. What is this invention? How are you involved in this whole dynamic energy displacement thing?"

"I'm not." She ran a hand over her still wet hair. "That's what's so bizarre. Phoenix discovered it, not Gordie or me. Phoenix said it worked off something called bounce back energy. Gordie's the one who created the amplifier that boosts solar energy to make the invention work better. So why kill either of them? It makes no sense."

"Is that what's on your laptop? This discovery?"

Her head bobbed. "It's Phoenix's laptop, and yes, I think all his other works are on it. Gordie's too." She sniffed, fighting tears. "I was there, Eric. I saw what that man did to him. I saw Phoenix... die."

Eric gripped her chin and said as sternly as he could muster, "But you're not there now." She needed to stay focused to recover from what she'd lived through. He meant to help. "It's up to you and me to get Berglund's discovery back to the States and keep it from Carlson and Abdul-Mutaal. That's our mission. Your mission."

"Wh-who?" she asked, wiping a stray tear away with her fingertips.

Softening his voice, Eric cupped her jaw in his palm. "Abdul-Mutaal. He's the latest whack-job out of Syria. He and Carlson both want to rule the world, only Abdul uses the sword to do it."

"That Abdul guy killed Phoenix and Gordie? Why? They never hurt anyone."

"I'm not one-hundred percent sure it's Abdul-Mutaal. He never said he wanted the laptop or your friends' invention. Only Finn. That's another thing." He smoothed his hands over her shoulders on his way up her neck. Cupping her chin in both palms, he tilted her forehead to his. "That was a gutsy move on your part to steal the SD card while he was still in the lab. I'm damned proud of you."

Tears welled up in her eyes. "I had to do something. I couldn't let him have the last say, not after what he..." A scary sad whine crept out of her. "I let my friend die."

Eric pulled her head under his chin, his palm now flat to her back. "No, you didn't, Shea. Believe me. There was nothing you could've done to save Phoenix. I'm a trained medic, and I couldn't have helped him even if I'd been there. Believe me. I saw the video. I'm just surprised Abdul-Mutaal was able to get him into the University in that condition."

"Classes were out. The World Cup, remember? The Netherlands lost to Germany. It was a huge deal in Amsterdam. Everything was closed for the holiday."

That explained a lot. All Eric could do was hold Shea close until she stopped shaking. Time would soften this ugly memory. Eventually.

She eased out of his arms and shook her head, her gaze far away. "After that guy picked up his camera and left, I ran. I called Gordie and told him what happened. He told me to go to an Internet café, that he'd find me, and we'd run away together. I already had the laptop, but he never showed." She swallowed hard. "I kept calling his phone, but he didn't answer, so I went back to our apartment, in case... in case he needed my help. Only I was too late."

"You saw the body, didn't you? You're the one who threw up."

"Yes." She shuddered as she relived another gruesome memory. "But there's more."

Just as I suspected. Eric leaned in, ready to finally get to the real reason for this miserable op.

"I'm an alcoholic."

That came out of left field. No way. "Since when?"

"Since I decided to drown my sorrow with booze." Her chin lifted a notch higher. "I'm not proud of it, and I'm recovered now. I decided I was only killing myself. I mean, I already knew that, but I needed something to, umm, stop the pain, so at first, I drank. A lot."

Her voice ended in a whisper. "But one day, I woke up, and this pretty little girl was on her hands and knees, and I was laying in the surf, and she was leaning over me. All I could see was her pudgy nose and two brown eyes and her hair. She kept patting my face, and I thought... I thought she was Cheyenne, only... she wasn't."

Shea stared off into the distance once more. "I thought I'd reached rock bottom when I woke up in Bagani's hotel room, but the day after, there I was again, falling down drunk and just as stupid. But what if it had been Cheyenne, Eric? What if she'd found some drunk in the surf and it ended up being me?" Shea's tone rapped into a squeaky whine. "How could I do that to my baby?"

Eric held his breath along with his heart. She needed to talk.

"So I cleaned myself up, and I found a job. Eventually, I found a better place to live. I bought a table and chairs. A bed. A computer. Video games numbed my brain, so I played when I wasn't working. Then I joined a couple gaming chat rooms. I went to Alcoholics Anonymous. I cleaned myself up. I'm sober."

He fingered the buttonholes at her neck, his brows furrowed. "Who's Bagani?"

Shea blinked, confused for a moment. "Basheer Bagani. He's..." She shivered. "He's a Saudi prince. I was drunk out of my mind, and I... I..." Her fingers curled into fists. "I've made so many mistakes, Eric. Now I've dragged you into this mess. I never should have—"

He swallowed hard, his chest on fire as if she'd kneed him. *Shit. Shea was with another man. What do I do with that?*

"Did you..." His dumb mouth started asking something he wasn't sure he wanted to know the answer to. Swallowing when it was nearly impossible. Trying to hold it together. Anger welling. "Did you and he…?"

Her eyes widened. "Oh, no. It wasn't like that, Eric. No, no, no!"

Her adamant declaration helped. He cupped her shoulder to steady his rising need to kill the bastard who'd touched her. "So…" *Big breath.* "…Bagani…" *The asshole.* "… took you to his room and you…"

She nodded. "And I was drunk. When I came to, he'd tied me to his bed. My ankles. My wrists. He had a table beside the bed and all kinds of… stuff. Straps. Cuffs. Knives. Lots of knives." Shea blew out a huff. "I Googled him, Eric. Some of his girlfriends have disappeared. I think he tortures them and kills them." A full-on body shudder crawled over her. "Oh, God no. I haven't been with anyone, not since… you."

"But you escaped?" he asked, needing to keep her talking. Bagani would die—very slowly—for touching Shea.

Her head bobbed. "I ran. When he stepped out on his balcony to take a call, I slipped out of the silk scarves, and I ran. I ran as fast as I could."

"Who were you staying with? Was there another…?" *God, help me get through this.* Eric bit his tongue, but he needed to know. *Another man?*

"No, no, no," she cried, her hands fisted under her chin. "I didn't want anyone else. This was never because I didn't love you."

Time to change the subject. *Got to keep her talking.* "What were you drinking?"

"Anything I could get my hands on. Mostly rum and coke, but no more. I quit. I haven't had a drink in months. I promise."

She met his gaze, and he believed her. Eric knew alcoholics. He'd lived with one. His father. In no way was she like him. She might have self-medicated, but one—maybe two—years in a drunken stupor did not an alcoholic make. Not in Eric's book.

"That was when I met Phoenix and Gordie. And Mother."

He'd nearly forgotten. Mother knew Finn. "Did you tell her you were my wife?"

"I couldn't. I wasn't ready. I was still, umm, hiding." She kept chewing her bottom lip. "At first, I thought maybe you'd sent her to find me, but I'm pretty sure she only knows me as Finn."

"I did look for you," Eric told her, his forehead pressed to hers as if he could pour all of his love into her through that mental contact and erase the last two years.

"You did?" Why should that surprise her?

"Yes. But you left no paper trail, and you'd left your phone behind. It was as if you'd disappeared."

Suddenly, she attacked, wrapping his head against her chest, holding him tightly. "I didn't think you would look for me," she cried, trembling. "I'd hurt you so bad, that I thought... I thought..."

Now it was his turn to wrap her up tight. "Of course I searched for you. Not until Cheyenne's one year anniversary did I..." He hated to say it. "...quit. But I figured you'd found a way to live without me, and what was the use of looking for you if you didn't want to come home? If you didn't want me..." And there he stopped, his heart still broken for all the time they'd lost. *God, this was so hard.*

Her tears wet his cheek. "I'm so, so sorry."

"God, baby, me too," he murmured, struggling for control. "I wish I'd known where you'd gone."

"I wish I'd told you."

The past was unfixable, but knowing she'd still loved him, helped. "You used your hacking skills, didn't you?" he asked, his voice drawn and tired. "That was how you stayed off the grid for so long."

Shea took a deep breath. "Yes, but I worked, too, and I paid everyone back. Except Bagani. Then Phoenix and Gordie got grants at the Amsterdam University, but they needed more money. They wanted me to come along—"

"You mean they wanted Finn."

She loosened her hold and tipped back enough to see into his eyes. The corners of her mouth twitched upward. "Yes, Eric. They wanted Finn, not me. You should've seen their faces the first time they met him. We'd only chatted online. I think they thought I was a woman, and once I told them I could get the funding they needed—"

"You funded them by stealing from…?" He let his question hang.

"Bagani," she said like it was obvious. "He's filthy rich, Eric, and he would've hurt me. Maybe killed me. Yes, I hacked his accounts to fund two enterprising college students who could actually do some good in the world. That was how I paid your boss, too, and I'm not sorry. Bagani needs to pay."

Eric tapped her knee with his index finger. "You do know hacking is illegal."

Her bottom lip stuck out. "So's torturing and r-raping women."

Ah, he loved it when she got her dander up. "The FBI will need to talk with you."

That took the wind out of her sails. The cutest frown wrinkled her brow. "I might go to jail, huh?"

"Don't worry about that now." *Because I will.* He set her back to her feet and stood with her. "Just so you know, the Legionnaires were looking for Finn when we left Rosie's, not some hot chick in a leather jacket. They got stuck with a pile of wet clothes, and... what was Finn made of, anyway? Some kind of foam rubber? Silicone?"

"That and cotton batting. Styrofoam pellets. A flesh colored Spandex body suit with a big gut and a bigger butt sewn onto it."

He grinned at the notion of his lovely lady buried beneath all that ugly. "Don't say that. Finn was growing on me. Where'd you find the poor guy?"

"Online." Her eyes widened. She gulped. Twice. "That's another thing you need to know." That tasty tongue of hers moistened her bottom lip with one deliberate stroke. "Mother taught me a few things about online gaming and writing better programs and—"

He'd already figured as much. "She taught you to hack?"

"She said I'm a natural, so I... so I..." Shea took a deep breath. "I practiced, but I only hacked Basheer Bagani. He's an ass, and he's filthy rich, and... and he owes me."

Eric raked a hand over his head. "Did he kill your friends?"

"No, Bagani's shorter than that guy with the sword. That might have been him on the bike, but he didn't kill Phoenix. That other guy's voice was—odd." The green in her eyes paled, letting the blue brim with tears. "I've been really stupid, Eric.

Leaving you. Binge drinking. Hiding all these months. How can you just sit here and forgive me?" She hiccupped, her fingers splayed over her lips. "I don't get it. All I've done is hurt you, but you... but you…"

Eric cupped her chin and tilted her face upward. He knew her tells, the way her fingertips tapped her lips when she was nervous. The way she licked them when she was in the mood. Shea wanted another kiss, and he intended to give it to her, but she needed something else at the moment. Settling up with that Bagani ass-hat could wait.

"Do you know how to stop time?" he asked quietly.

Of course, she didn't know where that bizarre question came from. "Wh-what do you mean?"

"We've done it before, Shea. It's easy," he murmured against those succulent lips. "Let me show you." His palms claimed the sides of her pretty face while his mouth claimed hers.

A soft moan lifted from her throat, and sparks ignited. Their tongues tangled and the magical Irish castle faded away, the rest of the world with it. There were no bad guys in that instant of stolen time, only two hearts alive with the same breath. The same love. And yes, the same grief. But time still stopped just as surely as it had every other time they'd lost themselves in each other.

Eric gave the woman he loved the last piece of his heart, as if it wasn't already hers, with his kiss. "I'll love you until the world runs out of time, baby. I always have. I always will."

CHAPTER SIXTEEN

Aishling came out of nowhere with a soft meow and a bounce. She scrubbed the side of her furry face into Eric's boot like a long-lost friend. "Where have you been, princess?" he asked as he lifted her into his arms.

Shea stroked the cat with one long pet, content for the first time in years. "This pretty lady thinks you belong to her."

"Not me. *We*. Here, hold her highness while I call Alex." Eric handed the cat over. "Don't let this nosy girl run off again."

Shea snuggled the black cat while Eric pulled his cellphone out of his backpack and thumbed the keypad. "Hey, Boss. Yes, I—"

She tried not to listen, but she could hear Alex's belligerence all the way from the States, just not enough to make out the precise words.

Eric's brow spiked. His jaw clenched. "No, I—" He stilled. "Yes. The client always comes first." Another tense pause. "No, *you* hold on. I've got—"

A shorter pause, and Eric jumped to his feet. "And I said no. As in hell no. Finn's been through enough. We're going to Dublin and we're catching the first flight home. I don't give a shit if Carlson flew all the way here to talk."

Her gaze dropped to Aishling. Eric hadn't told his boss who Finn was, but Alex wanted Eric to meet with Carlson? Why?

"You don't understand. It's not that simple." Eric turned his back on her. Either he'd outright lie to his boss, and he didn't want to look at her while he did it, or—

"Finn isn't the guy we thought he was," Eric said quietly. His shoulders squared. "He isn't a guy at all. She's my wife."

Oh, oh. Shea bowed her head. She hadn't cared what Alex thought or knew about her before, but she did now. The little she knew about him had come through Sasha. That was also when Shea knew she might have to go undercover, and turn herself into a chubby guy to avoid the incredible reaching power of The TEAM. *Small world.*

"It's a long story, Boss." Eric stilled once more, his hand cupped at the back of his neck. "True. Yes, that's right." Pivoting on the ball of his foot, he caught Shea's eye and winked. "It's no one's business but mine."

That sounded more positive. Sasha had often shared little insights into her boss, Alex Stewart, and his infamous temper, but she'd also declared he was one of the fairest men she'd ever worked with. Shea started breathing while Aishling purred beneath her fingertips.

"Okay. Got it. We might be able to pull that off," Eric stated, his voice calmer. "He say if Jordan was hurt? What about the others with him? The cabbie and Rosie O'Banner?"

Shea dared to hope. She'd heard those three shots after the French Legionnaires rolled the cab. Was it possible everyone was still alive?

Eric blew out a deep sigh. "Can do. Yeah. Let me talk with Shea and—" He nodded, his eyes on the ground. "Yes. That's her name. Shea Powers Reynolds. You're right, Boss. I should've told you. We'll talk later. Count on it."

The silence stretched. Apparently, Alex had a lot more to say.

"Finnegan's here?" Eric's brows lifted in surprise, definitely one of Shea's favorite expressions. His tanned forehead wrinkled in parallel wrinkles to his dark brows. The laugh lines at the corners of his eyes deepened. And she fell for him every single time. The man was pure eye candy.

"That will make the job go down a lot easier. Sure. Good to know." He'd come back to her side. The moment he rested a hand on her shoulder, Shea forgot Alex. She rubbed her cheek against Eric's arm, sending him her vote of confidence.

"Okay. Got it. I'll touch base with him and get back to you. Do me a favor. Don't tell Mother who Finn is. Ah-huh. Thanks. Copy that." Ending the call, Eric stuffed his cellphone into his pants pocket. He pulled her to her feet while Aishling wound herself around his boot like a feline floozy, purring loud enough to wake the dead.

A smile stretched over that ruggedly handsome face. "Come with me. There's someone I want you to meet."

The day that had started so badly was looking up. Eric pushed the bike over moss-laden undergrowth and around one long stone wall, also covered with moss. He hadn't started the

Harley yet. Didn't want to risk attracting any adversaries in the immediate vicinity.

For now, Shea carried Aishling. The darned cat didn't seem to mind being hauled around like a baby. That was another thing. *My wife needs a pair of sturdy shoes.* Pride filled his chest at the thought. *My wife.*

Alex had shared interesting intel. Of all the damned things, Eric's ex-boss from the Seattle office, Murphy Finnegan, owned property in Ireland. Who the hell knew that? Only Alex, it seemed. Jordan, Rosie and the cabbie had actually been *rescued* by those French Legionnaire guys—according to Carlson.

Rescued nothing. Eric wasn't falling for that line of BS, and neither did Alex. Carlson wanted the laptop, but he'd insisted his men were only in Dungarvin to *protect* Finn when they'd *accidentally* bumped into the cab. After all, the roads in Ireland were quite narrow.

Yeah, right. "Explain shooting at me then, you lying bastard," Eric muttered to himself.

"Excuse me?" Shea asked. "Did you say something?"

He glanced over his shoulder at her. She couldn't have looked better if she'd just stepped out of one of those modeling magazines. Okay, so maybe modeling for a camping magazine, but still. "We're going to the Rock of Cashel. Will you be okay riding that far?"

"I guess. How far is it?"

"Not sure." Alex had told Eric that Murphy would be waiting due north of Cashel, where he lived. He'd actually retired from the Alexandria, Virginia, TEAM office only to hit

Alex up for a management job a year later at the Seattle office. Seemed retirement gave him a little too much free time.

Eric stopped pushing the bike and jutted his left rear pocket in Shea's direction. "Reach into my pants pocket and get my phone. It's got a map app. Should tell us how many miles and the best route."

Wrong move. The second she set the cat down and slid her slender fingers into his pocket, his blood supply fled south. It took an extra *oomph* to get the Harley's wheels moving, but like most women, Shea seemed not to notice. She tapped the phone's screen as she walked, Aishling padding silently at her heels. "What's your password?"

Maybe this wasn't such a good idea. Eric didn't mind that he wore his heart on his sleeve, but she didn't need to know what a sap he was. He spelled out his closely guarded password. "C-H-E-Y-N-S-H-E-A."

"Cheyenne and me? We're your password?" The hint of a gracious smile graced her lips as she tapped a few more keys until she found, "Cashel. In the County of Tipperary. It's due north. Sixty-two kilometers away. One hour by automobile. Take R672 to get there. I think that's a road instead of a motorway. Ooooo, the Rock of Cashel is there. We should stop and see that castle."

He heard what she was saying. Barely. At least his eyeballs were focused on the way her delicate brows arched when she talked. The O shape of her mouth when she pursed her lips. Shea was a study in soft browns and creams accented with turquoise. But those lips. Petal soft. The palest mauve. Cherry blossom sweet.

"You're off the path, Eric." She'd stopped walking.

Well, so I am. By about ten feet. Grunting, he righted the bike and forced his wandering brain back to business. At last, they were back on asphalt and ready to ride.

Once more, he tucked Aishling inside his jacket. Shea donned her helmet and leather jacket, and this time, he didn't have to pull her forward on the Harley seat. She'd wrapped her arms around him and his cat, while the inside of her legs clamped against his thighs. There wasn't another guy alive who had it so good.

He kicked the kickstand free and those sixty-two kilometers, *give or take a couple,* flew by. Soon they rolled into the busy Irish village. Its claim to fame was the magnificent Celtic cathedral on the edge of town, the Rock of Cashel, complete with stone towers and walls. Impressive, but so was the sneaky feeling he was being watched.

Eric took a second look at the town. Shops galore. People walking everywhere. Nothing seemed out of place, yet the sensation persisted. Ducking the Harley into a narrow alley, he turned a sharp U-turn to face the street and pulled his cellphone out of his jeans pocket—*all by himself this time.*

"I see you made it," the older guy said upon answering.

Eric glanced over his shoulders, uneasy even in this quiet alley. "You see me, huh. Where are you?"

"Gray panel truck, just passing the alley you turned into. I've been following you the last couple of miles. Get back on the street. Turn right. Take the third exit at the next roundabout and head due north. Stop at the first red brick home on the left and follow the drive to the far west of the property. The garage will be open. Park your bike inside. I'll be waiting. Who's the chick? Alex didn't say anything about you bringing a friend."

"Copy that." Eric ended the call without answering Murphy's question. He might've caused that sneaky feeling, but Eric assumed nothing.

Traffic thinned once he cleared the roundabout and turned north. The road was blessed with trees on both sides of its narrow winding self as well as the ever-present stone fences. All that leafy green made for good cover, but it also provided a wealth of sniper hides.

He remembered too well being ambushed in Afghanistan's Nahri Saraj District, FOB Camp Bastion. A guy never overcame something like that.

Clenching Shea's joined hands, he pulled her closer. They were still inside that narrow window, when relief seemed so close a guy could taste it, but when things could still go damned wrong. A bullet could come out of nowhere. Or a rocket propelled grenade. An IED might take a lone rider out—or his passenger. *Not today, damn it.*

Adrenaline gunned the throttle. Only when he'd turned left alongside the red brick home did Eric allow a full breath. Once their feet were on the ground inside Murphy's open garage, he killed the Harley's engine. Shea removed her helmet while Aishling climbed up the inside lining of his jacket and meowed noisily.

Murphy activated the automated door, sealing them inside a windowless, concrete garage. Fluorescent shop lights overhead cast a bright glare on an organized, two-car garage. "Out of sight is always better."

Still seated on his bike with his legs spread, Eric made quick intros. "Shea, Murphy. Murphy, Shea." That was all he needed to know for now.

Sliding off the Harley, she extended a hand. "It's nice to meet you, Mr. Finnegan."

Always the gentleman, Murphy clapped both his hands over hers, his blue eyes bright. "So you're the woman this guy's been heartsick over for months?"

Eric could've smacked the guy for that comment, but Shea handled it with grace. "I'm his wife. I hope so."

Murphy shot him a wink. "You've got some explaining to do, but let's get inside first."

It was funny how everything had changed since the morning. Where then Eric had been agitated because his chunky client couldn't climb a fence, now, now he was riled he couldn't protect Shea like he wanted to. If Abdul-Mutaal had wanted, the ride up from Dungarvin would have been the perfect time to take her out.

Booting the kickstand, Eric dismounted the bike. He pulled his gear out of one of the saddlebags while Shea slipped her laptop from the other. Their eyes caught, but Murphy took over. With his arm around Shea, he set a quick pace from the garage to his back door.

Aishling meowed all the way.

CHAPTER SEVENTEEN

"But I *can* do it." Shea stood her ground, shaking but determined. Getting the upper hand with Carlson was just a matter of hacking into the castle's server.

A shower would've been nice. Clean clothes. Shoes and socks, too. There wasn't time.

She and Eric had only made it to the breakfast bar in Murphy's orderly kitchen, done in an old-fashioned Irish farmhouse style. High cabinets showcased granite sinks and counters. Dark wooden stools with round red cushions rimmed the breakfast bar. The white enamel stove and icebox caught Shea's eye. Those sweet babies were right out of the 1950s, and this was her dream kitchen come true. It almost made her want to whip up a bacon and cheese omelet, Eric's favorite, while the men talked.

There was a time she'd loved cooking, but there wasn't time for that, either. Once safely inside Murphy's sturdy cottage, all the news stateside had spilled out. On the surface, Carlson had certainly hit all the well-intentioned high notes. He was the one who'd initiated first contact to Alex. He'd adamantly insisted his men had *accidentally* run into the cab in the course of *protecting* Finn Powers from other unnamed parties.

Accidental, ha.

Jordan, Rosie, and the cabbie were supposedly under Carlson's care while he was staying at Ashford Castle. Who does that? Just suddenly show up in Ireland at the same time that the woman—ahem, woman in a fat suit—showed up with one of the world's best kept secrets? *Protecting Finn Powers, my foot.*

If anything he said was true, Shea hoped it was that Jordan and her friends had been treated for their injuries. But, given how Gordie's encounter with the billionaire ended, that was the question of the day, wasn't it?

The problem now was getting Jordan and the others out of Ashford without another *accident.* Shea wanted to help.

"No," Eric said, his voice taut with his conviction. "You did enough when you snagged that SD card away from Abdul-Mutaal. You're sidelined. Take a chair."

She climbed onto the nearest bar stool and hooked her bare heels to the bottom rung, sidelined maybe, but not done arguing her case. "Murphy, may I at least use your computer?" she asked, her hands clasped on the granite counter as if she were an obedient wife.

"I said no, Shea. I don't want you in more danger. You've got three different factions after you now, and they're all violent. Enough is enough." God, she loved Eric. Her sexy husband meant well, but as he lifted an imperious brow, as the wrinkles on his forehead echoed the ire he meant to convey, she nearly smiled. Eric should know better. No obedient little *housewife* would be in this much trouble.

"She's what?" Surprise widened Murphy's blue eyes. The sixty-plus Army veteran ran a hand over his thinning gray hair. "This I've got to hear."

Eric lifted his index finger, punctuating his side of the argument as if he'd already won. "Abdul-Mutaal, the ISIS terrorist, not sure who he's working for or with." Another finger hit the line-up. "Three Frenchmen who we're fairly sure work for Carlson." He spiked an evil glare at Shea when his third finger stood up. "An Arab on a motorcycle who knows how to shoot, and who might be working with Mutaal. We don't know yet." Finally, baby finger made four. "And oh, yeah, hacking is illegal. If you get caught—"

"Did Alex catch me? Did Mother?" she asked, trying hard not to sound as smug as she felt. What she wanted most was to lick those fingers, just not in Murphy's kitchen. "If I remember right, Alex was a few million richer the last time we talked."

Eric's eyes narrowed as if he was surprised she would challenge him. His lips pursed. His brows clashed, like maybe he was trying to intimidate her, but that'd be the day. She'd never been afraid of Eric, *so stop with the male posturing.* "I don't care. I'm not putting you in danger anymore."

Why didn't he understand that she shared that same fear when he put himself in harm's way? She had skills they didn't. Why not use them? "I'll be extra careful, Eric. Besides, I know more about Unix, Python, and PHP than either of you. I can manipulate most systems and talk with more processors than Mother. I can get inside Ashford and find him."

"Yup. You two are married." Murphy's eyes twinkled at the banter. "Mind telling me what the heck PHP is? That another designer drug I don't know about?"

That merited another dirty look from Eric, and Shea honeyed her words with a gentle smile. He'd eventually come around to her way of thinking, but she needed it to be on his terms. At least, she needed him to *think* that. "It's an HTML scripting language, a hypertext pre-processor. Web developers use it to design dynamic websites or to decode fatal errors. Think of it this way. When you hit the keys on your computer, it gives you exactly what you ask it to. If you type a Z, you'll get a Z. But with PHP, I can macro every keystroke to make it do what I need it to do, not just a single alpha or a numeric. One tap can contain an entire program. I'm not just typing when I, umm, *dabble*." Eric's brows hit an all time high at that selective word. "I'm using scalar declarations, null coalescing operators, and infiltrating—"

Mischief tweaked the corners of Murphy's mouth. "For crying out loud. Did Mother and Ember teach you all this mumbo jumbo?"

Shea ducked her head into her shoulders, guilty as charged. "Mother says I have a gift. I'd like to use it to rescue Jordan and Rosie." Regret took over then. "I couldn't do anything to save Phoenix or Gordie. I just want to help."

Eric's gaze narrowed in on her like a sniper, one eyelid nearly shut and her heart in the crosshairs. Shea dropped her lashes, not willing to challenge him. If he honestly thought he could do this without her, maybe she would make an omelet or something while she waited. *Like a good little wife.*

Murphy dropped his elbows to the counter between Shea and Eric. "Unless you've got a better plan," he said to Eric, "I think we ought to see what your significant other can do. She sounds pretty smart to me."

"Smart isn't Shea's problem." Eric exhaled a slow huff of disapproval, that full-on sniper glare on high beam. "These guys are vicious killers. They'll murder her if they catch her, Murph. I know you want to help your friends, Shea, I just can't—"

She reached across the counter for his hand. Like old times, his strong, manly fingers intertwined with hers like the lifesavers they always were. "I can do it right here if you and Murphy buy me what I need. You can watch. It won't be hard and it won't take long."

Eric's lips pursed as if he might be considering it, but Murphy winked at Shea. "Come see what I've got before we go shopping."

With a nod and a smile, he ushered them into a spacious office off his living room, another spectacular vision in Irish living. Heavy wooden furniture done in soft purples and mint green paisley patterns circled a stone hearth that invited the weary traveler in Shea to linger. It'd be nice to curl up there with Eric and watch football under that lush cream-and-merlot-colored afghan draped over the arm of the couch. What a paradise.

"Your wife has good taste," Shea murmured as she dropped to the office chair in front of a large wooden desk.

"She does," Murphy agreed. "Now show us what you can do, little lady."

Like a silly nineteen-fifties housewife, Shea peered around Murphy, needing Eric's approval before she touched the keyboard. Not once in their married life had he hinted she needed permission to do anything, but she wanted it now.

He lifted a forefinger to his right brow, his tell that he was considering his options. Then, "Go ahead, Shea. Show us what you can do."

She nearly teared up at his faith in his faithless wife. How did a woman ever forgive herself for running from a man like him? *Not now,* she thought. *Focus. Prove to him you can do this.*

Shea let her mind soar and her fingers fly.

"I don't know about this," Eric growled, obviously doubting because he wasn't in control of this breach.

To keep him aboard, Shea explained, "Don't worry. I'll protect Moira's system before I attack Ashford's." Her mind was already ten steps ahead, working the complexity of reaching into Ashford's remote server and circumventing its system administrator, ICMP protocols, operating systems, and firewalls. To find a way inside their server, she'd need to deactivate the hotel's OS detection, find their vulnerability. Maybe locate an open port that would provide access without detection. "Brute force will do it," she theorized out loud.

Eric leaned over, his cheek nearly against hers as he watched the screen. "Are you sure this won't get you caught?"

Just as she'd expected, her protective ex-husband had transformed into her willing cohort. Logic and honesty worked with Eric. She wished she'd remembered those simple techniques two years ago.

"Positive." She gulped, her fingertips on the keypad, but needing Murphy to understand what she had to do to his wife's computer. "Do I have your permission to replicate your operating system? I won't harm a single file, but I need everything of yours shut down and stored before I can maximize bash scripting."

Her heart thumped along with her tapping fingers. This was her chance to shine, to make up for the trouble she'd caused.

A twinkle lit Murphy's eyes. "You do know that I haven't got a clue what you're talking about, don't you?"

"It's a security measure," Eric cut in. "Shea needs all the operating space she can get."

"I'll be extra careful," she promised.

Murphy dropped into the nearest overstuffed chair, his hands folded over his stomach. "Sure. Moira won't mind. If she does, I'll buy her a new computer. How long's this gonna take?"

"Only as long as it takes me to bypass the castle's security protocol and insert my spiders. You won't be sorry." Shea drew in a deep breath. *I hope.*

With Eric peering over her shoulder, her fingers danced through macros, assembly languages, and interpreters. She knew programming, and once she'd partitioned Murphy's files, she ensured her programs remained virtual ghosts. Everything would be for naught if Carlson traced her *dabbling* back to Moira's IP address.

Shea set to work. She set up a virtual copy of her system that only she could delete, then installed firewalls to protect Moira's simple operating system. *Next, Ashford.*

Yes! Their system security was similar to the ones large departments stores used to ensure the confidentiality of customer financial data. *Tap. Tap. Tap.* Easy, peasy for a savvy hacker with nimble fingers.

One to go. Next, locate Carlson. Target his name, voice, or face within Ashford's enormous database. With one last tap of her index finger, she unleashed her elite spyware. Her spiders.

"Come back to me with good news," she breathed as a small window opened. Coding flashed too quickly for anyone to read, and—

Bingo. Primary target acquired. *Oh, look.* Along with Carlson's mug shot came a view of the three Frenchmen he employed. Ashford's front lobby security cameras had caught their arrival when they'd checked in at the front desks like normal people.

But she wanted more. A room number would be nice.

Ashford Castle boasted its own private cellphone mast given its reputation for pandering to the exclusivity and privileged tastes of its wealthy clientele. Her army of virtual spiders could detect radio frequencies from that tower, both transmitting and receiving. All Carlson had to do was use his phone, and she'd know precisely which room he was in.

"I love spiders," she murmured to herself just as her fingertips tripped over themselves at the sensual shiver of Eric's warm breath on her neck.

"You never used to like bugs," he whispered, the tease. Aishling prowled somewhere in Murphy's quaint Irish cottage home, but Eric? He stayed fast at Shea's side.

She stifled the urge to bump lips with him once more. "I'm working here," she replied, sure Murphy heard what she wasn't saying, which had everything to do with sex on this desk if Eric didn't stop—breathing. *Sheesh! How was a love-starved woman supposed to keep her hands to herself with him around?*

"Good girl. Now we know for sure those guys work for him." He might as well have licked the back of her neck. Her heart set to racing. The blood in her veins thrummed. Every last bone in her body was melting. She could so not concentrate.

"What am I watching?" he asked, his voice in her ear, his lips a kiss away.

Me melting under Murphy's desk. Want to join me?

Trembling with the sexual tension wiggling down her spine, Shea tapped out a new command for her spiders. "Right now, I'm inside Ashford's wireless phone system." *But I want you inside me.* She coughed to clear that husky tremor out of her voice. Blinking up into her ex-husband's honest gaze, she told him breathlessly, "It might take a while to hone in on Carlson's vocal patterns if he isn't using his cellphone." *Do you want to make love to me while we wait?*

"What are you using as a reference?"

"This recording." Licking her bottom lip, she minimized the coding window, highlighted another icon, and tried to wrench her mind back from the erotic abyss it seemed to be swan diving into with utter abandon. "I recorded it when Carlson visited the lab. I could use the GPS chip in his phone to track him, but this is more accurate. It'll all but put me, I mean us, inside his room." *Where he's probably got a bed we could use while we wait...*

Shea hit the previously recorded clip she'd stored online. One tap and Carlson's arrogant threat boomed as if he were there with her. "Do you think someone like you is strong enough to tell *me* no?"

The rancid arrogance in his demeaning threat killed the teasing mood.

"That's exactly what I'm saying, sir," Gordie had replied, firmly and politely. "This discovery's not for sale, not now or next week. We've just begun exploring the ramifications of bounce back energy. Think about it. It's been around since the beginning of time, and we never knew it until now."

Intensity shuddered off Eric. His breath caught as Shea rubbed the goosebumps off her bare arms at the rowdy clip of Gordie's New York accent. Hearing it almost made him seem alive.

"Nonsense!" Carlson again, right before he'd shoved Gordie against the lab's countertop. "This breakthrough is huge! Monumental! Too big for the likes of you sniveling lab rats. Only someone with limitless funding has the right to study it. Think about this, you little fraud. Five million! That's what I'm offering you right now. Take it or leave it."

Shea was still proud of her friend. Most would've caved in the face of blatant corporate greed, but Gordie had stood his ground because he'd believed in her and Phoenix. He knew they could work together, if only because they already had. They were Professor Grover's shining stars. "I'm sorry, but my answer is still no. There's nothing you can do to convince me to sell. Phoenix and Finn have put too much of their hearts and souls into this discovery. You need to leave, Mr. Carlson."

"You recorded the whole thing?" Eric asked, his palm squeezing her shoulder.

"Yes," she breathed, so damned distracted. His mouth was less than an inch from hers. His tongue had just moistened his bottom lip with one languorous slide that looked like an invitation. Pure admiration glittered in his eyes. Maybe even pride. Or lust…

She shrugged, struggling to stay focused, but man… This guy was making it—*dare she think it*—hard? "I… I was the fat man out, remember?" *And right now, I'm falling for you.* "P-people usually didn't see me, so yes. C-Carlson was just like everyone else, and…" Her tongue seemed to have forgotten how to enunciate. "Ph-Phoenix wasn't there, so I recorded everything. I knew Carlson was trouble."

"That's not what your buddy said!" the man roared just as the clip ended.

Shea froze. *Say what?*

"What'd that mean?" Eric asked, his palm alongside her keyboard now, the sizzle between them gone.

"I don't remember him saying that, but I was nervous, and I…" *God, Phoenix. What have you done?* She replayed that last segment. Then she played it once more as if repetition would change what Carlson meant by those words. *It can't be. I can't believe Phoenix would…*

Eric said it for her. "Is it possible Berglund was talking with Carlson behind your back?"

Shea shook her head. "No. That can't be." But yes, that was precisely what it sounded like.

"Jordan found a hole in the wall behind the refrigerator in your flat, did you know that? Is it possible Phoenix was hiding something there?"

"Like what? Drugs? Money? They both smoked a little pot now and then, but I can't believe he'd…" *No, no, no. Phoenix loved Gordie. He did. He wouldn't have gone to Carlson behind our backs. He wouldn't.*

Yet someone had certainly leaked this important discovery. Else, how had Carlson known to come looking for it? Her heart thudded with a hard beat deep within her chest. Someone was still out there waiting for her. Shea just didn't know who.

CHAPTER EIGHTEEN

Eric's palm on her shoulder brought them face-to-face. "Let's not jump to conclusions, Shea. Carlson's a sneaky SOB. He might've been casting doubt where there was none."

It was so like him to offer hope, but this was bad. Still, Shea tied a knot in the end of that lifeline he'd just tossed, and chose to believe in her friends. There had to be an explanation for what Phoenix had done.

"What else did you record?" Eric asked, reassurance on his handsome face.

"Things," she replied, quietly evading the question as her fingers wavered over the keyboard. Her heart was torn.

"So now we wait?" Murphy asked from his comfortable chair.

"It shouldn't take long," she assured, working on catching her balance. "He's an important guest."

Eric grunted. "At least he thinks so."

As if on cue, Carlson's smug voice slithered through Murphy's computer speakers. "Alex Stewart? Well, well, well. What can I do for you?"

"My man will contact you tomorrow morning," Alex informed their mark abruptly.

My man? As in—Eric?

Shea twisted around to Murphy, the guy sitting next to her with a cocky smile on his face, and his cellphone in his hand. "You told Alex to call Carlson?" She wished she'd thought of that.

"'Course. I might be an old fart, but I know how to text."

Straightening, Eric grinned as he rubbed his hands. "Good thinking. I'm ready for some payback. How far to Ashford?"

Murphy leaned forward, his elbows to his knees. "That depends. It's a good two hundred kilometers northwest of here if you plan on driving. Less if you want to fly. What's the plan, Eric?"

"You heard the boss. The plan is I go in and get Jordan and the others out."

"Shhhhh," Shea whispered, her index finger to her lips while Alex and Carlson continued sparring. Her heart was stuck in her throat at this unexpectedly quick resolution. Why did Eric have to be the one to confront Carlson?

Shea brought up a map of the interior of the castle and pinpointed Carlson's location. Her spiders had served her well. His room was located at ground level. West side. Oldest part of the castle.

She double-checked the spider's findings against the hotel registry. *My, my.* Carlson occupied the two adjacent suites as well. That gave him sole access to that entire wing, including a private side entrance. He could come and go as he pleased.

"Expect Agent Reynolds at daybreak," Alex snapped, "and trust me, he *will* be taking Hannigan with him when he goes. The others, too. They'd better be there."

Shea nodded at Alex's bold order. *You tell him.*

"Hold that thought," Carlson's gravelly tone pitched a note deeper. "I said I was willing to negotiate, but I'm not giving up my ace in the hole."

"I don't negotiate with terrorists, rich or not," Alex hissed.

"You do now. You want your man? I want Finn Powers. Deal?"

"You'll ensure Reynolds and Hannigan are safely out of Ashford by zero eight hundred hours tomorrow or—"

"Are you threatening me, Stewart? You? An American *has-been*?"

Silence. *Click.* Typical. Alex didn't waste time negotiating. He'd hung up.

"Arrogant prick!" Carlson hissed as his line went dead.

Murphy chuckled. "How much do you want to bet Alex'll be on the next plane to Shannon Airport to knock Carlson on his billionaire ass?"

Shea bit her lip while Eric and Murphy discussed their boss's temper. Carlson had been every bit as hostile with Alex as he had with Gordie. Maybe it was time he got a taste of his own medicine. Her fingers wandered the *world wide web* until—

Oh look, the mighty Hugh Carlson's website. With links.

She let her fingers do the walking all the way into his FAQs, his very pristine *About Me* page, his sizeable financial holdings…

Oh, look. I wonder how this happened. I'm inside his bank account. Make that, his bank.

Leaning into the monitor, Shea counted all those digits to the left of the decimal point in one of his many accounts. This guy could feed a few starving nations all by himself, and he could do it out of his petty cash—like never. Hugh Carlson wasn't about helping others. *But lookee here...*

"Don't do it." Eric's deep voice rumbled.

Busted. She swallowed hard. "I'm just looking, but see this?" She pointed at the screen and all those digits. "I could bring him down to our level..." She snapped her trembling fingers because they were tapping all over the screen. "...just like that."

"We don't want his money."

"True, but others could use it." *As in other countries.*

Eric placed a quick kiss to the side of her head. "One mission at a time. No."

Shea leaned into the warmth of Eric's male body to reassure him she wouldn't defy his wishes, but the instant she did, her body revved up like that Harley she'd just had between her legs. Every last ounce in her body sang at his touch. A shimmering flame pooled between her legs, scorching her until she had to cross her ankles to ease the ache.

"But I could. If you ever want me to wreck him, just say the word." *Because I really want to humble this jerk, and damn it. I need sex. With you!*

"Can you monitor his cellphone to track him at all times?" Murphy asked.

Shea nodded. She could monitor just about anything she wanted, and she could, *umm, dabble* at the same time. Easily, she skimmed Ashford's event schedule. Dinner in the George V Dining Room was served promptly at five pm. An acclaimed chef prepared only the finest dishes. Slow roasted *Rib of Beef.* Nyangbo frozen *Choco-latte Mousse. Blah. Blah. Blah... What have we here? A masquerade ball? Tomorrow?*

"So strategize," Eric declared. "All I know is I've got marching orders to be at Ashford at zero dark thirty."

She straightened in her seat, startled that she'd missed part of the conversation.

"And if Carlson refuses to hand over Jordan and the others?" Murphy rubbed a clenched fist over his chin. "We'll have to go dark, and that'll be a two-man job, Eric. We'll need to leave Shea here alone. Are you prepared to do that? Or do we take her with us?"

She shot Eric one of her looks. Despite the tension in the air, the corners of his mouth curled. Lust was simmering in the depths of those handsome eyes. She never got tired of looking at him. He was her worst addiction. Her crack. Her meth. All rolled into one, glorious hit. Stealing her breath like a sucker punch to her solar plexus with his sexy bod, and yes. They could both spell. *S. E. X.*

"I have an idea," she said, not sure how to approach him, but she was going to try. "What about going to a masquerade ball?"

The smile dropped off his face. "A what?"

Murphy leaned forward, his elbows on his knees. "Let's hear what she's got to say."

Her heart climbed up her throat. This idea might be more dangerous than she wanted to handle, but it might also be the perfect solution. "Well, umm, a masquerade party's scheduled for tomorrow at Ashford. It's for lords and ladies. Invitation only. Royal attire. Masks. Pomp and circumstance. The whole nine yards."

"Why do we care?" Eric asked, his head canted as if he knew where she was going with this. He always could read her like a book.

"I was thinking you guys could dress as lords to my lady and—"

"No." He took a full step back from her, his hands on his hips and shaking his head. "I'm not putting you into play, Shea. Not with this crowd. No way."

Murphy leaned into his comfortable chair, watching.

Shea didn't offer another word. If Eric said no, then she wouldn't argue. Not anymore. She wasn't a covert operator, although she had fooled Phoenix and Gordie for over a year, and she'd fooled Eric until Finn had lain down in a bog. Come to think of it, she'd fooled Jordan, too. At first. Still, Eric was her first priority. Whatever he said would go.

"Now hold on," Murphy muttered. "Your little woman might have a good idea. No one would suspect us if we're in costume. Where will this shindig be held? Any chance it'll be near Carlson's suite?"

"Yes. The reception area is also in the older portion of the castle, only it's in the lower level. It holds one hundred and twenty people, so it sounds like they're planning on a large party. There will be musicians and heavy hors d'oeuvers. An open bar." Palpitations set her heart hammering. *There'll also be danger. Too many eyes. Maybe a scimitar hidden in the sleeve of a billowing, black robe that wasn't a costume.*

"You can't be serious?" Eric asked, rolling both shoulders because she'd just trapped him. "Send in an inexperienced woman to do what, Murph? Face a madman and his three goons while she's wearing some stupid ruffled get-up and heels? Give me a break."

"No. I was thinking she could charm the pants off the old bastard no matter what costume she wore," Murphy focused on Shea. "Face it, Eric. Shea can accomplish what neither you nor I can. While Carlson's distracted by her, shall we say, *feminine persuasion*, one of us relieves him of Jordan, and we all hightail it out of there."

Shivers skittered up Shea's back. Murphy almost made it sound doable, all except for that *feminine persuasion* part. Carlson hadn't made a good impression the last time she'd seen him. How could she fake flirting with him? *What if he was like Bagani, or worse.* Her heart thundered. *What if he was the murderer in the black robes?* That almost felt—right.

"No." The cords in Eric's neck were tight, his jaw set, and Shea was beginning to agree with him. This was too scary for someone like her. "I won't allow it. She's not a narc or a merc, and she's not one of us. You're asking for trouble sending a novice into a black op, Murph. Besides, she's been through hell. You're asking too much. No."

"But she is good looking," Murphy said thoughtfully, "and, if I understand what went on during the last twenty-four hours, she had the nerve and the notion to outwit Abdul-Mutaal in the middle of a slaughterhouse. Most folks would've been too scared to move, but she one-upped the guy. And she managed to protect and smuggle out of Amsterdam the invention everyone's hot and bothered over. By the way, where is it?"

Eric jerked his head at the backpack resting on the floor by the desk, anger swallowing the glow in his eyes. "She's still not going."

Shea lowered her lashes. Now that Murphy had reminded her of the last gruesome twenty-four hours, she wished she hadn't brought the masquerade ball up. "Never mind. I can't do it. Eric's right. The last time I fooled anyone, I wasn't myself. I was some guy in a fat suit, not a fancy dress. Besides, what if Abdul-Mutaal is there? I'd never recognize him behind a mask." *I might get everyone killed.*

Murphy pitched forward, his elbows to his knees. "Exactly, Shea. Everyone's still looking for the bumbling oaf in the fat suit, not a gorgeous woman in red sequins. It's the perfect solution. Distract Carlson. Give him what he thinks he wants. Trust me. I know what happens when Moira slides into anything red. I have to fight off every guy in sight. They've all got their tongues hanging out. Funny thing, she doesn't seem to notice. She's like you. Single-minded. Eyes on one man and one man only."

Eric dropped to one knee beside her chair. "No, Shea," he said quietly. "It's not because I don't think you can do it. I know damned well you could. You've already proven you're smart. It's not you; it's me. I wouldn't... I couldn't survive if anything happened to you. Not now."

She cupped his jaw, touched at his blatant declaration of love. With all her heart, she yearned to prove to him that she was his single-minded woman again.

"Then it's settled." Murphy slapped his hands to his knees. "We do it your way. I'll stay here with Shea and keep her safe. You go get Jordan."

Eric pushed off the floor with a growl. He huffed. Pursed his lips. Chewed the inside of his cheek. He turned in a full, tight circle until—finally, he drew in a deep breath and snorted through both nostrils. "Oh, hell, fine. You're both coming with me."

Shea peered at him, not sure she'd heard right. "We are?"

He nodded at Murphy. "Shea might be scared, but she's smart, and she's right. Nothing dangerous, though. I want you standing close by, but not in play, so we all leave together once we get Jordan. That's all. No damned masquerade party and no damned red dress."

"Okay," she agreed, barely able to breathe again. Being separated from Eric was the last thing she'd wanted.

"Then times a-wasting. Let's get back on the road," Murphy said with authority as he got to his feet. "We've got three hours of driving ahead of us."

Eric pulled Shea out of her chair and into his arm. "Not until we shower. Where's the head? A new set of clean clothes wouldn't hurt, either, and Shea needs shoes. She's been barefoot all day. You got any extras around here?"

Murphy scrolled his eyeballs up and down Shea, a gentle smile breaking over his fatherly face. "Right, I should have thought. You kids must be hungry. I'll fix some soup and sandwiches while you take your showers, and I'll check Moira's closet to see what I can come up with."

Shea's heart set to beating. Food would be wonderful. A hot shower would be heavenly, but a shower with Eric? *Perfect.*

CHAPTER NINETEEN

Eric tugged Shea into the head with him, his skin crawling to be next to hers. To feel her slippery heat at the tips of his fingers. The taste of her honey-sweet mouth on his tongue. The bathroom door had no more than closed, when she attacked, climbing up his body and hooking her legs over his hips, the heat of her core against his belly. "I want you," she growled, deep and needy, her breath in his face.

Taking a step backward, he shifted both hands to her backside, clutching her ass while their mouths collided. His lady definitely had computer skills—and others, if those frantic fingers scraping his dirty shirt out of her way meant anything.

Gripping his head between her clenched fingers, she ravaged his mouth, swirling her tongue over his lips, and groaning. Devouring. Nipping. As if she couldn't get enough. As if she'd been starved and needed to feed. Right. Damned. Now.

The shirt flew. She ducked her head, her lips sucking a sweet trail of pure pleasure over his chin, down his neck to his chest. His head fell back as he wormed out of his jeans. He'd already left his dirty boots at Murphy's back door. Somewhere in the back of his mind, a mission countdown had commenced, but he couldn't remember what it was for.

His boxers went next. Need lifted its pulsing head, thick and heavy, coursing with blood and passion. Backing her to the counter, he set her at the edge. Her shirt and pants hit the floor, and they were skin to skin, both lost in a frenzy of searching hands and probing fingers, grabbing and tugging. God, he loved that she'd gone commando.

Eric met the intense stare of the guy in the mirror behind Shea, a damned happy man with his hands full. His gaze drifted down the reflection of her elegant bare back. The curve of her hips. The jut of her hipbones and the possessive grip of his darkly tanned fingers against the creamy cheeks of her naked ass. The delightful crack in that ass that never failed to inspire every last masculine impulse in his body. He groaned. No way was there enough time in the world for what he wanted to do with his wife.

Shea seemed bound and determined to have it her way. *Lead on, baby.*

With one clenching grip of her delicate hand, she'd reached between them. "Now, Eric," she whimpered, pulling him erect, her fingertips teasing the heat right up and out of him. Arching, she impaled herself with one stroke.

Already primed and on the verge of detonating, it didn't take much to close the deal. With one quick grunt, they came together. Hard. Fast. Steam covered the mirror, and he stopped watching.

"Oh, God. Oh, God, Eric," she whispered, her fingernails raking his shoulders, pulling him closer. Frantically, she slapped both palms to the counter, supporting her weight just enough to lift one leg over his shoulder.

Ever the gentleman, he lifted the other shapely leg and secured her foot next to his ear. The sight of her body opened wide for him ignited every last damned male instinct to claim his woman. He went deeper, matching her voracious appetite groan for groan. Thrust for thrust.

Her head fell back, her lovely neck exposed and her breasts bobbing. Closing her eyes, she demanded a fervent, "Now! More! Now!"

Ah, he loved it when she turned into a bossy dominatrix. Eric thrust forward as aftershocks rippled through her, eliciting tiny, sexy noises that seemed to come from her toes. He couldn't hold back if he'd wanted to. They came together in white-hot heat that obliterated every last thought or worry. Caution. Common sense. Decency.

Wrung out from the best damned sex he'd had in years, Shea collapsed, the top of her head to his chest. But holy hell, his legs were about to give out. Lifting her off the counter, he sank to the floor with her, thankful for the cold tiles on his bare ass, but not ready to let his lady go. Mind-blowing sex wasn't the best start to any covert mission, but He. Did. Not. Care.

Not one bit.

Whatever God in heaven had protected Shea these past years had also brought her home where she belonged. He knew it the minute he'd seen her in Rosie's kitchen. Shea was killing him with her love, taking one slice of his soul at a time, winding like the tendrils of a tenacious vine into the chambers of his heart. There was no life without her in it. No sense in trying.

Eric swallowed hard, still breathing heavy. He bowed his nose to the top of Shea's head. "I love you, baby," he murmured.

There was no better feeling in the world than a thoroughly loved woman in a man's arms. Nothing. All this unprotected sex might have repercussions down the road, ones he'd gladly embrace if the day came that Shea was pregnant. But what a way to make a baby. *Our baby.*

The particulars of *Operation Find Finn* came back to mind. Eric had no strength to rise, but rise he did. Setting Shea's feet to the floor, he kept an arm around her waist for support. She had to be exhausted after the day they'd had. "I didn't mean to go all caveman on you. I didn't hurt you, did I?"

Shea lifted her chin, her just-kissed lips swollen and pink. Wet. Inviting him. She grunted a soft kind of a grunt, almost sarcastic, if that were possible. "You've never hurt me."

Threading his fingers through her short locks, he closed the space between them and tasted her mouth, mumbling, "I hope Murphy found some clean clothes for us, because baby, I can't resist you when you're naked like this."

The corners of her lips lifted, and his sun came out. Shea lit up the whole room. "I've missed making love with you," she said, her hands on his chest, "and I've missed loving you. We're good together."

Lifting her hand to his lips, he kissed her palm, so damned glad that poor guy with the wart on his chin had asked for Eric.

Finally, they got down to scrubbing. Shea snuggled into Eric's wet body, the dark hairs on the arms wrapped around her perfectly combed by the water. She thanked the Lord for honorable men, especially the naked one filling this four-by-four space with his handsome body.

Muscled from head to toe, he'd always been her version of pure porn. The sexy smattering of dark hairs over his pecs and trailing down his lower abdomen to below, mimicked his short-cropped inky black hair. Eric had manly hands, wide and capable of fixing everything from cars that wouldn't start in the morning, to removing miniscule slivers from a little girl's dainty fingertips.

Thick-necked from carrying mega-loads of gear when he was active duty, he'd grown more chiseled than she remembered. The six-pack was more defined. His biceps bulged. He had thicker thighs. And that back. Eric's wide shoulders coiled with strength that narrowed to a trim, athletic waist, but the strong wall between? Pure manpower.

She wanted her hands on him again.

Other women used to ogle him. Shea knew they did. She'd caught them staring at his butt in the grocery store. Fanning themselves when he walked by them at the pool. Everywhere and anywhere they'd gone together, Shea's green-eyed monster had lifted its head, thinking, *Back off sisters. Keep your fingers to yourselves. He's all mine.*

He seemed not to know he was glorious to look at though, probably because he'd never stopped long enough to see himself. Just others. Their pain. Their broken parts. Why he now worked for a company of snipers was a mystery, him being a medic and all. Yet this career choice seemed to fit him.

"Why'd you start working for Alex?" she asked, her hands behind her so she wouldn't be tempted to grab onto his wonderfully clean male parts and get sidetracked once more. You'd think all their lovemaking in the middle of that ancient Irish castle would've been enough. Guess not.

One brown eye peered down at her while he rinsed his head, then turned the water off. His heated gaze mellowed with a sigh. "It's like this, baby. The last two years were hard for me, too. Then one day Alex called with a good job offer, thanks to that old fart in the other room."

"Murphy?"

"Yes, Finnegan got it in his head that I'd be a perfect fit for The TEAM. Go figure. He said he saw something in me when we'd first met, I don't know what. Anyway, the job pays good, but meeting Harley probably helped me the most at that precise time."

"Harley?" Shea asked. "Is he another agent?"

"Yeah. Harley Mortimer. Believe it or not, he's a recovering alcoholic and drug addict. Ex-Army K-9 handler. One of the best. Anyway…" Eric blew out a deep sigh. "He'd been out visiting the Seattle office, and we got to talking. Somehow, he knew I was struggling. The day he flew home, he dropped a Bible on my desk and told me to read it once in a while. So I did. I think the book was his own personal copy, because lots of verses were underlined or highlighted. The pages were dog-eared. Anyway, I started reading it, and then I started going to this little chapel in downtown Seattle. It helped. I'll take you there sometime." He shook his head, spraying her with the cast-off water. One brow lifted with devilish mischief. "Who knows? We might get some of that old-time religion."

Blam. A jolt of lust shot straight through her. Her hands went to his chest. Then her lips. Beginning with a kiss on his sternum, she nibbled her way up to his neck before his soapy hands slid down to her ass. Old time religion sounded very good, especially if it started now. With a baptism. Followed immediately with sex.

He chuckled hoarsely, "Hold on, baby. We keep jumping each other's bones like this, and Murphy's going to come and roust us out of his shower. Come on. Jordan's waiting. Let's go save him and Rosie, okay?"

Shea sighed. She gave him one last kiss before she opened the shower door.

Playtime was over. For now.

Eric wrapped a towel around his waist and peered into the hall. Sure enough, Murphy had left several packages on hangars on the bathroom doorknob. Scooping them up, Eric ducked back behind closed doors. Shea too had a towel tucked around her, but he needed her dressed before he climbed her bones again.

"Moira is my size. And look. Underwear. Still packaged." Shea dropped her towel and dressed, smiling all the way because, well, Eric didn't have a polite bone in his body at the moment. He couldn't make his eyes move off her. Didn't even try. Just grinned at her naked body while she slipped the red bikini panties up her bare legs and pulled the black T-shirt over her head. Sweetest picture ever.

"It feels good to be myself," Shea murmured, stepping into the jeans and tugging them up over her hips. She hopped, pulling the skinny jeans up higher until she could manage the zipper.

"I like you better this way," Eric agreed. Messy wet hair. Long-legged. Nipples on high alert beneath the cotton tee. Perfect. With a sigh, he dressed. The denim jeans were worn and a tad loose, and the gray T-shirt was one size too large, but he made do instead of doing his wife.

Murphy smirked the second they returned to his living room. "Took you two long enough."

Eric ignored the jibe. "You wouldn't have a pair of boots around here for Shea? Socks would be nice too if you've got extras."

Murphy pointed to the ensemble on the floor. Various boots, running shoes, sneakers. "Moira likes to shop. Help yourselves. I've got more unopened boxes and merchandise than I have space to put them." He chuckled, his gaze skating over Shea. "I see the jeans fit."

A prickly wave of cave-mannish need to knock Murphy out cold slithered up Eric's spine at his friend's open appreciation, but he stifled it. *Yeah, Shea looked good. Men are gonna look at her. Get used to it.*

She'd dropped to her knees to examine a pair of hiking boots. "May I try these on?"

"You bet. Socks are on the chair over there, too. I figured Moira's things would fit you. See what else I figured?" He pointed to the wooden closet on the other side of the room where a red sequined evening gown hung. Two ornate face masks. A tux.

"Not on your life," Eric growled. "I'm going in alone. You'll hang back and keep Shea safe. That's the deal. No ifs, ands, or buts."

"You ever think we might need a back-up plan?"

"We won't." Eric dropped to the couch and watched Shea try on a couple pairs of boots before she decided what she liked. Kneeling, he laced them for her, fighting the urge to smack Murphy for keeping this masquerade ball idea alive.

Murphy didn't argue. "I'll drive," the old guy announced, his hands to his knees, and the masquerade idea seemingly forgotten. "You two kids ride in the back and get some sleep. You both look like two sheets in the wind."

Eric snagged his gear bag and the laptop. "What do you think? Leave it here?"

"Sure. I'll lock it up while we're gone." Murphy opened the side door and ushered them outside, his brows knitted. "Let's make this quick."

Eric followed to the garage, Shea's hand in his. "What's up? You see anyone?"

"Not yet." Once inside, Murphy locked the garage door behind them. One deadbolt. One galvanized steel horizontal bar bolted into the concrete walls as opposed to the wooden doorjambs. And a panic bar that Murphy jammed beneath the Master Lock doorknob. "My security system hasn't given me any indication we've got company. I just like to be prepared in all things."

Eric knew the feeling, but he had no idea how prepared Murphy was until, with a flip of a switch, a metal floor panel slid open. Just as Murphy flipped a light switch to brighten the hidden bunker, Eric grinned. "You've got an armory, don't you?"

Murphy just grunted as he set a boot to the narrow wooden staircase. Eric held Shea's hand while they descended. There were shelves lined with canned foods and batteries. Cables ran the length of the ceiling. Twenty-gallon jugs lined the far wall. A portable generator. A small safe. He even had a television set next to a ham radio set-up. "Are you one of those doomsday-preppers?"

Murphy stood at a control panel near the stairs. "Like I said, I like to be prepared. Now put that there invention in here." He punched a button on the panel with his knuckle, and the steel cabinet to his left rotated outward like a door, revealing a larger safe. "That other's a decoy. Ammo's under the stairs. Weapons too. Take what you need. Your little lady know how to shoot?"

"I do," Shea asserted quietly. "Eric taught me. I'm a better shot than he is."

She had to let *that* cat out of the bag. Yes, she was a better shot, but only because he couldn't concentrate at the range with her around him. One whiff of her perfume and he was—distracted.

"That so?" Murphy winked. "Maybe I should've hired you instead of him."

"Maybe," Eric agreed. "She's got better eyes." He handed over the laptop for Murphy's safekeeping.

Once they were back up top, Murphy secured the metal floor panel and moved a heavy-duty work rug to cover it. The garage went back to ordinary. He gestured to his gray panel truck. "Get in. I'll be right back."

Opening the back gate of the truck, Eric ushered Shea up and inside. One bench seat lined the side, but better yet, a foam mattress had been spread on the floor along with two pillows in clean pillowcases and a blanket. Murphy had thought of everything. Eric climbed in, tired but not sure he'd get any sleep with Shea snuggled against him.

Murphy returned with a medium-sized aluminum suitcase, which he stowed behind the driver's seat. "Keep down," he warned as he opened the garage door and pulled the vehicle onto the road. "I don't think we were followed before, but just in case. Let's keep everyone guessing."

Eric got comfortable with Shea's back to his front. The truck swayed from curve to curve on the way to Ashford. He dipped his face into her hair when Murphy turned the radio to a local station. The last thing Eric remembered before he drifted off to sleep was having his arms around heaven.

Aishling snores?

Eric stared down at the purring beast curled in his arm. "What are you doing here? Where's Shea?"

Purr. Purr. Purr. Damned if the cat didn't look like she was smiling. Even her coal black whiskers tilted upward.

He stroked her silky belly. "Tell me. What'd you do with her?"

"Meow-fff," she answered in a hoarse little cat-whisper. "Meow-fff."

The dream swelled up around Eric. Why did he feel as if Aishling had just told him Shea would be purr... purr... purrfectly safe?

CHAPTER TWENTY

Shea opened her eyes when the truck stopped moving, surprised she hadn't had a nightmare. It had to be because she'd slept with Eric for the first time in a long while. With his bicep for a pillow and his muscular body half-blanketing hers, she'd been lulled into restful oblivion by the hum of the truck and the sturdy strength of his body.

But the engine had stopped, and he was no longer beside her. She pulled the blanket up to her chin and listened while he and Murphy strategized from the front seat. It had to have been well after midnight, but Murphy had the window between the shell and cab of the truck open. That was thoughtful, to be included in their plans.

"If you get the slightest inkling Carlson won't negotiate, you need to back off."

"I won't be asking," Eric said quietly. "The next time you see me, be ready to hit the gas. If I'm lucky, I'll be moving fast with three in tow."

"Same protocol as a black op?"

"That'll work, but whatever you do—"

"I know, I know. Keep Shea safe. Count on it. What if Jordan and your friends aren't mobile?"

Eric paused. "Then we're screwed. If I had a few Tattle Tales, I could plant them to keep track of what's going on inside or if they move Jordan."

"Humph," Murphy grunted. "I can get those in place no problem. I always keep a handful."

"You've got the app that goes with them?"

"And the laptop to monitor all video feeds, too. I've been to a few goat ropes before, you know."

"How about you go in first then? Plant as many Tattle Tales as you can, and once you're back, I'll go in."

It sounded as if Murphy drummed his fingers. "Things could still get ugly."

"We'll cross the ugly bridge when we get to it. When did you plan to go in?"

"Now. Hand me the suitcase behind my seat."

"I'm awake," Shea announced as she doffed the blanket. "What's up, guys?"

Eric tugged Murphy's small suitcase out from behind the front seat, handing it off as he talked. "Murphy's going into Ashford first to add a little insurance before I go in." The suitcase clasp unlocked and— "Oh, hell no. Not this again."

The suitcase had just revealed not only Murphy's laptop, but the red sequined dress. "What part about 'no' don't you understand, Murph?" Eric hissed.

Like before, his boss shrugged, in what Shea decided was his way of getting around stubborn people. And Eric could be very stubborn. "Just keeping all options open," he replied smoothly.

"No," Eric growled. "She stays, you go. Are you ready?"

"Ready as I'll ever be," Murphy answered as he snagged his jacket from the suitcase. "You kids be good while I'm gone. It might take a minute or two to get inside. Might not. We'll know soon."

"You got your ears on?"

Murphy tapped his head. "I'm on an active op, aren't I?" he answered with a hint of sarcasm.

"Just asking. I can't help you if I can't hear you. Don't take chances, Murph. This guy's a flaming bastard. We'll keep the light on."

The door opened and quickly closed behind Murphy. In seconds, he'd faded into the pre-dawn darkness and a lot of trees.

"His ears?" Shea asked.

"We wear Bluetooth earpieces when we go dark. Keeps us linked. Right now, I'm listening to an old guy walking through the trees and whistling."

"Where are we?" Shea asked. "Close to the castle?"

"No. We're nearer the next village over. Murphy's got a good two click hike ahead of him, then he has to get inside the castle without being seen." Eric drummed his fingers on the dashboard. "Come sit up front with me while we wait."

"First, I need to step outside."

He squeezed one hand over his wrinkled forehead, a quiet groan eking out of him.

"I just have to pee," she whispered. "I'll be right back."

"I know. I'm just tight. You've never been on an active op with me before, and it's made me hyper-alert. That's all."

"You can come if you promise not to watch."

"Good idea." He rounded the truck in record time, opening the driver's side door.

Accepting his outstretched hand, Shea climbed off the running board and landed quietly on the mossy ground. "Do you have some tissues?"

"Sure do." He pulled a few sheets from his back pocket, a smile barely cracking his face. The crazy guy steered her to a nice big shrub and stood guard while she took care of business. "Do you think someone would kidnap me all the way out here?" she asked once her pants were up and zipped once more.

He handed her a travel-sized bottle of hand sanitizer. What hadn't he thought of? "It could happen. I'm not taking chances. Not with you."

A little alcohol-based cleanser did the trick. Rubbing her hands together to help it dissipate, Shea gave the bottle back before she took Eric's hand. "Now you know how I'll feel when Murphy comes back, and it's *your* turn to face Carlson."

"I get that, but I'm trained. Like Murphy. If all goes well, those French assassins guarding Jordan will never know what hit 'em." Eric steered her to the grill where he pulled her back to his front, his arms around her shoulders. "I can't lose you again," he whispered in the crook of her neck. "How do you feel this morning?"

She wiggled her fingers in front of his face. "With my hands," she teased, needing to break him out of his somber mood. "But I can't lose you, either. What am I supposed to do while *you're* gone?"

"Whatever you do, do NOT put that dress on. I don't know what the hell Murphy's thinking. He wouldn't put Moira in play, and I won't use you to get to Carlson."

Shea gulped. Yeah. It didn't seem like such a good idea anymore. She couldn't believe she'd thought of it. And yet… "A masquerade ball would be the perfect way to sneak into Ashford."

"Maybe," he said, his fingers absentmindedly smoothing up and down her biceps, warming her in more places than just her arms. She captured his hands to still the heat climbing up her body. It didn't go unnoticed that he was already aroused.

The first streaks of dawn glowed in the eastern sky. The smallest birds in the forest had awakened and began chirping. The bigger birds would soon commence, but for now, Shea felt as if she'd awakened in paradise. Pulling in a deep breath of cool morning air, she relaxed against the hard body of the man who always had her back. When she'd let him.

"We haven't used any protection," he murmured, "and we've been humping each other like rabbits in early spring. When was your last period?"

Twisting to face him, she pressed her cheek to his chest. The thought to use protection had honestly not entered her mind. Not with Eric. He'd always been safe, but the thought of another baby and another death stole her breath. "Two weeks ago," she murmured, the consequence of her actions tiptoeing up her spine with ticklish, scary fingertips.

Her brain pulled up the necessary facts every woman knew. Mid-cycle. The perfect time to hump like rabbits IF you wanted to get pregnant. She'd been so starved for Eric's acceptance that she hadn't thought beyond their initial encounter. It had seemed so impossible for so long.

A tiny voice whispered, *'Deep down, you wanted this. Admit it."*

Maybe...

She turned in his arms, a hard knot stuck in her throat. "So what if we are?"

For the first time a smile blossomed inside those stained-glass windows to his soul. "Then I guess we'll have a brand new baby in our home. You'll come to live with me in Virginia. We'll build another life together. Would you like that?"

One problem solved. Another problem raised. *How can I love another child as much as I loved Cheyenne?* "I, umm..." She let her doubt trail away. *I. Don't. Know.*

Eric cocked his head, looking deeper into her eyes. She lowered her lashes, her mind full of this newest challenge she'd gotten herself into.

Folding her inside his arms, he simply held her, his chin at the top of her head. "Think about it, Shea," he murmured, a tinge of sorrow in his tone. "I know your heart. It's brave. It's full of love, and it wants to heal. You have everything inside of you to love another child. Our child. You just have to open your heart and let go."

A sob sneaked up on her. She couldn't speak. Brave was the last thing she was. Only a coward deserted her husband at the worst time in his life. He was the brave one. She was just a foolish woman who'd let grief get the best of her.

The sound of tapping lifted her teary eyes. Eric turned to look over his shoulder, giving Shea the same view. A tiny bird had lighted on the roof of Murphy's truck, and whatever bug it found up there, it seemed intent on catching. It scurried to the right, then back to the center, hammering its tiny beak as it went. Tap, tap, tapping to catch its breakfast, which didn't want to get caught.

"Life is like that little guy, it will always find a way, baby," Eric whispered. "Trust me. If we're pregnant, we've been given a second chance to pour some of that bravery of yours into another child. We've got another opportunity to be crazy-tired with around the clock feeding, piles of stinky laundry, and gooey burp cloths that never come clean. We get to be grumpy zombies while we adjust to slavery at the hands of a teeny, tiny tyrant who just might scream if we step out of line. It'll be fun. Call me crazy, but I'm up for it. How 'bout you?"

She smiled, her fingers absorbing the strength from his sinewy back muscles and her belly noticing the power in the cradle of his hips. The scenario he'd just described did sound familiar and somewhat appealing, all these second chances and lost opportunities. Eric had always gotten up with her when Cheyenne stirred as a newborn. He didn't just roll over and go back to sleep because he wasn't the one nursing. No. He made tea. Gave back rubs. Foot rubs. Ensured his girls had company in the wee hours of the night in case they needed anything. He'd said it was his pleasure to serve his queen and his princess.

Yeah. He was a rarity among men, an honest to goodness white knight.

Shea swallowed easier. She'd never been alone until she'd done it to herself. *No more.*

"What if, umm, it's a boy this time," she dared ask, not like it would matter to Eric. It was just a safe segue into what might be.

His cheeks moved against her scalp. She could tell. Her man was smiling. A. Big. Wide. Jack-O-Lantern smile. "Then,

Mama, you'd better sign us guys up for Little League, cuz this boy's gonna be a slugger just like you."

"But what if…" she gulped, afraid to voice the thought.

"No fucking way," he whispered. "Odds of another child of ours coming down with *Meningioma* are so slim, they border on impossible. We've been tested, Shea. Neither of us is genetically predisposed toward neurofibromatosis type 2 disorders, so put that worry out of your mind. What happened to Cheyenne was a one-in-a-billion fluke of Mother Nature."

That medical-ese tumbled off his tongue like nothing, but lightning did strike in the same place twice. Shea knew it did. She squeezed her eyes tight before her tears could fall. This was why she'd needed Eric to come save her. He'd always believed in her, and if he could look forward with faith, so could she.

"God, I could eat you up," she whispered fervently.

"Trust me, little girl." He did his best impression of a big bad wolf, the one that used to make Cheyenne squeal with delight. "You'd better get back in the truck before I make damned sure you're—ahem, we're—pregnant. Wouldn't that be something for Murphy to catch us at?"

Shea giggled, her body and soul on fire for her man. "I'll bet he's seen worse."

"But he's never seen better, and he's not going to now. Besides, there's something I want to show you."

"But, honey," she teased. "I've seen that before."

He smacked her ass. Just once. "Not that."

Eric knew it would make her or break her, but he hoped for somewhere in between.

"You've had this with you? All this time?" Shea held the metal case with Cheyenne's pretty picture, her eyes brimmed and her fingers trembling.

"Yes," he admitted quietly. "I keep it next to my bed. We talk every night, Cheyenne and me. I ask her to watch over you. She tells me to keep looking for you. Stuff like that."

A tiny 'oh' squeaked out of Shea. Her tears fell as her fingertip traced the face of their perfect little girl once more. "I didn't take one with me," she cried. "And me. You've got me in here, too."

Okay, this was not what Eric intended, not for Shea to fall apart. Tugging her other fingers to his mouth, he kissed them to distract her. "I just wanted you to know we never forgot you. That we both love you."

A hiccup wrenched out of her. "And this key. Is it…?" The saddest turquoise took him by storm.

"Yes. It's to the front door of our place on Vashon Island. I never sold it." *I couldn't.* He kissed the knuckle of her first finger. "A nice family's renting it. They take good care of it. You'd like them."

"B-but… but…" And there she stopped, heartbroken—not what he was going for.

"You know what?" He reached for the box. "This isn't helping like I thought it would."

Angling her shoulder between them, Shea lifted the treasure out of his reach. "But I want it," she squeaked. "Can I keep it from now on? Please? I won't lose it."

Like she had to ask? What could he say? Not much with the lump in his throat. "It's already yours, baby."

"All this time…" The saddest whine he'd ever heard.

"And longer," he promised.

Shea climbed all over him then, crying and kissing, whining and kissing some more. That was when Eric knew. They were going to be all right.

CHAPTER TWENTY-ONE

"Damn it," he muttered more to himself than to Shea. "I can't get into Murphy's laptop. This thing's password protected."

"Want me to hack into it for you?" she teased, her pretty brows lifted and that sugary-sweet, *I-told-you-so*-smirk tweaking her cheek. "I could, you know." One delicate brow arched.

"Yes, damn it." Eric handed the device over with a grumble. "I'd like to be on top of all the Tattle Tale feeds as soon as Murphy activates them."

Her fingertips were tapping before it settled to her lap. "Just what are these Tattle Tales you guys keep talking about?"

"Miniscule listening and video devices. Mother's inventions. She's a genius, you know." *And so are you,* he thought as his wife's very capable fingers worked magic on the keyboard.

"Ha. I should've guessed. What is it with you guys?" Shea handed the laptop back. "His password is as easy to break as yours. It's Moira911."

Coughing to mask his own internal sap, Eric keyed in the offending code—then entered it again because he'd fat-fingered it the first time.

Speak of the devil. Murphy ducked from the cover of the nearest tree, hot footing it to his truck. Shea slid out of the driver's seat to make room as he climbed in, panting but excited. "You haven't fired that gizmo up yet?"

"I'm working on it." Eric hit ENTER—again— and waited the prerequisite split second for the machine to boot up. "You want to do it?"

"Nah." Murphy pulled his arms out of his jacket sleeves. "I worked up a sweat hightailing it back here before the sun got any higher. You go ahead."

"Anyone follow you?"

"Nope, but I found Jordan. He kept my cover, but now he knows we're coming back."

"How is he?" Shea asked. "Are they taking care of him? Where's Rosie? The poor cabbie?"

Murphy pulled at his chin, now covered in gray stubble. "Sorry, but your friend and the cabbie aren't there. I'm hoping these Tattle Tales will tell us where Carlson's got them stashed, but yeah, Jordan's okay. He's got one arm in a sling, and he's tied to a chair in the suite next to Carlson's. He wasn't bleeding, but he's mad. I hated getting his hopes up only to leave him, but now he knows. Don't worry, he can handle it."

Eric knew better. Protective custody didn't include restraining an injured man. Maneuvering through the on-screen windows, he activated the app to monitor his buddy. Four smaller windows flashed onto the monitor.

Murphy leaned around Shea to point out, "See there? I only had time to place four Tattle Tales. One's at the side-entrance to the castle. One's in the hall. The last two are inside Carlson's suite. Should give us what we need."

"How did you get inside?" Shea asked, peering over Eric's shoulder.

"Easy. These rooms are all high-tech. After I, ahem, requisitioned one of the universal remotes for the rooms, I activated Carlson's sunblind. After a few minutes of listening to them argue because it kept going up and down, I knocked and asked if they were having trouble."

"You were probably wearing a staff uniform by then, too, weren't you?" Eric asked.

"Well, sure." Murphy tapped the monitor with his index finger. "One Tattle Tale is aimed at Carlson's bed. And that one—"

"I see him." The other Tattle Tale revealed Jordan. "You're right. He doesn't look happy."

"They've got him tied to the chair," Shea said, her voice tight, but Eric had other things on his mind. Like why the black eye? Why did it look as if Jordan couldn't sit still to save his life? Was he worried? In pain? Or scared?

Eric should've known better than to watch too long.

"Don't," Jordan croaked as he tipped back in the chair. "I've got nothing more to say."

A wide, muscular back covered the screen. "But you do," Carlson said, "and I want it all. The pass codes, addresses, and bank account numbers, if you've got them. Every last thing you can tell me about Alex Stewart and the two-bit, black op service he runs."

"Never," Jordan hissed. "I don't betray my f-f-friends."

"Stewart's your buddy, huh?" Carlson finally stepped away from the Tattle Tale and into view. The man was wearing a suit. One of his guards already stood beside Jordan's chair.

"Then why hasn't he sent one of his famous teams to save you? Or are you one of those expendables he purchases by the dozen?"

Jordan's gaze jolted from Carlson to the guard, just as the Frenchman stabbed a hypodermic needle into his thigh. "I won't talk," he ground out just before his body went slack.

"They're hurting him," Shea whispered.

Eric slammed the cover shut. Time to go. "Murph, keep my girl safe. I'll be back."

"Watch your step, young man," Murphy warned. "I'll be watching you."

"Promise me one thing," Eric said as he turned to Shea. "You won't wear that damned red dress."

She nodded, her eyes wide and bright. "I don't want you to go."

"I'll be back before you know it, and I'm bringing Jordan with me."

She flung herself against him, but he only had time for a quick kiss.

"Be safe," she said quietly as she released him. "I'll be here for you."

He smiled. "Do you know how long I've waited to hear those words? Trust me. I'm coming back as fast as I can."

The problem with marrying a USMC medic? They tended to forget they could also get shot. Or killed. Pressing her palm to the center of her chest, Shea willed the rising panic in her heart away, but it had a good, strong hold. The ugly scenes from the university lab and the bathroom in her flat replayed in her mind until she needed to scream. Or run after Eric.

She glanced at Murphy, not sure which he could handle, the tears or the noise. Stifling both, she slid into Eric's empty place, still warm from his body heat.

"He's running," Murphy advised. He hadn't taken his eyes off the monitor since Eric slammed the truck door.

Shea leaned over to watch the screen, but Murphy tilted it sideways so she couldn't see it. He'd also stopped chatting except for a rare update. Shea couldn't take the suspense. Another man was being tortured because of her. She couldn't catch a decent breath. Or swallow. Or think.

"Tell me," she ordered. "What are they doing?"

Murphy shook his head. "He's not bleeding, but they're rough on him. Whatever they shot him full of has made him cooperative, but you don't need to see this."

Biting her lip, Shea turned to the window. Damn Eric for being the noble one. For always putting himself last. For caring about people and acting like he was the only one who could help. Others could be just as helpful. He didn't always have to run to the rescue.

"I'm wearing that dress," she said vehemently. "If they even try to hurt Eric, I'm putting that dress on and I'm marching straight into that masquerade party and—"

"Honey, we don't even know if Carlson plans to attend the ball."

"I could find out."

Murphy closed the laptop and turned to face her. "I know this is hard, but let's let Eric do his job before we unleash the power of an angry woman, okay?"

"But he's walking into trouble." *Maybe death!*

"But you need to understand that your husband has a talent most other guys don't. I recognized it when I met him. He doesn't exactly walk on water, but he comes pretty damned close."

Tears flooded her eyes at this calm conversation. "Why is it always him?" she asked, hating that her voice sounded whiny instead of strong.

Murphy's lips curled with a tender smile. "Because Eric knows how to read people, Shea. He cuts through the chaff and gets to their heart of gold, if it's gold they've got. He can also detect a liar quicker than a fox can gobble up a field mouse. Just wait. Your husband's one in a million."

She sniffed. *I know that.*

"So how long have you two been married?"

"A little over eight years."

"Then why am I just finding out now?" he asked, his hand gentle on her shoulder.

"Because I... I..." Gradually, the story came out.

Murphy paused twice to provide an update to Eric's progress, and Shea didn't go into great detail, but by the time the telling was over, Murphy knew enough. He never batted an eye.

"We all go through fires in our lives, Shea. It's the way we're made and the road we're on. There isn't a one of us coming out of this life without a few bruises and hard knocks."

"Yes, but, I hurt him." *And now I'll get my just reward, to live alone like I thought I wanted two years ago.* It seemed the ultimate justice, Karma's tit-for-tat.

"Seems to me that bothers you a helluva lot more than it bothers him," Murphy said. "Hold on." He snapped the laptop cover up, his jaw cut into a hard angle. "He's at the castle."

Shea held her breath.

Murphy pursed his lips, his finger to his ear, but no status report was forthcoming.

Shea couldn't bear to watch—or not to watch.

"Sonofabitch." Murphy wiped one hand over his face. "That was close."

"What?"

Murphy held one palm to her face. "Shhhhh. I can't hear."

Damn it. What's happening?

"He's inside, but Carlson's men were wise to him. They must've gotten Jordan to talk."

Panic sidled into the seat alongside Shea. "What now?"

Murphy slammed the laptop cover closed with a resounding snap. "They've got him. Damn it to hell, they've got him. They knew he was coming. Where's that dress?"

CHAPTER TWENTY-TWO

Eric thought he was secure. Might even have thought he was invincible—for a second there. Now he sat restrained in Carlson's suite with Jordan limp at his side. At least Jordan wasn't bleeding, but he'd talked, and Carlson had simply waited. His thugs apprehended Eric in the woods north of the castle.

Angry at his arrogance and what this mistake would do to Shea, Eric lowered his chin to his chest. His cellphone had to be nearby. It enabled his earpiece.

"Murphy? Can you hear me?" Eric whispered as quietly as he could. Carlson might be listening—but he might not.

"Copy that," Murphy replied. "We're moving."

"No," Eric hissed. "Stay put."

"Sorry, son. You're compromised. Once they give you whatever they gave Jordan, you'll give us up. I can't let that happen."

"Don't bring her—"

The adjoining door burst open, and Hugh Carlson strolled in. Alone. *Shit.* "I understand you have something to say to me."

Eric swallowed hard, hoping Murphy was listening in. "You picked the wrong man to mess with."

"You must be talking about your boss. Stewart does spew a good line of B.S., doesn't he? But no, it's you I wanted. You're the one who got away from Dungarvin, something my men have yet to explain to my satisfaction." Shoving his suit jacket back, his hands sank to his hips, and he widened his stance. "You have one chance to tell me where Finn and his computer are. You were the last to be seen with him. Where did he go?"

Had this guy's thugs not seen Finn's remains sprawled all over Rosie's kitchen floor? Or were they just that dumb they couldn't put the fat suit and the sudden appearance of a woman together and come up with Shea?

"I'll tell you on one condition," Eric ground out, praying to hell Murphy was still online. "Tell her I love her." He stiffened his spine, prepared for the smack down headed his way.

Carlson cocked his head. "Tell who what?"

"Copy that," Murphy's voice came through soft and sad.

Carlson waved one of his guards into the room. "Show this fool I mean business."

"You again, eh?" the Frenchman's lip cured into a snarl. Worse—he held a hypodermic in his hand.

"You can't leave him!"

Murphy caught her hands before she could yank the truck door open. "I'm only moving to keep us safe. We're not leaving Eric behind. No sirree, Bob."

"We're not?" Shea stuttered. He'd passed on Eric's last words, and she should've known he wouldn't desert his men. She swallowed hard and tried to listen better, which was difficult with her mind pinging from one bad scenario to another like a wrecking ball. After what had happened to Phoenix, Gordie, and Professor Grover, Eric and Jordan's chances were so slim.

"When's that dance begin?"

Shea saw his lips move, but it took her a second to understand what he'd said. *What dance? Oh, the masquerade ball?* Freeing her hands from his grasp, she raked her fingers over her head as if ruffling her hair would help her brain to work. "Umm, let me think." *Now I remember.* "One pm! Today!"

Murphy slanted his shoulders to face her. "Now, you listen here, Shea. We've got two men to rescue, maybe more if I can figure out where Carlson's holding your friends. I know you don't want to hear this, but you need to settle down. You're no good to Eric if you're hysterical."

She focused on Murphy's tired, blue eyes. "I know, but…" She said the obvious, "We have to save him."

"And we will, but first, I need to get you to a beauty salon. I brought along some high heels and some make-up, but I don't think you're in any condition to apply blush much less all that shadowy, smudgy stuff you women like to paint on your eyes. And glitter. You'll need glitter."

Shea bobbed her head, willing to do anything.

"You and I are going to the ball, and we'll be early." Murphy's eyes narrowed. "I need you to focus, Shea, because the rest of this day will depend on you wowing every last man at Ashford. I need you to be radiant and giddy. Maybe even flirty. If a little buzz will get you there, tell me now, and I'll buy a bottle while I'm shopping, because you'll need to turn every man's head at that ball."

"No. I'm… I'm sober. I don't drink, but I can pretend." *I can do anything to help Eric.*

Murphy cupped her cheek, a tender light glimmering in his eyes. "You're one rare woman, you know that?"

No, I'm not. I'm scared.

Releasing her, Murphy stowed the laptop, muttering about needing fake identification and an invitation. A classy ride. A bigger expense account.

When the truck engine turned over, Shea clenched her fingers into a fist, sick at having to leave. "Hurry. He might not have much time."

"Don't worry," Murphy said as he maneuvered them out of the forest glade and onto the road. "Eric's been in tighter spots than this. Besides, Carlson probably used Sodium Pentothal to make 'em talk. Maybe Scopolamine."

"Are you serious?" That sounded so bad. Shea ran her fingers over her head again, her imagination providing all the worst-case scenarios Eric might be living through.

"Sometimes it's bad, yes. Sometimes, no," Murphy said calmly. "It all depends on the operator, but Eric's smart. He's got a good head on his shoulders, and he knows drugs."

The truck jostled and bounced as it wound along the country road, and Shea knew Murphy wanted to keep her talking, but she knew better. Truth serum was the least of Eric's worries. *No, no, no. Not torture.*

She hadn't yet detected the black-robed assassin, but he might have tracked her to Ireland. Everyone else had. *Think! Who wants me dead? Who besides Bagani and Carlson could've sent that killer after me?*

Murphy was headed south to Cashel when the answer struck. The assassin and Carlson both wanted Finn. Bagani only wanted Shea—if he'd linked her to his missing money. The chances of that happening were an incredible long shot, but it made no sense that he would've tracked her to Ireland. She wasn't Shea when she'd boarded the flight at Heathrow. Shea hadn't resurfaced until Dungarvin. The shooter on the bike couldn't have been Bagani. That meant...

Grrrrr! I don't know what anything means anymore! Eric's in trouble! That's all that matters!

Finally back in the village of Cashel, Murphy scanned the busy main street until he caught sight of a hair salon that boasted unisex hairdos. He parked at the curb and handed her several euros along with his jacket. "This is the plan. You're going in there and tell them you need a killer hair-do, make-up, and a manicure. I'll be back in less than thirty minutes."

"But—"

"But nothing." Sliding his right hand under his left arm, he retrieved a small pistol. "Keep this with you. I doubt you'll need it, but if you do, don't be afraid to use it. Got that?"

"Okay." Swallowing hard, she took the jacket, weapon and the money.

Murphy rested his chin to his forearm over the steering wheel, squinting at the busy street. "Thirty minutes, Shea. That's all the time you've got. Tell 'em you want to sparkle with red and gold glitter when they're done. And extra-long nails. Red. It's a masquerade ball, remember."

He meant to leave her. Alone. With a gun.

Shea steeled her nerve and eased the passenger door open. Dropping to the street, she glanced back. Murphy winked and headed south, leaving her to fulfill her part of the mission.

Turning to the salon's front window, she gathered her courage. A redheaded woman with her head half-shaved and the other spiked, greeted her with at the receptionist desk with a cheerful, "May I help you, doll?"

"I need, umm, a shampoo, and a cut and…" Shea ran her fingers over what scant hair she had to work with. "Never mind. Do you sell wigs? Hair extensions?"

"We do!" the woman all but squealed. "Right this way, lamb." Her steady endearments were more than a little off-putting, especially since Shea felt already like a lamb to the slaughter. Nonetheless, in two seconds, she found herself in a brightly lit room with a table of Styrofoam heads wearing all fashion of hairpieces on one side, a wooden chair that looked more like a throne facing the table, and a mirror the length of the wall behind the table.

She nearly turned back at the sight of all those body-less heads. Flashbacks of poor Phoenix lifted the bile up the back of her throat. *What was I thinking? I can't do this.*

"Is everything okay, love?" *Again with the sweet talk.*

"Yes," Shea hissed, dizzy enough to pass out, but determined. This was about saving Eric and Jordan. She could do it. *It's just Styrofoam and hair.*

"Why don't you have a seat, and we'll just see which version of lovely you prefer today, shall we?"

We shall. Shea sat in the throne with Murphy's jacket folded on her lap. The familiar smells of perm solutions and hair sprays calmed her nerves. There was no brute with a scimitar in the shadows. *It's just Styrofoam and hair.*

"So what's the occasion?" Miss Redhead lifted a blonde wig off its wig holder. "A wedding? A vacation?"

"No. It's just a party." *Of sorts.*

Miss Redhead chattered like they were old friends as color after color and style after style topped Shea's already shorn head. The blonde was just plain no. It bleached her already pale skin tone to pasty-gray. Purple? Green? No, but the coppery red was interesting. Shea flounced her fingers through the shoulder length curls, canting her head in the mirror, not sure. But no, it wasn't her, either.

Black? *No, too stark.* A sable brown pixie-cut? *Already have that, thanks.*

"I know just what you need, Princess." Her helpful salon artist reached to the far end, and, just that fast, she turned Shea into the longhaired brunette she once was. Having that particular shade, her own natural hair color, falling over her shoulders and down her back filled her with confidence and a touch of sex appeal. She shook her head, tossing the mass of spiraled curls along with it. "This one. I'll take it." *It's me.*

Miss Redhead beamed and told her, "That'll be a hundred fifteen euros, love."

Bless Murphy. He'd given Shea a dozen €20 banknotes, more than enough. Her confidence ratcheted-up another notch. "I need my nails done, too. And make-up. Do you have anyone on staff who can do my make-up, so I look, umm..." *Like someone else?* "...glamorous?"

Miss Redhead's smile grew larger. "Honey, by the time you leave, you'll be a brand-new woman."

Shea could only look at herself in the mirror and think, *I already am.*

CHAPTER TWENTY-THREE

Damn. Frenchy could hit.

Eric pulled his heavy head up from his shoulder, and twisting his neck, spat the blood out of his mouth. Carlson's guard had been working him over for what seemed like a year, but had probably only been an hour. Time didn't matter after the first fist in his gut. His spleen had to be jelly. Blood oozed into his eye from at least one orbital laceration. He could barely see.

The brutal Frenchman wore gloves to the party. Leather gloves. With razor sharp, cutting seams running up the back of each finger and over his knuckles. Guess flunking the truth serum class had consequences.

Eric figured he would die in this sonofabitchin' chair rather than betray Finn. *Finn. Finn. Finn.* He focused on that single name. Didn't let another flit through his wandering mind. No way. No how. Concentration was the only line of defense against the seductive lure of psychoactive meds. Most bullies used some kind of truth serum to bring their mark to the edge of Never-Never land. Too much would put him to sleep. Permanently.

Unfortunately, shooting a victim up also reduced his hold on reality. Eric had enough in his veins to be dizzy, incoherent, and seeing things. Just not enough to spill his guts.

The gloved fist looked like a giant hammer from cartoon land coming at him. *Ouch, shit.* His head flew back on his spine. Frenchy grabbed a handful of hair, jerking his face to the ceiling. Eric huffed through his mouth because his nose was too full of blood. By then, his eyes were too swollen to see the bastard, but what the hell. Time was on Eric's side. The human brain could only take so much before it shut down and lapsed into unconsciousness.

"Come on, Reynolds," Frenchie hissed. "I'm tired of beating your lazy ass to make you talk. You were the last one with Powers. Where'd he go? What'd you do with him?"

Eric pushed the tip of his swollen tongue to the back of his bottom teeth. All were loose, but none were missing. "Bog," he wheezed for the millionth time. "I hid him... at the bog. I think. You find him yet?"

He would've laughed, because his fuzzy brain found everything funny for some stupid reason, but he didn't. Last time he laughed, he got—

SMACK!

Yeah. That.

Another fist landed to his right cheek. Then his left. "Stop lying! There weren't no bog!"

Oh yes, there were. Umm, was. Aw, shit, who cares.

More spit and sweat flew. Blood. Maybe a brain cell or two. It made no difference. Eric could only endure what Frenchy dished out, so endure he did. But he had to know. "You going to the... ball, Sally?"

"Merde!" Frenchy about knocked Eric's head off that time. "The ball is Monsieur Carlson's problem. Stop calling me Sally!"

Eric let the twilight claim him with a whispered, "Good to know."

Murphy was as good as his word. He was back in precisely thirty minutes with what looked like a large coat box under his arm. He must've gone shopping for himself and gotten a shave too. Dark glasses concealed his eyes. An Irish tweed cap perched on his head and he wore a new jacket. He took a seat facing the manicure booth where Shea was being thoroughly attended to. The briefest smile graced his mouth as he rested the box upright against the wall by his chair.

Maybe he'd bought a rifle. Shea hoped. That would be better than any coat. They could go into Carlson's suite together with all guns blazing. Rescue Eric and Jordan. Find Rosie and the cabbie. Get the hell out of there. Lay waste to anyone who tried to stop her.

A fierce warrior wife had replaced the woman she'd been at the crack of dawn. She'd kept Murphy's jacket on her lap, but now that he was back, she wanted to run to Ashford and rescue Eric. *Had to be the hair.*

Murphy must have read her mind. He motioned her with both palms to *hold on.*

The two women doing her nails and make-up chatted non-stop with each other, which was fine with Shea. She had other things on her mind beside whose baby was being baptized on Sunday or the high price of lamb shanks at the local market. She yearned for her husband, trying hard to not think what might be happening to him while she played Disney Princess.

Finally! Her blood-red acrylic nails were dry. The last poof of glittery sparkle was applied to her face and hair. She couldn't get out of that chair fast enough.

Murphy was gracious enough to pay, although she still had all of the banknotes he'd given her. He didn't even raise an eyebrow when Miss Redhead gave him the final total. Moira must have trained him well.

Picking up the box again, which had a plastic handle now that she had time to really look at it, his eyes scrolled over Shea's new look. He helped with her jacket, then offered a cocked elbow like a lord would for a real lady. She rested her hand on his forearm, and the game was on.

They drove back toward Ashford, but this time Murphy drove right through the gate like he owned the place. "I asked for a room in the older part of the castle where Carlson's staying so we'll have some place to retreat to once we get our boys back," he murmured under his breath. "I'll need you to bring the suitcase while I take everything else."

"Okay. Then what?" *I'm so nervous!*

He didn't crack a smile. "Then we go dancing."

Gradually, the castle appeared through the trees. Breathtaking. The view looked as if it had been taken right out of a fairytale. Towers. Turrets. Gardens. White swans on the nearby lake. Utterly gorgeous in an overwhelming way. The epitome of decadent wealth. A veritable stone edifice of upper crust splendor.

Through the two stone guard towers they went and over the bridge to Ashford. Murphy parked along the front entrance to the lobby and instantly Shea felt shabby. If the cars in the parking lot were any indication, she was way out of her element. A McLaren. The Rolls Royce two cars down looked just as expensive. Latching onto the suitcase, she focused on her reason for being there.

"Can I get that for you, ma'am?" a smartly uniformed bell cap asked the moment she set both feet to the ground.

"No thank you. I've got it."

Stepping out of the way, he gestured her forward. Murphy took her arm and escorted her inside. "Smile. People are watching. As far as they know, you're my young wife and I'm a lecherous old bastard."

She glanced up at him. "That's the plan?"

A tender emotion shifted over his face. "Yes. I hope Moira's not here."

"Is she supposed to be?"

He chuckled, his voice softer. "I'm kidding, Shea. Loosen up. At least act as if you like me."

Shea pasted on a big smile and tossed her head, pushing her glistening mane over one shoulder. She latched onto Murphy's arm and stepped in closer to him. "I can do that," she said. To prove it, she tipped her head back and laughed as if she hadn't a care in the world.

"That's the spirit."

They cut across the parking lot and ran up the stairs between two stone Irish Wolfhounds. At the top step, an older gentleman announced heartily, "Welcome to Ashford."

While Murphy checked in, she stayed close by and gawked, thoroughly taken aback by the opulent lobby with its suits of armor and massive paintings.

"Will you be joining us for tea?" the woman at the counter asked.

Murphy tucked the stem of his dark glasses into his shirt collar. "We'd like to shake off the dust of our travels first if you don't mind."

"Right this way, sir." She stepped away from the counter and led them to their second story room. Shea was nervously impressed. The room was grand, but she had Eric on her mind.

The woman explained how to control their environment from the bed. The universal remote controlled everything from the power sun-blinds to the big-screen television. Fancy that. And in case they wanted to watch the movie, *Quiet Man,* just press star.

Murphy dropped the box and garment bag on the bed. He yawned. He stretched. Then he hinted. "Thanks, ma'am. I can take it from here."

As soon as she closed the door behind her, Murphy tossed a smaller box across the bed to Shea. A computer box. "I bought you a new toy. Now get your spider friends to work. We need to know where Carlson is in this joint. Then get dressed. I'll lay out the duds."

At last. Something she could do. But instead of spiders, this time she reached out to the frequency of Mother's Tattle Tales and narrowed the band-width until...

There they are.

The very distinct sound of men's laughter lifted up from the laptop's speaker. "If Reynolds doesn't snap out of it, I'm going to fill the tub with ice water and drown his ass. That'll open his eyes."

"What are you listening to?" Murphy leaned over her shoulder to peer at the screen.

"One of Mother's Tattle Tales. I'm inside Carlson's suite, but I can't get any video."

"Carlson won't approve," a definite smoker's voice rasped. "Him liking his showers like he does. You'll make a mess of that tub in there, and we'll never hear the end of it."

"I should've stayed in Africa," the first man groused. "Could've done as I pleased with the prisoners in Darfur. Didn't have no pretty boy screening my calls, neither. You know how long it's been since I been inside a woman?"

A snicker.

Shea cringed.

Murphy tapped her shoulder. "Your dress and shoes are in the bathroom."

She lifted her chin, but couldn't hide the tears. These guys weren't men. They were monsters. "He's hurt," were the only words she could squeeze out of her dry throat.

Murphy nodded somberly. "I get that, but I know that man of yours. So do you. He's a fighter, isn't he?"

But fighters got killed, too. So did heroes. It happened every day. *Just read the papers.*

Lifting her out of the seat, Murphy turned her toward the bathroom. "Happy hour begins in thirty. Let's be early."

She did as she was told, her fierce warrior persona subdued at what Eric was living through. Now was not the time to play dress up, but if this crazy scheme got her man back, then by hell, she would pretend she was *Madonna.*

Closing the door behind her, Shea turned on the light. There in steamy red elegance hung *the dress*. A silky pair of black French-cut panties lay on the vanity. Matching black heels stood near the door, ready for her to slide into them.

Murphy had thought of everything. Blushing, she slipped into the panties and then the dress, careful not to smudge her make-up or break a nail. She shimmied and jiggled until at last—she was in. All she needed was someone to zip her up.

Smoothing her fingers over the shimmering fabric, she looked at her reflection in the mirror. There was a day she and Eric had been the life of the party. They'd danced, they'd laughed, and everyone else had wished they were the charming lovers known as the Reynolds couple. No one was happier than they were.

But today, another woman entirely stared back at Shea. Smokey black eyes glittered with an almost feral excitement. Full red lips matched the fuck-me red dress perfectly. Flawless complexion. Long fluttering lashes drew attention to her deep turquoise eyes. The dark chocolate mane made her look more like herself again. Despite her nerves, that fierce warrior persona had elbowed its way forward, just not quite like Madonna.

A semi-hysterical chuckle bubbled up from the back of her throat. *Damn. I look like Jessica Rabbit.* Except Jessica had big boobs. Cartoon boobs maybe, but more than Shea's plum-sized offerings. The sleeveless dress was a bit much, but thankfully, the built-in underwire bra made her assets look like she owned at least some oceanfront cleavage. She'd turned into a thin-busted seductress with her shoulders bare and a lot of skin on display. *A lot.*

The front of the gown split at the bottom hem of her black panties, revealing most of her left thigh and leg. Shea turned to view her back. *Wow, that's a lot of me showing*. If those panties hadn't been bikini style, the top of them would be on display, too.

Resting her hands on her hips, she swished her backside. Thick fudge-colored curls tumbled over her naked shoulders like a waterfall. The smoky seductress in the mirror stared her timid self down. Red had always been her favorite color. *I may not be dynamite like Marilyn Monroe, but I can do this.*

Exiting the bathroom, she faced Murphy with her right hand on her hip, giving him her best shot. "How do I look?"

He'd changed into a tux and stood in front of the full-length mirror just outside the bathroom door, working at his bowtie. His jaw dropped as his eyes scrolled down to her feet and back up again. "Umm, good. You look… real good. Almost as good as my wife."

"Moira," Shea murmured, fully aware that his eyes had gone hazy. She turned to let him see the finished product. "Her dress fits me like a glove. Can you zip me up?"

"Why yes, it does, and I certainly can." Clearing his throat, he took two quick steps to her aid.

Warmth spread up her neck at this intimate act of kindness that husbands normally did for their wives. With the zipper undone, Murphy had a good view of most of her back and enough of her panty-clad backside. Without a doubt, Eric would've taken advantage of the moment and made sure those panties fit just right.

Murphy didn't even touch her skin, just pulled the zipper up, then secured the zipper pull beneath the fabric with a gentle pat at the extreme small of her back. "There you go. You're all set, little lady."

His voice had turned hoarse. When she pivoted, he took a step back, his eyes glued to her face instead of her bosom. Poor Murphy looked as guilty as sin. A little flushed, too. His tie still dangled at his neck.

"Do you need help with that?" she offered.

He shook his head and stepped farther back, both palms forward "No sirree Bob. I can manage." He coughed. "Damn, girl, you clean up real good. No one's going to recognize you at this ball."

"Isn't that the idea?" she asked, her palms sweaty at the thought of dancing as if she didn't have a care.

Tearing his eyes off her, he turned back to the mirror, chuckling to himself and still fumbling with his tie. "I could get myself in trouble if I'm not careful."

In your dreams, she thought as she swished past him, pulling the elegant gown's court train behind her. She checked the computer for Carlson's whereabouts before she turned to Murphy once more, anxious to get this masquerade over with.

Murphy glanced sideways, still tugging his tie. "There's something for you on the nightstand. Make sure you know what's in it."

A sequined red clutch purse beckoned to her, but the second she lifted it into her hand, she knew what he'd given her. Unsnapping the gold clasp, she removed the small revolver. A Walther CCP. Nine millimeter. Sleek. Black. *Just my size.*

Nine-millimeter rounds dealt significant knockdown power, something Eric had stressed she would need in a concealed carry piece. The weapon fit snug in her palm, the weight and balance perfect. Scrollwork etched the grip, but holding it in her trembling hands now frightened her instead of bolstering Shea's confidence. This was real tonight. Not practice and not a game.

Hefting it, she aimed out the window as the memory of Eric's arm around her when he'd first taken her to the range flooded back. They'd practiced for hours with a weapon similar to this one. Then they'd picked up a basket of fried chicken on the way home, and they'd made love on their living room floor. They'd laughed and spilled wine, and they'd loved.

Now that was a memory worth making.

"Shall we?" Murphy asked, intruding on her trip down memory lane.

Shea smoothed her right palm down over her hip to remind herself who she was tonight. Instead of a runner, she was the warrior-wife of the handsome man she intended to get back alive. *Damned straight.*

CHAPTER TWENTY-FOUR

Gliding down the hall toward the ballroom on Murphy's arm, Shea's stomach clenched with too much acid. He'd fastened her mask in her hair with combs. Simple in its elegance, the raven black mask had been decorated with red sequins, the wings at the sides of it creating the illusion of flight while it hid her facial features.

His was a simple black scarf, the kind Zorro might've worn. The Fox. More surprising were the butterfly wings he'd mounted to her back before they made their grand entrance. Sheer black and bejeweled with tiny red stones along the skeletal veins, she hesitated when he'd stopped her short of the door and told her to spin around.

"Where'd you find *that*?" she'd whispered, more than a little sarcastically as she smiled at the interested audience gathering to stare at her in the hall. The last thing she wanted was to look like some juvenile butterfly at an adult party. Honestly, this guy came up with the most amazing things in the last hour: a computer, a weapon, and insect wings —unless he carried them everywhere he went. She wouldn't doubt that he did.

He'd just smiled and made the circular motion with his index finger for her to turn. The appliance that held the wings in place was simply a clear plastic halter that hung over her shoulders and beneath her hair. He pressed a fifty-cent piece sized button into her palm. "Squeeze this remote when you want to flutter."

She shuddered instead. "Why would I want to do that? You've just made me a bright red target. With wings."

He tipped her chin up with two fingers, his eyes soft and hazy. "Oh, no. I've just made you the sweetest flower in the garden. Look at your competition, young lady." He turned her to face the hall where couples stood talking, goblets in their hands. Not a single gown sported wings, which proved her point, didn't it? "I can't go in looking like this." *Can I?*

"Trust me on this, Shea," Murphy whispered in her ear. "You're the woman people will want to be seen with tonight. They're watching us now. Shall we give them something to talk about?"

Murphy certainly knew know how to make an entrance. Sweeping her onto the dance floor, his hand dropped naturally to her hip, his other clasping hers as they swirled to the sedate rhythm of whatever waltz the string quartet was playing. The energy in the room seemed to change in an instant. More couples took to the floor, but her panic flared. Shea had no way to know who was who behind the masks. How could she get close to Carlson in this crazy get-up?

Until a man's hand clamped Murphy's tuxedoed shoulder and put a stop to their dance steps. Shea turned to the only man in the place arrogant enough to think he didn't need a mask. "May I cut in?" Hugh Carlson asked, bowing at his waist in a courtly gesture.

Rolling his eyes like a perturbed husband, Murphy didn't spare the megalomaniac a glance. "No. You may not. For hell's sake, Carlson, this is my wife, not some party girl you can hire for the night. Take off." Growling, he whisked Shea back into the crowd, chuckling and not a bit winded. "The bastard sure thinks he can take what he wants, doesn't he?"

"Wasn't that the idea?" Shea asked, her toes nicely warmed in those six-inch heels while she kept up with Murphy's sure footing. The man could've given Fred Astaire a run for his money as gracefully as he worked the floor. *Covert operators. Who knew?*

"Don't worry. He's had his eye on you since we started the ball rolling. He'll be back. Count on it."

Shea followed Murphy's lead and acted the part of a young wife enamored with her older husband. He was easy to like. Debonair. Gentlemanly and courteous to a fault. It was no wonder Moira loved him.

They laughed. They danced. When the musical number ended, he held her fingers in his hand as they made their way to the nearest empty table. "I'm going for beer. Sparkling water for you?"

"Yes, please," she whispered, her throat dry and her lips parched. Nervous or not, she'd needed that energetic dance to get her head in the game. It was almost fun.

Tapping her acrylic nails on the tabletop, she scanned the room, half-expecting Carlson to make another move. Instead, an elegant man of shorter stature and the caramel-colored complexion of the Mideast slid onto the chair directly next to hers. A gold mask lifted as he reached for her hand and lifted it to his lips.

Her lungs failed. Her throat clamped shut. *Basheer Bagani.*

"I've looked for you," he whispered in an all too familiar voice. "My little rabbit thought she could run from me, and I wouldn't come after her?"

Shea tried to swallow. Tried to think. "H-how…?" crawled off her tongue.

"Tsk, tsk, Shea Reynolds, or is it Hollister now? You move on quickly, but like you, I have my ways." He gripped her hand tighter. Hollister was the alias Murphy had registered under. Interesting. On top of her other problems, Shea was now an oil heiress.

"You gave it a good try, though. You almost fooled me. If not for Mr. Carlson's obsession with that buffoon, Finn Powers, I wouldn't have found you. I must say, I find that an interesting puzzle. Are you and Mr. Powers related?"

Jerking her fingers from Bagani's slimy grip, Shea shifted the Walther to her lap. There she was, caught between two killers, one who'd been searching for Shea Reynolds and had found her, the other still hunting poor Finn. Whatever happened next would be up to her.

Going for broke, she offered her left hand, palm up on the table. Inviting Bagani to take hold one more time. If he dared.

He did, but he'd no sooner latched onto her fingers, when his eyeballs fell for her oceanfront property, the perfect distraction. It gave her the few seconds she needed to make her point. Or points. By the time his eyeballs jerked back to her face, the Waltham was pressed to his crotch, and her trigger-finger twitched to blow Basheer Bagani's balls into the lovely decorated ceiling.

Oh, look. Cherubs with tiny little arrows. Wonder if they're as good a shot as I am. Of course, at this range...

He stiffened, but she wouldn't release her death grip on his fingers. Her warrior-self was back and pissed at being hunted by one too many jerks at the same time in the same freaking country!

"Basheer," she gushed. "So nice to see you again. It's been ages." *Who's the victim now, you jerk?*

Murphy returned with their drinks, but he froze six feet behind Bagani, his eyes wide as he took in the scene.

"Murphy, my love. Come join us," she said with enthusiasm. "There's someone I've wanted you to meet for the *lonnnnnnnnnnngest* time." *Right before I neuter him.*

Mr. I'm-Above-The-Law Bagani paled. Right there on the spot, he turned into a pasty white guy with black buggy eyes and a nervous tick in his right cheek. Possibly a nervous dick in his pants, too. His gold mask fell to the floor. He stood the very real chance of never being *long* again.

Murphy set the drinks at the edge of the table, but scanned the crowd instead of sitting. "You got your silencer on, dear?" he asked quietly out of the corner of his mouth.

"Didn't think I'd need it tonight, what with the dance and the music and all," Shea purred, not sure where all this bravado had come from, but willing to go with the flow. "But now I wish I did. Sit with us, honey. Basheer has something he'd like to tell you." She sent him a flirty chin nod, the kind a wife sends a husband who's on board with her game plan.

Murphy sat facing the nervous Arab. "Would that be the story of how he got you into his bed?"

Bagani's eyeballs darted to Shea. "I did? What? Who me? No. Never! I would nev—"

"Cut the bullshit," she spat. "You *did* abduct me, and you *will* do it to other vulnerable women the first chance you get, but that's not the story I want to hear tonight. Why'd you pay an assassin to kill my friends?"

"I what?" he choked. Sweat dripped at his temples. His upper lip glistened with it.

Murphy tilted into Bagani. "You heard the lady. Talk. Maybe she'll go easy on you."

"But I... I..."

"Tell me who killed Phoenix and Gordie?" Shea asked, digging the tip of the pistol into his crotch a little deeper. "He's your man, isn't he, the guy in the black robe with a scimitar? You sent him to kill me. He works for you, right?"

"Me, me, m-me?" Bagani seemed to be climbing the musical scale, only he'd gotten stuck on do-re-*me, me, me*. "I don't know what you're talking about. Yes, I followed Carlson's men from Amsterdam to here, but only to find you. Then I followed the other guy on the motorcycle, the one with the girl, but just because they were chasing him. I swear. I speak the truth. But you..." His brows clashed over his accusation. "You stole from me. In my country...!"

Murphy folded his arms over his chest as he leaned back, grousing, "Here we go."

"That was you on the motorcycle?" Shea meant to stay on the subject. "You were the guy shooting at us?"

He shook his head. "No, I was shooting at... wait. You were the woman on the back of that bike?"

"You shoot at all random people on bikes?" she volleyed back at him.

"Yes, I mean, no." Bagani ran his fingers over his black eyebrows. "I tracked Mr. Carlson's men to that bed and breakfast, but when I got there, they were already chasing some guy on a motorcycle, and they were shooting at him. I knew they wanted Powers, and I knew that somehow Powers and you were connected, so I followed. Once we hit the stone fences, I finally had the upper hand. It was an honest mistake. I wasn't shooting at you, only at the bike's tires. I thought—"

"You thought you could terrorize me all over again." Shea stabbed that Walther in as close and personal as she dared. "You have the nerve to accuse me of theft after what you've done to all those other women, you creep. After what you were going to do to me!"

Suddenly shaking in his fine linen trousers, Bagani whined, "Puh-puh-puleeeeze, don't shoot me. My father will be so—"

"You tied me to your bed," she hissed. "You're right, I stole from you, and I will again until you come forward and admit what a pig you are. I'll drain your accounts until you name every last woman you've raped or tortured with those disgusting toys of yours. Deal?" Another dig, and she was surprised at how powerful turning the tables on this creep made her feel.

Bagani's eyes hit the table as his head bobbed. "A confession. Yes, yes. I can do that." He lifted his left hand, for what that was worth. "I swear."

But Shea knew exactly what that left hand was used for in most Mideastern countries. She called his bluff. "Will you look at this liar, Murph? He can't tell the truth to save his life. I think it's time to get real."

Murphy grunted. "Damn it, wife, I told you to never leave home without your silencer. Now things are gonna get ugleeeeeeee."

Shea could've kissed him for playing along.

"No!" Bagani shoved away from the table, his eyes wide-open. "I'll leave and you'll never see me again."

Only Murphy wasn't playing. Crossing his arms with his elbows on the table, he faced the Arab. "You see, Bagani, that's just not good enough. I know my wife…" He winked at Shea, and coyly, she mouthed a kiss back at him, "and she's hurting for all those missing women you've left in your wake. Understand? She's got enough evidence to put you away for life. Now either I let her rip you a new one—and trust me, she'll do it—or…" His head lifted as his gaze shifted over Bagani's shoulder. "Hello, officers."

Retracting her weapon, Shea concealed it back in her purse as three beefy Irish police officers materialized behind the Arab. "Would this be the one, Murphy?" the closest officer asked.

"Yes, this is Basheer Bagani, the man you've been looking for. He's all yours. Thanks for following up with me."

"But, but… I have diplomatic immunity!" the arrogant playboy declared, his shoes barely scuffing the polished wooden floor with the police helping him walk like they were. He managed to twist his neck around as he bellowed, "I will be back!"

Murphy pursed his lips and let out a soft whistle. "No, you won't. Trust me on that one. Not where you're going."

The drama proved too much. Shea turned to *J. E. L. L. O.* Right there on the table. She laid her sweaty forehead on her trembling, folded arms. Didn't it figure? Her wings started fluttering.

Her husband-for-the-night cupped her quaking shoulder. "My hell, Shea," he whispered. "Does Eric know you've got the makings of a good operator?"

She peered up at Murphy, needing to throw up. "Is everyone looking at me?"

"Only because you're a celebrity now." Murphy scanned the dance floor. "Sit up straight. Relax. Throw me one of those screw-the-world smiles. Come on. You can do it."

Okay then. Still trembling, Shea tossed her head back and laughed. It almost worked, but the pitch sounded tight and strained. Trying once more, she threw her soul into this crazy masquerade as if Murphy had just told a funny joke.

Playing along, he tugged her close enough for a kiss to her forehead. "I knew you could do it."

"You've got actual evidence on Bagani?" she whispered into his chin. *Please, tell me you do.*

"No, but I've got enough questions for the Garda Síochána to keep him in a holding cell for a couple days until I get the evidence," he breathed in her hair. "Don't worry. Bagani has everything to lose, Shea. Not you."

"But those were the police." Would they now think to investigate her? What a mess!

"Forget about it. The night's young, Mrs. Hollister. Let's dance those wings off."

Exhaling a deep breath, Shea nodded. "First, how do I stop them?" The fluttering behind her back was driving her crazy.

"Just hit the button. You've got all the power in the palm of your hand, remember?"

No, she hadn't remembered anything, and the remote control wasn't handy anymore. But it was in her purse, right beside the Walther. Done and done. The fluttering ceased, but then her heart kicked in. Talk about jumping out of the frying pan and into the fire.

"I see your *father* has grown tired of the nightlife," Hugh Carlson said, his voice honeyed and insulting.

Shea held perfectly still as he approached from behind her. He needed to think she was just some young, addle-brained starlet with a daddy complex. Lowering her lashes, she let Murphy take the lead, but gripped her tiny purse—the one with a big boom—just in case.

Releasing her, Murphy tipped back in his seat. "What do you want, Carlson?" he asked with a twist, making Carlson's name sound insignificant.

"Murphy Hollister, I presume," Carlson drawled Murphy's fake-name-for-the-night with as much disgust. "Out of your element, aren't you? Shouldn't you be back in your Texas oil fields instead of dancing?"

Murphy scoffed, his arms crossed over his chest and his chin stuck forward. "Just because you own half the world doesn't mean you own me. And I'm her husband. Not her father." He tipped his beer to her. "Shea, darlin', this big mouth's Hugh Carlson. You might've heard his name mentioned once or twice on the news."

Carlson lowered into the seat next to her. The one Bagani had just vacated. "A beautiful name, Shea. Irish, isn't it?"

She faced him, her chin on her palm, mostly to keep her head from shaking. Aiming for disinterest, she traced the tip of her finger over the embossed design of the tablecloth. "Hugh Carlson, huh?" she deadpanned like a spoiled millennial would. "What do you want?"

It would've worked, but the man had the most incredible eyes. Gunmetal blue, his pupils dilated. This couldn't be the same guy who'd threatened Gordie. Up close, Carlson looked perfect in his trim, black tux, but the men's cologne he wore couldn't disguise the rank smell of the crimes she'd witnessed. *And I'm supposed to dance and flirt with you?*

A smile tweaked the corners of his lips. Probably botoxed. He had that too-good-to-be-true, airbrushed persona of a male-model. Tanned. Trimmed. Shaved and suave. Evil as sin.

Tenting his fingers to the table, he leaned in her direction. "I'd like one dance with the most enchanting woman on the floor," he whispered, as if Murphy was no longer there. "That's all I ask. Your *husband* looks a little, shall we say, winded?" Carlson offered his hand, palm up. His fingers curled, beckoning her to join him.

Shea shook her head, wishing Murphy would jump back into the conversation and tell this player where to go. But he didn't, because this was the reason she was here, to bait Carlson.

"Oh, hell," Murphy grumbled. "One dance. What will it hurt? Run along. Kick up your heels while I take a break."

Shea turned on him, hoping the pounding beat in her chest didn't show through her eyes. "But honey, I came with you." *And I don't want to be alone with this creep.*

"And you'll be leaving with me, too, young lady," Murphy grumped at her. "Now go. Let me drink my Guinness and rest my dogs a spell. Then I'll be the one keeping you up all night for a change." He dismissed her as if he were old, grumpy, and winded.

Shit. Shit. Shit!

CHAPTER TWENTY-FIVE

Reluctantly, Shea lifted her red clad butt from her chair, going for aloof and regal instead of frightened and cowardly. "Let's have that dance then."

A mouthful of perfect, straight teeth gleamed back at her. Carlson moved in, his fingers quickly splayed at the exposed small of her back, too close to her ass. "You won't regret it."

I already do. Shea shivered the moment he made contact. No man had touched her there except Eric. Even Murphy had been careful while they'd danced. Reaching behind her, Shea latched onto Carlson's wrist and moved his palm up higher. "Why, Mr. Carlson, you're very fresh."

He seemed deaf, but then his gaze was fastened to her plumped-up *Jessica Rabbit* boobs. *No. Chance. In. Hell.*

Unfortunately, the music kicked into a tango, her least favorite dance with a stranger. Had he somehow orchestrated this number? She knew the steps and the sizzle intended to go with them. The slow. The quick. The intimate way the dance partners' bodies were supposed to turn into each other with the heated tempo. But it should be Eric dancing this intimate, prelude-to-sex dance with her. It should be his knee between her legs. Not Hugh Carlson's!

"Can you feel the down beat?" he whispered hotly in her ear.

Not like I can feel the Waltham in the clutch at my wrist.

Distancing herself, Shea endured. The dance kept her close to Carlson's chest and against his muscular thighs, but her heart was one floor up with Eric. This masquerade ball felt very much like another betrayal.

"The tango is full of passion. It's primitive and wildly erotic. Hedonistic. Wouldn't you agree?" Carlson rasped, using all the right words. *Still getting nowhere.*

Shea turned her cheek to his lips, agreeing to nothing but this one dance. How she regretted coming up with this idea!

Carlson crouched just before he latched onto her waist and lifted her over his head, his hands sliding up her ribs until his thumbs anchored under her breasts.

Put me down, her heart cried. Shea gulped, feeling more like a tender morsel for a hungry lion than a dance partner. Taking a chance, she activated the tiny remote she'd kept in her palm. Her wings fluttered, turning her into a fairy. The attention they garnered didn't dissuade Carlson in the least. Instead, the other dancers stilled and clapped. Some idiot wolf-whistled. The room darkened as a spotlight sought them out. So not what she was going for.

Carlson's smile turned dark and haughty. His brow lifted as if he thought she was teasing him. As if!

A different side of the man emerged now that he was the focal point. His shoulders squared as he transformed into some exotic Latin playboy. He played the part to the hilt, lowering her sequined body slowly down the length of his until she lay at his feet. She stilled her stupid wings, wishing her jackhammering heart could cease flapping as easily.

Murphy had better have Eric and Jordan to safety by now, because he certainly wasn't sitting back and sipping a cold one. She knew. She'd checked.

Shea stalled, buying as much time as she dared while she lay there on the floor acting the part of his limp partner. Carlson was a study in showmanship. Very slowly, he dragged her up the length of his leg until she was back in his arms. "I swear I've seen you before," he breathed heavily into her face, one brow lifted. "Have we ever met?"

Oh, if you only knew. She batted her glittery, fake lashes and gave him her best, sickeningly sweet smile. "A girl can only wish."

The dance continued with a final set of slow-slow, quick-quick steps across the length of the dance floor, and there he stopped. He tipped her back until those damned wings touched the floor along with most of her fake hair. He held her in that position, his eyes darker yet. The stupid, stupid man licked his lips, as if he had a snowball's chance in hell of kissing her.

Tossing his head back, Carlson pitched the perfect Olympic ice skater pose, his arm curled over his head and his eyes on his audience. The only thing missing was a red rose in his perfect, straight teeth.

Since she had no choice, Shea let him have his moment. The applause continued while Carlson drew her back on her feet, but she dodged being pulled into his arm. The spotlight vanished as the houselights came on, but then he tipped his nose into her hair and whispered, "Take your mask off, Mrs. Hollister. For me. Must I beg?"

Beg all you want, Shea thought as she glanced to the dining room doors, her stomach lifting up her throat even as her fingers tightened around her dangerous little purse. *Where the hell are you, Murphy?*

Eric flinched at the ice-cold water splashed in his face.

"There you are. Come on son," a familiar voice murmured as a towel scrubbed over his head. "We don't have a lot of time. I'm going to lift you out of that chair you're hanging onto. Come on. Let it go."

"M-M-Murphy?"

Murphy didn't answer, just did what he'd said he'd do. Lifted Eric to his weak-kneed feet and draped Eric's arm over his shoulder. "I'd carry you if I could, but we've got to make this look like you're drunk. Can you walk at all?"

Eric bobbed his head, and God, he tried to walk, but Murphy ended up half-dragging, half-carrying him out of Carlson's suite. "W-Wait. Jordan."

"Already taken care of. Jordan's safe. Keep moving."

Two guys lay face down beside Carlson's king-sized bed. "They dead?" Eric tried his damnedest to care about Frenchy and his friend.

"Yes, now shut up. I'm supposed to be dancing with your wife, not you."

By then, they were out of Carlson's suite and halfway down the hall. Murphy leaned Eric against a wall while he called the lift. On the second level, Eric went over Murphy's shoulder in a fireman's hold. It hurt. Hell, everything hurt, but he refused to vocalize his pain on the short walk to Murphy's room.

Saving a man from the immediate battle zone often caused more damage to already existing injuries, but the groans and screams of a fellow soldier hurt a rescuer's feelings. Murphy didn't need to feel any worse than he already did.

Murphy toed the door shut and crossed the room. Very gently, he lowered Eric onto white clean sheets that weren't going to stay that way for long.

"Shea," he whispered, at last able to speak her name. "Where's Shea? Is she here?"

Murphy loosened Eric's belt and removed his boots and clothes, stripping him down to nothing but boxers. "Don't worry about your little wife. She's packin' heat, and trust me. She knows how to use it."

"How's... how's Jordan?"

"Here," Jordan answered thickly.

"He'll be fine," Murphy said. "He didn't take the beating you did, so settle down. I'm going back to get your wife, then we're leaving. Get some sleep." He dimmed the lights and left.

"You okay, bro?" Jordan's voice creaked from the other side of the bed.

"Yeah, man. I'm good." *At least, I will be when I see Shea.*

Carlson kept the façade of a rakish gentleman going as another song began, a slow dance number that agreed with Shea's aching feet. She could see how he might be a difficult man to resist. Overly attentive and silver tongued, he complimented her hair, the unique color of her eyes, her dress—her everything. But his eyeballs kept straying over her bare shoulders to her cleavage, when he wasn't ogling her exposed thigh.

Placing her right hand in his left, she accepted just one more dance, making sure to expose more of that thigh he seemed enamored with.

"Your husband doesn't deserve you," Carlson breathed into her ear, his cheek pressed too close for comfort.

"I love my husband," she answered back a definite truth.

"Then he's a lucky man." Carlson moaned. "A lucky man indeed."

She rolled her eyes. Oh, give me a break. The only reason this player had glommed onto her was his typical dumb jock vision of a naked fairy screwing the daylights out of him. There was only one man Shea planned on doing that with, but he wasn't on the dance floor.

Carlson's slick fingers slid down her back and came to rest on the exceedingly low-cut edge of her dress. *If you even touch my bottom...* Both hands sank lower until his palms cupped the globes of her ass, pressing her body in closer until she could feel—him. All of him. Through that sequined dress.

She swallowed hard. Yes, *hard* all right. Everything about this ridiculous night was *hard*. What else could she do? Run? To where? Play the offended wife? That held merit, but until Murphy returned, she needed to keep the very sophisticated tomcat at her fingertips distracted.

Lifting her face, she fluttered her stiff, fake lashes against Carlson's chin, giving him the tiniest hope. He sure as hell wasn't getting anything else. But she was fairly sure that thing in his pants had just twitched. *Eww. So not going there.* Just the thought of arousing him sent shivers over her bare arms and shoulders.

Her overly attentive dance partner murmured into the top of her head, "You're cold, Mrs. Hollister. May I ply you with a buttered rum or an Irish Coffee?"

"Why not?" She let loose a drawn-out sigh and played the offended wife. "My husband seems to have wandered off. What's a girl supposed to do with a man like that?"

Carlson ducked his head to peer into her face. "Your husband's a fool. An old fool." The tip of his tongue skated over his bottom lip. "You deserve someone more virile who can keep up with you."

Shea tightened her hold on her clutch, and without meaning to she eased back.

"It's only one kiss," he assured.

And I have a gun in my purse that will take your head off if you try. Her lungs shut down. She couldn't swallow. *Don't make me shoot you, because, trust me. I want to.*

Carlson must have misinterpreted the jackhammering in her heart for arousal. Lowering his head, he closed the distance.

Shea closed her eyes, lifted her purse, and—found herself jerked out of Carlson's grasp and those perky Jessica Rabbit boobs banging into Murphy's rock-solid chest.

"Damn it, woman. I leave you for one dance and the next thing I know, you're kissing the biggest man-whore on the planet. Am I gonna have to spank your ass again?"

Heat flamed her face at the spectacle Murphy was making, but yeah. She'd settle for a spanking from him over a kiss from Carlson any day.

Carlson's head went up as he snapped, "The day will come that she leaves you, Hollister, and I'll be waiting for her."

"Well, until it does, keep your hands off my wife. Capiche?"

Carlson stepped into Murphy's comfort zone. His chest swelled as he pulled his right arm back, but before he had the chance to strike, Murphy hauled back and decked that mouthful of straight, white teeth with a mean right hook. Something flew when Carlson's head dropped back on his spine. Could have been one of those perfect teeth.

"Murphy! Stop!" Shea shrieked, tugging Murphy's forearm like any good, little wife would, when secretly, she wanted to slap Carlson herself.

His glittering eyes mirrored encouragement until she launched herself at him. "I told you I was married, but you had to keep pawing me. You think every woman's your plaything, well, I'm not!" She stamped one six-inch stiletto to make certain she had everyone's attention. The music had stopped. Why not give his adoring fans another show? "Keep your hands off me, Mr. Hugh Carlson!"

Turning to Murphy, she hooked her hand over his arm. "Come on, honey. Let's never come back here again." She would've torn her mask off and tossed it for the sake of drama if Murphy hadn't squeezed her arm, signally her not to get too carried away. Shea turned to her *husband*. "I want to go home, honey," she whined in her best spoiled-brat imitation.

He nodded in his fatherly way, offering one last spiked brow at the billionaire before they walked away. Once out of sight, they picked up their pace.

"How is he?" Shea asked, the beat of her heart matching the clip of her heels on the hardwood floor.

"He's dazed, but he can walk. Kind of."

The fear of being caught ran with them. Shea couldn't get to their hotel room fast enough. Murphy passed the cardkey through the door lock and Shea ran inside, kicking her heels off and discarding the mask and purse on her way by the desk.

And there she froze. Tears flooded her eyes at the sight. "Eric!"

Eric gritted his teeth at the tender fingertips on his battered face. He honestly didn't know which part of him hurt the worst, but those fingers weren't helping. "Let me be."

An angel fluttered overhead. He heard the wings. Had to be an angel, didn't it? More fluttering mixed with muffled sobbing. Cool water graced his brow, and damn it. He could barely keep his bleary eyes open, much less make out what was going on.

But the fingers wouldn't leave him alone. He growled a threat to leave him alone, but they stayed. Cupping his chin. Combing through his sweaty hair. Over his pounding head. The sweetest lips touched his, and it was raining. Tears. He peeled his eyelids open, and there she was. Floating above him, a vision in red and… *wings? What the hell?*

"Shea?" he rasped. "That you?"

"I'm here," she answered, her sweet voice the best thing he'd heard in a while. "We have to move, Eric. Can you walk at all?"

"Sure," he lied. To prove it, he barely lifted his head.

"I'll take him," Murphy said, firmly pulling Eric to the edge of the bed. He eased him into a bathrobe, then onto his feet and over his shoulder. "Get Jordan up. Let's move."

And move they did. Out the door and down the hall, then to an elevator. This wasn't exactly how Eric saw himself leaving the grand estate, but he was humble enough to accept the rescue. He ended up in the rear of Murphy's truck on the foam mattress. Damn. Even softness hurt. Shea climbed in beside him with a hurried, "Ready."

"Rolling," Murphy announced as he hit the ignition. The truck rumbled. Lights flickered past the windows, creating shadows and light that both did a number on Eric's eyes. He closed them to the soothing touch of Shea's fingers.

"I'm good," he assured her, wishing he could prove it.

"Yes, you are," breathed against his cheek.

While Murphy drove, Shea cleaned and bandaged what she could reach. Her touch almost made everything worthwhile. The scent of antiseptic filled the truck. The sound of Irish ballads as well. Eric drifted, safe in the knowledge that Murphy was one of the best covert operators the Vietnam War had produced. Damned if Aishling wasn't there, too. He heard her; he just couldn't see her. The truck swayed and hummed until it finally came to a halt. No lights. No sounds. Just Shea kneeling at his side.

"Where's my cat?" Eric asked.

"She's back at Murphy's, remember?" Shea answered.

"Take it easy," Murphy muttered, his voice more gentle than Eric had never heard. "I'm going to pull you out of the truck now. I've got a wheelchair, so we'll go slow."

Shit, I'm hurt that bad? Eric doubted it, but he went willingly. The wheelchair bumped along a dark concrete path and up to a small thatch-roofed cottage.

"Wait. Where are we?" he asked at the door he didn't recognize. This wasn't Murphy's place. What was going on?

But over the threshold they went, into the soft golden glow of a kerosene lamp set on a sturdy wooden table. Had to be someone's hunting cottage. Primitive. Almost rustic. A strange man stepped out of the shadows. "Is this the patient?"

"Yes," Murphy replied. "Eric Reynolds, one of my agents."

"Bring him this way," the man waved them into the adjoining room where Jordan already sat on the edge of the bed, a blonde nurse at his side.

"Where's Shea?" Eric asked.

"Right here," Shea answered while Murphy lifted him out of the chair and got him situated on the bed. But Eric couldn't sit, so Murphy leaned him back onto the pillow and lifted his feet off the floor. Eric bit his lip as his clothes were removed and the lights dimmed. This was so much bullshit. All he needed was a good night's rest, and he'd be better.

Ah, ha. So he had seen an angel in red. Shea was wearing that dress. But wings? Those were new. He blinked to be sure his lying eyes were telling the truth. "Didn't you have wings before?"

"I did, but I got Bagani," she said, her pretty eyes dark blue with unshed tears.

"How?" He wanted to care more than he did.

"Like I said," Murphy cut in. "This little woman has a few tricks up her sleeve. By the time she was through with Bagani and Carlson, they were damned glad to get away from her."

"Hmm," Eric breathed, his eyes closed once more. *Where's my cat? She was just here. I swear.*

"Carlson will be hunting for us, though," Murphy worried. "Not like I give a shit. I've got a round with his name on it if I ever see him again."

"Me, too," Eric whispered, wanting to hear more, but fading fast.

The last thing he felt was Shea's tender lips on his swollen, mashed mouth. "I love you, Eric."

He groaned his *I love you* back to her, hoping she could translate. A tiny sting hit his left bicep. The pain in his chest lessened as his lungs filled with air. The dark reached out and Eric drifted away to a land of talking blue-eyed cats and angels in sparkling red.

A man could get used to—breathing.

CHAPTER TWENTY-SIX

Shea wiped her tears. Eric's two broken ribs were now banded and the excess blood had been siphoned out of his lungs through an incision the doctor made between two of his ribs. The poor man would have more scars than he deserved, but Eric breathed easier now. The oxygen cannula strapped to his face made sure of that.

Eric's physical fitness had served him well. For the most part, he needed rest and time to heal. The kindly Irish doctor, a close personal friend of Murphy's, assured Shea that all would be well.

The nurse, Miss Day, was a godsend. Young and athletic, she seemed an efficient woman who expected people to do what they were told so she could do what she did best: Keeping these two men alive. She wore her hair in a short bob, the back cut high, the front longer. Tiny red freckles dotted her pixie nose. Blue eyes. Her nurse's uniform was different than the ones Stateside. Tan slacks. Tan button-up shirt. Some kind of a gold pin on her collar.

Jordan said he'd passed out when Carlson's thugs injected him with the truth serum. That explained why they hadn't made the same mistake with Eric. But because he hadn't talked like they'd wanted, they'd beat him. Shea doubted those

Legionnaires got anything useful, though. Eric could be stubborn when he set his mind to it.

She'd finally changed out of Moira's gown and into the borrowed clothes Murphy had thoughtfully brought along. He'd proved the true mastermind behind the dubious success of this operation. Not only had he packed extra clothes, he'd also fed and watered Aishling before they'd left his home near Cashel. The man truly believed in being prepared.

The early morning sunlight filtered through the window. No sounds of busy traffic or other mechanical noises lifted to her ears, only the chatter of nosy jackdaws and the melodic whistles of finches.

Standing outside Eric and Jordan's room, Shea stared at the lovely scene while her brain worked the never-ending puzzle of this operation. Bagani was the motorcycle rider who'd chased her and Eric. He wasn't the money behind Abdul-Mutaal. Then who was? Surely not Carlson. Yes, he could certainly hire as many assassins as he wanted, but he had his Legionnaires, what was left of them, to do his dirty work for him.

Shea couldn't shake the disquiet lurking in the back of her mind that she'd missed something important, that all was not as it seemed. Other than Bagani, she had no link to anyone from the Mideast, so why had Abdul-Mutaal killed Phoenix and Gordie to get at her? What was the link she wasn't seeing?

The warm hand on her shoulder drew her back to the cottage. "Well, Mrs. Hollister, what do you think?"

Shea tipped the side of her head to Murphy's broad shoulder. "I think it'd be nice to be Mrs. Reynolds again."

"Don't worry. Eric will be able to fly in a few days. Jordan can now, but I'm guessing you'd rather go home with the right man."

"Yes, I'm ready." She sighed, never so sure of anything in her life. She would still be inside with Eric and Jordan, but Miss Day had ushered her out to give both men a much-needed sponge bath.

Eric had yet to open his eyes after his surgery. Shea counted him lucky not to have suffered a collapsed lung. As it was, he should've been admitted to a hospital, but somehow, Murphy knew all the right people.

The door creaked open behind them. "You can see him now," Miss Day announced.

Shea turned away from Murphy to go to her husband's side. Eric had lost a shade of his handsome tan overnight, but his eyes were open. Black and blue. Swollen. A little red where the white should've been. But open.

He lifted a weak hand and let it drop back to the blanket covering him. "Murphy says you've got skills. Talk to me. What happened?"

Twining her fingers with his, she went over her encounter with Bagani, hitting the highlights, but making sure Eric knew Bagani was now incarcerated. Next came the story of the Tango with Carlson. Disgust rippled up her spine knowing what she knew now. For two cents, Shea wanted to go back in time and shoot Carlson the second he'd laid a finger on her.

Eric's eyes grew heavy, but he still squeezed her fingers. "Love you," he whispered.

She laid her head gently on his bandaged shoulder, needing to be closer to him than his condition allowed. "Not as much as I love you."

He huffed, on his way back to sleep. "You owe me a dance. In a red dress. With wings."

Shea placed a soft kiss on his lips. "Count on it."

Eric lost track of time. The only constants in his current state of delirium were a beautiful elf in a shiny red dress that took extra special care of him, and, oh yeah, a cat that talked. Aishling came up with the weirdest things, assuring him he'd live one moment, then saying something off the wall like, "Gordie's back," the next. Even a delirious man with a fever knew headless guys just didn't do *that*.

At last Eric woke. The room spun and damned if that black cat wasn't sitting square in the middle of his chest. He peeled his gritty eyes open and stared at her.

Aishling purred, her pretty blue eyes half-open, as if too comfortable to stir. Her nose twitched. "Avoid travel," she whispered in a soft, kittenish voice. Half air. Half make-believe.

He wrinkled his whole face at that nonsensical comment. There was no logic to anything this cat said. Talking felines? Just plain weird.

"Go away," he groaned, wishing he had the strength to put her back in that Harley saddlebag.

"Ah, you're up." Shea lifted out of the nearby chair. "What did you say?"

He closed his eyes and shook his head. "This cat talks, you know. She's bugging me."

Shea leaned over him and planted a kiss on his forehead. "What cat? There's no cat here. Aishling is back at Murphy's. How many times do I have to tell you that?"

Eric patted his chest with both hands. Sure enough. Aishling was gone. Damned good thing. He shoved a hand over his face, needing a shave and an aspirin for his headache. "What's that smell?"

"Gun cleaner," Shea whispered, nodding toward the open bedroom door. "Jordan's obsessed. He's cleaned your weapons three times already this morning."

Eric lifted his head to view his buddy just outside the doorway. The poor guy looked like shit with his arm in a sling and one black eye. But damn, he was earnestly absorbed in his work, his head bent over a disassembled pistol.

It was called field stripping, the process of partially disassembling a weapon to clean it. A man broke his rifle or pistol into its biggest components: barrel, slide, rod guide, frame, and magazine. Then, with cleaning rods and bore brushes, little wads of patches and solvent, each piece got meticulously scrubbed until those patches came out clean and mostly dry. Then lubricants. There wasn't much to it, unless a guy developed a titch of hyper-awareness and over-compensated by cleaning the same four weapons over and over again. Like Jordan was doing.

Obviously, he needed to focus on a work well done, even a simple job. That was why he cleaned and re-cleaned. It was his way of putting the past behind him.

Simple logic. After every mission failure, lost battle, or loss of life on the warfront, when a guy was feeling like crap and his squad was sure they were a bunch of losers, their commander called them together. Sometimes they got their butts chewed. Sometimes the chaplain was there to talk about—stuff. But after that come-to-Jesus hard line meeting? The CO assigned hours, maybe days, of menial, back breaking labor. Housework. Scrubbing barracks, walls and floors. Swabbing decks. Redundant FOD walks on desert AF tarmacs. Simple chores, done right always restored confidence and boosted moral at the end of a blistering, sweaty day. Any jarhead knew that.

Shea busied herself helping Miss Day in the kitchen. Delicious aromas overcame some of the smell of the solvent. Bread baking. Some kind of soup, maybe chicken noodle.

Eric pushed his tired bones up from the bed where he'd lain too long. He needed away from the smell of solvent. By the time he'd pulled on a clean pair of jeans and shrugged into a dark blue T-shirt, he could barely manage a slow shuffle to the bedroom door.

Shea came to his side, one arm at his waist, the other on his chest to hold him steady. "You're up."

"For now. Sit outside with me?"

No sooner said than done. Miss Day took over kitchen duties while Shea dragged a chair outside. Shuffling past Jordan and his gun cleaning station, Eric paused. "How's it goin'?"

Jordan grunted without looking up. "Almost done."

"You ought to do this outside. Come on. The fresh air would do you good. Join me and Shea for a breather."

"Nah." He wiped the clean pistol in his hand with a soft cloth before he lifted his eyes. "I didn't give you up, bro. I wouldn't do that to you, at least I don't think I did."

Eric waved the apology off. "I don't hold grudges, not when truth serum kicked both of our butts."

Jordan pushed off the floor, his emotions etched on his face. Instead of a handshake, he pulled Eric into a man hug. They slapped each other's backs, and Eric winced, but called it good. "Is one of those clean enough for me?"

"Sure." Jordan clapped a full magazine into one of the pistols and handed it over, grip first. "Yours. Loaded. Ready to go."

Eric tucked the weapon in his waistband and gave Jordan a fist bump on his way to all that fresh air. "How many days have we been here?" he asked Shea.

"Just three."

"Three's too many." He dropped his butt into the chair on the porch, tired of being sick and sick of being tired. A man needed to work to stay sharp, damn it.

Shea lowered to the top step of the porch. Tipping back, she peered into the kitchen. "Dinner's almost ready. Are you hungry?"

He nodded, grumpier than he'd expected. "Think we can walk to the road and back first?"

She bounced to her feet, a genuine light in her eyes. "Sure. Ready?"

And that was another thing. He hadn't felt a single spark for his wife since he'd gotten beat up, and it bugged him. He wanted his old mojo back, every last inch of it. Groaning out of his chair, Eric kept both palms on the armrests like an old man with bad knees. Finally upright, he wobbled, but damn it. *This weakness bullshit stops here.*

It took an extra minute to take that one step to the ground, but Shea was patient. Didn't that irk him too? He didn't want a nurse. He wanted his woman. In bed.

The afternoon sun had grown warm. By the time he'd gone a few feet, Eric felt better. Straightening his back, he cocked his elbow like a gentleman, and he took his pretty wife for a real walk. "You like Ireland," he observed.

"I do. Right now it's peaceful and everything's green. Ireland has as many wild flowers as Washington State. And look at the wild rhododendrons. They grow two stories tall here." She pointed to the cascade of purple flowers to their left, her voice filled with contentment.

"Shea. Look at me."

"Yes?"

Warmth flooded his chest, the good kind of warmth. "Nothing baby. I just wanted to see those pretty eyes. For a while there, I thought I might never see them again." He zeroed in on a post at the side of the road, his turning point.

She clenched her fingers around his. "Murphy went to the market to buy a pregnancy test kit. I want to know if we're going to be parents."

Just hearing the excitement in her voice lit a familiar fire in his belly. "You're ready?"

She nodded. "Yes. I want us to be a family. Will you marry me?"

That took his breath. He stopped short to tug her under his arm. "I never signed those divorce papers, baby. We're still married."

Those pretty turquoise pools turned misty. "But I think it automatically takes effect after a while if you don't sign it, doesn't it?"

He wrapped her up in his arms. "I don't know and I don't care. I never agreed to divorce you, so there."

A cry hit the back of her throat and suddenly, his body sprang to attention. She clutched his chin and tilted up on her tiptoes to reach his mouth. Threading his fingers through her short hair, he reeled her in to his lips. *God, I hope we're pregnant.*

They kissed. More like they devoured each other. She tried to be gentle, but her rowdy nature kept getting in the way. Eric wanted to pick her up, but his broken ribs protested too much. At last, he came to his senses. There was no convenient place to lay her down and molest her from head to toe. He had to calm his raging hard-on for now.

Easing her feet back to the ground, he murmured, "I want you" to let her know this was not over. Just postponed.

A lighthearted giggle lifted out of her. "Miss Day will be wondering where we sneaked off to."

"Let's head back."

He'd no more than faced the cottage when a creepy feeling slithered up the back of his neck. The rule was simple. If you sensed you were being watched, you probably were. "Go to the cottage," he ordered, his inner sniper on high alert. He shook her fingers free and grabbed his pistol. "Run, Shea. Go! Now!"

"But—"

"But nothing?" He stabbed a finger at the cottage. "Get inside!"

The bullet came out of nowhere. Eric never heard it. One tap to the head. Just like he would've done.

"Let me go!" Shea screamed, throwing her elbows into the muscled wall behind her. She was desperate to reach Eric before he died. "Jordan! Help me! Help!"

An idling engine sounded nearby. A gloved hand covered her mouth. The man who'd grabbed her grunted when her elbow connected with his throat. She threw another, but had no traction, not off the ground like she was.

Jordan's angry face appeared at the cottage window, then at the door. "Shea!"

Miss Day ran to his side, a shotgun in her hands.

The idling engine drew closer.

A black bag descended over Shea's head, and still she struggled. The brute that had hold of her shoved her to her knees into a vehicle. She hit the seat face first before he laid a solid hand on her ass and pushed her to the floor.

The door slammed just as Jordan hit the side of the vehicle. "Give her back!"

A gun discharged. Then another. Shea cringed. *Not Jordan! Please not Jordan, too!*

Panic climbed up her throat. Thrashing, Shea was still determined to run, but her kidnapper caught her left wrist and twisted it behind her back. Then her right. He snapped something onto each wrist, and she was immobilized.

An awful scent filled her nose. She'd come across it just once in her life. *Blood.*

She'd been caught by the man in the black robe, Abdul-Mutaal.

The vehicle came to a grinding halt when another gunshot sounded, and Shea dared to hope. But then it roared forward, fishtailing as it screeched onto asphalt.

Then she knew where she was going. Straight to Hell.

CHAPTER TWENTY-SEVEN

"Then tell me what happened," Murphy demanded somewhere off in the ether. "Because no one—NO ONE!—should've been able to find this place. It's not on any maps, damn it! Not a one!"

Cuss, cuss. Swear, swear. Murphy was one angry son-of-a-bitch. He kept stabbing at Jordan's chest. Jordan kept backing up. Didn't seem to matter. Murphy clearly wanted to fight someone. "Pull your head out of your ass, Hannigan. Are you a black operator or not! You were supposed to keep her safe, not let them get her."

Eric lifted his head, dizzy, and not sure why it felt as if it had split wide open and all his brains were poured out. He pushed up from the bed, needing to know what had pissed Murphy off. His words kept rolling in Eric's skull like a penny in one of those department store games that goes around and around.

Keep her safe.

Keep her safe.

Keep her safe.

"Shea!" He jumped to his feet. Not a good idea. The floor bucked beneath him, but he stayed upright. Clinging to the wall, but good enough. "Where is she?"

Murphy turned on him. "Why the hell did you have her outside? What are you, Superman? Hell, I almost lost you, too. Could've lost all three of you damned stupid kids! What were you thinking?"

Eric had no answer. Murphy needed to pick a spot and hold still. Jordan, too. The two of them kept bobbing like prizefighters. It took a few seconds to realize that he was the problem. Dropping to his knees, Eric rolled to his butt before he fell down. He'd been shot, his hard head grazed. *Upper left quadrant. Stitches. Ice pack. Painkillers.*

"Where is she?" he bellowed until his head split wider at the sound of his own roar.

Murphy crouched at his side. "Now, take it easy, son. You've been shot and—"

"Where is she?" Eric demanded more quietly, sick of the bullshit. "Tell me."

Sucking in a deep breath, Murphy let it go in a huff. "She's gone, damn it. I'm sorry, but she's gone, and I don't have a stinkin' idea where they've taken her."

"Who did it?"

Murphy lowered his gaze to the floor. "I don't rightly know, son. Jordan tried to stop the car. Mercedes. SUV. V-8. Bronze."

"You get a plate?" Eric knew better than to ask.

Jordan hadn't yet shaken off the effects of the truth serum overdose. He shook his head, his eyes wide with guilt. "I got to her as soon as I heard the gunshot, but he already had her inside the car."

"Who, damn it?"

"A big guy. Mideastern. Dark skinned like… like…"

Shit. "Like Abdul-Mutaal?" Eric asked, his voice thin and brittle.

"Yes," Jordan croaked. "Only I don't think it was him. Look." He handed Murphy a dried piece of a branch and Murphy passed it to Eric.

Something tan smudged one whole side of it. "What is this?"

"Grease paint. You know. Make-up," Jordan answered. "Whoever that bastard is, he just wants us to think he's Mideastern. Whoever killed your wife's friends staged it. He's not the real ISIS leader."

"Their deaths sure as hell weren't staged," Eric snapped. "Neither were the tortures."

Jordan shoved both hands over his head and down the back of his neck. "God, I'm sorry. It all happened so fast. I shot at the driver, but bulletproof glass, man. Elsa fired, too. These guys were prepared. The back windows were blacked out. No license plates, either. They knew exactly how this had to go down."

And now that bastard has Shea.

"Elsa?" Eric asked, his brain throbbing.

"Miss Day. The nurse," Jordan answered.

Another sledgehammer coursed through Eric's hard head. He lowered his chin to his clenched hands, both elbows on his knees. Weary as hell. He did the only thing a desperate man could do. Eric pushed up off the floor, dizzy and spent, but focused on getting Shea back.

Breathing hard, he planted his feet to shake off the nausea that accompanied the minor concussion of a head wound. A man kept going, damn it. Cocking his head at Murphy, he growled, "I need one AR, and an eight-inch blade. Extra ammo. You got 'em?"

Murphy knew better than to argue. He opened what looked like a basement door just off the kitchen and disappeared through it.

Eric held out his palm to Jordan. "My pistols. Extra mags. Now."

Jordan scooped them up from the floor, the pistols already tucked in a double holster. "I'm coming with."

"I was hoping you'd say that," Eric growled as he slid the holster over his shoulders.

Murphy was back by then with more weapons than what Eric had requested. Apparently he thought he was part of this op, too. He spread them on the kitchen table with an apology to Miss Day and a curt, "I'll be in touch."

She nodded, but didn't obey. "You'd better have a holster there for me."

Eric looked at her then. Diminutive, but athletic. Close to the same height and weight of Shea. Bright blonde hair. Blue-eyed. A dimple in her right cheek. Drab gray scrubs. *She'd taken a shot at the getaway vehicle?*

"Who are you?" He had to know.

Her chin lifted as she stared him in the eye. "Miss Day to most people, but Elsa Finnegan to my friends. Uncle Murphy's my dad's brother. You didn't think I was just a nurse, did you?"

Eric looked to Murphy, but the old guy just shrugged. "I told you I like to be prepared."

That actually explained a lot. Eric stiffened his spine for the chore that lay ahead. He needed Shea's tech-savvy skills now more than ever. Using the landline, he called one of the only other hackers he could think of.

Mother picked up on the first ring.

"Find Hugh Carlson for me," he ordered.

"Yes, Eric," she replied without her customary nosy questions. "Hold please."

"What are you thinking?" Jordan asked. "That Carlson tracked us here?"

"No way," Murphy groused. "I checked before we left the castle. He couldn't have. My truck is clean. There was no tracking device stuck to it anywhere. Check it again if you don't believe me."

Eric nodded once at Jordan to go and do just that. A tracking device would pin Carlson's ass to the wall. "Take a flashlight. It's dark out there."

Elsa took the hint and grabbed a flashlight out of the kitchen drawer and tossed it to Jordan. He caught it in midair and left through the front door.

"Carlson's at Shannon Airport," Mother reported in his ear.

Murphy stabbed the speaker button on the phone so all could hear.

Eric's chest squeezed off. "Do you have any way to view Shannon's security monitors? What flight's he on? Is there a way to stop him?"

"Ember's online with their security system now. They may not like it, but they're about to be—"

"Hack 'em, damn it." Eric's patience evaporated along with his opinion of hacking.

Ember's voice came on the line. "Hey, Eric. Don't worry. I've got him on my monitor. He's standing at an Air France gate. It boards in ten, oh, wait. It's been cancelled, darn it. Wow. I don't know how *that* happened."

Eric could've kissed mother's genius assistant. She'd just manipulated Shannon's scheduling system and cancelled Carlson's flight. "Thanks," he murmured. "Keep his ass in Ireland 'til I say he can leave."

"What's going on?" Ember asked, her tone filled with genuine concern. "Does he have Shea?" God, the woman was psychic. Alex must've updated his team, at least his two techies.

"Yes," Eric ground out. "I think. Is anyone with him?"

"No female. Just a beefy bodyguard in a beret and desert cammies. I'm checking the cargo hold, just in case."

He hadn't a clue how she could do that, but good on her. Thermal imaging came to mind. Ember had a world of resources at her fingertips. Assholes were known to smuggle children and women in trunks after they'd drugged them for the sex trade. He squeezed his heart closed at the other things criminals did to their victims.

"All clear in the cargo hold," she said after a couple of endlessly long minutes. "I've tagged him for constant surveillance, though. Don't worry. We'll find Shea. Mother needs a word with you."

"Eric, I'm rechecking all satellite imagery from last night and today. Give me your global position and tell me the last time you were with your wife."

My wife. God, he's got my wife! Eric gulped, this conversation getting tougher with every personal question asked.

Murphy offered precise coordinates quickly, giving Mother what she needed to hone in on Eric's location on those satellite images, and hopefully, Shea.

"This might take a second…" Mother drew out her last word, and Eric knew without a doubt he had The TEAM at his six.

"I can't believe she fooled me all these months," Mother murmured. "Ember just input her pretty face into our facial rec program, too. We will find her, Eric."

He couldn't speak. He'd seen the fake Abdul-Mutaal's work. What would that bastard do to a woman as sweet as Shea?

"Thanks," Murphy spoke up, his voice gruff and no nonsense. He read off a list he'd written on his hand. "Those are burner phones. Keep us informed, you gals."

"Eric," Mother called out before he hung up.

"Here."

"Shea's a very intelligent woman. She's the only reason you're there now. Remember that."

He clenched his jaw. *Tell me something I don't know.*

"Keep your phone in your shirt pocket. It won't take long to run back through these images now that I know who I'm looking for. I *will* be contacting you soon." Mother hung up just as Jordan returned. He slumped into the house. Gray-faced. Holding one hand to his chest.

"What now?" Eric snapped.

"I was under the truck looking for any tracking devices when I saw it." Jordan blocked the entrance with his arm. "W-w-watching me. Don't go out there."

Murphy made it to Jordan first, but Eric pushed past them both, needing to know what the hell his buddy was talking about. He didn't get far. There on the ground behind Murphy's truck…

Facing the cottage…

Staring…

Fuck! That damned Aishling was right. Gordie Mikkelson *was* back. At least, his missing head was.

CHAPTER TWENTY-EIGHT

They killed him! God, they killed him!

Shea sat alone in the dark, scared for her life, and shivering with her heart crushed. Her wrists were bound behind her back with a sturdy Flexi-Cuff, the kind police and military the world over used to subdue their prisoners. It worked.

She'd kicked like hell when the man who'd abducted her took her boots and dragged her out of the vehicle by her ankles, scraping her butt and shoulder blades against the gravel. She'd bucked and cursed him when he tossed her down several stairs and into an earthen cellar. But there was no way to fight the chill of an Irish midnight. Or the despair welling up inside.

It didn't matter now if she lived or died anyway. What was the use? In a little over two years, she'd lost both Cheyenne and Eric. She'd seen the hit to his head, and the blood. She'd watched Eric fall while trying to protect her even though he should've been in bed. He would've still been safe in America if not for—*me.*

Shea gulped against the tears still pouring down her face. The spiral of grief she'd been caught in had finally delivered her to this lowest point. She'd only been lower once before, on that beach when she'd thought she'd seen Cheyenne.

Even now she wasn't sure she hadn't. A mind played terrible tricks when a person was at the end of their rope, but that beautiful trick was a once-in-a-lifetime kind of trick. It wasn't happening once more. Cheyenne's sweet ghost wouldn't suddenly appear in this cellar like the ghost of Christmas Past. There was no happily ever after. Only regret.

"I'm sorry," she whispered to her child and husband. "This is all my fault."

She'd expected threats or bragging once Abdul-Mutaal had finally caught her, but the creep hadn't spoken a single word. Not even a grunt once he'd forced her to the floor of that car. Neither had the driver.

Throughout the hour-long drive, Mideastern music had played loudly, probably to mask the traffic noises. She'd expected to be beaten or beheaded at the first chance, but the man in the backseat, whom she assumed was Mutaal, had only trapped her to the floor with his boot on her neck. Nothing else.

There was no crack around the door to let in a glimmer of light. No windows. After all she'd shared with Eric, sitting alone in this concrete prison seemed her just reward. To die in the dark with a splitting headache from crying.

Her heart hurt, making little sucking pains in her chest like it couldn't catch its breath, either. Like a fish out of water, gasping for air. A heart out of time. A dying soul without its mate.

Shea bowed her chin to her chest and let the bitterness of her mistakes drip down her cheeks. Life had played an awfully cruel trick on her. It let her think she'd been forgiven, then dashed her hopes in a most cruel comeuppance.

The scene back at the cottage replayed. Shea hadn't been able to let go of Eric's hand until he'd shaken her off and yelled, "Run, Shea. Go! Now!"

He'd wasted his last breath. *On me.* At the end of everything, he'd thought only of—*me.*

"He wanted me to live," she told the spirit of her daughter. "You wanted me to live that day on the beach, too. That other little girl only brought you to me, but I know it was a message from you. You're who saved me."

Shea stilled.

"You wanted me to live," she told her dead husband. To simply give up now because everything seemed bleak was an insult to his final gift. It seemed an impossible feat to hold on to hope in such awful circumstances, but Eric had laid down his life to save her.

"I'm going to live," she whispered to herself with no hope of rescue. No hope but—*me.*

Shea wiped the tears away on her arms and shoulder. Her captors had already made a mistake when they'd given her too much time to think. Her sorrow distilled into anger. Then revenge. If she couldn't have the people she loved in her life, at least she could avenge them. The pig that'd murdered Eric was going to pay.

Pushing to her knees, then one foot, Shea lifted to her feet. Sitting there and waiting to die was a waste of whatever time she had left. Cheyenne and Eric had rescued her for a reason, and if they believed in her...

There had to be a way out of this cellar.

Bumping along with nothing but her bicep and butt for tactile sensation, she found that three of the four walls in the cellar were concrete. The other was a slanted wooden door, five steps up. What did Murphy like to say? Time's a-wasting? *No shit.*

Shea repeated the drill, using the side of her face as well as her body to feel for that one flaw in this prison. *There has to be one. No plan is foolproof.*

Again, she came up with nothing. The concrete walls were smooth and cold. The stairs rough sawn wood. Panic flared. Time was not only wasting, but running out.

On her third attempt, she rubbed harder against the walls, and she moved slower, using every exposed cell and nerve as she turned herself into one giant sensor, carefully molding her flesh to the divots and textures of the concrete in hopes of—anything. At last, near the door, something dug into her bicep. She jerked away from it, thrilled to be bleeding if it meant freedom.

Backing into the doorjamb, she lifted both bound hands to feel for that sharp thing again. A slender piece of what felt like rusted metal met her fingertips. Less than a half-inch of it extended past the wooden jamb, but the top edge was sharp. *It just might work.*

The awkward angle of the slanted door was problematic. Shea had to stand backward on the highest step, bent at the waist with her bound arms raised behind her, leaning forward to reach the metal. Off balance and dizzy with nothing to focus on, but—well, nothing—she shifted her butt against the door to anchor herself.

Hooking the plastic cuff over the sharp edge, she tilted forward and backward just enough to work the Flexi-Cuff over the jagged slip of metal. It took a while, and she kept her ears tuned on high alert for any sounds of her captors returning.

At last, the cuff gave, a blessed relief to her numb shoulders, shaking legs, and aching back. Encouraged at this small success, she straightened and tossed the plastic restraint aside. The cramped cellar didn't seem so cold anymore.

After another nervous search of walls, floors, and ceiling—with fingers and hands this time—she knew exactly how to escape. The wooden joists overhead were reachable. Nearly a foot deep, the space between the parallel boards was a good foot wide, the perfect nook for a woman with no feminine curves to hide between. On top of that good fortune, the space over the cellar door offered a six-inch shelf above the doorjamb. All she had to do was climb up there and keep quiet until someone came along and let her out.

Then, if her luck held out, she could get the drop on him. Or them. Shea dropped to her hands and knees. A slim chance was still a chance, damn it. What did Eric always say? Keep on keeping on? Good enough.

Clinging to his USMC mantra, she fluttered her fingers over the floor to locate the discarded cuff. It wasn't much of a weapon, but it might make the difference between life and death. *Got it. Great!*

Satisfied she'd done all she could, she stuck the cuff into her pants pocket. Using the overhead joist for leverage, she pulled one knee onto it, then braced her body into the long narrow space that would serve as her final hiding place. Her one slim chance.

Tucked in tight, she laced what was left of the Flexi-Cuff through her fingers with the sharp edges sticking out. It wasn't a knife, and she couldn't kill anyone with it, but it could scratch a face or an eyeball. That was all this insane escape plan was about anyway. Buying time. Getting a head start. *After all, I'm good at running.*

If all she accomplished tonight was to escape, she promised herself that somehow, Abdul-Mutaal *would* die, and she—Mrs. Eric Reynolds—would keep on keeping on.

It was Elsa who elbowed past Eric and Murphy to deal with the grotesque discovery. Lifting the rope tied around Mikkelson's forehead, she set it inside a large, zip-lock plastic bag and marched back into the cottage.

Eric stepped aside and let her enter. She went straight to the refrigerator, opened the sliding freezer drawer, and deposited the grisly package. Turning, she peeled the gloves off her hands and dropped them into the trash receptacle. With a cocky toss of her blonde head, she dusted her palms together and stared the men down. "There. That's done. We know two things. We have substantial evidence and Abdul-Mutaal doesn't keep trophies. He meant that little display to shock you. Did it, boys?"

Well, yeah. It took Eric a minute to shake the shock and horror off. Jordan had fled to the head, umm, bathroom, and, at the moment, Eric couldn't come up with one good reason why the Navy used *head* for any-damned-thing.

"What now?" Elsa prodded, her brows lifted. "Anyone else need to puke their guts up or can we get down to business?"

Damn. She was heartless in a sneaky, smart way. Eric recognized another black operator when he saw one. "Who'd you work for before you became a nurse? The IRA?"

She lifted one brow. "Now why would you think I worked with them?"

"Because you're good." *Too good.* The Irish coat of arms, the gold harp against a dark blue shield on the wall behind her, suddenly took on a different meaning. As did the tricolor flag of green, white, and orange displayed above the front door of this quaint little cottage. "What exactly does that mean to you?" he asked, pointing to the Gaelic inscribed below the flag.

Murphy slapped Eric's back. "Don't ask questions you don't want to know the answers to, son."

"*Fe Mhoid Bheith Saor.*" The Gaelic rolled off Elsa's tongue without hesitation. "*Sworn to be Free.*" Something about that tilt to her chin declared it was more than just a national motto to Elsa. It sounded like her *Pledge of Allegiance.*

Eric nodded, not wanting to get her hackles up. He was plenty touchy about how some people in the States treated his flag, too. "You Irish Army or Air Corps?"

Her stance softened. "Neither."

"G2?" Eric couldn't resist baiting her, just a little. The G2 was the Irish Army's top-secret intelligence section during World War II. Their claim to fame grew out of their uncanny detective skills at locating and arresting German Nazi spies. He was pretty sure the G2 was still around.

Elsa winked, her way of neither admitting nor denying.

And suddenly, they were four operators—if Jordan could stop hugging the porcelain.

Eric took a seat at the kitchen table, his head pounding like a mother and his stomach as queasy as his buddy's. "Listen up. We know where Carlson is. Mother will keep an eye on him, but I doubt Ember will find Shea soon enough with her facial rec program. It's up to us."

He rubbed the side of his head where he'd been grazed. Elsa must have taken that as a hint. She kicked back into nursing mode and retrieved what she needed to clean and bandage the wound. She offered him several tablets and ordered him to, "Swallow."

He tossed his head back and downed the tablets dry while she cleansed and re-bandaged his wounds. "Our only hope is what Mother finds on the satellite images. We wait, unless…" he turned to Murphy, "you know something I don't. You're the one who's always prepared. Where do you think Abdul took her?"

Jordan joined them at the table. A little shaky. A little embarrassed. But functional.

Murphy pursed his lips. "I don't think they can get her off the island unless they have a private plane. I've got people watching all the airstrips. They move her, I'll know."

"And?" Eric pushed.

Elsa intervened. "And I've alerted all Irish Defence Forces. They already have eyes in the air and on the ground searching for her."

Eric nodded. "Good to know. Thanks."

"And if Mutaal intends to punish her the way he did her college buddies, he'd need the location and the privacy."

Eric growled. *Not much help, Murph.* Brutality happened anywhere and everywhere. Even Catholic churches and rectories weren't safe anymore.

"But," Elsa said as she took her place at the table, "I don't believe Mutaal abducted her just to hurt her. Somehow, he's made the connection that Shea is Finn. He wants her for a specific reason, which is why he killed to get at her in the first place. I find it unreasonable that he'd kill her the moment he got his hands on her."

That made scary, painful sense.

"So you need to tell us," Murphy slanted his body to Eric. "What has Shea been up to the last two years since she ran away? I know about the booze and the hacking. She's got a talent the folks at Quantico would love to get their hands on. We've already dealt with her friend Bagani back at Ashford. What else?"

God. What else was there? Eric shook his head. He didn't know, but he knew someone who might. "Give me the house phone."

Mother picked up on the first ring. "Yes, Eric?"

"You taught Shea to hack," he said pointblank. "Is there any way you shared files or something? Can you tell me where she is?"

Dead silence.

"Damn it, Mother! I know you taught her how to get into bank accounts. Talk to me. I need to know everyone she hacked and who she stole from. Can you help me or not?"

"Aww shit!" was the last thing Eric expected to come of out of Mother's mouth. "She wouldn't have."

"She wouldn't have what?" His heart rate spiked. What the hell had Shea done now?

"Hold," Mother barked before he had a chance to stop her.

She put me on hold! Now? At the worst time of my life!

She came back on the line before he could mentally curse her. "She only stole from Bagani, but Eric. I'm scanning some of her files now, you know, the ones she sent me for safe keeping. I swear, that wife of yours has a data bank for a brain. Anyway, my new anti-virus software picked up a piece of code she probably didn't notice she had, not with her limited operating system. It's a tracking malware that replicates itself. Anytime she activated an executable file, whoever infected her computer with that malware, knew precisely where she was, and what she was doing."

"Who?" he asked. "Abdul-Mutaal?"

"There's no way to tell. Let me try something though. Just... hold... on..."

Eric buried his forehead in his hand, not sure what hurt worse, his head, his broken ribs, or his heart. That malware might explain how Mutaal had caught up with Shea. He'd zeroed in on her at Murphy's home in Cashel, then again outside of Ashford. Once he had a visual, he knew who Finn was, and any covert operator could've followed Murphy's truck. Possibly by air. The United States military wasn't the only worldwide force with state of the art technology.

"Hang on another... second..." Mother murmured.

I am so fucking tired of hanging on.

"I've hacked, umm, excuse me, I've *broken* his algorithm. He's got a—damn, I'm good...."

Adrenaline laced with angst overloaded Eric. *Just tell me!*

"Almost... got it…"

His fist needed to hit something!

"Eric!"

"What?"

"Whoever he is, he's online right now. I'm looking at his keystrokes. Go to these coordinates! Hurry! Save Shea."

He hung up on Mother with the coordinates in his hard head. "I know where she is."

CHAPTER TWENTY-NINE

Finally! Heavy footsteps sounded from the other side of her prison door.

Shea tucked her gut in and held her breath. If this ruse worked, it'd be the biggest miracle ever. Her arms trembled so hard, because the ledge was so narrow that she had to physically brace her body in the tight space between the joists. All her abductor had to do was tip his chin up, look directly overhead, and she'd be caught.

Sweat dripped around her neck, trickling between her breasts. She blinked the sting of it out of her eyes, daring to believe in miracles.

Something heavy slid over the wooden door, maybe a bar. The distinctive clack of a metal chain. The door lifted. Cool night air filled her cell. Then the stark bright beams of a flashlight invaded her creepy, crawl space.

"No, no, no! She can't have gotten out of here!" an angry baritone voice boomed as a sleeved arm extended into the doorway. A large male body concealed in a black robe followed. Every cell in her body shrank from the evil just inches below her. It was him. Abdul-Mutaal. But why was he speaking with a clipped British accent?

The beam searched the far corners of the cellar. Top right. Top left. Back to the floor once more. Tucking the flashlight under his arm, he fumbled with his robe until he drew a cellphone from its folds. "They've taken her." He paused. "I know it can't be, but it is! Someone's been here, chap. Believe me. I'm looking at a room full of nothing!"

A drum roll exploded in her chest. *Yes, yes, I'm gone.* She hoped. *Now leave.*

He did, mumbling again in English. Not Arabic. *How very un-Mideastern of him.*

She stilled in her ceiling hiding space until the sound of him walking away diminished.

Then the clock really started ticking.

Shea rolled off the ledge and cleared those five steps. Into the chilly night air she went, running for her life. Across the crisply mown lawn. Over a low hedge. She hit the wrought-iron fence next, the thing topped with sharp spikes that cut the palms of her hands. It slowed her down, but it didn't stop her. Nothing could. She was on her way home!

"There she is! Quick. She's getting away!" the same clipped English voice bellowed behind her, but Shea had the fear of death on her side. She balanced for a precarious second at the top bar of the fence, one bare foot between two deadly spikes before she pulled the rest of her weight up enough to clear it.

An engine rumbled to life in the courtyard behind her. She dropped to the other side of the fence, her knees punching her chest and momentarily knocking the breath out of her. *Go! Go! Go!*

Fighting for air, Shea pushed off. The forest across the dark road offered escape and she took it, intent on distance and speed. Her feet suffered the abuse of thorns and rocks, well, let them. She could heal later. *Run. Run. Run!*

"Don't let her get away!" Okay, that voice belonged to someone else. It sounded almost American. She logged that insignificant detail and kept going.

"What do you think I'm doing out here?" Abdul-Mutaal growled.

She almost stopped to see who had spoken to him. One of those voices seemed so familiar, but a four-wheeler had already cleared the gate, and it could definitely catch her. Deeper into the trees she ran. Zigzagging like a fox and barely seconds ahead of her pursuers.

The taste of blood filled the back of her raw throat. Pain as sharp as a knife stabbed her side. Barreling into the wide trunk of a tree, she dashed behind it, struggling to catch a breath. "I can do this," she whispered as she aligned her body to the far side of the tree, needing just a few more seconds of airtime. Licking her lips, she froze in place, not willing to break cover unless that bastard got off his ATV and came looking for her on foot.

Quietly panting her fear away, she stilled. She'd seen the size of that arm of his, though. What were the odds that a guy his size was also light on his feet? She willed herself to remain calm and find out.

The vehicle stopped yards from the tree she'd hidden behind, but the engine continued to idle. A laser-bright beam cut the forest around her. Searching. Probing.

Flattening her shaking body even more, Shea became one with the tree. She stopped breathing, scared to death Mutaal knew right where she was.

Footsteps approached. A man's heavy breathing. *God, he's right behind my tree.* She cringed, sure that her jackhammering heart was loud enough to give her away.

"I know you're out here," that same British voice declared, so close that she jumped. "Just so you understand how this will go down. You can't get off this estate, Shea or Finn or whoever you are today. I've activated all of the electrical fences. Next, I'll call the boys, and I promise you'll not like what they'll do to you."

She gulped, steeling her throat muscles to keep it quiet. *I don't like what you did to me, either.*

"Or maybe you'd rather I spoke," a distinctly Arabic voice chimed it. She dared peak around the tree trunk. Only one man stood there, his hand on his hip and the flashlight in his hand pointed away from her. Like Finn, Abdul-Mutaal was a fraud, a Brit hiding behind a black robe. Wasn't Karma a bitch?

But he hadn't seen her yet. He turned to his left, the beam bouncing over scary looking ferns and ghoulish bumps in the wooded glen. She held herself perfectly rigid, barely breathing. This was what Eric did. He hid in plain sight. If he could do it, so could she. *Keep on keeping on.*

The footsteps and the beam retreated to the ATV. A radio crackled. "I know she's right here under my nose. You don't have to tell me that, but I can't bloody well get her to run. Send the dogs. Let them drag her back. You don't need this little rabbit in one piece to get what you want. All you need is that fucking laptop."

Her stomach pitched acid up her throat. *The boys were dogs?*

"Nonsense," the other voice spoke again, but not over the radio. No. He was there. He called to her because—he knew her. "Let me try. Finn Powers? Is that you?"

Professor Grover? How could this be?

"Come on in, Finn or Shea or whatever your real name is. No one will hurt you, dear. I'll make sure of it."

Shea rethought all she thought she knew. *He's not dead. He must be captured. Like me. Or is he?* It felt right, but it made no sense. He'd had a stroke. She'd been sure of it. Those Legionnaire guys had burned his house down. Hadn't they? Eric said they did, so that much was true. Still...

The sound of barking lifted through the dark from a ways behind the ATV. Crap. That meant the dogs were loose and she doubted they were poodles. There was no choice. Quivering with all out terror, Shea stepped out from her safe tree and peered into the glare of headlights.

The dark silhouette of the man standing near the ATV beckoned to her. "There she is. Come, Shea. Come to me."

"Professor?" she asked, just to be sure.

"Yes, yes, it's me. Come quickly now. The boys will be here soon."

She held her position. *But you're here now.* "He killed Phoenix and Gordie, or did you already know that?"

"Why don't we discuss all of this over a nice cup of tea? I'm dying to hear how you managed to live in that fat suit all those months." He certainly sounded like the professor she'd thought she knew.

"I thought you were dead," she told him without taking a step forward, her hand still on the tree trunk. "Where's your friend, Abdul-Mutaal?"

Professor Grover shrugged. "We can talk about that inside. Once the dogs get here, I can't help you. Those two Dobies can be very mean."

Yeah. Definitely not poodles. Shea took one step forward, her internal alarm roaring in her ears. And there she stopped. Dogs or not, she wanted answers before she would believe.

She never got them. A sharp sting hit the side of her hip, and down she went. *Tasered.*

Murphy's truck only went so fast, not that driving one hundred kilometers an hour was a given on dark, narrow Irish roads that had once been old sheep trails. The truck's headlights rarely offered more than a view of another twist in the winding road. Or the walled fence alongside. There were no shoulders, and nowhere to pull over if the need arose. It was no wonder Jordan was hanging out the rear side window.

Eric rode shotgun since Murphy knew the roads. Elsa sat behind him and next to Jordan, her window rolled down too, most likely to keep the air current fresh and steady.

Even if Carlson wasn't behind Shea's abduction, it all came back to the same thing: Dynamic energy displacement. Eric should've known. The reason Carlson badgered Mikkelson in the first place was to get the new technology. Shea's abductor must want it as badly because, at this very moment, that bastard was less than three clicks from Murphy's home north of Cashel, nearly where Eric had hidden Mikkelson's laptop. Those were the coordinates Mother had given Eric. Imagine Murphy's surprise that Shea was back at his cottage, or at least near it.

"It doesn't make sense. An older British gentleman owns that parcel next to mine," Murphy worried out loud. "I haven't spoken to him in years. Why would he do this?"

Eric didn't care. He just needed to get to Shea. Every turn in this crooked road spilled more fear into his gut and ramped up his adrenaline until he needed to hit something. "What's his name?" he asked to zero his mind.

"Dang, I knew you'd ask, but it's been so long since I've seen him. I can't remember. Let me think."

Eric faced straight ahead, willing his head to cease throbbing and his gut to stop churning. The road didn't seem to bother Murphy. He drove like a professional stock car racer with brimstone on his six.

Eric fingered the grip of the pistol resting under his left arm. Before this night ended, it would be a damned hot piece of metal, just like the one under his right arm. He'd stuffed enough extra mags into his pocket to burn Hell down if it meant getting Shea back alive.

"Damn. I remember now," Murphy growled, jerking Eric back to the business at hand.

"You remember what?" he had to ask because he'd forgotten what they'd been talking about.

"My neighbor." Murphy slapped the steering wheel. "Don't know why I couldn't think of it before, but you know how it is with us old guys. Your memory's the first thing to go."

Eric sighed, not wanting to have to ask a second time.

"Morell Grover. The old gent's name's Morell Grover, and he's quite the—"

"Say what?"

Murphy shot Eric a look. "That name mean something to you?"

"Grover was Shea's professor in Amsterdam. He mentored Mikkelson and Berglund. Shit! If he's behind this—" Eric punched the dash, his heart thrumming with an overload of fear.

"The bastard set his own house on fire. He's behind the murders. Not Carlson. Step on it!"

CHAPTER THIRTY

Shea woke up sputtering to a blinding spotlight and cold water pouring over her face, shivering uncontrollably in this new version of Hell. Her lungs locked down in panic. Her nostrils closed reflexively to keep from drowning. Icy chills skated over her drenched jeans and shirt. A fan on the floor blew cold air up her legs and over her body.

"Stop! Stop!" she sputtered, not able to catch a breath. Thrashing against the wooden chair that held her, she shook her head to see through the water to the asshole drowning her. "Stop it. I… I… can't… breathe!"

But the water kept coming.

A whimper lifted out of her. Here she would die. Held captive and tortured until she gave up whatever Morell and his friend wanted. But they had yet to make a sound and they hadn't asked a single question!

"What… Wh-what do you… want?" She kicked at the floor, frustrated and helpless. Shadows loomed in close, and still the freezing water poured.

Suddenly, Cheyenne's bright giggle filled the room with a pure bright light, and Shea knew she was seconds from drowning. There was no way to win this battle.

I'm coming, baby, she told her brightest angel. *Mama's... coming...*

Murphy latched onto Eric's forearm before the truck rolled to a stop. "We play this smart and we do it right," he cautioned. "Jordan, hand me that case behind your seat."

Dragging a black weapons case up off the floor, Jordan unlatched the snaps and flipped the lid open. "You're shittin' me. NVGs? Sweet." He handed two upfront, but Eric set his aside. Night vision goggles were cumbersome. They limited a guy's peripheral, and something as small as the flare of a match or a handheld flashlight could blind a guy at the worst possible time.

Jordan and Elsa both donned a pair. Murphy didn't.

"Okay then," he said. "Elsa and Jordan will go in ahead. Once they give us the all clear, Eric, you and Jordan will go in hot. Shoot whatever moves unless it's running away. As soon as you've got Shea out of there, meet us back here at the truck and we'll retreat to my place. Elsa and I will cover you. Understood?"

Why did Eric have the feeling these instructions were intended for him more than the others? "Copy that," he acknowledged as he strapped on for war. Over the shoulder holsters pocketed his SIG Sauer nine millimeters, keeping them close and accessible. Another holstered SIG tucked snug inside his jeans at the small of his back. Extra mags went into his pockets. A seven-inch blade hid in his right boot sheath.

The AR he kept close to his chest, the extra mag for that dangling on a clip off his belt.

The rest of his team were likewise prepared by the time he'd finished.

"One last thing," Murphy offered before they set out. "You kids be safe out there. Come home like you're supposed to."

"That goes for you too, Uncle," Elsa said, her chin up.

Enough. While Jordan and Elsa headed out through the trees, Eric and Murphy trailed them by a few yards, providing cover. Using the NVGs, Jordan and Elsa could detect body heat signatures outside the grounds and around the mansion directly ahead. The trees were thick, but the four of them moved like trained shadows through the woods, never breaking formation.

Jordan's fist came up at a right angle. *Hold. Danger.* He dropped to one knee, while Elsa moved forward, her weapon pointed ahead. Two fingers to her eyes, she signaled at the house, and Eric wished to hell Murphy'd had Bluetooth earpieces in all that doomsday-prepper stuff in his bunker. It'd be nice to know what was going on.

Elsa disappeared into the shadows while the rest of them held position. In minutes, she returned and gave them the thumbs up signal. The danger, whatever is was, had been secured or disabled.

Eric and Murphy advanced to where their buddies had halted. *What do you know?* A silvery thin wire shimmered at waist level, something Eric wouldn't have spotted. How anyone saw it was the question of the night. No doubt it was part of Grover's security system. Impressive. *Good catch, Miss Finnegan.*

A dog growled from somewhere nearby, and damn it. Eric didn't want to, but the second he saw those two sleek Dobies charging, their noses skimming close to ground level, he dropped to one knee and fired off two rounds. It hurt to have to kill any animal, but Jordan and Elsa were his first priority. As it was, they never saw the animals tumble snouts-down into the dirt.

Round one. First contact had been made. Murphy clapped Eric's back with a single atta-boy, and they kept going.

A ten-foot high wrought iron fence surrounded the estate grounds. Straight up nasty, the fence boasted intermittent spikes topside. Its rolling gate had been left open. That alone made Eric uneasy, but he blew it off.

When a mercury vapor light switched on over the center double doors, everyone froze. Jordan hissed as he doffed his NVGs. Elsa's pair already dangled at her hip.

A man whistled at the door, probably looking for his two besties, now sleeping beyond the fence. "Brutus. Max," he called out.

Eric didn't want to end him, too, but if Dog-guy came looking for the Dobies, he would.

Grumbling, the man stepped onto the porch. "Brutus! Max! Damn it, where are you?" He stood with his hands on his hips a moment longer, then stepped back inside and closed the door. The light went out. First encounters with the two-legged enemy signaled round two had begun.

The rest of the infiltration went like clockwork. Jordan and Elsa took the right of the home, Eric and Murphy went left. They rejoined in the backyard.

"The immediate yard is clear," Jordan whispered. "There's a root cellar on the east side of the garage. It's empty, but check this out." He handed Eric a pair of Flexi-cuffs, the plastic smeared with what could've been blood.

Eric held the cuff to his nose, wishing he had half the olfactory senses that Alex Stewart's ex-EOD dogs had. It'd be good to know if these cuffs had been used on Shea.

A light flashed on at the rear of the house, providing a clear view inside while making anyone standing in the dark outside all but invisible. Dog-guy again. He stood a good six-feet tall. Maybe two hundred pounds give or take. Gray sweatpants. Gray T-shirt. He'd opened a door in the hallway, and stood there looking in, talking to someone unseen. The door opened outward to his right, shielding most of him from Eric's view.

"You guys see another light on in this place?" Eric asked quietly. *Because I sure don't.*

His team members fanned out and returned quickly with three negatives.

"Then who's he talking to?"

"You want me to kick up a diversion?" Elsa asked.

"Not yet." Eric pulled up his binocs out of his pack, needing one hundred percent intel before he entered ground zero. Dog-guy had hold of a metal door, if those heavy-duty hinges meant anything, and metal doors meant security.

"Floor plan," Jordan muttered, jerking something up out of his pocket. "We need the blueprints to this place, and I've got an app for that."

Unbelievable. "You do?" Murphy asked.

"Sure. You're not the only boy scout in town." Angling his body, Jordan shielded his cellphone as he worked the screen. "Give me a sec."

Eric held position, already planning how to breach the rear entry. Which hall to take first. Which level. The mansion was a massive building. There had to be at least twenty rooms inside. This had to be done right.

While Jordan worked, Dog-guy scratched his head, then entered the room and eased the door shut behind him. Eric watched for it, held his breath and hoped for it. At last. The door settled, still a crack open. By now, Murphy peered over Jordan's shoulder, his face backlit by the screen. "I'll be damned."

Jordan's head popped up. "That metal door leads to a basement room with no concrete walls and no windows."

"A safe room," Elsa hissed.

"It might not be breachable," Murphy worried.

"Then we need to move fast." Eric nodded at Jordan. "You ready?"

"To the end," Jordan replied, pocketing his phone while his rifle shifted back into position.

Without waiting, Eric advanced on the single-windowed rear door, watchful of trip wires and security beams. Nothing seemed out of the ordinary. If any alarm system had been activated, it was silent—or lying dead beyond the front lawn. Time would tell. Eric just didn't plan on being inside this place that long.

Carefully testing the exterior doorknob, he found it unlocked, so he entered first. Jordan followed on his six, both with compact rifles snug to their chests. Close combat could be tricky. Once inside, Eric shouldered his rifle and pulled both pistols front and center. Jordan followed suit.

The place was quiet. There wasn't time to do a room-by-room, and Eric didn't intend to. Trusting his gut, he tested the handle to what he now knew was a basement level safe room. Built to withstand fire or armed assault, most were constructed of concrete, reinforced steel beams, and sufficient staples to survive weeks of confinement, if necessary. The ones Alex Stewart built into all of his safe homes included state-of-the-art surveillance equipment, and damned tight locks that could withstand a blowtorch. They were the definition of unbreachable.

The key to getting Shea back—if she was in that basement room—would be to move fast. Fortunately, Dog-guy didn't seem to be trained in black ops. He hadn't shut, nor locked the door behind him.

Peering down into a narrow wooden staircase, Eric reported back to Jordan with two fingers, one for the visual of Dog-guy standing at the bottom of the stairs, facing right, the other for the unseen man or men he was talking with. While Jordan kept watch at the basement door, Eric lowered one boot to the first step, his senses flared forward.

Apparently bored, Dog-guy complained, "Can't even get a decent signal this far from town. How 'bout you? Got any bars?" He latched onto the overhead doorjamb at the bottom of the stair as indiscernible muttering answered him.

Eric cocked his head and took another step. Listening. Waiting.

"Yeah, well he should." Dog-guy muttered. "A satellite dish out here would make a helluva difference in this crap hole.

I ain't Einstein. What's he expect me to do, read something outta his fancy library? Shit. I hate reading. It's a waste of time." His shirt rode up to expose a tattooed lower back and a sloppy gut. "How long's she been out this time?"

She? Eric took three steps toward Dog-guy that time.

"You ain't got nothing outta her yet?" Pause. "You're kidding. You still ain't asked the bitch where the shit is? Damn. How long are you gonna wash her down 'fore you get to business?" He shifted his feet. "Still coaching, huh? That crap ever work?"

Eric gritted his teeth, fighting for the restraint to not blow Dog-guy to hell and storm this safe room. *Coaching, my ass!* Standard CIA lingo for interrogation, it amounted to water-boarding a suspect before asking questions. Sometimes for days. By the time *coaching* was complete, the suspect—guilty or not—was ready to crawl out of their skin to answer anything and everything their coach asked. If they'd survived the lesson.

Shea! They were water-boarding Shea for god's sake!

"Eric," Jordan whispered, halting his progress with a firm hand on his arm. "Elsa's at the back door signaling us. Come on, man. Pull back. Something's up."

Like hell. Dog-guy had a double-tap coming and Eric meant to deliver.

"Don't do it," Jordan hissed, but Eric had no room in his heart, not even for his buddy. *Not now, bro. I'm not* that *guy anymore.* He jerked his arm free of Jordan's grip and planned to murder an unarmed piece of shit.

Dog-guy kept shooting his mouth off. "When's the professor gonna get back? Do you know?"

Whoever chatted with Dog-guy needed to speak up, but at least Eric now knew Grover wasn't onsite.

"We've got plenty of time then. You want a Guinness? A Heineken? Professor's got both on tap." A pause. "'Kay. I'll be back, but I want to see some action when I do. Shit. Strip her naked if you have to. Let's have some fun before she comes to. I'm past due."

Eric's thin hold on composure evaporated. He took another step down that dark basement stairway to—

Jordan jerked him backward by his collar, a ballsy thing to do in the middle of a showdown. Eric found his back to the wall on ground level again, beside the still open security door with his buddy's fist in his shirt. Nose to nose, Jordan growled, "Stand down, Sergeant. I swear to God, we're not leaving Shea. We're just making sure we do this right."

Eric blasted him with a blistering, "Fuck off!" The image of Shea struggling while some ass straddled and water-boarded her triggered his deepest rage. God, she'd be scared to death—or close to death. Jordan needed to get the hell out of his way. Now!

Instead, he jerked Eric around the corner just seconds before Dog-guy cleared the doorway, cracking his knuckles and oblivious to the fact that he had company inside the house.

Jordan hovered like a righteous fullback in the middle of Eric's emotion driven quarterbacking, his fist under Eric's chin. "Trust me. We go in smart," he said quietly, his eyes ablaze. "I know this bullshit's killing you, Eric, but if you off this meat sack too soon, we might not be able to get Shea out of there alive. You feel me?"

Eric blinked, not understanding one word that had just come out of his buddy's mouth. His eyes were on Dog-guy. The dumb ass wasn't following any covert rules Eric knew. He'd hiked the front of his T-shirt up and slapped his hairy belly like bongos, rapping in time to some piece of crap lyrics about *doing a bitch, do her 'til she screams, ba dunk, ba dunk, bad-da-da-da.*

Jordan's observation should've meant more to Eric, but all he wanted to do was rip this motherfucker's heart out and make him eat it. He would've if Jordan hadn't still been strong-arming him, holding him to the shadows.

At last, Dog-guy strolled past the corridor where they were standing. Down the hall he went like a teenager whose parents were out of town for the weekend. Either these guys were over-the-top-confident that they thought they were untouchable, or they were complacent as hell.

Eric's gaze dropped to that bulging ex-Army Ranger's arm muscling him in place. He'd never noticed how strong Jordan was before. Or how right. They still didn't know how many were down in that basement safe room with Shea. To go in guns blazing could get her killed. Eric had to get his head back in the game. Swallowing hard, he calmed enough to be civil to the one man in as much danger as he was.

"What then?" he ground out, forcing slow, even breaths.

"Now I go see what's up with Murphy and Elsa. You good?"

Hell no, I'm not good. "Make it quick," Eric said, his gaze on the light down the hall. The second Jordan stepped away, he lifted his SIG back to the direction Dog-guy had gone. *Come to me, you bastard. You'll never touch that gut of yours again. Or my wife.*

But Eric was smart enough that he held position until Jordan returned with news that, "Alex is on the ground."

Like that meant shit. "So? Is he here? Is he close enough to get here in time?"

"No, but Elsa also has two more guys in her sights outside, and Murphy's sure there's more. He wants us to pull back before we ruin our one shot at saving Shea." Jordan sucked in a deep breath. "But it's your call, brother. You stay, I stay."

That word. *Brother.* Eric knew Jordan would lay down his life for him or Shea tonight, but Murphy should've known better than to ask. Pulling back wasn't an option. "I won't leave her."

Jordan nodded once. "Knew you'd say that. Let's do this thing."

CHAPTER THIRTY-ONE

It took longer coming to this time. Shea tried to lift her head off her shoulder, but the thing was heavy. For now, the torture had ceased, but her limbs were ice. Her feet were numb. Wet clothes plastered her body. She couldn't feel her fingers. Worse, there was no way out of this concrete chamber.

The last time she'd felt this bad had been on that beach when Cheyenne appeared to her in the angelic guise of that other little girl. The one who'd patted Shea's bloated cheek with the tender touch of an innocent and said in the sweetest voice, "Hi, Mama. I found you."

Only now Shea knew the little girl had probably said to her real mother, "Hey, Mama, look what I found." That scenario made more sense, but for that one split second in time, Shea's heart had believed. That one spark of hope was all she'd needed to remember the life she'd tossed away.

"Cheyenne," she murmured, wanting that hope back again. How like her father Cheyenne was, both saviors, but on different dimensions in the grand scheme of things. And now she'd lost them both.

Voices buzzed around her. Angry voices. She tried to make sense of it, but the cold won. She yearned for freedom, but knew better. She would die in this chair. This was the end. And yet…

Across the room, her blurry eyes locked with—*Eric?*

There she is!

Shea sat strapped to a wooden chair bolted on the concrete floor over a large metal grate. Barely conscious, she was drenched and pale. Wide plastic restraints circled her forearms and ankles.

Two men sat in front of her, their backs to Eric. One smacked his open palm with a baton, the other finger tapped at his computer tablet. The son-of-a-bitch was taking a break. Playing a video game. Didn't that add gasoline to the blazing fury already stoking Eric's rage? Not one flicker of remorse entered his mind when he advanced on the whisper-quiet feet of an executioner. Until everything went south.

"On your right!" Jordan yelled just as some guy came out of nowhere and sent him flying. The heavy security door at the bottom of the stairwell clanged shut when Jordan hit it, shutting Eric and him inside the safe room with Shea.

Spinning around, Eric brought his AR front and center as a meaty fist hit him squarely in the face. Not enough to knock him down, but enough that he lost hold of his rifle and his nose gushed.

The man who'd hit him was a hulking monster in a black robe and brandishing a scimitar just like in the video. Bulky arms crossed over a wide, thick chest. He wasn't the real

Abdul-Mutaal though. He wasn't even Mideastern. No way in hell. He was a punk-assed white guy with a thick, red beard who had smeared his clown make-up.

The guy was quick, though. Using the handle of that scimitar like a pair of brass knuckles, he punched Eric hard in the chest with the side of it and knocked the air out of him. Once. Twice. The guy pummeled him, shoving him backward with every blow.

Muscle training took over. Shifting his AR over his shoulder and out of his way, Eric countered with an uppercut that clipped the bastard's chin and knocked his head back. One, two, three more fists to that whiskered face, and the wannabe fell back a few steps.

Eric reached for his right holster, but came up empty. He'd lost both pistols in the scuffle, and he barely had time to grab the blade in his boot, a pitiful match against a three-foot sword that could take his arm off, if and when this extremist got serious. The guy seemed to be holding back.

"You came for your wife," he taunted, the scimitar now poised in his right hand, his feet spread wide. "Come get her if you think you're man enough."

Yeah. Not an Arab at all. Liverpool, maybe. Still going to die.

Eric jumped at the guy, feinting to the right. Startled, the Brit pulled his sword arm back, needing more room to swing than the low ceiling allowed. Wrong move. Bigger didn't necessarily equate with better. Or faster.

In the time it took him to wield that three-foot blade, Eric charged, slicing the Brit's arm as the scimitar parted the air at his left with a whistle. He dodged, but not before landing a solid kick in the Brit's ribs.

The big guy lost his balance with a grunt, but stuck a solid three-point landing, one palm to the floor. Reaching into the folds of his robe, he came up grinning with two bleeding fingers. His tongue snaked out to lick his own blood. "That all you got, Yank?" he asked, his eyes wide.

This guy might just be on drugs, Eric thought as he shot back, "I'm just warming up." His inner warrior wanted all ten of this freak's fingers. Maybe his head, too. It seemed a fair trade.

Pushing up from the floor, the Brit toggled those same bloody fingers for Eric to come play. The scimitar shifted hands. "You must do better than that, Reynolds, or soon I'll be licking your sweet little wife." His lips puckered as he blew Shea a kiss. "Want to watch?"

Keep playing with me, asshole, Eric thought as he stomped a boot forward again, *and I'll carve those lips off your ugly face.* Parrying a stab and a fake punch, he refused to let his emotions rule no matter how crass this clown got. This pompous Brit needed to think he had the upper hand. It kind of felt like he did.

Jordan was on his feet and heavily engaged with the two that had been sitting with Shea. He looked like he was holding his own, but Eric was too busy to go to his aid. Charging the redheaded killer, he drew up just short of that slashing blade. The tip of it caught him this time, slicing his chest, cutting shirt and skin. But that was what Eric wanted, to be inside that down stroke. Seizing that split-second window of opportunity, he thrust his blade upward, into the Brit's bicep and he twisted. Now it was Eric's turn to taunt. "That all you got?"

The liar groaned, but the handle of that damned scimitar caught Eric across the side of his head. He landed face first on the floor a good ten feet away. Blood trickled into his eyes. He wiped it off, along with some stars and a few flashing comets. Holy shit, this guy was built like a bull, all rock-hard muscle. But once more, the Brit had held back.

It was time to recalculate and re-strategize. Eric sucked in a deep breath, buying time. He might be faster and more agile, but his previous wounds were wearing on him. *This is no way to save Shea.*

Rolling to his side and breathing hard, enlightenment dawned on him. *Damn it to holy hell. This is just foreplay.* That was why the Brit hadn't used his scimitar as effectively as he could have. He was toying with Eric. Playing. He meant for Eric to live just long enough to break Shea. Torturing and beheading her husband in front of her would surely do it.

That shit's NOT going to happen.

Eric dragged his tired ass up off the floor like a guy who'd given up. He knelt on the concrete. His shoulders sagged like a weakling's. He groaned. He frowned. Didn't bother to wipe his bloody nose. Let the Brit get his hopes up.

The asshole stomped one boot. "You call that a fight?" he bellowed, smacking his chest with that fisted blade. "Come on, Reynolds. Up with you. Fight like a man."

"I can't. I give," Eric wheezed like the pansy he was not. He lifted his hands, palms forward, not taking his eyes off this jerk for a second, but willing to play the game. "Damn it.

You're bigger than me. I can't win. I give. Who… who *are* you?"

The Brit's bushy brows lifted. "You Americans. Quitters! All of you! Nothing sporting about the lot of you. As for who I am, I'm your worst nightmare, Reynolds. The name's Lord Piers Yeoman, if you must know, though it will make little difference at the end of this day. You'll still be dead, but not before you serve my purpose."

Knew you'd say that. Eric blew out a big breath. *I was right. He intends to torture me to break Shea. I've never killed a lord before.* "Why… why the torture?" he gasped, going for broke. "Why water-board a woman? Looks like you've got her where you want her." *You flaming asshole.*

The man's right eyelid twitched. "Why not? All is fair in war and…" He glanced back at Shea with a salacious leer, "love. Wouldn't you say?"

Eric let him get two steps closer before he jerked his ace-in-the-hole off his back, where it had been beating the ever-loving shit out of him this whole wrestling match. Tough guy didn't look so smug all of a sudden with a Sig Sauer pointed up his big ego. Funny how life can change in the blink of the eye of one pissed-off husband.

"That's my wife!" Eric bellowed as his trigger finger wiped the smirk off Lord Yeoman's ugly face.

It took four body shots to knock the bastard down. His shiny scimitar hit the floor first. While the Brit collapsed like an accordion within all those black robes, Eric sent a round into one of the men beating on Jordan. That freed Jordan to finish snapping the last guy's neck.

"You good?" Eric asked when the battle was done, keeping his pistol ready.

Jordan sank to the floor, his bloodied hands on his knees, nodding and wheezing. "Yeah. You?"

"Will be," Eric muttered. It took a second to get to Shea, but the plastic restraints on her forearms were thick. A metal lock secured each Flexi-Cuff, but time was running out. Eric attacked the ones at her wrists with the tip of his knife, his ears tuned to any indication of more trouble headed his way.

Still in battle-mode, Jordan returned to Eric's side. Stabbing his blade into the locks at Shea's legs, he muttered, "Never met one of these I couldn't break." With a snap, both locks opened.

"Thanks, man." Eric wiped his face, wishing his hands were clean for this next part. "Speak to me, Shea," he coaxed as he pulled her off the chair and into his chest. Folding her fingers in his, he brought them to his mouth to warm them. No response. He might as well have been breathing on icicles.

Jordan secured Eric's weapons and nodded at the hidden panel next to the steel door. "No wonder Abdul Fucking-What's-His-Name got the jump on us. Look. A secret panel."

Eric glanced at the dead poser who'd ambushed them. That Dog-guy hadn't come running to assist the Brit meant one thing. With the door shut, this room was soundproof. The sure knowledge that she'd suffered in this concrete dungeon and done it alone nearly broke his soul. "Get us the hell out of here."

"Stay close," Jordan replied. "I'll clear the way."

Cradling Shea's head under his chin, Eric climbed the stairs behind Jordan, his pistol still in his hand. At the top step, she huffed into his neck, his first sign of hope.

Jordan had barely opened the door when his left arm blocked Eric's ascent. "Shh. Your friend's still here."

All Eric heard was Jordan taking the silenced shot, followed by glass crashing to the floor and a heavy thud. Eric wished he could've watched when Dog-guy went down. *Just because.*

"Cheyenne!" Shea screamed bloody murder all the way back to Murphy's, ramming her head into Eric's shoulder until he was sure his collarbone was broken. He'd already pinned her arms. She couldn't hurt herself, but the terror in her voice wrecked him. Every time.

She was still cold by the time Murphy lowered his garage door. Jordan hustled and provided cover from there to the house in case they'd been followed. Elsa scrambled inside as Eric hurried Shea into the guest bedroom. While Elsa provided several blankets, he stripped Shea to her birthday suit and wrapped her as tight as he dared.

Elsa took over so he could grab a quick shower. "Go on with you," she ordered. "I'll try to get some tea into her. Hurry. You can't have her seeing you like that."

Tea. The Irish cure for everything.

Elsa was right. The man staring at him from the bathroom mirror looked pretty damned scary. Eric had a black eye he didn't remember getting, a bloody path on the left side of his head from being shot, a purple, swollen nose that didn't work so good anymore. The thin slice across his chest from the scimitar was the least of his worries.

By the time he'd showered, he could breathe through his nose—barely—but some. Rummaging through Murphy's medicine cabinet, he found a first-aid kit. Six butterfly bandages took care of the scimitar slice across his chest. Two more closed the split over his left eye. His nose? Well, that was another story. Wincing, his eyes watering, he managed a single strip of flesh-toned adhesive tape over the top of it. At least it wasn't bleeding.

"Poor, poor thing," Elsa murmured when he returned with a towel wrapped around his waist. "Jordan brought a cup of tea for her, but she's still incoherent. We may need to transport her to a clinic. There's a fine one in Cashel."

"No. I'll take it from here."

"But Mr. Reynolds—"

He shook his head. "Leave us alone. Please. She'll be fine."

Elsa had the good sense to close the door behind her.

Eric dropped the towel wearing just his boxers. What Shea needed couldn't be found in a clinic. He climbed into bed with her and wrapped her up warm and tight, using his body heat to raise her temperature.

That was his first mistake. Shea bucked and kicked, thrashed and twisted, screaming "Cheyenne!" His baby girl's ghost was suddenly present, if only to tear at her mother's heart.

"I've got you," he crooned, squeezing Shea just enough to let her know she was safe. That he was there. The same mistake-made-twice got him another head-butt. He shed real tears that time, but he wouldn't let her go.

Rearing back, Shea struck his forehead with the back of her head, panting and fighting to get free. Frantically sucking in air as if her lungs weren't working. As if those bastards were still water-boarding her. The single word kept pouring out of her mouth in one long, shrill wail to the universe, her terrified keening enough to wake the dead. "Chey—enne!"

A lot of guys would've gotten frustrated and slapped her at that point to snap her out of it. Not Eric. He understood where her need to fight came from. Instead of using force, he did what he should have done two years ago. He held on.

Murphy hovered in and out of the bedroom. "I've got a bad feeling. Soon as she's warm, I want you kids down in that bunker. Something's wrong. I can't reach Mother. Alex, neither," he grumbled. "Do you think she'll take a little broth?"

"Not yet." Eric gathered the blankets under her chin.

"I'm sure sorry, son," Murphy said as he left.

Eric hadn't the time to worry about Alex, because the man posing as Abdul-Mutaal had done what he'd set out to do. He'd broken Shea. But that feeling of impending doom? Eric had it since they'd left Grover's place. He couldn't shake it. They might have taken Berglund and Mikkelson's murderer out of the picture and maybe a few bad guys, but the professor was still out there. With Bagani and Carlson eliminated, Grover had to be the one in control.

Shea lay quiet for the moment with her back to Eric's front, but whining to be let loose, her fingers fisted beneath her chin.

Still crying for her baby girl after all these years. Either she wanted Cheyenne to come back to life—or she wanted to join her.

"You're not leaving me, baby. Not this time," Eric told her in no uncertain terms. He couldn't tell if she heard, so he began at the beginning.

Once upon a time there were three little pigs. Those rascals loved to play in the mud. All day long they built mud pies and mud castles. Mud mountains and mud rivers. If there was water and dirt to be had, there were three dirty little pigs smack dab in the middle of it.

But more than the mud, they loved the cinnamon bunnies from the baker. And strawberry shortcake. Sweetmeats. Cotton candy, and well, they loved everything as long as it was extra gooey and nutritionally bad for them.

Shea used to smirk at that extra long word in the middle of a child's bedtime story, *but work with me here,* Eric had told her. *Medics love to use extra-big and long words. It makes us look smart.*

He paused. "Do you remember who Mama Pig was, Shea?"

No answer other than a huff through her nose, but at least she was quiet.

Okay, so one morning the three dirty little pigs woke up with a start. They heard someone in their dirty little-pig kitchen, and that person made a lot of noise. Whoever it was rattled pans and spoons and—hummed?

Eric pinched his nose and hummed a nonsensical ditty the same as he had for his daughter at this point in the story. Cheyenne used to giggle and squeal. Not Shea.

With their little piggy eyes squinting so they looked extra-scary, and with their little piggy ears cocked forward like tiny radar dishes, the three, dirty, little critters sneaked into the kitchen. Extra sneaky like. Piggy hoof by piggy hoof. Big pink piggy ears twitching. Curly little piggy tails extra curly.

Eric smoothed a palm over Shea's shoulder, needing her to want to live.

What a surprise! A bigger than life Mama Pig was standing at their stove and…. and…she was using it!

"I didn't know it worked," said one little pig.

"Me neither," said the second.

"What's a stove?" asked the third silly little pig.

Then something magical happened. The most delicious aroma drifted up into their little pig snouts. Their little pig mouths watered. This wonderful mama pig was cooking!

Eric pressed a kiss behind Shea's ear. "You always gave me such a dirty look at this part of the story. Honest, honey. I wasn't assigning any gender specific roles for Cheyenne to live up to. It's just a fairytale."

No answer. Eric went on with the story. *Suddenly, Mama Pig stopped humming. She spotted the dirty, little piglets. Her eyes grew extra large and round, and the funniest thing happened.*

"Do you know what was so funny?" he whispered, his heart too tender to go on with the telling. "Do you remember?"

Cheyenne's spirit seemed to have drawn nearer with very word of that often-repeated fairytale. If there was a heaven, she had to be leaning over the edge of it and listening to her favorite story right now. At least, Eric hoped, she was watching her father struggle to hold onto her mother. "Cheyenne still loves you, baby. I know she does, but so do I."

Eric mashed his nose into the side of Shea's head, no longer able to hold back the tears. At the end of all the stories and fairytales he'd told Cheyenne, he'd always made certain there was a happy ending. Children deserved to be innocent as long as they could. They deserved to believe in magic and Santa Claus, Rudolph and the Tooth Fairy—all those tender lies parents gave credence to for as long as they could. Children deserved to believe in the stability of their parents' marriage, too.

He'd set the example in his house. If Shea was having a bad day when he came home, he fixed it. If she needed a break from a crying baby, if she simply needed a time-out and a bubble bath, he provided. That was his job and his rule. The prince and princess lived happily ever after in his kingdom. They went to bed together, they ate dinner at the table, and that was the way it was. For as long as they had Cheyenne in their lives, she'd believed in the magic of her parents' love. He meant that vow he'd made at the foot of that altar; to love, honor, and serve.

But now... Eric wasn't so sure how this story would end. He couldn't make the one woman in the world whom he adored with every beat of his heart love him back. He couldn't fix this.

It was up to Shea to decide whether she wanted to stay in this life or—leave.

CHAPTER THIRTY-TWO

Afraid to wake up, Shea floated. Her hysterical mind couldn't wrap itself around her new reality, so she stayed suspended in this secret place where she was warm and safe. Until a soft baritone murmured in her ear, "I want you to make love with me again. Dance with me. Get silly with me. Just one more time. Please come back. Choose me too, Shea." As if *he* knew exactly how to reach her, he began humming the Marine Corps anthem.

She stilled, not believing. Could it be possible? *No. I saw him die.* Shea turned in his arms, nuzzling his neck, needing the scent of his skin in her nose to be sure. She was that coke addict, desperate for a fix. "Eric?"

Warm kisses rained over her forehead, down her nose, and over her cheeks. "Oh, baby, you're back at Murphy's, and everyone's worried about you, and…"

"S-s-save me."

"You're already saved," he assured, breathing life into her even as she burrowed under his chin.

"Don't let them get me," she cried, frightened out of her wits that she'd never be free of Grover and his assassins again. That they would always hunt her. That she couldn't run far enough or fast enough. Desperate to be sure, she twined her arms around Eric's neck, her fingernails digging into his shoulder muscles.

"Deep breaths, Shea. Breathe with me. Slow and easy," he soothed, his arms around her, one hand cupping the back of her head. "That Abdul-Mutaal wannabe is dead, so are the other guys who were with him."

"G-Grover? C-Carlson, too?" She knew his answer by the way Eric's hands pressed her against him in a suffocating squeeze. This thing wasn't over.

"Not yet, but we're flying out of here as soon as you can travel. Elsa's made arrangements. Trust me, Shea. Someone else can clean up this mess. You need to be home."

The tsunami of terror dissolved as she wept against his neck. "You came for me."

"Always," he promised with a growl that seemed to surround her. "Damn it, Shea. Always."

A nine-millimeter round made a helluva noise.

"We've got company," Jordan called out from the other room. "Grover's here. Any word from Alex yet?"

"Not yet," Murphy answered tersely. "He won't pick up his phone. Mother, either. Something's not right."

Eric shifted his weight to one elbow and listened to the muffled exchange through the closed bedroom door. Shea lay with her back to him, one hand splayed to the pillow. She'd fallen into a fitful sleep from exhaustion and the extra-strength ibuprofen he'd given her to help her relax. The poor thing needed some serious downtime to decompress, a couple weeks of R&R at least. Instead, she'd soon wake to the sounds of battle, not good therapy for a person suffering from serious shellshock.

Murphy knocked softly as he opened the door. "How's she doing?"

"She's sleeping. Grover's here?" Eric rolled his shoulder, ready to knock that SOB to kingdom come. "Give me five."

"No, you stay here with your wife," Murphy ordered. "I wish you two were in the bunker. You'd be safer there."

"You know better. I'd like Shea down there, but I don't hide. Besides, you'll need my rifle." There was no way to avoid this showdown. The professor wanted Shea, but he couldn't have her. Simple as that.

Carefully, Eric eased his feet to the floor. A clean change of clothes lay folded on the end of the bed. Typical TEAM wear: Camouflage pants, a black T-shirt, black cotton socks, a tactical vest, and his holster, two SIGS already loaded and tucked in its pockets. Better yet, pre-loaded .308 caliber clips for the AR tipped barrel-up next to the door. Extra magazines. *Good man.*

Dressing quickly and quietly, Eric strapped on and ramped up his inner sniper. If Alex were in Ireland, now would be a good time for him to show up. Somehow, Eric doubted that would happen. Alex wasn't the cavalry.

Shea mumbled in her sleep, and for once, she wasn't crying. Eric dropped to one knee at her bedside and placed a kiss on her cheek. "I won't be gone long," he whispered. "Dream for me, baby."

Aishling peered out from under the bed. As if she knew it was her turn, the crazy cat climbed up and curled her fluffy black body into Shea's chest. Shea didn't wake, just cradled the cat like a baby in one of those automatic motherly responses, and for that, Eric was glad.

Stretching one lazy arm, Aishling rested a paw on Shea's chin, almost as if giving her stamp of approval. Or possession. Damned if she didn't look like she belonged there.

"Take care of her while I'm gone," he whispered, his fingers smoothing over Shea's forehead. Of course the cat didn't answer, but the same odd feeing he always got with Aishling, whispered around Eric. When he was a kid, he used to believe in guardian angels. This cat certainly fit the bill. All she needed was a pair of wings.

Eric strapped on his boots, shrugged into his holster, and steeled his heart, needing the dirty job ahead of him and his team done, once and for all. Another shot sounded. Then another.

Time to move.

Closing the bedroom door behind him, he unholstered his pistol and went in search of his guys. War might have come for Shea, but it was going home empty-handed.

"And I said get the hell off my property." Murphy's chin lifted, his rifle already targeting the gray-haired gent in a sweater standing at the end of the driveway, the one with ten or twelve beefy guys at his back, all sporting short stock rifles. Had to be Grover.

A hefty camouflaged six-by-six five-ton cargo truck blocked the drive. "Take your boys and leave," Murphy ordered. "You're only going to find trouble here."

Still standing out of sight at the corner of Murphy's house, Eric scanned the yard. Jordan stood at Murphy's left with his rifle to his cheek, but Elsa was missing. Not acceptable. As good as she was, Murphy needed her on his right. At least, on his six.

Before joining the standoff, Eric took stock of the immediate area. He scouted the stone fence that lined Murphy's place, the opposite side of his cottage, and the stand of trees that shaded it. Eric spotted Elsa's long barrel at the same time he spotted the sneaky bastard hiding in the shadows of the cargo truck.

Elsa had chosen well. Ornamental pampas grass made a fine sniper hide for a gal laying on her belly while lining up her next shot. But damned if that guy playing hide-and-seek wasn't Hugh Carlson. Just as Eric had suspected all along.

Now that he knew where everyone was, Eric stepped out front and took position to Murphy's right. He didn't recognize the men willing to die for the professor, but mercenaries were like that. Once you've seen one, you've seen them all.

"That Grover?" he asked out of the corner of his mouth.

"In person," Jordan muttered from Murphy's left. "That's the rat bastard who tried to kill me at the hotel."

"Grover was there?" Eric hadn't known that, but it made sense. Birds of a feather, and all that shit.

"But neighbor…" Still standing at the edge of Murphy's property, Grover waved one hand toward Murphy's house and lawn in a magnanimous gesture. "Do you think I'd let you stay here now that I know you have the goose that lays the golden egg?"

"What the hell are you talking about?" Murphy hissed. "The only thing I've got for you is the first round out of this muzzle, and trust me. It's not made of gold. Come get some."

Eric grunted in agreement. Didn't matter what the braggart wanted or how many men he'd brought with him, Grover wasn't leaving with anything but lead in his ass. Certainly not Shea.

"But Mr. Finnegan." Grover kept trying. "Let's be reasonable. We can work this out." His head bobbed like it was already a done deal.

"Let's not." Eric zeroed in on that other sneaky bastard, the one who thought he was clever. *Guess again.* "Get your ass out in the open where we can all see you, Carlson."

Damned if the billionaire playboy didn't step out from behind the five-ton like he was told to. Dressed in a business suit as if he didn't plan on getting dirty, Carlson fingered the cufflink on his left wrist as he sauntered into view.

"What's he doing here?" Murphy asked. "I thought he was waiting for a flight."

"He's the money behind all this." That much Eric knew for certain.

"Ah, Mr. Reynolds," he said, still without meeting Eric's eyes. "What poor timing you have. You, too, Finnegan—or should I call you Hollister?" He lifted one shoulder. "Not that it matters, but if you'd stayed in your country and minded your business, none of this would be necessary."

"None of what?" Murphy asked.

Carlson toyed with the cufflink, still not man enough to look his three adversaries in the eye. *What an ass.* He still thought he could walk in, snap his fingers, and the world would bow to kiss his feet. *Not today.* "Have you contacted your superior yet, that prick, Alex Stewart? His staff? Anyone in his office?" he asked. "Anyone on the entire Eastern seaboard for that matter?"

Murphy growled, but didn't answer.

Carlson proceeded past Grover and his string of goons, still not willing to make eye contact. "Let me answer that for you," he told his cufflink. "No. You haven't been able to contact him, and you never will. Why? Because my chip, the one that every cell service in the world is currently required to incorporate into their products, is now in charge. It's taken over the world, so to speak. It's tracking every last deadbeat with a social network account or an email address. Your fragile little republic across the pond has gone back to the Dark Ages. You couldn't call home if you tried."

Eric steeled his jaw. He'd never been as tech savvy as Shea, but this sounded about as bad as it could get.

"What the hell are you talking about?" Murphy snapped. "Stop bullshitting and spit it out."

"Patience, old man." Carlson preened like the peacock he was. He flicked an invisible something off the lapel of his high-priced suit. Finally, his head came up and his eyes locked on Eric. "I should've killed you at Ashford. Where is she?"

"Safe," Eric bit out, shifting one boot forward in preparation for the pounding kickback his rifle would soon deliver. His rifle contained a built-in shock absorber in the butt-stock, but ballistics being what they were, his shoulder would still be damn sore at the end of this fight. "You honestly think I'd bring her here? How stupid are you?"

Carlson's eyes narrowed. His head bobbed once in one of those cocky guy-moves, the ones shitty winners traditionally gave sorry losers on the basketball court. The gloves off nod that says: *I don't have to play fair because I own the refs.*

Eric answered back with the laser dot of his Leupold scope dead center on Carlson's forehead. *I'm not playing.*

At least, he had the good sense to stop advancing. He might own the world, just not the zone between his brain and the business end of Eric's rifle. Carlson still thought he had a dog in this fight, though. Brushing his high-end jacket out of the way, he rested both palms to his hips as he scanned Murphy's house and garage. "We both know where she is. You should have taken her into that bunker of yours, old man." He blew out a breath, shaking his head as if making a tough decision. "I'd rather not burn this quaint little cottage to the ground, but I will. I'm not leaving without her."

"Try it," Eric hissed. "I may not be rich, but I can promise, you'll die first."

"And then what?" Carlson barked, his dark brows arrowed. "You'll go down in a hail of gunfire? Trust me, all of your men will die too, and in the end, one of my guys will still get her. Do you honestly think I've come this far without a back-up plan? Who's stupid now, Reynolds?"

Carlson cocked one elbow as he lifted his index finger to his chin. "Even if I were to, say, have a massive heart attack tomorrow while teeing off at Pebble Beach, she'd still be MY corporate asset." Fisting that same hand, he thumped his chest like a Neanderthal, his gaze still on Eric. "Don't you get it? Someone like your wife can only belong to a man like me, Reynolds. I'm the only one who can hone that remarkable talent of hers. Like it or not, she's mine."

God, none of this made sense. It hadn't from the start. "Why the hell do you want her?" Eric hated having to ask, but it gave him something to do before he turned Carlson's head to mist.

"Because I can break him, Eric, my one true love," Shea's sweet voice answered from over his right shoulder.

The pitch of his rifle would've dropped if not for the genuine gleam on Carlson's smirky face inside the crosshairs. The bastard eyeballed Shea like she was the most precious creature on the planet. Or his next greatest investment.

"Get back," Eric hissed at her, not daring to take his eyes off target. "Please, baby. Go back inside."

Of course, she didn't listen. "I know now why you paid that guy to torture me and kill Phoenix and Gordie. It wasn't for the invention. You didn't want Gordie to work for you, did you, Mr. Carlson?"

How could she be on her feet already, much less be so polite to this monster? Eric shifted his stance, ready to end Carlson if he took one step in her direction.

"God, you are a true beauty," the pompous man gushed.

"Answer the question," Shea returned. "Why did you have my friends killed?"

He glowed. The bastard glowed as if Shea had made all of his wishes come true just by showing up. "That's not precisely accurate, Mrs. Reynolds. May I call you Shea?"

"Mrs. Reynolds to you," she bit out.

You tell him, baby.

"Fine then. Mrs. Reynolds." He offered a courtly head nod. "That day in the lab, I wanted Finn, but I fell for that disgusting disguise you'd created. Frankly, I couldn't bring myself to hire anyone so repulsive looking as you were then." He waved one hand to his nose. "You carried it off quite well, you know. I never suspected that a lady as elegant as you lay hidden beneath the folds of all that fat and poor hygiene. Well played."

"Then why kill my friends?"

"Because of what that fool Mikkelson said."

"Explain," Shea ordered.

Carlson folded one arm over his chest, the other cocked with his fingertips skimming his chin. "He called you the genius behind them. Why would I want him when I could've had you, even as disgusting as you were then? His rejection that morning forced me to rethink my strategy. I couldn't just turn and proposition someone like Finn, even as brilliant as he, ahem, you were. It was obvious you three were bound together by something more than science."

"So you thought if you killed my friends I'd be desperate enough to come crawling to you with their invention?" When her elbow brushed Eric's forearm, he shifted to make room for her between himself and Murphy.

Carlson cocked his head. His smirky mask drooped as if he'd suddenly realized something. "You bitch!" he hissed, his brows spiked like ugly rainbows. "You didn't discover it, did you? You have nothing to do with dynamic energy displacement, do you?"

She leaned into Eric as if for strength. The poor thing was shaking. "Wow. For a smart guy, it took you long enough to figure that out. No, I don't have a clue how Gordie and Phoenix's energy displacement thing works. They were the geese that laid your golden egg, Mr. Wizard. I just came up with the funding that allowed them to run with their dreams as far as they could. They were two of the most genuinely, loving people I've met in my life, but—you killed them."

Eric caught a quick glimpse of her in his peripheral. Forest green sweatshirt and pants. Trembling. Sweating. Murphy's open laptop shifted in her left palm, her right hand poised over the keypad. Her index finger hovered on the ENTER key like it was a trigger. One she couldn't miss. *What a sight.*

But Eric had to know. "You'd already bought Phoenix Berglund by then, hadn't you? You paid him off. Why?"

Professor Grover had the nerve to smile. "I made him a little deal, you see. He was supposed to hand over Finn, but then he backed out. Now I know why, don't I? He never planned to go through with it, did he?"

Eric could feel Shea tremble at this new betrayal. "You… you paid him to sell me out?"

Grover's shoulders lifted along with his bushy eyebrows as if he thought it were no big deal. "It's called insider trading, my dear sweet girl. People get away with it all the time. It's just good business."

"It's called backstabbing and murder, you ass," Murphy hissed.

A dainty snort huffed through Shea's nostrils. "And now, because of your greed, the world will never know about dynamic energy displacement." She took a step forward, shaking, but with her head raised high. "The discovery of the ages is lost, Mr. Carlson, because you killed to get what would never be yours. And yes, I have Phoenix's laptop, but you'll never get that, either. It's as lost to you now as your twenty-seven offshore bank accounts and every last penny in them. Your cozy home in Cap d'Ail, France. The mansion in Mallorca, Spain. That godawful thing you call a home in Dubai. Your billion-dollar Swiss chalet up high in the Alps." Her voice ratcheted higher with every exclamation. "How much money *did* you have, Mr. Carlson?"

Carlson's eyes were nearly bugged out by the time Shea finished. He shuddered as much as she did. Half turning to Grover, he muttered out of the corner of his mouth, "You told me Finn was the genius."

"But he is," Grover mumbled. "He, ah, I mean, she's the only reason I accepted the other two. They were a packaged deal, but she's the one, damn it. I know she is. Can't you see? She's been pilfering millions out of some Saudi prince's account for months, and now she's bankrupting you."

Carlson bit out, "She isn't that smart—"

"How'd you know?" Shea interrupted. "Professor Grover, how'd you know about… that?" She bit her lip and Eric was glad she hadn't divulged Bagani's name. Grover had enough dirt on Shea. "Are you spying on me?"

"I've got my ways," Grover murmured, his eyes shifting to his feet then back to her.

She stamped one foot in frustration. "You never had a stroke, did you? Everything you did was a lie, wasn't it? I trusted you. Gordie trusted you. Are you even a real professor?"

Eric winced. The regret in her voice was palpable.

"Of course I'm a professor. I'm tenured. Not everything I said was untrue," Grover answered in that singsong voice he had. He cocked his head, his fingers clasped over his belly. "You'll always be my favorite lucky star."

"I'm not your anything!" Shea spat. "They're dead, and you're as guilty of murder as that creep who killed them!"

"Shut up!" Carlson bellowed at his buddy in crime. "I don't care about her pilfering some loser's money! Where's the damned dynamic energy displacement model you promised me?"

CHAPTER THIRTY-THREE

"Let me get this straight," Eric interrupted only because he wanted to rub it in. "You wanted Shea because you thought she invented dynamic energy displacement? That was why you had your Abdul-Mutaal knock-off assassinate her friends? The ones who actually invented it? How stupid are you?"

"Discovered it," Grover corrected. "Phoenix and Gordie actually dis—"

"Shut up!" Carlson roared, the lines of his face rigid with frustration.

Murphy chuckled. "Well, I'll be dogged. You two are a couple of flaming jack-holes. Don't you check your sources, Carlson?"

"I did," he hissed, his pallor a little on the deathly side of pale.

Shea's fingernails still tapped at her keyboard, and the one thing that had been made irrefutably clear. She had not only the means and the motive—she now had all the power.

Eric wrapped a steadying arm around her waist without taking eyes off his target. She needed to know she was not alone. He planted a quick whisper kiss to her cheek. "I've got your six, babe. Do what you have to do."

The poor thing shivered despite the hold she had over Carlson, but her voice rang out as clear as the 4pm closing bell at the New York Stock Exchange bell. "Your chip is a fraud."

Damned if Carlson didn't get paler. All that rich-boy-on-the-block cockiness evaporated. He took a step back, shaking his head. Blinking.

Shea kept going. "I cracked your code, Mr. Carlson. You buried a level-eight replicating worm in it, didn't you? That's why Murphy can't reach Alex or... or anyone else in the United States. But I've got news for you. Right now, Interpol's looking for you. They want to question you about the blackout that took out the eastern power grid in the United States, half of Canada, and Quebec today. They've tracked the blackout to *your* chip."

"How do you know that?" He challenged.

Shea stuck her chin at him. "I just told you. I cracked your chip. Isn't that what you always wanted? One Nation. One Network. One World? That's what's at the other end of this little plastic ENTER key. Your whole world," she ground out.

Carlson's eyes hit the dirt. He jerked his thumb over his shoulder and snapped, "Move out," to Grover and his goons.

"Oh, no, you don't." Shea took a full step forward, away from Eric and out of her comfort zone. "You don't get to walk away from this, Mr. Carlson. Not today. You killed my friends. You and Grover paid that Abdul-Mutaal look-alike to drown me." Her shoulders shook with fright while Eric's heart swelled with pride. "I found everything I needed to know about you on the *World Wide Web*. I didn't even need to hack your personal accounts for that."

Jordan exhaled a hearty, "Damn, she's good," from Eric's right.

Shea drilled Carlson. "Were you there when your hired-killer was drowning me? Were you there when Gordie begged for mercy while your assassin cut his fingers off?" Her voice wrapped to a high pitch. "Do you know Phoenix cried when your evil minion flogged him within an inch of his life? Ask me how I know this, Mr. Carlson! Ask me how I know that you murdered your first wife?!"

Holy shit! didn't begin to describe the jolt to Eric's heart. His sweetheart had just taken a scary turn toward becoming one of those evil minions who thought they could take over the world. "Shea," he whispered, needing to reel her in before this attack of hers blew up in her pretty face. "You don't want to do this."

"I do," she answered with a stomp of her bare foot. "I really do. I ran from my problems once, but I'm not running anymore. He killed her, Eric, and she was pregnant! He killed his unborn baby!"

Man, this twisted nightmare just kept getting worse and worse. Shea still suffered from losing her own little girl. The murder of this unborn child was now the last straw that just might push her over the edge.

Eric could tell Shea was crying by the wretched crack in her voice, and because he knew his woman, he stopped being her hero, and he let her take the lead. This was her show, her decision point to make. He wouldn't betray her trust by offering one solitary excuse why Carlson should be allowed to live. Eric couldn't honestly think of one, not after how Phoenix and Gordie had suffered. But everything—his heart, her life, and their future—was on the line. If this plan of hers backfired…?

"I can't lose you again, baby," Eric murmured out of the corner of his mouth, praying Carlson couldn't hear him, but that Shea would understand what he hadn't said. *Don't get yourself killed trying to end Carlson. The man isn't worth it.*

"Wh-what are you going to do?" Carlson asked, like he didn't already know.

She cleared her throat, her eyes on her target. "I'm transferring every last penny out of your accounts—all of your accounts—to people who really need it."

His hands come up. "No, stop—"

"Too late!" she shrieked, the tip of her dainty index finger hovering at a ninety-degree angle over the ENTER key. "I hate everything you stand for. You're nothing but another Hitler in disguise. A Pol Pot! You're a disease, and you know what happens to diseases?"

"No!" He took a step forward. "Wait. Jesus Christ, don't do it! I'll make you rich—"

Eric stepped to Shea's side, his finger snug in the curve of that trigger. "Don't come any closer."

"I don't want money!" she shrieked, her neck stretched forward as if she needed Carlson to know that a lowly woman had bested him. "You've got nothing I want because You. Are. Nothing!"

Carlson's shoulders stiffened. "At least think about it, Shea, I mean, Mrs. Reynolds. Come on, be reasonable," he couched his words in despair even as his shoulders lifted like a little boy who was still working to get his way. "Think what you and I—"

With a toss of her shorn locks, Shea took a deep breath, her spine straight, her beautiful neck erect, and her head held high. Yeah, this was so going to happen. Eric couldn't have been prouder—or more worried.

"Viruses," she said quietly, the hate and anger suddenly under control. "Viruses that cause disease get eradicated, Mr. Carlson. Something bigger and better comes along, and Mother Nature wipes them out."

Sometimes, it was the little things that mattered the most. The dime-sized pad of Shea's fingertip hitting the stamp-sized ENTER button on Murphy's laptop. The fraction of a second for a tiny thing like her to bring a bigger-than-life monster to his knees. Or the wisp of a gasp from her small, compromised lungs when the deed was done. The twitch of despair that contorted Carlson's brilliant, privileged mug. In the end, it all came down to—*One. Little. Tap.*

"No, no, no!" Carlson lifted his clenched fists to his temples. "You didn't!"

But yes, yes, yes. Shea did. By the time Murphy's laptop fell to the ground at her feet, the deed was done and Carlson was ruined. "There. Now you're as dead as Gordie and Phoenix," she told him, her chin still up. "How's it feel, Mr. Carlson?"

God, don't taunt the guy now that you've poked his eye out. Eric pulled her back into his side, his rifle still aimed for a headshot if Carlson so much as breathed wrong. Without looking, he sought her cheek with his lips. Damn, he was proud of his wife, but scared what might go down next.

Carlson snapped his wrist forward as if tossing an invisible towel into the ring. Grover pivoted to his left, motioning with a sweeping gesture across his neck to his guys. Murphy and Jordan closed ranks with Shea squeezed in tight. It happened too quickly to know precisely which one of them fired first, but *HOLY SHIT!*

Any gunfire was swiftly overcome when, with a screeching bellow, the five-ton cargo truck pitched up from the ground in a heaving ball of flames. All doors popped open. Black smoke belched out from shattered windows that instantly resembled empty eye sockets. Grover's men screamed and ran, some of them engulfed in flames. Murphy's cottage windows blew, too. Eric slammed Shea into his side, protecting her with his body while the wreck spewed whistling, burning shrapnel.

Murphy knocked them both to the ground, covering them with his body as well. Jordan joined the huddle, while Eric tried like hell to maintain a protective barrier over Shea, his elbows locked at the sides of her head to keep the weight of his friends from crushing her.

A tear dripped straight out of his eye and onto her pretty face. It trickled down her cheek, and their gazes locked. This was it, damn it. The end. Between the hail of gunfire, the fireworks, and the shrapnel from that five-ton, it wouldn't take long before Murphy or Jordan took a hit. Then him. But not Shea.

"I've got you, baby," he ground out. His elbows dug painfully into Murphy's concrete patio. "I didn't mean for it to end like this."

"Me neither." She reached one hand up between their bodies and wiped her thumb under his eye, cupping his jaw.

God, she was a study in peace and calm, her nightmares at last revealed and dealt with. "You're hurt."

He shrugged it off. "Yeah, well, it's been a tough day."

"You've always been my hero, Eric," she said, her eyes brimming. "I only wish I could love you longer."

"How about forever?" he asked. Because that was what lay ahead. Death. Then forever. With her and Cheyenne. Except for the dying part, it almost seemed inviting.

More shots rang out. He waited for Murphy or Jordan to flinch from a hit, or for the bullet with his name on it to find its way through them and into his ribs or skull. He kissed his wife one last time, her lips quivering as he stiffened his neck and shoulders to not bump heads with her. He pressed his lips to hers and absorbed the tender flesh one last time. There was no better way to die than protecting her to the bitter end. If this was to be his final moment on earth, it was enough.

"Close your eyes and hold onto me," he ordered, gritting his teeth. "Even if I get hit, hold your cover until the shooting stops. Let me shield you until the end. Then I want you to live for me, Shea. No matter what, never forget how much I love you, but live, damn it. Find a way to be happy. Go back to that desert island and live."

"No," she said, a sob caught in her throat. "I go where you go. That's the deal." She pressed her face into the breathing space beneath his chin, her breath warm and moist on his neck. "I'm never leaving you again."

So be it then. Eric closed his eyes and waited for the end, while Murphy and Jordan still hugged the living shit out of him. Hell had come to Murphy's quaint little cottage. The groans and shrieks of falling rubble filled the yard. The rancid stench of burning diesel clung to every breath, coating his tongue, until…

All at once—silence—except for the roar of flames from the burning rig, and the groans of a few injured men. Eric didn't dare hope the shooting was over. When nothing else came except a grumbly, "Damn, girl. Are you finished yet?" from Murphy, Eric pushed out from under his guys.

Lo and behold, Elsa Finnegan stood there with the butt of her rifle on her hip, and an army of three stalwart young men at her six. They had that same devil-may-care glint in their smiling eyes as she did.

God, don't tell me the IRA just saved my life, Eric thought as he pushed to his feet with Shea plastered to his side. Yet it surely looked as if that was what had gone down. Grover's men were on the ground, some by fire, some by gunshot. A gray sweater smoldered over a dismembered body. Carlson's body was indistinguishable in the debris.

"You Americans," Elsa muttered, her right cheek pinched into a smirk. "Why are you hiding like a bunch of school children? Did I nah tell ye that I have friends in high places?"

Ah, he loved her Irish brogue. Eric would've kissed her himself, but Jordan beat him to it. One of her brothers-in-arms belted Murphy's upper bicep a stiff one. "'Tis a fine barrel of Jamison you'll be owing your niece for saving yer sorry arse now, Finnegan. Let's have a go 'fore she's done mugging the hired help and drinks 'tall herself."

Elsa eased out of Jordan's clutches long enough to mutter a quick, "Knock it off, Sean. Go secure the prisoners if there be any left alive." When Jordan dropped his hands, she snagged his collar. "Not you, my handsome man. I have plans for you."

Now that the danger had passed, Shea couldn't seem to stop crying. Her friends had stood with her during that daring face-off with Carlson. Not only Eric, Jordan, Murphy, and Elsa, but Phoenix and Gordie, too. She'd felt them. Even Cheyenne was there—in spirit. They'd all filled her with confidence that evaporated the moment she'd hit that ENTER key.

After quick introductions with Elsa and her team, Eric carried Shea into the cottage and straight back to bed. He set her on the edge of the mattress and removed the tennis shoes she'd borrowed while she struggled to compose herself. Winning should've felt better than this, but all that noise. All those men dying. It was a horrible way to end this... this mission.

Sliding his palms up her thighs, Eric tugged her borrowed sweat pants off. The sweatshirt went next, before he wrapped her in the blanket and gathered her onto his lap. Finally, he settled against the headboard, and there he stayed, breathing hard with her pressed under his chin. "God, baby, you never cease to amaze me."

"I told you I could wreck him," she croaked, for the first time free of the death threat hanging over her. Ruining Carlson financially seemed enough of a fitting punishment, but Elsa's solution honestly felt better. Carlson deserved to die.

"Were you serious? Carlson's chip is a hoax?"

"It's actually not, but it is designed to leave a port open on any security operating system it encounters. That was how he brought the eastern seaboard down. He's got someone on-line at this very moment hacking more power grids than just our country's. Whoever Carlson's computer tech guy is, he or she is as dangerous as Carlson was."

"And he killed his first wife?"

She nodded. "For a genius, he wasn't very smart. He kept three ghost files on his desktop. One contained a video clip that looked like it was taken from a scope. It showed Prentiss Carlson through crosshairs at the railing of a ship. Remember when she went missing on that cruise? The guy who did the job tossed her body overboard after he killed her and her baby. That clip was his proof of death so his hired assassin could get paid."

Shea whined, her heart breaking for that other lost child, the one Carlson hadn't wanted.

Eric whistled under his breath. "What was in the other two files?"

"Sheesh, eric, I didn't have time to look at everything. I needed a kill-switch to all his accounts before you guys got yourselves killed." A yawn came out of nowhere. Shea ran her fingers through her hair, shuffling it like a handful of playing cards. "And I know where Rosie and the cabbie are. They're at another one of Mr. Carlson's mansions. Look for the castle north of the *River Suir*. At least they're safe."

"Remind me never to get on your bad side," Eric murmured as his large hands skated down her back to her ass. The man had no idea the surge of warmth that flooded her at his intimate touch. It usually excited, but this time, it was the perfect gesture. Eric had literally held her life in those powerful, tender hands. Cheyenne's, too.

"Tell me a story?" she asked because that might be the only way to get him to stop with the questions.

The sound coming up from his chest rumbled like pure honey on her favorite hero pancakes. He kissed the top of her head, but she only lasted long enough to hear, "Once upon a time, there were three dirty little pigs..."

CHAPTER THIRTY-FOUR

"No fucking way," Jordan hissed. "That's who you are?"

Eric lifted his head from the pillow; surprised he'd dozed off, but positive of the cuss word from beyond the guest room. Easing his aching body out from beneath his sleeping wife, he rolled her onto her side. The poor thing didn't budge. He tucked Shea into bed before he joined the warriors gathered in Murphy's living room.

"What's up?" Eric asked quietly, shutting the bedroom door behind him.

"Them," Jordan said from where he sat beside Elsa on the sofa, his arm behind her, his gaze fixed on the men sitting cross-legged on the floor.

Eric took a good, hard look at Elsa's team with their short haircuts and straight postures. The same dark trousers. Same button-up shirts. All sported a golden winged angel pinned to their collars. That seemingly insignificant detail explained Jordan's F-bomb. Elsa and these men were not just Ireland's version of Army Rangers. They were military intelligence, the infamous G2. In person.

And that angel depicted on the pins? None other than God's right-hand man himself, Gabriel, the bringer of tidings of great joy as well as the bearer of dire consequences. Gabriel was the archangel with Daniel in the lion's den during ancient times. He'd protected God's prophet while, at the same time, he'd foretold the downfall of wicked Persia and Greece. Yeah. That guy. "Military Intelligence, huh?" Eric asked.

The nearest man climbed to his feet and stuck out a hand to Eric. Discerning blue eyes twinkled. "Agent Sean Denning at your service, Agent Reynolds. You've a bit of the old sod in ye, do ye nah?"

"Both of my parents," Eric said as he returned the strong grip, "and my wife."

"Aye, the Powers hail from County Kilkenny as I'm sure ye know, the Reynolds from County Dublin. What took yer ancestors to America? 'Twas the famine?"

"One of them," Eric admitted. "Thanks for having our backs out there. I'm glad none of you were hurt."

By then, the others were on their feet. "'Twas our pleasure," one of them said. "I'm Gary Dunne and this lad here's Brian O'Macken. 'Tis a good day when we get to save an American's arse."

"And this American is damned glad you did," Eric returned. "Come visit me the next time you're stateside. I'll show you around."

"I'll bloody well take you up on that, mate," Gary said. "Me wife's family lives in Boston. You might be seeing me sooner than ye think."

"While you've been tending to your wife, the rest of us dealt with the authorities," Elsa piped up, her palm comfortable on Jordan's thigh. "The coroner and his technicians are still gathering the bodies, and the constable wants to speak with

Shea and you. I told him that wouldn't be possible, that you need to leave Ireland by nightfall."

That was considerate. "And...?" Eric waited, his mind racing over what he thought he knew. Could leaving this country be that easy?

Elsa winked. "Get your wife ready to travel. A private helicopter is standing by to fly you to Shannon Airport. Once there, you'll transfer to Aer Lingus. You're booked first class. You should be able to sleep and do it in comfort."

Eric raked his fingers over his head. Sleep was the last thing on his mind. "We're taking the laptop with us."

"As you should," Elsa said without batting an eye. Lifting her left wrist, she checked her watch. "We leave in thirty minutes. Can Shea be ready by then?"

"You bet."

"I'll get the laptop that caused all this trouble," Murphy said, pushing up from his easy chair. Elsa's three men followed him out.

"Come sit, man," Elsa declared once the room cleared, chin nodding at the chair beside her. "What else do I need to know before you leave?"

While Jordan settled back with his eyes on Elsa, Eric took the chair to Elsa's left and he divulged what Shea had shared. The ghost files on Carlson's computer. The clear-cut evidence of the first Mrs. Carlson's assassination. The fraud known as the Carlson Chip.

"But nothing about the dynamic energy displacement model, eh?" Elsa pressed, one brow lifted. By then her elbows were on her knees and her hands were clasped. It was obvious she had her eye on the prize as well. God bless Murphy for not divulging that bit of intel to his niece. It would've been easy enough, as close as they were.

"I have no idea," Eric hedged. He didn't know for certain and Shea had never said, but he suspected the DED was on Phoenix's laptop. It was good to know that the guy had put his life in danger trying to do—at the end—what was right. With Carlson's millions waved under his nose, what twenty-some kid wouldn't have been tempted?

Mental note to self: Ask that courageous woman of mine where she transferred Carlson's money. That would be nice to know.

"Your wife is very good with a computer," Elsa stated the obvious. "NCSC would like to speak with her. Sooner than later." Another blatant hint.

Eric nodded, but Ireland's *National Cyber Security Centre* could take a number. The FBI folks at Quantico would be *speaking* with Shea first. Possibly last.

"We're all in this together." Elsa softened her tone. "All of us who stand on the side of freedom, that is. *Fe Mhoid Bheith Saor.* Sworn to be free—or die, remember?"

"You don't have to tell me, but Shea's not cut out for this job. She's lost enough."

"Then let's get her to that land of liberty you're so proud of." With her palms to her knees, Elsa pushed to her feet, a genuine smile on her face. "You look ten sheets to the wind."

No kidding. In the last week, he'd survived a rollover and a beating. He'd been shot and possibly suffered a minor concussion. Not to mention all those damned airline flights he'd taken while he'd tracked Finn. Jordan didn't look a whole lot better, but what worried him at the moment? "Can you take care of my cat?"

A big, shitty grin cracked Jordan's mug, but Elsa winked. "Aye, I can do that for you. Uncle Murphy told me about yer Aishling. 'Tis the perfect name for her, don't ye think?"

Eric cocked his head. "Excuse me?" *She's just a cat. A clever cat, but still...*

"You didn't know? Aishling is Gaelic for dream, Eric."

Was that supposed to mean something? He had to ask, "Does she seem odd to you? As if she knows what you're thinking?" *As if she does walk in dreams?*

Elsa winked. "I would nah be surprised. The cats of Ireland have always been linked to the magic of the Fae. Why else would she be here if she had nah known you needed her?"

"I needed her?" Not likely, but now that he had time to think about it, Aishling was a most curious animal. *And those crystal blue eyes...* He brushed the Fae explanation aside as nonsense akin to the Irish folklore of leprechauns and elves. "You'll keep her until I can send for her then?"

"You know I will. Uncle Murphy's going back to America with you, so I'll transport her back to Dublin when I leave here. I'll keep her safe until you call for her to join you."

Eric offered his hand. "We wouldn't have survived this without your assist. I hope you know that."

Elsa came forward, her handshake as firm as a man's. "Aye, you would, so don't go thanking me just yet. 'Twas Jordan who set the perimeter charges before Grover showed up with his feckin' five-ton. All we did was finish the job."

Eric hadn't known that. "You did?"

There sat Jordan, as humble as ever. "I let you down once, brother. I wasn't doing it again. I owed you. No one, and I mean, no one, was getting your woman again."

That binding word again. *Brother.* Civilians who hadn't served would never know that it was enough to make a grown man cry.

Eric had Shea dressed and on her feet in ten minutes, groggy, but mobile. "And you," he murmured to Aishling, who was stretched out on the bed, soaking up what was left of Shea's body warmth. "I'll come back for you, so don't go getting your lovely self lost."

Damned if the silly cat didn't wink. *Uncanny is what she is. Damned uncanny. Dream, huh?* Eric closed Aishling inside the bedroom, so she wouldn't sneak out and get lost, not that he thought a door would stop her.

Elsa's promised helicopter sat waiting in the pasture behind Murphy's cottage. While Jordan loaded their gear, Elsa chatted with her uncle. "You'll be back next week then?"

"Moira and I are flying into Sword Sunday night. If you and your guys are free, meet us there for dinner," Murphy said as he stowed the laptop. "You know the place."

"Aye, that carvery you like so well, and no doubt, a pint of black beer," Sean declared easily.

More backslapping. More handshaking. Once Jordan finished mugging Elsa, he climbed onboard, and the helicopter lifted. Eric should have felt a measure of relief, but he'd seen too many Black Hawks brought down on their way to shelter. Still antsy, he watched for lingering signs of trouble in the soft green meadow below. The sun's glare off a sniper's scope. The skulking shadow of a killer at the tree line.

At Shannon, an armed security guard accompanied them from the helicopter to a nearby airliner waiting on the tarmac. When they boarded without incident, the smallest whisper of peace breathed hope into Eric that this op was truly over.

Because he had Shea to care for this time around, the transatlantic flight went by quickly. She slept most of the way, but near the end of it, she roused in a steadier frame of mine. Elsa must've alerted the crew to her delicate condition. The two flight attendants couldn't seem to do enough for her.

God, the Statue of Liberty in New York Harbor was a welcome sight. "I'm home," Shea whispered from where she was tucked in under his arm. "I'm finally home."

Eric planted a kiss to the top of her head. He'd given her the window seat for this precise moment. The first glimpse of America was always a heartfelt rush after deployments. "Almost. We still have to catch an express into Reagan, but you're sleeping in our bed tonight."

"Our bed?" she asked, that beautiful glint of disbelief in her eye. "The same one? You kept it?"

How could he tell her what a sap he was? That bed was the place he'd prayed and cried for her every night since she'd run away. He couldn't get rid of it any more than sign that damned divorce decree. Eric settled for an extra moist kiss to her forehead. "Our bed, baby. The house is different, but the bed..." He choked. "The bed's sacred, baby." *It's where we made love and I'm never getting rid of it.*

Shea snuggled into him, her hand on his chest and the scenery forgotten. "I so hope I'm pregnant," she whispered at his neck.

What a marvelous, hopeful thing to look forward to. Eric held his wife as the aircraft circled the city before it landed at JFK. The fairytale ending Shea deserved was finally in reach.

"There's something you need to know before we go home," Eric whispered on approach.

His wife's lashes lifted as she looked up at him. "Yes?"

"We've got three dogs now."

Her eyes lit up. Her shoulders scrunched. "We do?"

"Yeah." He pressed his forehead to hers. "Bogie, Buddy, and Beau. They were strays. I got them from the shelter. They're boarded now and I'll have to stop on the way home to get them."

"Aww, the three dirty little pigs," she said, her fingertips on his cheek, making him wish they were already home and in that bed.

"The house was empty and I... I..."

"And you filled it up," Shea finished for him.

"Something like that," he admitted. His throat closed at the memory of all the lonely nights that left him feeling like he lived in a morgue. Bogie and Buddy joined the solitude first, but then he'd spotted little Beau quivering in the farthest corner of a big empty kennel, so now he was a no-kidding dog owner. Between them and Harley's Bible, things were almost bearable until that South American op when he thought he'd lost his picture of Cheyenne. It wasn't the only one he had of her, but it was the one he'd talked to. Cried with. *Yeah, that.*

"I can't wait to meet them. What kinds are they?"

"Bogie and Buddy are brothers, brindle pit bulls, but Beau's the boss. He's some kind of a Chihuahua mix. Looks a little like a Jack Russell with whiskers all over his face. You should see him chase his brothers. He thinks he owns the place."

"And now we'll have Aishling," Shea murmured. "We'll have a house full."

Eric slid his palm over Shea's flat belly. "I hope."

Just then the pilot announced their arrival. Sixty-three degrees and scattered showers in New York City. He thanked everyone for flying Aer Lingus and landed the flight with barely a bump or a rattle. *Give that man a standing ovation,* Eric thought as he pressed one last kiss to the top of Shea's head.

"There's a limo waiting for you on the tarmac," one of the flight attendants said. "Courtesy of a Captain Finnegan of the Irish Guarda. Do you know her? She said the limo was on the house."

That elicited a growl from Murphy. "That girl's making too much money."

Eric kept his opinion to himself. Throwing a little money at the hacker who'd gotten away was a smart move on Elsa's part. It was a small token of one-upmanship in the face of the formidable FBI, but it was classy. Damned classy.

"I'm good with it," Jordan said brightly.

Of course you are, Eric thought, *you hound dog. It's a send-off from Elsa. Why wouldn't you be good with it?* "How long before our connection?" he asked the attendant.

"Three hours," she replied. "That should be enough for you to grab a decent lunch."

"And a pint or two," Murphy added.

"And I need to call Ireland." Jordan didn't seem to know when to leave well enough alone.

"Not to my niece, you're not," Murphy shot over his shoulder as they disembarked.

The showy limo, a black Lincoln Town car stretch, was a nice change from the usual airport shuttles. The uniformed driver stood at crisp attention as they made their way down the steps. With a curt nod, he ushered Jordan and Murphy in first, then assisted Shea to the side-bench. Amenities of the highest order greeted Eric once inside. Plush white leather seats, as soft as butter. A sidebar with Irish Crystal decanters, matching lowball glasses. A Bunn push-button coffee thermos. Irish Coffee cups with crystal handles. *Chic. Very chic.*

All exterior limo windows were tinted dark to ensure anonymity, the privacy screen between the driver and the occupants as well. Once the driver closed the passenger door, he was out of sight and out of mind.

As the engine left the runway in its rearview, Eric tugged Shea into his side, content to hold her on this last leg of her harrowing two-year journey. The driver had placed her next to the privacy screen, but Eric wanted her in his arms. "Almost home," he whispered against her temple.

Her answering squeeze on his thigh jump-started a fever in his blood that he couldn't wait to put out. The Reynolds family was finally back together, maybe with a baby on the way. Except for his report to Alex, *Operation Find Finn* was over. Berglund's laptop with its dynamic energy displacement model was in safe hands, Murphy's at the moment. *God, it's good to be home.*

Jordan kicked his long legs into the center aisle, his head tipped back. "I had no idea G2 had these kinds of funds. Man, Murph, your niece is spoiling us rotten. I think I'm in love."

"You do know I'm right here, don't you?" Murphy growled. "Keep your paws off my niece, Hannigan."

Jordan lifted a brow, his grin wide and relaxed. "She started it."

"Hey, Eric, why don't you call up front and find out where we're going?" Murphy asked.

"Knowing, my girlfriend, we're probably on our way to a fine Irish pub," Jordan added. "I'd wager there's plenty of them in New York City. Are you good for twenty, Murph?"

Murphy landed a smack to the backside of Jordan's head. "She's not your girlfriend, you bone-headed lout."

"Sorry, old man. That's between me and my girl."

"She's not your girl!" Another smack did nothing to dampen Jordan's wicked grin.

Depressing the call button, Eric asked their driver, "Excuse me, sir, but exactly where are you taking us?"

The privacy window lowered. A pistol lifted into view.

"To hell if I've got anything to say about it!" Hugh Carlson roared.

CHAPTER THIRTY-FIVE

"Give me the damned model," Carlson growled from the mangled mess that used to be his face. "Where is it? I know you have it."

Shea's heart dropped at the wretched sight of the man riding shotgun. How had he gotten from Ireland to JFK ahead of them? "What are you doing here?"

Instead of that salacious sneer Carlson was known for, saliva dribbled over a raw bottom lip as he spat, "I'm not as dumb as you idiots think."

Red seeped through the already bloodstained bandages on his hands and forearms. Charred hair and an oozing scalp turned him into a ghoulish sight. There was no hint of the arrogant brows. Worse, he seemed to have trouble gripping the weapon that bobbed with deadly intent, if not accuracy, in his right hand.

Eric leaned forward to protect her, but the second he went for his bag, Carlson bellowed, "Touch it and I'll blow her head off!" A dollop of spit slid over what was left of his lower lip, but he seemed not to notice. "Where is it? Give it to me."

"You should be in the hospital, Hugh," Murphy countered.

No. He should be dead.

Carlson fired once, straight up, blasting a hole through the limo roof. "Give it to me. Now!"

Murphy lifted his hands, both palms forward. "Now take it easy. I'm just trying to help—"

The gun jerked on him. "You say one more word and I'll blow you to hell. I swear I will."

They were barely off airport property. Surely someone heard that discharge. Eric wouldn't like it, but Shea knew what she had to do. All of these men would die for her if she didn't act. She couldn't bear it. Leaning away from the front seat, she murmured, "I'll take him to where it's hidden."

The distraction worked. Carlson's face turned towards her, and as quickly as it did, Eric's boot connected with Carlson's hand as Eric pulled her back under his arm with an angry, "Like hell you will!"

The pistol slipped, but just as quickly, another weapon appeared in Carlson's right. Damned if it wasn't a .44 Magnum, Israel's powerful semi-automatic, a Desert Eagle. With its six-inch barrel, it was one hundred percent blow-your-head-off deadly, just like the one in Eric's gun safe at home.

Carlson aimed at Eric, the barrel wavering like he couldn't see straight. The silvery flash of a blade in transit from Eric's right hand was all she saw until—*THUNK*. It landed.

Before Shea could catch her breath, Jordan scrambled past her and grabbed the weapon from Carlson's limp grip. "Pull over!" he commanded, pointing the weapon at the limo driver.

Like the fierce protector he was, Eric palmed the side of her face, forcing her to look away from the grisly view. But Shea needed to see the knife in Carlson's throat. She had to witness the desperate plea for help flickering in his lying eyes.

She had to hear his gurgling death rattle, so much like poor, sweet Phoenix's, just before he'd died. Shea had to know Carlson couldn't hurt her or anyone she loved ever again.

Shoving away from Eric, she angled past Jordan's beefy shoulder enough for one last look. "Die," she commanded Hugh Carlson on behalf of her murdered friends.

Eric kept a tight hold on her forearm as she aimed her hatred at the brutal financial genius who'd stooped so low as to kill his unborn child. "Die! God damn you, die!"

As if in defiance, Carlson gasped, "But I... I just want... Finn."

"Then take him!" Shea screamed, poor Eric holding her back with both hands now. "Take him to hell with you because I'm. Not. Finn! I'm Mrs. Eric Reynolds and you can't have me!"

God, it felt good to say that.

As Carlson collapsed to the floor, the limo bumped the curb. Murphy and Jordan tumbled out and restrained the driver, while Eric pulled Shea to the nearest storefront, his heart pounding as loudly as hers, still blocking her view.

Spectators gathered. They called their friends. They snapped selfies. Murphy bellowed for someone to, "Call 911, for god's sake!" Rain began to fall in a gentle drizzle then.

Shea lifted her face to the leaden skies. She'd finally reached the end of her rainbow and she'd found the pot of gold she'd been searching for in the heart of a man named Eric. Even now he wrapped her in a gentle hold with her back to his chest, his chin in the crook of her neck.

Together they faced their reflections in the plate glass window of—

Shea looked overhead to the sign. *Kelsey's Diner.* Hmmm. After all this time running for her life in Ireland, she'd expected something more mystical, like one of Rosie O'Banner's Irish blessing. At least something that signaled the end of her long odyssey home.

Eric nuzzled the ticklish spot behind her ear. "Are you ready to go home, wife?"

She pulled the manacle of his strong arms tighter around her, never more sure of anything. "I am home, Eric. Home is right here, with you," but then she added, "and I do want a baby. *Our* baby."

The sexy man's smile reflected in the glass couldn't have been wider, or his rakish eyes darker. "That I can do, Mama. That I can do."

EPILOGUE

The thing about being a greedy, billionaire bastard was all that money. After a guy died, it had to go somewhere. Now Eric knew where.

Mysteriously, the birthplace of modern democracy was able to turn its failing economy around. Who knew, right? The islands of Greece made for a beautiful second honeymoon, too. Secluded sandy beaches. Ancient, mystical ruins. The most amazing cuisine with tasty cheeses, olives, and wines, not that Shea could have any alcoholic beverages at the moment. Not with the next Reynolds bun in the oven. *Make that buns.*

The moment they'd hit Northern Virginia, she'd wanted one of those OTC pregnancy tests kits. Eric stopped at the nearest drugstore to oblige. She made her quick purchase, ran into the restroom, and all but glowed when she'd returned and showed him that little pee-stick lit up with the magic word: *pregnant.*

Talk about the understatement of the year.

Eric smiled at the prominent baby bump between her bikini top and bottoms while she soaked up rays on the beautiful, secluded Zakynthos Island. Apparently humping like bunnies in Ireland was magical. Shea was only three months along and already showing like five. *Triplets will do that to a gal.*

Call it luck. Call it another paradox of sly Mother Nature. Hell, call it the residual effect of dynamic energy displacement. But yeah, they were expecting three babies this go round. He couldn't have been happier. After he'd filled out his final report on *Operation Find Finn*, he'd re-married his pregnant wife and booked a cruise to the Med for their second honeymoon.

Alex was back from Ireland by then. It seemed he'd gone there not so much to bust Carlson's chops as to hunt down the diabolical hacker who'd brought most of the world, along with a good portion of its power grids, to its knees. He'd found the guy, thanks to Mother's and Ember's sharp tracking skills, inside one of Carlson's many corporate offices, this one in Belfast.

As a result of Carlson's bombastic ego, his chip was now illegal. His monopoly on communication had been broken, and all was well with the world—at least until the next megalomaniac lifted his or her ugly head.

As to how Hugh Carlson made it to JFK before they did? Eric hadn't the nerve to tell Shea yet, but she hadn't truly divested him of all his wealth in her dramatic stand-off with the evil narcissist. He'd hidden assets in so many shell corporations—some in his deceased wife's name and some in his unborn son's name—that all he had to do was make a call and the minions who owed him favors came running. Which proved once again that money can buy just about everything— but happiness.

The dynamic energy displacement gizmo? Safe in the hands of McCormack Industries, where it could be carefully studied instead of weaponized. Carlson was right on that point. Phoenix Berglund's discovery needed substantial funding, and with the country in economic crisis at the end of every fiscal year, well, Jed, another billionaire, was the man for the job. He promised full disclosure. Didn't every politician?

An inquiry into Carlson's first wife's death blew up all the gossip rags for a day or two. Prentiss Carlson's murder evoked a passionate discourse between Hollywood and Washington D.C. about gun control, but in the end, as usual, there was nothing to be done. The sniper for hire who'd assassinated her wasn't a U.S. citizen, so the second amendment debate didn't apply to him. He ended up being one of Carlson's ex-*Berets Verts*. France wanted him back. The United States was happy to oblige.

Carlson's other two ghost files? The Justice Department was knee deep in that little mess.

"Lose the suit," Eric ordered the National Security Agency's newest hire in their cyber-crime department.

Shea rolled to her side and lowered her Raybans with one fingertip. "Excuse me? Here? In public?"

He scanned the solitary beach from his chair. "I don't see any public, but I do want to see your bare ass. Now strip."

She lifted up from her towel and faced him with her hands on her hips, and her feet spread just enough to complete the perfect triangle. Two long legs that led straight to heaven. "What if someone sees me?"

He pointed to the sand between his bare feet. "No one's around for miles, and you know it. Drop that string you call a swimsuit and get over here." He almost said *please*, but stopped himself just in time. *Please* gave her a way out. Not this time. Not the way the sun kissed her golden skin, and not with her biting that lower lip like she was. He wanted his wife naked and he wanted her naked now.

Shea cocked her head, coy all of a sudden. Shy. Had to be because of those triplets and the fact that her body was changing in the best ways possible. Sometimes she actually thought she was unattractive. Her? The sexiest woman on the planet? *Oh, hell no.*

She shrugged the strap off one shoulder. Then the other. Bending forward, she dropped her bikini bottoms, her full breasts on display and—

He needed more room in his swim trunks.

"What now, husband?" she asked as she straightened, her tone deepened. She moistened her bottom lip, then clamped down on it with her top teeth. The way she sometimes clamped down on him.

Eric lifted out of his chair and discarded his trunks. He sat again and patted his thighs, his ankles together. "Come here, baby."

She tiptoed across the warm sand, her eyes hooded. The sway of her hips and the bounce to her breasts enflamed him all the more. Pregnancy looked good on Shea.

Planting one foot at each side of his chair, she straddled him. He palmed her backside, spreading her until he had her right where she belonged. Tilting forward into his forehead with a soft sigh, her sun-swollen lips begged to be kissed. The tips of those perfect, perky breasts skimmed his pecs. When he palmed her swollen nipples, her body tightened around his.

Fire licked up his body, filling him with the need to rock into her. Her body echoed his natural rhythm. Rocking. Deeper. Closing the deal until…

Squeezing her eyes shut, she clenched his manhood with a grip that made him hiss, and—damn. He slammed home. Coming home. Again and again.

Shea matched him every inch of the way until their bodies melted together under the pleasant Greek sky. It was hard to know where he left off and she began. Aftershocks trembled up her spine, clenching him. Clenching her.

At last spent, and for the moment sated, she settled under his chin. Eric closed his eyes and gathered her into his arms, blessed by the sun and triply blessed by the woman straddling his lap. This was as close as he'd ever get to his unborn babies, but he couldn't fathom anything better than being inside of her body with them.

Cheyenne's three brothers or sisters were tucked between two brave souls who'd conquered more demons than most people would face in a lifetime. And they'd done it together. He smoothed one hand up Shea's sun-warmed back as the wild Aegean Sea lapped at the shore.

She tipped back in his palms, her hands on his collarbones and her eyes bright with mischief. "Skinny dipping?"

He chuckled. "Ah, now you're brave."

Before she could answer, Eric pulled her into his mouth, hungry once more. At last, he planted a sealing kiss to her forehead and muttered, "Let's."

Lifting his wife to her feet, he took hold of her hand. The wind ruffled her short locks, and Eric knew to his soul that not all runners were cowards. Surely, not Shea. If anything, she'd proven her bravery every step of her two-year journey back to him. It took time, and yes, it was hard, but that was the epitome of courage, wasn't it? To be strong enough to admit to making the worst kind of mistake, then to face the person she'd hurt most. To be humble enough to beg forgiveness when forgiveness was what she'd most needed to give herself. To leave herself vulnerable to hurt once more. To believe.

Even there under the blue Mediterranean sky, Shea stood at the edge of another scary adventure. Motherhood. Of triplets.

But for now, the sapphire surf beckoned them to come play. Eric lifted her hand to his lips and together they ran like Adam and Eve into the rest of their life. This was after all, the way any fairytale worth the telling ended.

Happily. Ever. After.

THE END

Sneak Preview of Jake

Book 16

In the Company of Snipers

"For gawd sakes! Can't you walk no faster?"

Jake Weylin silently accepted the whining rant of his good buddy, Jamaal McCune, and picked up the pace. Both Marines out of the Corps and down on their luck, Jamaal made the difficult street life he'd chosen worse by drinking his troubles away. This afternoon's rant evolved from his hangover of the night before. It hadn't lessened with the stubborn guy's application of more alcohol. By ten, he was long past inebriated. By noon, he should've been flat on his back and snoring like the banshees of Jake's ancestor's homeland.

No such luck.

By four in the afternoon, Jamaal was falling-down-sloppy-drunk and crying because he missed his mama. When the big guy decided to put one away, there was no keeping up with him. Jake didn't blame him. He used to drown his sorrows almost as often as Jamaal did his, but the bigger problem at the moment was the two-inch gash on Jamaal's right butt cheek, proving once again that even the smallest flask of cheap red-eye did not belong in a man's back pocket. Why Jamaal had a mini-bottle stashed in his pants was another story not worth telling.

"The place'll be closed by the time we git there if'n we don't hurry," he grumbled while shuffling along, one big palm holding the wad of blue paper towels from the service station on the last corner to his bleeding backside. The Good Samaritan Free Clinic on Good Hope Road was five blocks away from their present hangout in the basement of what used to be an IGA grocery store. With only two blocks to go, Jake knew every step of them would be loud and painful.

"The clinic never closes," he offered meekly.

He didn't fight or argue anymore. There was no sense in it. The war in the Mideast had taken the last of his aggression and most of his self-confidence. He didn't look people in the eye these days and the only reason he'd come to Anacostia was to find Jamaal. He'd never intended to stay, only to look up his buddy and talk about the could-have-beens, the what-ifs, and the whatcha-gonna-do-nows. Maybe see if Jamaal had a spare room to offer a buddy for a night or two. At least that was the plan.

But everything changed when Jamaal opened his front door, blubbering his eyes out. He'd been evicted. Jake almost hadn't recognized the once proud black man he'd deployed with. Jamaal had sunk into serious depression after his mother passed away, but numbing his pain with booze didn't pay the bills.

They'd been on the streets ever since because the bond between brothers-in-arms ran strong. It all came down to the fact that Jamaal refused to leave his childhood neighborhood, and Jake refused to leave Jamaal. It was an odd pairing at best:

two bedraggled alcoholics who had once belonged in the company of the few and the proud. But there they were, one average-sized white guy and one bigger-than-life black guy, hanging out together in one of America's toughest neighborhoods and drowning their sorrows every chance they got.

At first, Jake had stood out like a sore thumb on the mostly African American side of the Anacostia River, directly south of the nation's *Oh-Say-Can-You-See* capitol. But Jamaal set the local gangbangers and riffraff straight. He'd told them Jake was a trained USMC scout sniper who'd gone crazy during a firefight in Kabul, Afghanistan. Bragged Jake could shoot a man's head off at two thousand yards, that he'd killed four men with his bare hands in a sneak attack. That he was stark-raving crazy and could snap at any moment. *Best watch your backs and be careful.*

At least Jamaal got one thing right. Maybe not the stark-raving part, but Jake was pretty sure he was leaning on the down side of crazy. Wasn't everybody who'd been in the sandbox?

Jamaal jerked to a stop and pointed his index fingers on the hand not holding his butt, at a gray Subaru parked alongside the clinic. "Who dat?"

Jake cringed. After a binge, Jamaal's grasp of the English language deteriorated along with his good sense. But who indeed was that slender woman standing at the open door of the parked Subaru, clutching the car's doorframe like a shield to ward him off?

The chilly December breeze shifting through the alley alongside the clinic pulled a loose strand of her hair out from the big black clip on the top of her head. He saw the problem clearly. The clip was too small for the bounteous mounds of brownish, reddish curls she'd tried to restrain. Good glory in the morning, but she was a breathtaking sight to behold. His heart damn near forgot to kick in with another beat the moment his eyeballs latched onto her.

She seemed frozen in place. He'd stopped dead in his tracks, too. The stupid thing in his chest did another funny kind of sucker punch, shutting off his windpipe and wiping his whiteboard clear of all intelligent words, like *hello* or *good evening* or *hey*.

"Huh," was what fell off his lips. He swallowed hard, certain that he was making a fool of himself. Like that was news...

She'd parked in one of the parking stalls marked *Employees Only*. Did that mean she worked at the clinic? Jake hadn't seen her here before, and with all the trouble Jamaal got into, he was here plenty. Was she new? Just visiting? Moving into the neighborhood?

A man could hope.

Another puff of the breeze set the rest of her hair loose to billow like a cloud behind her head. A halo formed around her delicate face at the same time her right brow lifted. Capturing her unruly locks with a quick handful, her nostrils flared. Her shoulders squared and her chin stuck out with defiance. Was she making a stand? *Against me?* It sure felt like it.

Damn. What a sight.

Just who the hell was she, another mean volunteer nurse at the clinic, or some fiery warrior goddess come from the halls of Valhalla? The sun at her back added to the illusion of fierce, feminine power, the kind that could back a man up as fast as if she'd stuck an M40, bolt-action, USMC scout sniper special up his nose.

Without thinking, Jake took a step away, yielding the alley to this alpha female. She could have the street too if she wanted it. He didn't. Then he took another step back in case she didn't believe him the first time.

"Hell, Jake, I'm gonna bleed to death if we keep walking backwards like we is," Jamaal complained, shifting his weight from one big flat foot to the other.

"Shhhhh," Jake whispered, his hand on his buddy's thick bicep to prevent further altercation. This Amazon warrior already had Jake by the balls, and she hadn't so much as said hello yet. Or go to hell and get out of my way, but hey. A guy could dream. "'Sides, you got plenty of blood. Let her get into the clinic first." *Nice and easy. Don't scare her. I'm liking the view.*

Jamaal huffed and grumbled. He whined, but held his position.

The woman pulled a backpack out of the squat vehicle, shut the door, and very deliberately headed straight for them instead of the door. Jake stopped breathing, like he had a choice in the matter. The closer she came, the surer he was that he might pass out. Hunter green eyes scrolled over him like he was actually visible to the naked eye, and he was acutely aware that he needed a shave and a trim. *A month ago.* He smelled like every other guy who lived in an abandoned building. *Bad. Really bad.*

Nonetheless, his spine straightened, and he didn't break eye contact with his target. Dread itched up the back of his neck, warning him. Or was he the target?

"Who are you?" she asked, looking at him—*just me*—as she broke the spell.

His gaze fell to where that simple question had come from. Had sincere concern just passed through those delectable, kissable shells that looked good enough to eat, like the sugary red roses on the top of wedding cakes? God, the closer she came, the more breathtaking she was.

It wasn't hair on her head, but was some kind of exotic spun sugar that refused to be ignored or controlled. Reddish gold strands of it caressed the pink blush on her high cheekbone, twisting under her chin like tendrils of some loving vine until she captured it and made it behave. The longest darkest eyelashes fringed pretty green eyes, but it wasn't welcome he saw there. More like, *'Who the hell are you and what do you want?'*

"Ah… ah… I'm Sergeant Jake Weylin, ma'am," his dumb mouth declared who he used to be to diffuse the situation.

Jamaal grunted and groaned. He was such a baby when he got hurt.

"You're Marines," she guessed correctly, stuffing her hair back into its plastic alligator jaws, her sharp eyes cast to the street behind them. "Do you guys live around here?"

Jake nodded, not sure where she was going with that question. Was she going to pay him a visit? Not likely. The transients came to her, not the other way around.

Of all things, the love song from the musical *West Side Story* showed up in his head with joyous exclamations of,

'Maria! Maria! Maria!' That refrain was followed immediately by the USMC men's choir belting out a raucous, *'We are proud to claim the title of United States Marine.'*

His brain worked like that, forever lost in timeless ballads he couldn't forget. That was the problem with a lot of guys like him who came back from the sandbox. They couldn't remember, but at the same time, they couldn't forget... *stuff.*

"We, umm, live over there," he said, motioning vaguely toward the east behind him, where the broken down grocery store stood like a skeleton in a graveyard of broken neighborhoods.

"Well, why are you waiting out here?" she asked bluntly. "Get inside. The last I heard Dr. Jarrett doesn't perform surgery in the alley."

He would've snapped to at her brusque order, but a shadowy current of—something—shivered between them. The woman gulped one very noisy gulp, giving herself away. Oh. Now he got it. All that bluff and bluster was more worry than challenge. *She's scared of me?* That didn't make sense. A has-been was no one to waste time thinking about, much less fear.

"My buddy here's Jamaal McCune," Jake offered quietly, making tentative eye contact so he didn't come across as threatening. Small talk always worked in delicate situations before. "He sat on some broken glass, and he might need stitches in his, umm, his..."

The woman peered around Jamaal's considerable rear end, her fingers nervously working—back and forth and back and forth—at the straps of the backpack she'd kept between her and Jake. Yeah, he'd called it right. She was scared, probably because she'd been outnumbered by two halfwits.

Jake tried once more. "You're new here."

Her brows went up, but she extended a hand. "Yes, I'm the new CNA here at the Good Samaritan. Lacy Wright."

Lacy, huh? That's a pretty name. I like it.

"What's a… C-N-N-N-N-N-A?" Jamaal slurred.

"It's a Certified Nursing Assistant," Lacy explained, the edge to her voice replaced with the pleasing lilt of patience. What a difference a couple of minutes made, huh? She almost looked friendly. Well, friendlier.

Jake wiped his fingers on his dirty jeans and extended his hand, ashamed that was the best he had to offer a lady. "Nice to make your acquaintance, Miss Wright," he said very politely, so damned thankful he wasn't drunk. Come to think of it, he hadn't had a drink for more than a week. That ought to count for something.

Her fingers felt small and breakable, a china doll's fingers caught in the callused confines of his, but her handshake was seriously firm and determined. She might be smaller than him and scared of him, but she meant to be taken seriously.

I can do that.

Loosening her grip, she nodded toward the clinic's rear entrance and the flashing red sign that clearly said: EXIT when it should've said: EMERGENCY ENTRANCE, or something profound like that. "Let's get your buddy inside where Dr. Jarrett can treat him, shall we?"

We shall. Jake let go of Lacy Wright's hand, instantly aware how cold the wintery afternoon had grown. How lonely. How weak the fading sun in the western sky had gotten. His index finger rubbed the rough pad of his thumb, missing the satiny whorls of her fingerprints against his.

She must have noticed. A genuine warmth curved the corners of her lips, spilling sunshine all over Jake. It had finally happened. There he stood. In the middle of Anacostia. Him. A nobody. Warmed from the inside out and all because a beautiful woman smiled…

At me.

Thank you for reading Eric!

Be sure to check out the rest of the guys and gals of Irish Winters' series: *In the Company of Snipers*

Other Irish Winters' books:

King of Hearts, Deuces Wild Series, *#1*

Joker Joker, Deuces Wild Series, *#2*

Smoke, Hearts and Ashes Series, *#1*

Ash, Hearts and Ashes Series, *#2*

Coming soon!

Seth, In the Company of Snipers, *#17*

One-Eyed Jack, Deuces Wild Series, *#3*

YOU are the key to this book's success!

Please tell other readers why you liked Eric and Shea's story by leaving an honest review at the retail site where you purchased it.
Recommend it to your friends. Lend it.
Most of all, enjoy it!

The best way to keep up with my new releases, giveaways, and actionable intel is to sign up for my spam-free newsletter at IrishWinters.com.

About the Author

Irish Winters is an award winning, Amazon best-selling author who, when she isn't writing, dabbles in poetry, grandchildren, and rarely (as in extremely rarely) the kitchen. More prone to be outdoors than in, she grew up the quintessential tomboy on a dairy farm in rural Wisconsin, spent her teenage years in the Pacific Northwest, but calls the Wasatch Mountains of Northern Utah home. For now.

She believes in making every day count for something, and follows the wise admonition of her mother to, "Look out the window and see something!"

Connect with Irish!
On Facebook: https://www.facebook.com/author.irishwinters
On Twitter: https://twitter.com/irishwinters1
Or at www. IrishWinters.com